# DELIVERANCE

*(Fourth Book of the Kahana Chronicles)*

## THE FLAVIUS JOSEPHUS JOURNAL PART ONE

**A family historical novel by
Allen E. Goldenthal**

First Published by Strategic Book Group, P.O. Box 333, Durham CT 06422
ISBN: 978-1-61204-642-6




Second Edition by Val d'Or Publishing
ISBN: 978-0-9942559-9-0
Released November 2020

# LETTER FROM THE EDITOR: 2<sup>ND</sup> EDITION

The story of Flavius Josephus has managed to survive for almost two thousand years since the time it was first published as an autobiographical attempt to explain how the most feared general of the Judean army could transition from freedom fighter to being a Romanizing adjunct of the Imperial Household.    To the Jews of his time, he was the Benedict Arnold of the nation, except unlike the American Revolution which was actually won by the revolutionaries, in Joseph's case, he did end up on the winning side.    His betrayal    was seen    by those    that survived    the war as the primary causal factor for the loss by the rebels. This certainly made it easier for the Pharisaic movement to explain how they could have lost after years of preaching that God was most definitely on their side and would almost single-handedly win the war for them. Being the populist movement of the time, the Pharisees had gained the hearts and minds of the youth in Judea, Samaria and Galilee with their radical concept that God would reward those that dedicated themselves wholly to his service. A promise that they would be rewarded with all that their hearts desired, including freedom from their oppressors.    In a theocratic society, where the rule of law had been exercised by those that were also the hereditary servants of God, the Pharisees were not only advocating a break from Rome but also a complete overhaul to the religious observances as established by Moses over twelve hundred years earlier.    So essentially, the war of liberation against Rome was not just a fight for political freedom against an occupying force, but more accurately an internal political struggle to control the religious institutions within the country. Until this time, the Saduccees, the hereditary priesthood held the religio-gubernatorial offices, creating a pseudo-elite aristocracy that allied itself with Rome, and therefore these Pharisees, forming a new class of religious thinkers that referred to themselves as 'Rabbis' or teachers, were able to disguise their thirst for power by directing the people to overthrow the Roman occupation, knowing that if successful, it would unseat the Saduccees and wrest the power from them simultaneously.

From the onset, it was a foolish gambit.    The Roman Empire had by that time conquered half of the known world, and one tiny little province on the eastern seaboard of the Mediterranean was hardly going to change that, but by instilling the belief that God would be taking an active part in the uprising, created an illusion of invincibility.    Once ingrained    within    the    hearts    and    minds    of    the    people,    it    proved easy for the Rabbis to preach that they were the only ones with a direct line of communication to the Almighty, negating the need for a priestly intermediary, which was the sole purpose of the Aaronic priesthood.    What the people failed to understand was that by following these Rabbinic teachings, they were acting in total contradiction to the scriptural laws as laid out by God to Moses, which was integral to the survival of the nation. The Levitical Priesthood served primarily as an institution to remove the burden of the laws from the common people by placing the onus of observance on a designated group that would then perform all of the rituals on behalf of the populace, thereby granting them a universal absolution for their sins, since their current city and town lifestyle ran contradictory to many of the rigid laws that were originally designed for a community having a more nomadic agrarian lifestyle. This cosmopolitan, urban commercial civilization that now existed twelve hundred years later certainly was not a perfect fit for the ancient laws.

The promises of a more socialistic society, where the voices of all would be heard equally by the supreme being, and all would share in the rewards provided by God certainly had a tantalizing appeal, but it took advantage of the less educated people that populated the cities, they themselves having no knowledge of international affairs and certainly not appreciating nor understanding how Israel as a minor chess piece on the world board was constantly being rotated as part of a much larger game played by revolving empires. The false impression provided by the Pharisees with their biblical lessons to the people that Israel or Judea were masters of their own destiny were not only naive, they were completely false. Somehow during the intervening years from the ancient Kingdom of David to the arrival of the Romans, the Jews had been repeatedly victorious via the hand of God against every external enemy they faced. But this interpretation of God's intercession in history on behalf of Israel fails to deal accurately with the history. In fact, the intervening thousand years between David and Rome was nothing more than a constant tale of occupation, survival, subjugation, revolution and then recycling all of these events upon the arrival of the next occupier. The Saduccees certainly understood it, and as a result they practiced a well rehearsed conservative standard of civil obedience, which they knew would guarantee the survival of the country long after the present occupier faded away and the next one arrived in his place.

Having created this unattainable concept of freedom, where a tiny nation surrounded by hostile forces representing the Empire could actually survive without being reabsorbed into the Empire, the people actually forced the hand of Rome to take action in subduing any suggestion of insurrection before the spilling of blood had an opportunity to become excessive. Therein lay the failure of all involved in understanding exactly what were the stakes they were fighting for. To the Romans, it did not appear to be anything more than a small group of rebels that they assumed could be eliminated without much effort. To the Jews, it was a battle they presumed God would fight on their behalf and they would simply wait for the miracle. Neither side ever imagined it would be an epic battle that would threaten the existence of both combatants.

This series of books known as The Kahana Chronicles has become more than just a history of my family; more than just a personal effort to preserve the loss of failing memories and counteract the natural distortion process that occurs over time. They have become essentially a moral tale for all of mankind, in which to partake, share and ultimately find purpose within our own lives. They are stories of survival, of persistence, of determination, but most of all they are valid reminders about the inexhaustible human spirit to be free.    I dedicate this book to my son James, whom is blessed with the most admirable sense of morality of what is right and wrong.    In a world where all the lines have been blurred beyond recognition, this commendable attribute will serve him well. This book is also dedicated to Flavius Josephus, who long ago recognized that death offers little in which to rejoice even for those that claim to be the victors but is still a cost we must willingly pay if we choose to live. Even so, death is nothing more than an end of existence and it should never be considered a solution if another choice is available.    It is our duty as human beings to live, while respecting our mandate to survive, and in our constant battle for freedom, we must never surrender to death quietly but only when we have no other choice.

.

Dr. Allen E. Goldenthal

# PROLOGUE

There is a stench to all that is Roman. A decaying, gnawing foul odour that eats at your innards until your belly is swollen with gall. For all that is Roman is not to be considered enlightened, or precious, or inspiring, or deserving to be praised and cherished. Instead it is a festering sore, which rots from the center outwards until there is no flesh left to feed upon. If ever there was a crime against humanity, it is their crime of ignorance, their inability to understand neither the world they rule nor the people they have conquered. They are not our masters!

Its legions come offering gifts of civilization and Prometheus' fire but they choose to never comprehend how those they have come to embrace find no solace or comfort in their offerings. This has truly been the sin of Rome's emperors and senators from their time of conception. Though desired, they can never understand that which they have lusted can never be fulfilled because one man's passion is another's hatred. This is Rome's true gift to the world, unbridled hate; a fiery, all consuming, unimaginable hatred that is destined to leave millions dead in its wake. Remember well the day that wind from the west came to the far eastern shores of our great sea, not as an army to pillage but as a friend, specifically asked to give aid to a battered priest. Our priest-king Hyrcanus, embattled in a war against his own brother in a never ending struggle to wrestle the kingdom and the throne. And remember it well that when the dust had finally settled, there was no longer a kingdom, but a province, ruled not by either of the two brothers, but by a vassal that danced a merry jig to the songs sung by generals and Imperators of the most powerful empire that ever ruled. And recall that when these vassals proved weak and inefficient, they were replaced by men of the equestrian order, knights of Rome, that were sent to this far corner of the world so that they could reward themselves with treasures, rape our women and desecrate our most holy of places. Remember them well, for they have reduced us to this pitiful state where we are beggars in our own land.

And none have shown us favor since the first of the procurators was gifted by Tiberius to herald our doom. Neither Caligula, nor Claudius, nor Nero that has followed saw it any differently. We are to be made to suffer by the hands of this breed of men that they have sent to rule over us as their procurators. Cruel and spiteful, bitter as this land of rock and hot sand that they have been rewarded with as their prize for all the years they have served dutifully. This bitterness has turned their hearts black and these men of the aristocracy, these nobles of ancient families have turned their venom against the very people they rule. They line our roads with crosses from one horizon to the other with the corpses of our people hanging until the flesh is eaten by the birds that dot the sky overhead.

Where are our leaders to raise their voices against such atrocities?    Our messiahs to bring a strong right arm against such brutality. Too many have fallen beneath the mighty hand that these procurators wield, and too many have been clamped in chains and sent to Rome, to stand before the Emperor to answer for crimes they have committed against this evil and corrupt Empire.

Now is such a time.    Now is the time for us to fight for all that we believe in. This is where our war begins.    We are at the junction when all that lives under oppression will rise in a single voice to shout that we will not suffer any longer. We will not remain helpless victims of a foreign occupation.    It is time for all men to finally look deep within themselves and find that inner strength that long ago separated us from the beasts of the field.    There is but one word that whispers over and over in our heads until we cannot hold it inside any longer and have to shout it out loudly for the entire world to hear.    We cry out for freedom, and when enough of the people shout that word together in unison, then we will become a force that will settle for nothing less than achieving that dream.    There are those of you that say we are not ready.    The time has not yet come.    The Lord God has not sent us a sign.    I say to thee, nay! He has sent us a thousand signs; a thousand upon thousands but we have been blinded by our own ignorance.    And even if the Almighty has been deaf to our plight, when he hears the shouts of our voices for freedom, he will be deaf no longer!    Let the Empire of Rome tremble in our wake.    Let all who bring death and destruction to the seed of Abraham know that in so doing they curse themselves.    We are the children of Israel, and we have no master to lord above us but God.    And with a mighty hand He will crush our enemies.    Hear me my brothers!    The breath and spirit of the Lord shall lead you!

Hallelujah!

Jonathan Cayapha

# THE KAHANA CHRONICLES
## BOOK FOUR

VI

# CHAPTER ONE

## JERUSALEM: 63 A.D.

From behind the hills the drifting cloud of dust lay thick against the budding horizon as the morning sun just peeked above the terrain. At first, it went unnoticed, nothing more than the desert wind scurrying across the scorched earth, but with time it finally caught the attention of the half-dozing guard standing watch on the north tower. In one fluid motion, the horn was at his lips and the piercing sound of three rapid blasts shattered the     stillness in the air.

Scabbards chimed against pleated leather skirts of the riders, rhythmically sounding the gallop like the endless roll of a snare drum. In their brass grieves, embossed chest plates and horsehair plumed helmets, the six riders approached the city in a dazzling display of prismatic light and color. Circling the valley's edge, their progress was carefully scrutinized by the sentries manning the iron reinforced perches built into the stone walls of the city. All eyes on the parapets were fixed nervously on this small unit of unexpected visitors.

The standard-bearer carried the small force's insignia aloft. It was clearly the combined wolf and eagle, symbols of the Legate of Syria and that meant this visit was official whether prearranged or not. Another series of quick blasts from the trumpets in rapid succession and the massive bolt retracted and the iron gates swung open on their corpulent hinges. Within moments the riders had passed through the gates and the guards strained to close the iron doors behind them.

"Hail, Tribune Gaius Marcellus Capito. We were not expecting you. What has brought you to our fine city, the land of diseased whores and leprous religious madmen?" The commander of the guard crossed his chest with his right arm in the standard military salute while chortling at his own joke.

"Cut the pleasantries, Rufus, there's nothing more that I could have wanted than to avoid coming to this festering city of yours. As we are both aware, there are over a half million of the sons of bitches heading towards Jerusalem at this precise moment and that means it's time to collect the head tax for the Legate. Unfortunately, I drew the short straw. But I'm certain that Albinus had made the necessary preparations for our arrival and has matters well in order to commence immediately? Someone in this forsaken cesspool had to at least expect that we'd be coming?"

"Are you telling me or asking me?" the commander scoffed. "Since when do they consider me of any importance that they keep me informed? And I'm certainly not the Governor's keeper! It's pretty obvious though that you're going to need to rely on my legionnaires to assist you with handling the taxes," the commander smiled greedily then winked knowing that tax collection meant there were perks of slipping the odd stater into their pockets from time to time. "That is unless you believe the six of you are going to manage it all."

"Obviously, I will need your help."

"At the usual commission for my senior staff?" the commander both asked and insisted.

"Of course."

"Then, welcome to our city, my men are at your service," the commander shouted with fond camaraderie.

"I thought they would be, Rufus. Now, for my next question. Where will I find Procurator Albinus? I'm certain he'll want to know that I have arrived safely even if he wasn't aware that we'd be coming."

"Now that could be a problem," Rufus cautioned. "He's secluded himself in the Antonia fortress on the east side of town; too many Jews in the city for the festival for him to remain safely in his Upper City palace. The man's no coward but he's no fool either. You know how these Jews can get when you put a mass of them into close quarters. Before you know it, knives slashing this way and that and you can't even find who did it. They'd gladly be nailed to a cross before they give up the name of one of their own."

"Shit!" the Tribune spat. "That's way on the other side of the city!"

"Oh, yes," Rufus confirmed.

"And how I'm going to get through the throng of people to get there? It could take hours!"

"Well, you could wait until the evening. The Jew's have their Sabbath tonight. Won't be a sole left in the streets once they go to their prayers. All these years I've been posted here and it still amazes me. One minute there's thousands in the street and the next you can't even find a street urchin. Downright spooky if you ask me!"

"I'm not asking and I can't wait that long. We'd be looking at almost twelve hours of sitting idle. As much as I enjoy your company Rufus, I don't really enjoy it that much."

The commander of the guard laughed at the insult. He and Capito had been trading them for years. "Of course you could always enter by the Lion Gates; easier to go around the city than through it," the commander suggested.

"You must be joking Rufus. Between the time I exit this gate and then ride the distance to the other side, my men and I will be open targets for anyone with a sling or arrow lying in wait along the Kidron. I don't feel like running a gauntlet through the valley. I'm not in to advocating suicide!"

"Well in that case, there's always the alternative involving beating a path straight through the heart of the city. For a slight service fee, of course." A broad smile scrawled across Rufus's round face.

"Perhaps a little support could be useful Rufus?"

"Most certainly dear Capito. Porcius assemble a cohort of men immediately," Rufus barked an order to his next in command. "Short Spanish swords and Gallic shields should do the trick."

"And if anyone refuses to move out of our way," Porcius inquired.

"Then move them. Any way you deem fit."

"Yes Sir," the centurion saluted his commander enthusiastically.

Within minutes the men were assembled, forming into two columns, spearheaded by a fortified wedge. Placing his riders to the rear of the armed infantry, Capito bid Rufus a short but hearty farewell. Two drummers beat out a march to which the soldiers kept step. The resounding beat served two important purposes; one was to maintain the orderly march the Roman military machine had become famous for, the other was to send a clear warning to all that crossed their path that any who dared to block their progress would be carried away and dealt with harshly, for such was the nature of the occupational force exercising its authority to govern. The Jews of this city had grown accustomed to the oppression and they had come to know the sound of the beating drums very well.

In little under an hour, the cohort had covered the distance to the Antonia fortress. Most of the citizenry had been either smart enough or fast enough to steer clear of the tips of the Spanish short swords, but a few had to be forcibly manhandled and brushed aside by the round leather Gallic shields that struck with the sting of a bull whip. Those were the lucky ones. If the shields caught bone when swung on their edge then they easily shattered an arm or a leg into fragments. The injured were quickly dragged from the path of further harm by friends and family. Once the battalion disappeared behind the fortress doors, the flood of people in the marketplace returned as swiftly as it had receded. No trace of the passing unit could be seen. It was as if they had never been. But those that had purposely witnessed the Tribune's arrival made note of every detail of his men. These were troubled times and information was the most valuable commodity to be traded in the streets.

# CHAPTER TWO

## WHANGAREI: PRESENT

"So, what do you think John," I asked of my companion as we walked along the fence line of my farm.

"I never expected that this was where you were going to end up Doc. Seems pretty provincial and remote. Didn't take you for a hermit. Guess I was wrong!"

"I thought it was getting time to retire. My entire life I've been globetrotting, saving the world as I called it, and I think I finally realized I've had enough. I was told you how I could understand and appreciate my ancestor, Professor Jacob at the University of Vienna much better once I had lived his life. But as you'll see when I write his story, he didn't finish off too well. Maybe that was the lesson I was meant to learn. That his life wasn't all it was cracked up to be. You just have to look at the parallels between our lives and its shocking."

"More GLEEM?" Pearce questioned.

"Heaps of it," I responded. "Here was a young man that left home around eighteen and never looked back, just like me. Or maybe it's me like him? Whatever. He puts himself through university, illegally I have to admit, not like me but still, he pursued a course or direction in life that family and community was against, and that was just like me. He marries, only to leave behind a wife with two boys as he heads off to life in Vienna, which one could say was very much me, as I left Canada to journey to New Zealand. This was followed by two more marriages and more children and again I have to admit doing the same thing."

Pearce shook his head. "Sounds like a strong coincidence if you ask me, Doc."

"Well, I can only describe it as extraordinary. It was beyond extraordinary. It was as if I could only make decisions that would parallel his own life. He had a passion for history and science while he taught as a Professor of languages. I have a passion for languages, while teaching science at two universities and history privately through my books. He was a major author on Jewish topics and I consider myself to be a well read author on the same subject matter. So you can call it a coincidence all you want, but I have to think it is

5

something far more.    Something ingrained into my own specific DNA as much as it was incorporated into his. So I guess that's the reason you're here, to finally get that story from me."

"What makes you think that," Pearce challenged.

"Oh, just a hunch when your editor calls me about doing a book on Jakob before you arrived.    You already said a year ago that there was a fair bit of excitement being generated about my ancestor's little tryst with the Empress Elisabeth. Or should I say, possible tryst. So, I think we can turn it into some first class tickets for all of us."

"Who exactly is all of us?"

"Well, my wife of course.    You don't expect me to leave her behind, do you?    Bad enough I'm always flying around for my work and leaving her behind. Do you know that last year I was probably home a grand total of about ten weeks.  The only good thing about CoVid is she's had me home most of this year for the first time in our marriage."

"And you think my editor will actually shell out for this trip of yours?"

"I told you a while ago, Pearce, nobody could care less about Jacob for over forty years of my life, and suddenly, they're all fighting, pursuing, cursing each other to find out what I know. Everyone loves a scandal, even if it happened a hundred and seventy years ago.    It still becomes front-page sensationalism. Think of it this way.    Whatever I can recall is probably only a fraction of what I can't. In that regard, I may very well have all of the answers to what everyone's looking for. And that's why I'm guessing your editor will pay for this little trip."

He turned to me and very slowly after a moment's consideration nodded. "I know.   He'll want that story.    But you're going to have to give me something more to deliver if you want that trip."

"What is it that you think I must deliver in order to get the seal of approval from your boss?'

"Something controversial."

"You mean something that makes him think there really was a conspiracy."

"Not having a record of whether or not someone sold the house on Postgasse Strasse that you once told me about just isn't going to do it," Pearce commented as he shook his head. "Maybe his third wife sold it, for all you know."

"Not that house. That was his hideaway.   His home to get away from the world and even away from his wives."

"Or so you believe." Pearce was still not willing to afford me any leeway.

"I believe it because I know in my mind it's true.   His third wife was Rosalia Horowitz   She had her own home that she resided in.  I'm not quite sure why he married her.   She was twenty-one years younger than him.   Not exactly from his world of debutantes and aristocrats but a military background instead.   Perhaps he already realized he need some degree of protection."

"Well isn't Ying almost twenty years younger than you?"

"Only eighteen," I corrected him.   "And that's different. We married for love.   The truth is, I don't think Jakob actually knew what love was.   He desired the Empress and every other woman was merely an attempt to conceal his longing for Elizabeth.   The only woman that spent any time in his home on Postgasse was his stepmother and that is a peculiar story in itself."

"Are you suggesting he had a thing for his stepmother?"   Pearce sounded a bit shocked, which was kind of surprising considering all the things he had already heard about my family.

"There was just over twenty years between them.   And you can imagine what a woman that preferred to be called Babette must have looked like during the nineteenth century."

"Probably like someone nicknamed Candy in the twentieth century," Pearce surmised. "But it's still a far stretch from suggesting he had a thing for his stepmother."

"I didn't say he did, only that it is somewhat suspicious that considering he had the money to build a luxurious tomb in the cemetery for his entire family, he decided to bury his second wife, Anna, in a far off corner of the cemetery while he had himself laid to rest in the same grave as Babette."

"You mean in the grave beside his stepmother," Pearce tried to correct me.

"No.   I mean in the same grave.   Two bodies in the same hole in the ground.   She died a few weeks before he did."

"Well…does sound a little strange, Pearce admitted.

"You think?"

"Okay.  A lot strange but still what does that have to do with proof that he never sold the home along the Danube?"

"Because as I see it," I advised him, "He had no idea he was going to be dead a few weeks later.   And if he's anything like me, and I think he is, then he didn't bother to make out a will in his fifties.   According to the family history, we all die closer to ninety or over.  So he had no expectation to die at fifty-three."

"Are you suggesting he didn't die from natural causes?" Pearce was finally getting a grasp on what I was telling him.

"Did you know that susceptibility to tuberculosis is familial?" Pearce's blank stare told me that he didn't have a clue as to what I was talking about. "It is well known that about one in nine families has a susceptibility. That means if you look at a family that has experienced a case of tuberculosis, you will find that throughout the family tree, they're going to have a numerous deaths recorded that can be attributed to the disease because they lack the natural immunity found in eighty-nine percent of the population. So if my third great grandfather died from tuberculosis, then I should see in my family tree which contains hundreds of names from the eighteenth century onwards, at least a handful death reports marked tuberculosis. Other than Jakob, I don't have a single report with that cause of death. So you tell me what you think he really died from."

"I don't really know," Pearce failed to provide an alternative.

"Well then, you're just going to have to wait until I tell that story in order to find out. So taking that in consideration and the fact that I find some of his children still registered as living at twenty Postgasse Strasse, then I'm pretty certain the property was never sold."

"Still doesn't rule out that the children didn't sell it."

"Almost all of Rosalia's children ended up in Theriesenstadt, John. Do you think the Nazis told them to take their time to sell their home first and then show up at the concentration camp later. I don't think so. There was no sale! It was confiscation most likely, but no sale What more could your editor possibly want?"

"It still won't be good enough for him," Pearce warned.

"What could he possibly want more than that to justify a trip to Vienna. There's a human interest story there. Nazis, stolen property, and a happy ending rolled into one if I get it back. People love that sort of thing," I explained.

"Still not good enough!"

"Give me a suggestion then," I demanded.

"It's got to be juicier," Pearce counseled. "The readership has to be able to sink their teeth into it. Give them that and you'll probably have your trip. People want something sensational. They want more. Much more!"

"Okay then, what about all Jakob's records disappearing from the university files?" I suggested.

"That's getting warmer. Would you like to expand on that point exactly?"

"Great, I see that I finally caught your interest.   You know, the Austrians are meticulous in their record keeping.  They have catalogues that catalogue their catalogues.  You know what I'm saying.  That's how passionate they can get about their records.   So you don't expect to find records disappearing."

"Which ones in particular?"

"That's the funny part.   Pretty much all of them."

"Can you verify that they went missing?"

"Actually Herr Kurt Muhlberger the archivist for the university library can verify that.   He was probably more shocked than I was when he found them all missing.   He told me that it's never happened before.   Files just don't disappear at the university   They're very pedantic about their files as I said."

"And when did this happen?"

"He couldn't tell me.   It wasn't one of the more popular files that gets requested frequently by the public. In fact until I came along, no one he could ever recall requested it to be opened.   He walked into the back rooms expecting to find them and they just weren't there. So he figures the loss must have predated his arrival at the university."

"The Nazis then," Pearce suggested.  "Didn't they try to destroy all the Jewish    records of any Jew that was noteworthy?    That would be the obvious reason    they're    no    longer    there."    Pearce    felt    certain    he    had uncovered the reason behind the missing files.

"Yes they were guilty of destroying a lot of the historical Judaica, but not in this    case.   Not in Vienna.   They never desecrated Vienna to the degree they did elsewhere.   Probably because the Austrians threw their lot in with them right at the beginning.   I guess that was one of the perks for being supporters of the Nazi party.   But even the allies avoided doing any damage to Vienna, though they bombed the hell out of every other place in the Reich."

"So what then?"

"Let me paint a scenario for you John.   Try to imagine this.   You are married to one of the most beautiful women of the time and for whatever reason, you can't bring yourself to lay in the same bed with her."

"I'd be a fool then," Pearce responded.

"Yes you would be.   So how else would you describe the Emperor Franz Josef   barely laying with the Empress and preferring several other women that didn't hold a candle to Sissi. But even more interesting is that when he did have children from these mistresses, they all tended to be female.   Seems like good ol' Franz Josef lacked the necessary Y sperm quantities to produce an actual heir to the throne. So not only is the Empress not getting much, so to speak, when she does have her children, one turns out to be a boy. Sounds like she may have had a lover of her own. I happen to think that my ancestor Jacob may have been the one busy providing the sperm for the next emperor." I figured why waste time. Might as well throw Pearce a bone and see how he'd react.

"Oh, this I think could definitely raise the stakes as far as my editor's interest."

"I certainly would hope so," I commented.

" Can you provide proof?"

"You should know that when discussing Franz Josef and his sex life, then almost everyone knows you actually have to look outside the palace and focus on his extra-marital affairs. Every historian knows about Helen Baltazzi, Anna Nahowski and Katharina Schratt. The Emperor had his stable of women from the day he was married to Elisabeth."

"Actually Doc, I don't know a thing about any of them."

"Okay, doesn't matter," I advised him. "I said historians. I obviously wasn't including you, no offense intended."

"No offense taken," Pearce reassured me.

"So let us agree in general that the Emperor didn't spend that much time with the Empress, either before or during their marriage. And coincidentally, after the death of my third great grandfather in 1868, Josef definitely had to get his excitement elsewhere as far as his wife was concerned. She apparently shut the door so to speak and took to traveling through Europe rather than spend any time with her husband."

"So you're suggesting because of your ancestor's death, the Empress was heart-broken and couldn't touch another man afterwards, not even her own husband?"

"No, I'm suggesting she thinks Josef was responsible for Jakob's death and couldn't stand to even look at her husband any more," I corrected him.

"Really?" Pearce sounded shocked.

"No, I just wanted to feed you that line to see how you'd react! " I said as my words dripped with sarcasm. "Of course really."

"And…" Pearce wanted to know the outcome.

"And you swallowed it like a fish, hook line and sinker. But bottom line is that all this will be explained in time when I write that book. So all you need to know right now is that the Emperor did have illegitimate children by some of his mistresses, but once again, they're all born female. Actually, let me correct that.

The one mistress, Anna, she did have one son but it turned out it wasn't by Franz Josef. Guess being the Emperor of Austria didn't grant him any exclusiveness in her mind. But where were we before I digressed?"

"All of your ancestor's files missing…," Pearce filled in the gap.

"So, you can obviously understand why they made this effort to remove all of his records from the University files. You can imagine the repercussions if they allowed any of these suspicions to leak out. I bet that even now it would prove to be a major embarrassment to Viennese society to admit to an event like this."

"So is this a hunch thing that they did it intentionally, or is it something more?" Pearce still wasn't willing to accept the explanation at face value.

"Do you know that if you go to the old University of Vienna Campus, down on Universitat Strasse, right in the middle of town, in the heart of the old building is this beautiful atrium, with the portico built all around it? And it's not even so much an atrium as a forest of busts and statues. And as far back as they can go, you have these lifelike busts of all the heads of the departments, deans, professors, everyone! It's a remarkable experience but having gone through every nook and alcove, there's one professor, one head of a department, one winner of gold medals in both London and Paris conspicuously absent. Well, I guess it's conspicuous when you're purposely looking for him and he's not there! So that's why I know the loss of the files isn't a coincidence, or an accident. Jakob Goldenthal has been officially erased by the State. Combine that with what I can see in my mind through the magic of GLEEM and there's another best seller on the horizon."

"How can you be so certain?"

"Mayerling!" I fired back.

I could see by the grin on Pearce's face that one name had fueled his interest further. He was excited about the story line now. I was actually surprised that he even heard the word before.

"You've got the key to unlock Mayerling, don't you?" He cocked his left hand like a pistol shooting in my direction.

"More than a key," I responded to his gesture. "You let your editor know that when I unlock this Pandora's Box, nothing will ever be the same when it comes to the history of the Habsburgs. That dynasty for all intents and purposes was heading for extinction as soon as Jakob arrived in Vienna."

# JERUSALEM: 63 A.D.

A head coiffed with masses of curls popped above the white-washed stuccoed wall as the young man called out to his brother who sat by the portico of their one story    villa.    "Joseph, Joseph, quick come see.    There's a unit of Romans marching their way through the city.    Come see!    I think they have come from Galilee.    It could be    evidence that it has finally begun!"

Stifling a yawn, the twenty-something short-bearded man waited until his younger brother came through the garden gates before responding.    "Don't get your hopes up Matthias.    As usual, I think you may be a little premature.    The time is not yet right."

Matthias drew up beside his brother and poured himself a cup of water which he immediately poured over his head to counteract the heat of the afternoon sun and his short run home.    "You know Joseph; you have this bad habit to play down everything.    One day we will rise up against these animals and you'll miss it because you'll just sit here as usual doing nothing."

"And one day we will all be dead.    Both may be inevitable but neither can be predicted as to when they will happen.    Be patient brother."

"Bah! Patience! That's all that we hear being preached from our leaders. We suffer, we are slaughtered, and all you hear is have patience.    There will be none of us left if we remain patient much longer."

"I believe you might be accused of exaggerating slightly, brother.    The Romans have been here for four generations now.    I'm certain we could survive a few more if necessary.    Wouldn't you agree?"

"There will be a spark in Galilee.    You will see.    Our northern brethren will teach us that which we are unwilling to recognize here in the south."

"The only thing the Galileans will show us is how to die on the edge of a Roman sword.    Just give it some thought, Matthias. When has there ever been a leader from Galilee for whom we haven't suffered as a result?    God's got a design on what will happen.    Let Him decide as to the place and the time.    Who are we to make the decision for the Lord?"

"You sound like all the rest of the politicians in Jerusalem. You all sit in your fancy villas with fresh water piped into your homes and there's always food on your table.    So why should you care?    You're no different from them!"

"Don't forget my hot-headed little brother that you happen to live in this house of ours too and I don't recall you ever being absent from our dinner table.    It's easy enough to defend an ideology when you don't have to make a sacrifice yourself. I think I'd have more sympathy for your cause if I actually saw your suffering. I don't understand this attitude among this generation. We reject everything about our society as if somehow it is responsible for all the wrongs of our world. You want to know the reality. The reality is you have good armies and then you have even better ones.    And the better ones win.    And the better ones rule.    And that's the way the world is.    You believe somehow you and your friends are going to change that?"

"At least we're willing to do more than just roll over and wave our asses in the air inviting the Romans to sodomize us."

"Hey, in case you can't remember we refused to let the Greeks stick it up our asses, only to go to war, beat them and then put some of our own into the royal palaces only to find out pretty quickly that it was our own kings that reamed us from behind.    That's how the Romans got here in the first place.    We invited them here to save us from our own kings.    Why don't you and your friends pay some attention to our own history lessons?"

"We have learned our lessons.    There won't be any more kings.    We'll go back to the way it was in the time of the judges.    That's the way God wanted it to be."

"Are you trying to take us back into the prehistoric ages?    We have a modern society now.    We can't live by the same rules of a nomadic existence. Look at all the conveniences we have now.    Would you choose to give them up too?"

"You still don't understand!" Matthias yelled.    "You are enamored by all the trappings that these invaders have brought with them."

"No! I'm just not prepared to go back to living in thatched huts and drinking my wine out of a goat's stomach.    Enough of this foolishness!    Let's go inside and start preparing for the Sabbath.    Father would not be pleased if he overheard us talking in this manner."

And with a mastered ease of handling people, Joseph displayed a manner that others could only admire, slipping his arm around his brother's left shoulder and leading him into the villa.    No sooner did his arm fall across his back; Matthias felt all the pent up anger and rage drain from his body. That was the power that Joseph held over all that had come to know him.    No one could ever harbor an evil thought against Joseph for very long.    His magic weaved a spell of harmony and tranquility to which none were immune.    Perhaps it was a gift from God, or the fact that his voice never changed in inflection or tone when prodded or pushed to anger.    In fact, no one could ever recall Joseph losing his temper.    The patience of Job, some said.    The hypnotic gaze of David claimed the others.

"Oh, I almost forgot," Matthias piped up.

"Forgot what?"

"The leaders of the Sanhedrin are coming."

"When?" Joseph prodded for his brother to complete his train of thought.

"Before the Sabbath.    In fact they'll be here shortly."

"And by them you mean...?

"Damneus.    He told me."

"And    this    event    you    almost    forgot    to    tell    me?"    Joseph shook his head.     "The High Priest tells you personally that he's coming to our house and this escapes your mind.     Brother, we must have a talk.     But first we must let our father know that we have guests coming. He will want to have some refreshments ready if they're walking all the way from the Temple grounds."

"I don't know why.   It's only Damneus."

"Joshua     Damneus     if     you     please,"     Joseph     responded     in a tone that purposely sounded as if he was scolding his younger brother.   "That man is the most powerful man in this country other than the Roman governor. You better remember that."

"He's just our cousin, Joseph.   By an act of fate it was his line six generations   ago that inherited the high priesthood instead of ours!"

"Six generations or sixty, it doesn't matter. He has the power, you do not. Better remember that!"

"How can you respect a man that goes by the surname of Domen?"

Joseph waved a finger cautiously at his little brother.     "Do not underestimate why he's called Doomyah, Matthias. If he was to overhear you refer to him as a piece of shit rather than his real title, he'd teach you very quickly how he received the cognomen of "the grave and silent one."   He's not one to be trifled with.   Not even his father could bring him to heal and there were few people that were powerful enough to resist Caiaphas."

"Caiaphas, Caiaphas. Almost two decades later and all people want to do is talk about Caiaphas," Matthias lamented.    "You'd think if he was so great we wouldn't be in the mess we are now."

Joseph shook his head, admitting there was little he could say that would arrest his brother's cockiness.    There was even less of a point to try to even persuade Matthias to examine the matter more balanced merely as a favor to their father; best to say nothing and pray that Matthias wasn't given the opportunity to speak during the meeting for all their sake.

# CHAPTER THREE

## WHANGAREI: PRESENT

"So, somehow this story is going to have something to do with Caiaphas," Pearce speculated. "I thought we had finished with that story. You know, did that, done that, sort of thing. After all, we rewrote the entire book last time we were together. What more do you want to do?"

"Everything has to do with Caiaphas," I explained. "I thought you would have figured that out from our last little get together."

"Don't get me wrong Doc. Sales for us have never been better. I must admit that I underestimated the potential for that book when you first mentioned we were going to do a rewrite. But I'll take it all back now. It's been a doozy. And you've become untouchable to boot. I've never seen anything like it. There are people practically willing to lay down their lives for you should anyone try to squirrel you away as a lab rat."

"And I have you to thank for that John, and don't think that I don't appreciate it. It was nice of your editor to run those articles on the government plans for people that might be considered in possession of certain unnatural attributes. Even though those stories were unsourced, they appear to have made the agency reconsider any intentions it may have had for me and any others like me. I just feel sorry for all those with special gifts that they experimented upon in the past. Now I can finally get back to living my life in the open without needing to look over my shoulder all the time."

"That's the readers you have to thank for that," Pearce was convinced. "When it comes right down to it, the people still hold the balance of power. It just takes some clever manipulation to bring them together as a united force."

"I thought that's why we have politicians. Manipulate the masses. You've obviously picked up some of the same tricks."

"But in a good way."

"Oh definitely in a good way. I wouldn't think your establishment would behave in any other manner," I winked knowing that the press could be just as bad in its intentions as any government.

"After all, we don't make the rules, we just play by them," Pearce smiled devilishly. "Best to beat them at their own game, if you're asking me. Put the spotlight on them rather than you and they broke under the heat. But going back to the Caiaphas issue, somehow the story you're giving me today has obviously evolved from the death of Jesus? Is that the connection here?"

"You could say that. But I think what actually triggered this memory was my middle son."

"Evan?"

"Let's go sit over there by the pond and I'll explain." I led Pearce over to the fish pond that was the central feature of my back yard. "Have a seat and I'll tell you what happened."

"So you must have spoken to him?"

"Relax, I'll get to it. Yes, I spoke to him. Called him a few days ago. He's a family man now. Two kids."

"I didn't know that."

"Why should you? Do you think I tell you everything?"

"Yeah, I did!"

"Mostly everything," I reassured him. Pearce seemed relieved by my comment.

"So what's he doing now?" Pearce moved the conversation back to my son.

"You can appreciate this in light of everything you know about GLEEM," I had to laugh "He's working on his PhD thesis at a Jewish University in medieval Jewish history."

"So like what you write about but from the other perspective," Pearce was quick to point out.

"He wants to be a professor in the studies. Does this sound familiar to you?"

"Sort of like your ancestor Jakob," Pearce surmised.

"Sort of? Let's see; trained in a religious institution in ancient languages and history, studying general Rabbinical and Karaite Judaism and examining the philosophers. At some point he's going to come face to face with his own family's past. Whether he handles it in the same way that Jakob or I did will be the million dollar question."

"So you're suggesting that GLEEM has predetermined his path."

"Would look like it, though I doubt he'd ever see it that way."

"Then if that's the case, what did he do to trigger this story from your memories?"

"I think it is the fact that he has his own children and it reminded me that whether or not we accept it, we are just one continuous circle of life, which resembles a slinky more than a circle."

"A slinky?"

"Don't tell me you've never seen a slinky John? How's that even possible? Imagine a large coiled spring but the metal is pretty flexible, so it bends and turns and does all sorts of things, like walking down stairs, even though it is just this one continuous circle."

"Okay, got it."

"So I'm thinking, how we can have different viewpoints from generation to next generation, never seeing the stark reality in the same way, yet we are still this continuous line of descent. What changes our viewpoint is the environment we're exposed to. That's when I began to think about my grandchildren, wondering what will be their exposure in this crazy world we no live in and how will that influence their beliefs. Will their Judaism be like their father's, or will it be like mine. Or perhaps it will be something completely different all together."

"But aren't your traditions pretty much the same as your sons?" Pearce asked.

"I wasn't referring to our traditions John. I'm referring to the orthodox teachings in which my son is being trained and raised. I'm referring my Karaite beliefs that every one of our tracts is to be individually interpreted but always practiced based on that interpretation. Failure to maintain that flexibility is what led to the dogma eschewed by those same orthodox rabbis that have repeated ly caused our downfall for over a thousand years. You see, they've preached that there is a distinction between themselves as Jews and the rest of the world as non-Jews. That it's okay to treat non-Jews as something less than themselves. They applied that same rule to Karaites as well, calling us dogs and anything else they could think of. They forgot the ancient teachings of Hillel when he advised them not to treat anyone badly by saying, "Do not do until others as you would not have them do unto you." But they didn't think that applied to anyone other than their fellow rabbinical Jews. They have lived their lives according to this false interpretation and are still committing the same offenses to God that got them into trouble time and time again. Moses' first rule he gave us was to befriend the stranger because we must never forget that we were strangers ourselves in a strange land."

"So Doc, are you saying somehow the fact you now have an expanded family it is in some way related to this entire episode of GLEEM. How does doing something nice for a stranger relate to this story?" Pearce, as usual, was somewhat confused.

"The world my son lives in, where the Rabbis are continually pitting us against other civilizations should have died out two thousand years ago but they're still doing it today. That's why I was wondering what will be the beliefs instilled into my grand- children from Evan a compared to those of my son Joshua, who is more secular in his beliefs. Will they be the same as their parents or will their religious beliefs evolve into something completely different. Will they be part of the present world, or still clinging on to a world that expired long ago?"

"And I guess from *Zutra* we know what the Rabbanites thought of your beliefs as a Karaite as well," Pearce was quick to comment. "So that's probably off the table."

"Oh, that is probably a given. I think you have to experience the other forms of Judaism before you come to the realization that Karaism is the true path."

"Okay, so I follow you that the choices your son has made in life would have an emotional and historical cognitive effect, but why would it trigger this particular story?"

"Can't you see John?   It is the same issues playing over and over again.   The prejudices of Jew against Jew, against half-Jew, against Samaritan, against Galilean, and even those Jews that wanted to embrace the Greco-Roman world. Nothing has changed and those very same prejudices led to this devastating event that practically exterminated us.   It was also the start of the major split between my family as Zadokites and the rabbinic Judaism that emerged following the destruction.   Essentially, I have the same microcosm occurring in my own personal family experience."

"So where's the Jesus factor in all this?"

"You see, the entire country was devastated by the events of the prior thirty years.   These included putting the high priest on trial in Rome, the assassination of King Agrippa, the arrest and exile of leading members of the Sanhedrin, and not to forget the crucifixion of Jesus. All these were considerable destabilizing factors.   Everyone thinks of Jesus' death in the context of the birth of Christianity but you have to remember, that really didn't take place until almost the turn of the century, sixty years later. Prior to this, what they had was nothing more than another Jewish messiah being killed and leaving behind his Jewish followers.   They certainly had experienced a number of these. For all intents and purposes, Jesus was nothing more than an internal Jewish affair.   So, as I said, everything that happened consequently evolved from these series of events, which Caiaphas was a prime factor."

Pearce became very quiet, contemplative to the point that I realized he had some serious misgivings.

"Is there a problem?"

"Sort of," he responded.   "I promised my editor that we'd give him something really different this time.   Don't get me wrong, he knows that your stories have been extremely successful to date, but he's looking for something with adventure and romance.   Sort of more like *Zutra*.   In truth he was hoping this time you would talk about your ancestor with the Empress of Austria.   That has the makings for a really good story. Not to say that this won't, but we've done the Jesus thing to death.   No pun intended. You want to write about something that has pizzazz."

"Pizzazz?   You're beginning to sound like the critics that told Mel Gibson not to waste his time or money on a movie about Jesus in a dead language."

"Well he shouldn't have, the movie was a disaster both at the box office and to his career."

"He should have tried telling the truth.   He might have found the audience a little more receptive if he did."

"Forget about Gibson, you know what I mean.   Something that will keep the reader on the edge of their seat.   Throw in a little soul-searching to boot and we've got pizzazz."

"Well I'll give you this, John, you are a sly devil.   All this time you had me practically begging to have your editor send us on a trip to Vienna to do that story and you knew all that time that he wanted that story and only that story. That's pretty low, even for you."

"Aw, Doc, give it a break. I just liked seeing your beg. So are we going to get it this time?"

"No. I'm going to give you this story. You'll get the other in good time John. Tell your editor he'll have that story, but I have a few things to get off my chest, so to speak. This one especially has been haunting me for a long time even though it just surfaced now because my son has triggered it, so I have to let it out."

"Haunting?"

"Nightmarish to be exact. That's one of the downsides to GLEEM. Sometimes you remember too much; every time death was cheated and every time that it wasn't. I have to get this story out! There's just no two ways about it!"

"Okay then, this is a 'have to,' so go for it. But my editor won't be happy about it. I can tell you that right now."

"I appreciate that John. I promise you that your editor will not regret this story. He wants adventure, he's going to get it. Intrigue, murder, romance, the works, this story has it all. This was one of the most important events in history. Bar none."

"Then let's go for it Doc. I'll get my trusty pen and pad out and we're away." Pearce bent over and rummaged through his brief case. Finding what he was looking for, he sat upright with that enthusiastic grin wrapped across his face that I had come to recognize whenever he prepared himself to dream about winning a Pulitzer. He placed his recorder on his lap and pressed the record button. "Okay, let's start."

"It's going to take awhile," I cautioned him.

"Yeah, so what's new? I brought lots of tapes."

"I'm not going to do it all at once," I added.

"Not to sound unappreciative here Doc but what good is a book to my publisher if you don't give me the full story?"

"You'll have enough to publish, just not the entire story at once. It's a trilogy at minimum. Perhaps even a four-parter or even a five-parter at max."

"Maybe I'm being dumb here," Pearce scratched his head, "But how do you insert a trilogy into what already is a series of books?"

"Just call them A, B and C, I don't care. Give each one its own title. I'm certain your editor can figure it out!" I provided a quick solution for him to think about.

"In case you haven't noticed Doc we've been labeling your books one, two, three, etc. already. A trilogy just doesn't fit the mold."

"Well, make it fit. This is a multi-part story inside a series. I don't have a problem with it so why should you?" I sat back against the hard boards of the bench and sighed with a deep exhaling breath.    This one was going to take a lot out of me.    There were so many crossover memories to sort out in order to assemble them into a cohesive structure that would make sense; a lot of painful memories, persisting over a multitude of generations.    The cold hand of death had choked the souls from so many of my ancestors in such a short time.    This was GLEEM at its absolute worst!

---

# JERUSALEM: 63 AD

Evening twilight was still two hours away when the procession of priests and court officers were seen transcending the arched bridge to the upper city, where the house of Matthias was situated.    In their flowing robes and peaked turbans, they immediately caught the interest of all they passed.    Everyone knew instinctively that it must be a very serious matter indeed for such prestigious and prominent leaders to risk violating the Sabbath by having the sun set upon them while engaging in business.    To be caught so far away from their homes on the Sabbath eve would have been enough to send the entire city into turmoil.    After all, who would officiate in the Temple that evening if the High Priest was to allow the sun to set without being within close proximity to the holy    sanctuary?    To even consider it was deemed sacrilegious.

They stopped outside the portico to the villa and waited to be officially greeted.    Proper respect had to be paid on such an auspicious occasion. Without it, they would immediately conclude their business, turn and begin the march back to the mount without ever setting a foot inside the house.    Principles always exceeded necessity as far as they were concerned.    That had always been the difference between Damneus and his father.    Caiaphas believed that the opposite was true and the two of them could never agree.    And even after his father's death, Damneus still insisted that he was right.

The senior Matthias bowed in reverence to the High Priest.    "My house is greatly honored by your presence Excellency.    May I offer you and your colleagues some light    refreshments."    Matthias clapped his hands and immediately his house servants brought out several trays of diced lamb wrapped in pastry, assorted fruits and cups of pomegranate juice.    Another set of servants stepped forward, one holding a laver of scented water while the other proffered a towel with which to dry their hands after dipping them into the bowl.

"We are most appreciative of your hospitality Matthias.    There was a hot wind in our faces all the way from the Damascus gate.    But we cannot stay long with sunset approaching.    Therefore I must conduct our business as swiftly as possible.    Do not be offended if we do not find the time to partake in little else than your refreshments."

"How is it then that I may serve my honored guests from the esteemed

Sanhedrin?"

"Actually Matthias, you cannot help us at all." Damneus cared little that his comment could be misconstrued as an impolite dismissal of the elder Matthias. "It is your son Joseph that can best serve us."

"I don't understand?"

"As you are well aware, there are several of our esteemed leaders from am ong the Sanhedrin that our being held in Rome under house arrest. For security reasons as the Romans would like to describe it. In reality, they are hostages being held to ensure our cooperation. I believe it is critical that these men be returned to Judea. The country grows restless and Rome has to understand that these prisoners represent one of the sources of that growing resentment. Some like Ben Phiabi have been held in Rome for almost nine years. It is time they come home."

"So what does my son have to do with any of this?"

"We believe he represents our best chance to retrieve these men."

"Joseph?" inquired his father, looking somewhat confused by the entire episode.

"Never have I seen anyone with his aptitude for both languages and law. From the time he was a young boy and sat in the portico of the inner court he has amazed us with the brilliance of his intellect. Ever since then I have watched him closely. His mastery of Greek and Latin is flawless. We need someone that is fluent with the both but more so we need someone that can get inside the minds of these Romans and comprehend how they think. I've seen him in the marketplace dealing with the foreign merchants. He knows exactly how to deal with them ... as an equal."

"I will not deny that. My son, if anything, has been too Hellenized to my way of thinking. There are times he prefers their philosophy to the Torah. He's a rebel although I say that with great pride. At his age I was the same in my father's eyes. I never imagined that this pursuit of foreign culture in some way could serve us, could serve our nation."

"Oh it does Matthias, it most definitely does. He is the key to the lock on those prison doors. One of the seers has even confirmed that it is so."

"I still don't understand how he is to do this. He's never been away from us. Other than Galilee, he hasn't been anywhere else."

"Don't worry. He will not be alone. There is a delegation waiting upon his arrival. They will provide him with the proper connections and audiences, but it will be up to Joseph to secure the priests' release through the use of that glib tongue of his."

"But he's just a youth," Matthias pleaded, reconsidering the request and growing reluctant to see his son placed into what could possibly be a potentially dangerous situation."

"Since when is twenty-six considered a boy? David was already ruling from Hebron by that age," the High Priest quickly negated Matthias' objection.

"It just that…"

"I know, Matthias," the high priest interrupted. "It's hard to think of them as anything but our children. But they don't stay children forever. Sometimes fate makes it happen sooner than later."

"There are others," the senior Matthias insisted. "What about your son, Jonathan?" he pointed towards Jonathan Cayapha barely visible among all the priests huddled near the entrance to the salon.

Damneus gazed over his shoulder briefly to see his son smile back at him upon hearing mention of his name.

"Let's be serious," the High Priest cautioned. "My son has his good points but let's not give him too much credit." Damneus spoke softly, but still audible to those standing close. It would not have bothered him had his son overheard his comments. Jonathan Cayapha was well aware of what his father thought of him. He had made it very clear on more than one occasion. "No, Matthias, there is only one choice if this mission is to prove successful."

"Still, I will have to let you know my decision," Joseph's father insisted.

"May I speak father," Joseph spoke up at last, breaking the silence as he rose from the seat he occupied in the corner of the salon beside his brother. "I do not believe this is an issue for debate. If it be the will of the Sanhedrin that I go on this mission, then who are we to quibble with their decision. After all, the collective wisdom of the holy fathers is beyond our ability to fathom, and they have judged me as the one to best serve the interests of our country in this endeavour. Father, who are we to argue with their decision?"

"You see Matthias,' Damneus remarked, "That is exactly what I was talking about. He talks like a lawyer and that's when he's not even thinking about what to say. It comes natural to him."

"There are many that talk like lawyers, with a lot more experience than Joseph, and able to converse in Latin as well," Joseph's father still argued.

"That is true but there are other reasons that I want your son to go."

"And may I ask what these reasons might be."

"They are for me to know and although you may ask, I will not tell you at this time. Trust me Matthias. When he returns successful in his mission, all will be clear. He will be the first to understand why I have entrusted him with this mission. As for the rest of us, we must trust in God!"

"How long until he leaves?"

"The day after the Sabbath."

"But that is in two days. It's not enough time to prepare properly. No, no…it's not reasonable. We need more time to prepare."

"Yes, it is possible. We will be back in two mornings. Have your son ready for travel on the road and a voyage to Rome. A single bag should do. Everything else will be provided once his boat docks in Puteoli. We will provide him with enough money to ensure his comfort so you need not trouble yourself with that at all.    I appreciate your support Matthias."

Before Matthias senior could even utter another word, Damneus had already turned his back and was heading towards the door.    Within half a minute most of the visiting party had disappeared through the doorway.

"But he's never been on the sea..." Matthias' voice trailed off into the emptiness that was left behind as soon as Damneus passed through the fence gate.

Joseph placed his arm around his distraught father.    "Don't worry Avi, I'll be okay.    God will look over me.    You'll see."

"Let me tell you a secret Joseph.    God hasn't been as reliable as one could hope.    You wouldn't be on a mission to Rome to rescue a handful of priests from internment there, if He had been.    God expects us to get through our dilemmas on our own before He intercedes.    And that can often take a lifetime."

"Avi, I really will be okay.    I don't expect God to intercede on my behalf. Merely provide guidance from time to time when I might need it."

"Perhaps it's just me, or maybe a result of all my generation has endured over the last fifty years.  Kings have come and gone.  Messiahs appear only to disappear.    But there has been one constant throughout all those years, and that was Rome. No matter which way you turn there is the heavy hand of Roman oppression.    It is hard to believe in the mercy of God, when he lets those that don't believe in Him rule the world."

"Who are we to understand the ways of God," Joseph calmed his father with a hand upon his shoulder.

"Ah, perhaps I'm just becoming a cynic in my old age.  But you'd think if He was truly aiding you on this mission He would have given Damneus enough sense to land you in Ostia and not strand you hundreds of miles away in Puteoli."

"Avi, don't worry about that.    God has better things to do than manage the ship schedules.    And you don't have to worry about becoming a cynic, you've always been one.    And we still love you!"    Joseph poked fun at his father as he patted him gently upon the shoulder.

# CHAPTER FOUR

## WHANGAREI: PRESENT

"You okay Doc?"

I found myself being drawn so completely into the memories that my head felt as if it was spinning uncontrollably. I steadied myself against the side of the bench, gripping the arm rest firmly until I could almost feel my fingers sinking deeply into the metal.

Pearce grew concerned when I didn't answer him. "Hey, everything okay?" he repeated.

I was able to anchor myself to the sound of his voice, drawing my mind slowly back to the real world, like a man climbing a rope hand over hand. Wiping the sweat away that broke out on my forehead, I turned to Pearce and smiled. "Boy, that wasn't easy. I haven't had that happen for almost fifty years now."

"What's that?"

"Sometimes the memories are so vivid, that my mind becomes confused. It can't separate out which time line I actually exist within. It wanted to believe that two thousand years ago was where I belonged. It's almost as if it was calling out to me."

"Doc, what happens if you can't snap out of it? What happens then?"

"That's what I thought was going to happen when I last experienced it fifty years ago. It was as if the mind could be peeled away from the body like removing the shell from a nut. But without the shell, there would have been no way I believe that I could return to the reality of this world. I fought hard to reclaim my existence. I did it but I still wonder what would have happened if I let my mind have its way and dwell in that other world?"

"This is getting too weird for me," Pearce struggled with the concept. "I mean you hear about people with these out of body experiences but not having undergone one myself, I can't relate to it."

"Remember how I once described to you how the mind could move through time because thoughts could actually move at a speed exceeding light-speed?"

"Yea, I remember," Pearce agreed. "That was in that John Robert Colombo book, **Ghost Stories of Canada**, right?"

"Well, this isn't much different. In both cases the mind has separated itself from physical containment. And if it can do that, then it can also remain separated."

"Sounds pretty risky if you ask me," Pearce commented. "You would have probably ended up in a padded cell with drool hanging from the corners of your mouth?"

It wasn't a pretty picture that he just painted but it caused us both to break out in nervous laughter. My world was pretty crazy just dealing with what I deemed as normality. But I couldn't see it getting much worse at times. I think Pearce realized that too. What happens when the mind separates completely from the body was beyond even my comprehension. Not something I wanted to explore or find out either.

"There's got to be safeguards in place that prevent it from happening", I suggested. "Otherwise I think I would have been lost a long time ago."

"So what's so special about this time," Pearce inquired. "The genealogy you provided for yourself has nothing to do with this Joseph guy. So where's the connection between you and him?"

"For that, you're going to have to pay attention to what I tell you. There are several linkages that exist; some through the male lines, sometimes through the female ones. But as to why this episode in history is so vivid I think has to do with the women that were involved."

"Through the female lines then?"

"Not exactly. Through love. The most intense emotion there is besides hate, and most of the woman that were intertwined with Joseph had this emotion in a double dose."

Pearce nodded his head in agreement. "I can agree with you there. I can still see all those times me and the missus were at our best and at our worst. You don't forget things like that. And even if you tried, my missus would make certain she reminded me so I didn't forget them as long as I live."

"No, you never forget the women you love, even if they span over two thousand years."

"I'm wondering Doc, if you know about all these loves that have existed throughout your family's history and as you said once, there are others that are also affected by GLEEM, does it ever happen that ....you know...like you find each other or something like that."

"We've already been through that one a long time ago John. Remember how I once described the coming together of people that react to each other without even knowing why. Well, it's not that unusual that you have a situation where both of the people involved also have what they think is déjà vu. That's when you know that both of them are being influenced by their ancestral memories and subsequently fate, coincidence, whatever you want to call it, brought those two descendants together in the same place and at the right time."

"Any things like that happen to you?" Pearce inquired.

"When you consider that my first wife's family and mine have come together again after two thousand years, and that of my second wife was after a thousand years, and both times we were immediately attracted to each other, it only leads me to conclude that it happens more than you think."

"What about your present wife, Doc?"

"You think because she's Chinese there couldn't be a connection. Then think again John. Zutra married Ti-ping or did you forget?"

"Are you saying Ying is a descendant of Ti-Ping?"

"I can't answer that. Her family never kept records and with all the turmoil in China over the past fifteen hundred years, it's unlikely we'd ever find such records. But like Ti-Ping, my wife can certainly sing. So perhaps that is a sign that she is somehow a descendant."

"Lot's of people sing, Doc," Pearce easily dismissed my comment.

"That is true," I agreed. "But it is food for thought. There was an interesting study done on personal connections. You may have seen it. It was on TV not too long ago. It was showing the links between people based on nothing m ore than out of six people that they name as friends, there's a link to one of six friends that someone else knows, and so on and so on"

"Yea, I did see that. Fascinating program. Six points of separation I think they called it. Didn't believe it at first until they started demonstrating it and then it was like this web that kept growing and growing. But I don't get it. What's the point you're making?"

"Don't you see?" I practically pleaded. "The world's not as big as you may think. If it was that easy to show links between people we know and practically everyone else in the world, then why would we think it so impossible to encounter people that our mutual ancestors came across. Most people generally stay in the same region or country for many generations. So even if you were playing the odds, they're stacked pretty high in favor of frequent contact between old acquaintances. And should two of those people happen to meet that had an intense relationship sometime way back in their family trees, just stand back because the fireworks will be mind blowing."

## JERUSALEM: 63 AD

The procession of elders reappeared at the gates that led to the outer courtyard of the house of Matthias on the day after the Sabbath but they did not enter. Joseph was already waiting at the portico with his bag over his shoulder when they arrived.

"Joseph," his mother pleaded with him "You don't have to do this."

"Yes, I do, Ima."

"Tell him he doesn't have to go," she cried to her husband. Matthias held his wife tenderly, restraining her from running to her eldest son. "Let him go Sipora. There comes a time when every chick must leave the nest. This is his time."

Joseph turned and began to walk through the courtyard to the outer gate.

"Joseph," his brother ran forward grabbing his arm. Embracing, the you nger Matthias gave his older brother the wisdom of his youth. "Give 'em hell when you're there brother."

Joseph smiled then lightly punched his brother. "Always the dreamer, Matti. This is going to be a piece of cake. I'll be back before you know it. And I'm not about to declare war on the Roman Empire while I'm there. Take care of Mamma while I'm away. She'll need you more than ever now."

"I will Joseph. I promise."

"And Pa too. He won't admit it, but he's taking this pretty hard as well." Joseph glanced back to see his parents still intertwined, clutching each other for reassurance as they watched him walk away. "Farewell Matti."

"Hurry now," Damneus shouted. "We don't have forever. You have a lot to do in a short time."

"He's an asshole," young Matthias whispered to his brother.

"And he always will be," Joseph admitted. Letting go of his brother's arm he ambled towards the elders that waited impatiently, refusing to turn back as he knew it would only make it harder to leave. Especially if he saw his mother's tears as she buried her face into his father's shoulder.

The High Priest looked on with disgust. "You're almost twenty-seven," he commented. "Did they think you were going to live with them forever?"

Joseph never bothered to respond, merely taking his place among the part y of the Sanhedrin and beginning the long walk towards the Joppa Gate in the western wall of the city. For the longest time not a single word was passed between any of the men, and none even bothered to acknowledge Joseph's presence. Then the silence was broken when Damneus' son, Jonathan Cayapha drew along side of Joseph and spoke cryptically. "It won't always be like this. There will be those watching over you."

"What?" Joseph was unable to discern what his distant cousin was saying.

Seeing that the high priest was now paying attention to what these two might be discussing, his son played it coyly. "The Sanhedrin has arranged for representatives of the Jewish community of Rome to meet with you when you disembark. They will watch over you," he repeated.

It was obviously not the same message that he initially tried to relate, Joseph was certain of it. Jonathan was definitely holding something back but when your father is Joshua Damneus, there's probably a lot you learn to conceal rather than encounter the high priest's wrath.

"Jonathan, what are you filling Joseph's head with?" Damneus demanded to know in that humorless tone of voice that was the only tone he ever seemed to use.

"Only to let him know that we have taken care of every necessity while he is in Rome."

"I would have explained all of that to him at the appropriate time," Damneus thundered.

"Yes Father."

"When we reach the gates, you will be handed over to the protection of Michael Corvasus. Corvasus has lived a good portion of his life in Rome and has been a most reliable servant of the Sanhedrin on other business. Be certain to do everything he advises you. His experience is most invaluable. Once you arrive at the port of Puteoli he will take you to the home of one of our agents that he is familiar with. Arrangements will be made to provide you with a line of credit at all our banking houses. Try not to abuse the privilege. Afterwards you'll be introduced to our people in Rome that have the ear of the Emperor Nero."

"And what am I to say to them."

"All that is taken care of in this epistle." Damneus withdrew the letter from the sleeve of his robe and handed it to Joseph. "Do not open it until you are safely with our agent in Puteoli. "It will make it clear exactly what we are prepared to offer for the safe return of our incarcerated priests. Whom and when will be detailed in letters that he will then dispatch to those that will aid you. All that you have to do is speak eloquently on our behalf as I know you are most capable."

"I don't understand your eminence. If everything has already been arranged, and you have your representatives in Rome why do you need me?"

"Because there are certain people that have the balance of power and you're the key that will persuade them to help us."

"How can that be, they don't even know me."

Damneus smirked, "Ah yes, but we know them. And you are most certainly the key. Of that there is no question."

Joseph was going to continue to pursue the issue but he recognized the look that the high priest flashed him. Damneus had said all that he was going to say and any further attempts would be a waste of time. From then on they walked in silence until they reached the huge stone gates that arched over the road to Joppa. These gates were ancient, rumored to be as old as the city itself, but no one knew exactly how old that actually was. A thousand years ago, David had taken the city from the Jebusites. How long they had ruled was unknown.

"As I mentioned, just outside these gates you will be approached by Michael Corvasus. You will give him this other letter." Damneus pulled another letter from his robe. "It secures the balance of his payment from our bankers in Puteoli. He is a man that, let's say, remembers his allegiance to his homeland only at a price. Be wary of someone whose loyalty can be bought."

"I thought you said that he had a history of being reliable," Joseph challenged Damneus' earlier comments.

"Do not confuse reliability with trust, my son. That is a serious error my father made that I swore I would never repeat myself. Trust in God, but don't waste your time searching for it in men. Take this bag. It contains enough silver denari and gold aurei to smooth your path with reliable people until our agent makes other arrangements for you. Be careful that you keep this bag well concealed during the voyage at all times. A life can become very cheap when it's weighed in the scales against money."

Taking the bag, Joseph used its draw strings to tie it to the inside of his cloak. "I understand," Joseph confirmed.

Moving to the centre of the gate, Damneus waved his hand over his head to signal a group of riders that watched from a knoll in the distance. Immediately one of the riders broke from the rest and came charging towards the gates, leading a riderless horse behind.

"You said nothing about horses," Joseph groaned. "I don't ride horses," he declared openly.

"Then learn," Damneus growled at him. And with that comment the men of the Sanhedrin turned and reentered the city, leaving Joseph behind with his new companions.

---

Most of the distance to Joppa had been covered before a saddle sore Joseph decided to break the unnerving silence. "Does anyone here know how to talk?"

"What would you like us to say," the one that Damneus had referred to as Michael Corvasus responded. Everything about him was Roman. His hair, his dress, even his accent. It was obvious to Joseph that he labored very hard to mask his Semitic origins.

"How about, 'It's a pleasure to be on this mission together' or something to that effect?"

Corvasus twisted his mouth into a wry sneer. "You assume a lot. What I do is purely business, pleasure has nothing to do with my motivations. You are nothing more than a contract. Ensure your safety to Puteoli, arrange for you to meet the Sanhedrin's agents, and collect the other half of my money for a safe delivery."

"Fair enough. I can accept that. You get me there safely and I'll go do my thing for the good of our people and country."

"Your people, your country. That's why they hire me. Because I live in that other world. Theirs is the dominant civilization, not yours."

"So you turn your back on your world, your culture, and everything that we've striven for, for over a thousand years."

"Because I chose not to strive any longer. You'd think after a thousand years we would have figured out that we were backing the wrong faction."

"I didn't know God picked sides."

"That should have been obvious. We haven't exactly been master of our own destiny for near on seven centuries now. How much longer do you think we need before we all figure it out?"

"So why do you even bother dealing with us at all?"

"The money's good. I can bridge two worlds and get paid for it. Doesn't get much easier than that."

"Damneus obviously forgot to mention that cynicism was one of your greater virtues."

"In a few weeks I'll have you safely at your destination and you and I never have to deal with each other again. Does that satisfy your curiosity?"

"Not completely. What I'd really like to know is how it feels to betray one's own people."

"Only a fool would see my choice as betrayal. That's why as Jews we're ultimately doomed to fail. We refuse to evolve. We can't seem to accept that the world is constantly changing. The Romans understand it. They have come to grips with the need to change. Why are we such a stubborn people that we refuse to accept what everyone else has come to understand? You explain that to me and then perhaps you may have some justification to point a finger at me!"

Casting his gaze downwards, Joseph admitted that he didn't have all the answers.

"I didn't think so," Corvasus gloated. "And don't expect to hear anything from our companions. Good men but they've lost their tongues a while back. They were all gladiators. Some of them were actually pretty good but they didn't want to wait until they were granted their freedom. Got involved in a slave revolt and typical of Roman humor, they were given their freedom in a sense once the revolt was put down. But they exchanged a few body parts in the bargaining process. And freedom only meant that they were sold to someone that was interested in them even after their punishment. I still considered them to be quite useful, so I bought them. Obedient and quiet. A very good combination."

"You're trying hard to disgust me, aren't you?"

"Let me know if it's working."

"What's your problem?"

"Overly ripe, holier than thou, pompous, highly judgmental, self-emulating, narcissistic aristocrats."

"Anyone I should know," Joseph retorted in a display of humor that Corvasus had not anticipated. It caught him completely off guard and he couldn't help but laugh.

"There may be some hope for you yet, Joseph ben Matthias."

Joseph turned his steel gray eyes towards Corvasus, flashing him a fleeting smile as he did so. They're worlds apart he thought to himself, but even so, there might be some tie that binds them together. This pretender to Roman culture was an interesting contradiction of birth he thought to himself. This would be a challenge. It was a long trip. Perhaps there would be enough time to return this lost soul to the fold. Ahhch! The thought soured in his mouth. Still thinking too much like a priest and that entitlement was no longer part of his inheritance.

As an ambassador, it wasn't his responsibility to try and save the sheep lost from the flock. Michael Corvasus was someone else's concern. No, all he had to do was tolerate the heretic for a few weeks and then forget about him.

---

Once safely outside the walls of Joppa, Corvasus handed each of his six servants a small leather pouch containing a good number of sesterces and sent them on their way.

"Where are they going?" Joseph questioned.

"They're just taking the long way home."

"What is that supposed to mean, the long way home?"

"You don't think I'm going to use the money I'm being paid to book all of them passage on the ship too. No, they can take the scenic route by land and wait for me back at my villa. Oh yes, my villa. Have I mentioned it before? I do get paid well for what I do. Nice spot on the Peloponesian shore overlooking my acres and acres of olive groves. Perhaps you can understand me a little better now."

"What I understand is that you're not adverse from taking money from those that you find an embarrassment."

"I may be somewhat embarrassed by my heritage but I certainly have no encumbrance when it comes to money. So what motivates you, Joseph ben Matthias? What is it that you're willing to lay your life down for?"

"I don't understand…"

"You may not like what you see when you look at me, and I certainly don't like what I see when I look at you but I'm thinking there are probably qualities that you have that if given half a chance, I could admire. So here's an opportunity for you to impress me by telling me what one of them might be."

Joseph kept his emotions under control. His instinctive response was to take a swing at Corvasus but logic told him that it would be a foolish thing to do. His adversary appeared to have had some military training in the past, not to mention that physically he was bigger and probably stronger. Then again, Joseph thought to himself, it wasn't that big an insult. It wasn't as if he had been sworn at. All Corvasus said openly was that he didn't like his character. Was that something to fight over? No. Joseph let it pass. "I'd do it for freedom!"

"Freedom? Freedom you say!" Corvasus howled with laughter. "So you consider yourself a freedom fighter." He was laughing so hard now that his sides felt like they were splitting. Michael wrapped his arms around himself as tears began to well up in his eyes.

"I'm no freedom fighter," Joseph replied sternly. "But if my freedom was being challenged I wouldn't hesitate to fight."

"I guess we'll never know that for certain, will we?"

Another veiled insult that Joseph knew he was going to have to let slide if he was going to even get started on his mission. "Don't you think we should perhaps find our vessel rather than stand about debating what I would or wouldn't do?"

"First we'll head towards the market and sell of our horses. We won't have need of them any longer," Michael suggested.

Finally, Joseph thought to himself. He'll be underway and off to Rome and he won't have to listen to this inane prattle any longer.

Leading their horses down to the market place Joseph found Joppa to be a thriving city with stalls and warehouses, overflowing with wares and foodstuffs imported from all around the Mediterranean. Like a child opening presents, he was enthralled with the variety of goods that he had never seen before. "Quick, over there," Joseph shouted and then darted towards one of the merchants.

Reluctantly, Corvasus followed, having to care for his charge no matter how difficult that might become. Catching up to the son of Matthias, he grasped his shoulder firmly. "Until we get to Rome, you have to listen to me. And one of the first lessons is you don't run off anywhere without my say so. Do we understand each other?"

Joseph brushed the hand from his shoulder. "Yes, we understand each other. But understand this. You were hired by the Sanhedrin. I'm empowered by the Sanhedrin. You work for me. Understood?"

Corvasus just shook his head and snickered. "Don't get smart with me. You need me far more then I need you. You're just one more job in a long list of them. You may not realize it, but there are a hundred things that can happen to you from here to the docks. And we're talking bad things. Most of them entail losing your money, your clothes, or your life before you ever reach that ship. That's why I've been hired to watch over you. Because for the hundred things that can happen to you before you set sail, you can double that for what may happen aboard ship, and multiply it by ten once you set foot on shore in Puteoli. You're chances of reaching Rome alive without someone like me guiding and protecting you are zero. So now that we have that clear, let me rephrase my directive to you. Do not run off because you are placing yourself in grave danger. And I don't need my job made harder than it has to because some backwater provincial aristocrat gets excited the first time he gets a glimpse of the real world. Now what was of such great importance that you had to see this stall?"

"You wouldn't understand!"

"Try me."

"You just know how it is. We backwater aristocratic folk just can't help ourselves when we see pretty shiny objects."

"But this is a fruit merchant," Corvasus advised his charge.

"Oh, fruit too, that's big for us primitive folk," Joseph grinned sarcastically.

"I guess I overdid that last comment," Corvasus responded as it dawned on him that he had now become the butt of Joseph's mocking humor.

"Yeah, you did," Joseph agreed. "You and I are from different worlds. On that much we agree. But don't for a moment think that where I come from, for that matter where you came from, is in any way inferior to the glitter and glory that's almighty Rome. We have something here that just doesn't exist in that world. It's too bad you never saw that."

"Don't try to get moralistic on me Joseph. I know what you're world's all about. I've seen its dark underbelly. Only difference is Rome wears its sins on the outside where everyone can see them."

"Then I'm sorry for you. If you can't see the holiness that seethes through every pore in this land then there's no way we're ever going to find a common ground."

"Good! Now finally I think we finally understand each other." Crooking his head towards his companion, he gave it a slight nod to silently suggest that they were actually on that elusive common ground, just not the way Joseph had anticipated it. Turning his attention to the owner of the stall, he inquired as to where they could find someone that would purchase their horses for a fair price. The man pointed them towards a platform closer to the waterfront. It was off in the 'L' formed by two shipyards, having its own alley that jutted off from the main road. There they would find the flesh merchant, a trader in all things living. Whether it was horse, cattle, or even human, he bought and sold it all from that platform.

As they approached the merchant's stall, Michael turned to Joseph and instructed him to remain silent. "I'll do all the talking. Don't say a word; this has nothing to do with you."

"Don't worry," Joseph assured him. "They're your horses after all."

"That's right. They are mine, so just stay out of it!"

The merchant could be overheard inspecting his merchandise from behind the heavy linen curtain that hung towards the back of the platform, creating a semi-enclosed tent that he could take shelter in out of the hot sun.

"Yo!" Michael cried out. "Is anyone there?"

The curtain pulled back ever so slightly from one side and the barest sliver of the merchant's face could be seen peering back at them. "What is it you want?" he replied.

"I was told you buy horses," Corvasus responded.

Stepping from behind the drape the merchant was glad to be of service. He was Syrian from his dress, the heavy turban twisted around a conical centre and his bell shaped coat reaching down to just an inch off the ground. "Yes, I trade for horses," he replied. "Perhaps that is what you heard?"

"No," Corvasus returned his comment. "I definitely heard that you buy horses. I'm not here to trade." He was use to the game and understood the rules completely. This was all part of the preliminaries. They would joust back and forth; sizing each other up until the deal was struck. To the merchant, there was as much enjoyment in the barter as the actual sale or purchase. To not play the game, Michael knew would be an insult and would result in no sale at all.

"But I really do have some fine merchandise. Two young men like your selves really should not be alone. It's always good to have women take care of your needs."

"We don't need any women."

"Oh, I see. Are you Greek then?"

"You know damn well we're not Greek," Joseph interjected, a touch enraged by the suggestion.

"Be quiet!" Michael instructed his companion. "No, you don't see! We're about to go on a voyage. There's no place for women on a ship."

"Then perhaps menservants to watch and stand guard over you while you're on board your ship. I have some fine Nubians. You cannot get a better body guard than a Nubian."

"That happens to be my purpose on this voyage. I wouldn't want to have to deal with the competition, especially since it is well known that the Nubians are proven to be excellent body guards." Corvasus was playing the game well.

"This is a waste of time," Joseph muttered. "Let's go find someone else."

"Don't be in such a rush, my young impetuous friend. I'm certain we can find a proper exchange for your horses."

"Pay him no heed," Michael drew the merchant's attention back to himself. "They're my horses, so you don't have to deal with him at all."

"I know, chickens! I have chickens. You'll be on your voyage for weeks. Nothing better than having fresh eggs when you want them, and a chicken to stew when you're hungry."

Michael shook his head and laughed. "No my friend, I don't think we'd need that many chickens. It would take hundreds just to cover the cost of these horses. Why don't we talk silver?"

"You know, I really do have some fine women. Let's not be hasty in saying no and let me tell you about this special one. Fresh from the desert. I just secured her today in fact, earlier this morning from a trader's caravan. She is positively beautiful. You'll absolutely fall in love the moment you lay your eyes upon her. I promise you, you will not be disappointed. Just wait a moment. Let me go get her and you'll see for yourself."

Michael was about to say 'no' but before he could even utter the word, the merchant had ducked back behind the heavy curtain. The two of them stood silently dismayed as they watched what appeared to be a struggle from the marked impressions visible on the linen surface of the tent. With a final heave, the merchant flung the defenseless girl onto the outer platform.

"My apologies gentlemen. She didn't want to co-operate at first. As I said, she was just sold to me this morning and I haven't had the opportunity to teach her any manners."

Joseph felt the bile rising in his stomach.    As the girl tried to regain her composure and dignity, raising herself from where she had fallen, he could see the welts and bruises that ringed her wrists and ankles.    Wherever she had come from, she had not come willingly and he sensed the anger intensifying in his every fiber.

"Isn't she beautiful," the merchant crooned.    "Look at those eyes! Have you ever seen eyes like that before.  You can get lost in those eyes.  They are like dark moons.    And such magnificent hair.    Auburn locks that fall like the wings of angels upon her shoulders.  You are very lucky men to have this opportunity. She won't be here for long, I can assure you.    It's not often that I have a slave of this quality.    And I bet you're thinking to yourself, how be it that such a goddess could be a mere slave girl.    It can only happen if in real life she was a princess."

"That's    enough    of    this    fable,"    Michael    insisted.    "Granted she's beautiful but she is not a princess.    Now let's talk about how much silver you can press into my hand for my horses and be done with it."

"Ah, but that's where you're wrong. Look at her dress, my friend. This is not the clothing of a peasant.    The embroidery alone would have cost a week's wages.  And let me tell you how she was found.    In a caravan.    In a bridal caravan belonging to Mithridates of Parthia. This girl was obviously one of his daughters about to be wed to some desert prince.    When the traders saw the caravan,    they    charged    down    from    the    hills.  All    of    the    royal guards fled, leaving behind this princess sitting alone and defenseless in her carriage.    Such cowardice is unbelievable, but it's true, they left her all alone.    The traders had no choice but to take her captive for her own safety."

"The raiders knew like everyone else does, that she was nothing more than a decoy.    Somewhere out there was the real bridal caravan and had it been attacked, the guards would have fought to the death, every last one of them. The Parthian Royal Guards are not cowards.    That I can assure you from my own experience.    She's no more than one of the princess' slave maidens."

"No, it's not true!    No princess would keep a maid that outshone her in beauty.    And for the princess to be more beautiful than this girl would be impossible.    Therefore    by    careful    logic    and    deduction, she has to be the princess."    The trader was    solid in his belief that she could not have been a decoy.

"Easy enough to prove," Michael challenged the merchant.  "If I prove it to you, will you just pay me the silver for my horses and we can be on our way?"

"Alright," the trader agreed.    "You prove it to me and I'll give you forty-five denarii each."

"They're worth at least eighty apiece."

"Yes, they may very well be, but I'm in the business of buying and selling.    I have to have my margin."

"You're    certainly    a    hard    piece    of    work,    aren't    you?"    Michael commented. "Okay, forty-five then and throw in a half dozen chickens."

"It's a deal, my friend.    Tie up your horses over there by my crates, and I'll count out the money and then you show me your proof and it's yours."

Pulling Joseph close to him, Michael spoke softly so as not to be overheard. "I'll go hitch these two up to the post but you keep an eye on our sticky fingered friend here and make certain he count's the coins out correctly."

No sooner had Michael started leading the horses across the square, the merchant leaned over until his face was mere inches from Joseph's. "I can tell you're enthralled by the girl, young master.    There's nothing wrong with what you're feeling.    She can be    yours.    Just yours!    You don't even have to share her with your friend."

"Get away from me, you sick piece of filth!" Joseph screamed as he gave a shove that forced the trader to stagger backwards and almost topple over.

"I'm wounded by your harsh words. They are like an arrow to my heart," the trader motioned with his hands, pretending to plunge a dagger into his chest. "How    could    I    be    anything    but    a    man    overwhelmed    by    such unparalleled beauty?    I am nothing but a normal male."

Joseph was torn between walking away and tearing the trader to pieces, limb from limb.    He couldn't ascertain why he was reacting so violently as he could not concentrate long enough to find the answer. The feelings he bore were totally unfamiliar.    His entire life he had chosen to follow the teachings of Hillel and practice passivity.    But now passivity was the furthest thing from his mind.

"Perhaps you have not seen enough?" The slave trader shouted a few words in a foreign tongue to the girl but she made no response.    He shouted again.    And once again she refused to acknowledge his instructions. The trader lurched towards her and grabbed the top of her dress, shearing it from her shoulders with a swift tug.    She frantically crossed her arms across her exposed breasts bursting into tears as she did so.    "How's that for quality, young sir?"

"You bastard!"    Joseph surged forward at the trader, leaping on to the plat form    and seizing him by the throat.    "She's not an animal," he screamed while tightening his grip until the merchant began gagging for breath.

Racing back towards the two of them, Corvasus grabbed hold of Joseph's arm and attempted to tear it away but with no luck    "Let go of him you fool," Corvasus ordered his companion but Joseph refused to release his death grip.    "God damn it," he bellowed as he took a few strides backwards and then charged into Joseph knocking him off his feet.

"Help, help me," the trader began screaming as soon as he felt the rush of air flowing into his lungs once more.    "Someone call the guards.    I've been attacked!"

"No wait," Corvasus urged, trying frantically to calm the man down.    "This is merely a misunderstanding.    You don't need to call out for the soldiers.    It's all a misunderstanding."

"Misunderstanding, nothing! You're friend's a crazed lunatic. He tried to kill me. Look at his eyes! He's out of his mind. He deserves to be locked up."

"No, take our horses. You don't have to pay me a thing. We'll call ourselves even. He obviously didn't know what he was doing. He's a priest, he doesn't understand these things."

"He's a maniac, that's what he is."

"Do we have a deal?"

"Fine, now get out of here before I change my mind and have you both arrested. You're both crazy. And your priest friend is a danger to everyone. Take him far away from here and lose him."

"No," Joseph shouted, "not without the girl."

"Are you truly crazy?" Corvasus reacted.

"How much?"

"Twelve hundred sesterces." Suddenly the trader had forgotten completely about the incident and was holding out his hand to complete the deal.

Joseph reached into his pouch and withdrew the equivalent amount in gold aureii. "Here!" He slammed the money down on the counter in front of the trader his pouch now lighter by about fifteen of the precious gold coins.

"This is insane," Corvasus screamed up to the heavens his fists clenched as he did so. "What do you think you're doing? That's like three hundred denarii. That buys you a quarter acre of good farm land. You're jeopardizing everything! The Sanhedrin didn't give you that money to buy a slave. That was money to ensure your comfort all the way to Rome."

"There's no way I'm going to let this piece of filth put his hands on her again. There's more money waiting for me when I get to Rome. I can do with this pouch as I please. Don't look at me in that way. Slavery is inhumane and I will not tolerate the abuse of any human being in this manner."

"Maybe in your perfect world it doesn't exist, but in this reality, it most certainly does. What are you going to do? Buy up all the slaves? It's a fact of life! Get over it!"

"Only because you're willing to accept it but Jewish law clearly says there are no slaves, only those that sell themselves into servitude to pay off their debts and even if they haven't paid it off, when the seventh year rolls around they are released from their servitude. That is God's law. You were a Jew once, you should know that!" Joseph repeatedly hammered his fingers against some imagined spike in the air as he dictated the Mosaic law to Corvasus.

"Take a good look around you Joseph. Have a dose of reality for once in your life Roman law is in force here. There's no place for God's law here. You better learn to accept that if we're going to survive this mission."

"It matters not; we're not leaving without the girl. Her family will want her back. She's the daughter of a king. They'll be grateful to us for her safe return. I'll get my money back."

"She's a Parthian slave girl for heaven's sake. She's no princess. No one wants her. No one is looking for her. She's just lost chattel. The stuff that slaves are made from."

"How can you say that? Look at her clothes. Look at the goods from the caravan that they captured. You heard his story that he told us. It had to be a bridal caravan."

"Oh, of that I'm certain. She could be wearing a gold tiara and it wouldn't be needed to prove that it was a bridal caravan. It's just that it wasn't 'the' bridal caravan. Just the decoy like I said. She's no princess." Grabbing the girl's right arm, he rotated it so that her palm turned upwards. "See that tattoo on her right palm, that's her slave mark; property of the house of Mithridates. You just bought yourself a very expensive bride's maid but not the bride."

"But a lovely one at that," the trader interjected, back in good humor as he hefted the gold aureii in his hand, taking enjoyment from the sound they made as they clanged together.

"Oh shut up," both Joseph and Michael responded in unison.

"Well, tell her she's free then Michael. I'll send her on her way; she can find her way back home to her mistress. You said you spoke Farsi, so tell her what I said."

"No need to," Michael informed him. "She heard you well enough the first time. She's a slave girl, which means she knows Aramaic as well as you and me."

"Well then," Joseph helped pull the dress back across her shoulders and knotted it behind her neck, "you are free to go. I'll give you some money to help you on your way and there's no need to thank me."

With tears in her eyes, she clung to his tunic. "You are sentencing me to death," she pleaded. "Better that I stay here in the slaver's tent than go alone on the road in this barbaric country. Do you have no pity on me that you'd do such a thing to me?"

Dumbfounded, Joseph glanced at Corvasus for an answer but his companion was too busy shaking his head in disgust to pay him any mind. "I don't know what else to do," he grabbed her hand trying to gently force her into releasing his tunic. "I have to sail to Rome today and I have no choice but to leave you to fend for yourself."

"Let me come with you," she suggested at first, then pleaded and cajoled until Joseph sensed his resistance waning.

"Oh great," Corvasus spat. "Not bad enough I have to look after one of you, now I've got two to wet nurse."

"I'll keep her out of your way," Joseph promised. "I'll sort something out once we reach Puteoli. "I'm certain the agents there can help her."

"You just do that," Corvasus warned him. "If I find in any way her presence threatens my carrying out my instructions from the Sanhedrin to protect only you,

I will not hesitate to feed her to the fish."

Frightened by the threat, the girl clutched even tighter on to Joseph's tunic. "He wouldn't do that, would he?"

"I'm afraid he's no better than the raiders that robbed your caravan. You actually may be safer trying to make it back to your homeland on your own."

"You will protect me, won't you?" She glanced upwards into Joseph's eyes and when he looked into hers he felt himself melting into the black pools that held him captive.

"I'm Joseph," he said finding it difficult to form the syllables of his own name, his throat dry and struggling to swallow.

"My name is Osirah," she smiled, moving her body closer to his, seeking the protection that he offered.

# CHAPTER FIVE

## WHANGAREI: PRESENT

I could tell that something was deeply bothering Pearce by this time. It's funny how you learn to perceive these things about other people after knowing them for some time. It's an intuition that they don't even have about themselves. You see it, you feel it, but if left to themselves, they never express it because they're never quite able to    put their finger on it.

"So what's the problem now?" I asked.

"No problem," he immediately responded.

"C'mon now! It's written all over your face. If you've got a problem with the story line, then let me hear it because if you have a problem, then thousands of readers are going to have a problem as well."

"Well, it's not quite a problem…"

"John, it either is or it isn't.    We've worked together too many times for you to go mute on me now.    Let me have it.    I'm a big boy, believe me, I can handle it."

Reluctantly, Pearce finally was persuaded to speak up. "After all we've discussed together, you'd have to say that by now I have a fair understanding of this whole GLEEM thing."

"That's a fair assessment," I commented.

"And I'm not saying that I can even imagine a tenth of what you must go through with all these memories swirling around inside your brain, but…"

"Okay, go ahead, but what?"

"Well, GLEEM works because you've inherited packets of memory incorporated into your own genetic makeup.    And nobody's disagreeing with you there. But this story that you're spinning now, it's not even your direct ancestry.    And I know you said that it's got more to do with female relationships and you'll explain it all as you go on, but what you're giving us now is pure fiction.    There's no GLEEM to support what you're saying. I'm pretty sure that I'm right here Doc."

"Sometimes you got to have faith John."

"You've always been a stickler for the facts," he pointed out. "Science was how you've tried to explain everything.    So I find it kind of surprising that you're now willing to accept something as real purely on faith and asking me to accept it on the same basis."

"As much as I'd like to believe there's a scientific explanation for everything, there have been times I've had to accept what my eyes were seeing entirely on faith.    I know you may find that hard to believe but it's true.    There are times I know that something happened even when there's no way I could ever prove it."

"So what kind of faith we're talking here?"

"Blind faith.    The kind where you have to suspend everything you hold dear and just accept it.    The most unscientific kind there is."

"But Doc, weren't you the one that told us that there was no way that you could accept the 'Outer Limits' type stuff and even though that incident about you witnessing a thirty year old murder was recorded in that book, you still went out of your way to prove it couldn't have been an apparition but most likely a slip in time.    So if you weren't prepared to accept the obvious then, why are you so willing to do so now?"

"Because there are things that happen that no matter how hard I strain to apply logic and reason they defy every physical law I can conceive of.  There's no other explanation other than the metaphysical or the paranormal and when I have to admit to myself that such a thing can exist, then I'm left with no other choice but faith that there is a greater power in the universe than I can fathom."

"Wow, I never thought I'd hear you say that."

"It shouldn't be that great a shock.    Just look at my family history, John. Ninety-eight generations since Aaron.  My ancestors actually talked with God.  They were given a bunch of colored rocks to play with inside their pouch under the ephod and with those they were able to divine answers." Pearce looked at me strangely when I mentioned the rocks, so I figured I'd better explain in greater detail.    "The urim and thummim of the bible, John!    A bit like rune stones.    So if they were being instructed directly by God for all those generations, who am I to doubt them."

"But do you really believe they talked with God?"

"Isn't that the essence of the entire bible? That in times of need God actually      speaks directly to a human being and instructs him on how to save His people.  You know, I always found it funny.  If a man is known to talk to God, he is  said  to  be  pious,  religious,  upright  and  righteous.      But  if  a  man said that God talked to him, we'd say he's crazy, a lunatic, and certifiably insane. How come he's only sane if God doesn't answer back? Don't you think it's funny how we're prepared to make that distinction?    Something's wrong with our way of thinking if we're willing to accept it in one direction but not the other."

"Good    point!"    John    asserted.    "I'll    have    to    remember    that one next time I hear voices."

"I guess the underlying fundamental rule of being the ninety-eighth generation means I have to be prepared for the unimaginable. I'm at that threshold of the hundredth generational promise to my ancestors that God was going to restore his order on this planet."

"So, one of your grandsons is going to be the one to rearrange the world?"

"Not necessarily. We were going to lose everything in the way of the promises to Aaron but that was only to last for the hundred generations. It didn't say that the hundred and first would have all the glory returned in one fell swoop. It could take hundreds of years for that to be rebuilt. It's just that it starts from that generation."

"And what's going to be the defining point that causes this turn around?" Pearce asked scoffingly but wise enough not to completely disbelieve what I had to say.

"It's already been happening, John. In case you haven't been paying attention, you and I have been that turning point. That day you showed up at my door several years back was the threshold and ever since you've been helping put what's in my head into print and circulating it to our readership around the world. That was the monumental day when change began to take place. So, sometime in the not to distant future, when they look back into history to see when the rebuilding all began, they'll see your hand in it. You're making history John."

"I think you might be getting a little carried away there Doc."

"Do you really want to know how a person realizes they have faith? This is how it happens. I must have been about thirteen at the time, perhaps almost four teen to be more correct. I remember the time frame because the event was related in some respects to the fact I already had my bar mitzvah. You know, when you become a man by joining the congregation. Sort of like communion in your church. There I am, in bed, experiencing that twilight sleep that you sometimes enter. You know, when you're not awake, but you're not quite asleep yet either. We all tend to experience it"

Pearce nodded his head. He knew exactly what I was talking about. Most people do, they just don't know how to properly explain their experiences while they're in that state.

"I rarely talk about this, so you better pay attention because there is a very good likelihood that I'll never mention it again. As you may or may not recall, I once explained to you that there's still some tribal allegiance existing in Judaism but it's only to the one tribe, that being Levi. Everyone else is lumped into Israel or Judah, because they haven't kept the records for almost two thousand years, ever since the expulsion from Judaea. So, two thousand years ago, people could still tell you that they were an Ashurite, or a Simeonite or a Benjaminite and so on. Paul of Tarsus for example knew he was a Benjaminite. So this whole lost tribe thing is more of a modern day fallacy. It actually got lost because the system of recording tribal origins broke down as soon as we didn't have our own country any longer. But the Levites always maintained the records. We had to. Before Rabbinic Judaism was able to evolve from the Pharisaic entity, the priests were still responsible for maintaining religious order and structure. And so the records of whom was a Levite, a Kohen, or even the Kohen Gadol, also known as the Kahana by certain families was strictly recorded. Even though the system has been displaced as the Rabbis have no use for inheritable privilege since it actually challenges their own authority, there is still an honor in the synagogue to be recognized as part of the tribe of Levi, and especially if you're of the Kohen orders. At the time of your bar mitzvah, your heritage status is to be announced to the entire congregation as it is essential that you can be ordained into manhood according to your appropriate family title. That never happened for me. I was entered into the congregational register as Israel, just a part of the regular masses. Why, because I never knew I wasn't. I was never told what my ancestry was. And this is where everything becomes a bit strange."

"Oh, like everything else you've told me over the years hasn't been incredibly strange already," Pearce challenged my comment.

"Stranger. Much stranger."

"So what was the problem that they didn't know?" Pearce was curious.

"You have to remember that my father was gone from my life when I was only nine months old. Of course, he knew that we were Kohanim but he wasn't around to tell the rabbis that I was a descendant of high priests and my mother couldn't be bothered as she tried to erase anything that had to do with my father."

"Sort of what you were describing not too long ago with your sons," Pearce interjected.

"Sort of. I guess it's fairly common in family breakups. But anyway, back to what I was explaining. So like I said, I'm in that half sleep that people often experience and in my head I hear this voice."

"What was it saying?"

"Just hold your horses, I'm getting to that. Just wait a minute. So there's this voice and it's repeating, 'Koom Kahana, Kahana Koom!' Which translates as Rise up Kahana, as a command for me to follow. Now my first reaction was to respond to this mysterious entity with a question, 'Kahana who?' I had never heard the term before. At the time it was quite meaningless. But I pictured myself getting up and following in the direction of the source of the voice. I was no longer in my bedroom but in what appeared to be a vast desert of dunes and very little else. Up ahead I could see the sands begin to swirl apart so that what used to be a dune was being burrowed, revealing the hard ground beneath it. I stepped forward to the uncovered earth and there was a stairway leading down. I could just make out the shadow of someone standing at the bottom of the stairs waving for me to follow. Whoever it was wasn't the source of the voice, but most certainly was acting as its agent. Now I recall part of myself saying in my head, none of this is real, you're at home in bed asleep but the other part is saying this is very real, you've crossed the threshold into an existence you cannot even attempt to understand."

"So what did you do next?"

"Exactly as I was told, I followed down the steps and into a huge hall. I never got any closer to the entity that was waving to me to follow. Never got to see what he actually looked like, other than knowing he was enshrouded in dark robes and a hood that masked his features completely. The hall I enter is empty. It's illuminated by some unnatural light without any identifiable source. I could see a single pedestal at the far end of the hall, and on it sat a large book. I knew instinctively that it had been waiting there for me all this time. I open it up but all the pages are blank. There was nothing written in it at all. 'I don't understand,' I heard myself cry out and then that same voice that had instructed me to rise and follow said, 'You will.' That's all it said and before I knew what happened I found myself sitting by the edge of a small stream. When I look into the water, I could see what appeared to be the outline of an underwater cave entrance. Whereas the banks everywhere else angled and sloped to the centre of the river so that you could clearly discern their surface, there was this one area that was completely black and seemed to angle in the opposite direction. So I did what anyone would do under those circumstances."

"What was that?"

"I swung myself over the edge and entered the cavern. It was almost as if I had been there before. I knew that I had to swim straight for about thirty or so seconds before I could resurface. And that's exactly what I did. I came up into a room hewn from the bedrock. At this end of the room was the edge of the stream and at the far end was a narrow flight of stairs carved from the rock leading upwards. The room was used for storage to safeguard precious items. The stairs were familiar as well. I knew immediately that they led to the court of priests with in the Temple, emerging beneath the marbled steps that were to the rear of the great laver sea that stood on the backs of the bronze oxen and to the front of the Holy of Holies. And in this storeroom were the robes of the High Priest. The silver and blue threads, the tiny pomegranate silver bells, the ephod with its precious stones. It was all there, and I spoke out to no one in particular and stated into the emptiness, 'I am Kahana.' That's when I heard the emptiness answer in a voice responding, 'Authi Kahana, you are my Kahana.'"

"And that's when you knew, right?"

"Pretty much, but I needed to confirm it for myself. The dream or whatever it was had ended but not the legacy of what it left behind. The next morning I confronted my mother. It was kind of bizarre when I think about it. I said to her, 'I'm from the priesthood, aren't I." And typical of my mother, her response was, "Yes you are, so what? That and fifty cents gets you a ride on the TTC." The TTC was the city bus operation in Toronto. So you can see, she didn't exactly think it was anything too important. Well, I was very upset. My father didn't leave me much when he disappeared when I was just a baby, but he obviously did leave me a heritage; a birthright that my mother chose to completely conceal and obliterate by not telling me. Now do you understand my embarrassment that I referred to involving my bar mitzvah? If it was a court of law, then I had been sworn in falsely. I wasn't given my dues. You'd have to probably be one to understand it but I felt totally ripped off."

"I think I can get the gist of it Doc. No one wants to feel

overlooked. So why'd your mother do it?"

"For the same reason she had told me for years my father was dead, even though I found out later that he had actually contacted her a few years earlier to see if he could visit with my brother and myself. Because she couldn't come to grips with my father and her relationship with him, she did her utmost to erase any element of his existence from our lives."

"Geez, that's a crying shame," Pearce consoled.

"Yes, it was and this dream, revelation, or whatever it was, was the way in which I was being given back my inheritance. So, you see, John, there are some things that defy explanation. Once I confronted my mother, she broke down a bit and told me a little more about my father's family. That there were these stories about them being big shots, or machymachs, as she referred to them, back when the family was in Europe. But then she had to finish off with the comment that as far as she was concerned they never had two cents to rub together and she had no reason to believe for a second that the entire bunch of them weren't full of shit."

"That's all nice Doc, but that ain't exactly a rock solid reason to believe in the inexplicable as you labeled it. In fact, I see it as just one more substantiation for your entire GLEEM theory. Something triggered in your mind and you simply recalled some old memories handed down by your ancestors that told you exactly who you were. Fits nicely, don't you think."

"It would, except for what transpired afterwards. There's something I've never told anyone except a religious scholar that my ex-father-in-law introduced me too. His name was Nazir, he's a Palestinian Christian. It was a strange meeting to say the least. Here am I, a Jew, discussing with an Evangelical Christian, who happens to be a Palestinian, events that must have seemed so bizarre that even a fiction writer couldn't have dreamed up a similar plot twist."

"And you're going to let me know what it was, right?" Pearce eagerly inquired. His reporter instincts weren't going to let me slide off the hook on this one.

"I will tell you about this one event that happened seventeen years later just as I told it to Nazir. And this is when I knew that most of these events had nothing to do with GLEEM but relied solely on faith; faith in a God and another world that we're not privy to except on very rare occasions."

"Sounds interesting, so let's hear it already!"

"It's about two in the morning and I'm sleeping on a couch in the living room. My life with my first ex-wife isn't going to well, which you may have already guessed by my sleeping on the couch reference. Trust me when I say, you get strange thoughts when you reach that point in your life. Desperate thoughts, like life stinks and why do I bother with it at all. Thoughts like I'm better off dead and then she'll be sorry. I know, they're stupid thoughts and I was quick to realize that the only one that would be sorry if I was to die would be myself. But you don't think like that at the time. You're rarely rational when it's happening, otherwise you'd respond quite differently."

"You know Doc, you should probably write those negative events in your life into an autobiography one day, just to get it all out of your system. Be like therapy, especially considering you've been there a few times," Pearce suggested.

"Are you attempting to say my marital life has been a mess and you'd like to read about all the sordid little details, John?"

"Not me," Pearce quickly denied. "I'm thinking for your sake. Just so you don't carry around bad vibes for the rest of you life. The type you were just talking about. I think it would be therapeutic."

"You're probably right, John, but you're a little late with your suggestion. Been there, done that!"

"Oh, you never told me you wrote it down." Pearce seemed disappointed that I actually did things without informing him of every little details.

"Not just wrote it down," I informed him, "But published it too! It made quite a humorous little novel, so to speak. And it was very therapeutic to boot!"

"I don't recall seeing any book of that nature come across my editor's desk," Pearce stated as a semi-warning. "You know we have an exclusive contract with you. Anything you write with your name on it has to pass through our publishing house first," he recited the details of our contract.

"You're right," I agreed, "But this didn't have my name on it. "You should get yourself a copy. I think you will enjoy it. It's called *Wedlocked* and published by this small publishing house in the UK called Finger Press. Just happens to be released under my pen name of Dr. Alexander G. Valley, that's why it didn't have to go to your editor first.

"That's downright sneaky Doc. But I have to admit, pretty clever. G. Valley as in Goldenthal or Golden Valley when you translate your name from the German. Not to hard to figure out."

"Not hard at all but you guys never caught it, so it was obviously successful."

"So was it therapeutic after all?"

"Extremely," I admitted. "It made me realize, why should I give up the best years of my life just because my wives were making them miserable for me? Get rid of the source of the problems and life's immediately better. But it isn't easy to accept at first. It takes time to comprehend. So going back to the story concerning my first wife, I was pretty down on myself and having a good time at my self pity party. Nevertheless, I'm laying there and I feel a hand on my left shoulder and then there's this hot breath on my ear accompanied by what I interpreted at the time as being a sinister voice."

Pearce was practically falling off the edge of the seat leaning so far forward that I thought he was going to be in my lap at any moment. "And..."

"Here's what it said.    'Lamah Kanini, Avivu Ishu Shealtani.'"

"What does it mean?"

"Ah, therein lays the problem.    I didn't have a clue.    I knew it wasn't Hebrew.    Close, but not Hebrew.    Something similar.    But I was inspired to put it mildly.    I suddenly forgot about all my personal problems and was focused on figuring out exactly what had been told to me.    I had a friend who operated a pharmacy.    His name was Eldin.    He was a Sunni Muslim from Iran.    Nice enough    fellow but you can imagine we had some pretty intense debates about religion at times.    So I told him what had happened the previous night.    At first he didn't' believe me but when I showed him the yellow ochre bruising on my left shoulder, he had to admit that it looked very unusual.    The color was something he couldn't explain and when he looked carefully at it he felt he could make out the outlines of childlike fingers where they had made contact with the skin.    So this well educated man, who believes in jinn, had to admit that perhaps there was an element of truth to my story.    Then I told him what I had whispered in my ear.    That's when he became acutely interested.  He thought he recognized the language as ancient Aramaic, a language that had died out almost two thousand years earlier.    After writing it down, he said he'd get back to me with what he thought would be the translation."

"So what did he find out," Pearce inquired very impatiently, rubbing his hands
unconsciously back and forth across his knees.

"He told me that it meant, '*Why do you pester me, if you persist I will hurt you.*'    It was a warning or so he thought."

"And was it?"

"At the time I had no reason to doubt him.    So you can imagine I was pretty petrified by the fact I had just been threatened by some spirit.    Not only was I despondent about what was occurring in my life but now I was receiving threats from the other side.    That's enough to scare the shit out of you."

"But that's not what it meant, did it?"

"How do you know that?" I was curious why Pearce would have doubted it.

"I don't know, I just know."

"Well, actually it didn't but it wasn't until ten years later that I found that out.    It didn't sit well with me either when Eldin told me that translation.    Sure, an unknown entity making a threat goes pretty well with the bruising on my shoulder and the visitation late at night.    It's the stuff they would write into horror flicks but the fact was that if it was an evil entity, there would have been no better time to cause me to suffer both physically and mentally.    Why stop with a pretty minor threat?    Didn't make sense.    So I never really bought the translation fully.    But like I said earlier, my ex-father-in-law mentioned out of the blue to me that he knew    of    this    young    Palestinian    Evangelical    preacher    that was visiting the Cross Roads Church.   Would I be interested in meeting him?"

"The Cross Roads Church?" Pearce was surprised.   "But you're Jewish!"

"Tell me about it," I mused,   "It's an interesting scenario when you look at it superficially.   Why would I, as a non member of this Church, not even a card carrying Christian for that matter wish to meet this person? No real reason that you could immediately come up with, right? But on the other hand I felt compelled to say yes immediately. Another little voice inside my head told me that I most definitely wanted to meet this person. And the rest I'm betting you might be beginning to figure out."

"You asked him to translate that message from ten years earlier, didn't you?"   Pearce was pretty confident he had guessed correctly.

"Turns out it wasn't Aramaic at all. So obviously Eldin's translation was incorrect. It was a closely related language though.   Nazir recognized it as Syriac. Still spoken by a few thousand people in the mountain regions of Syria and Iraq.   He got on to the phone to a professor in ancient languages right away and got me my translation.   It didn't translate exactly into English but the intent was there.   It was funny, because he was apologizing for being unable to provide a literal translation but when he provided what they thought it meant, it made perfect sense to me.   It all had to do with what you and I are doing now but he had no way of knowing that.   **Ishu**, the word in the phrase is a direct reference to Jesus.   It's how they pronounce his name in that part of the world.   Considering in Hebrew it's Yeshua, there isn't much difference.   I should have spotted   that right away.   The rest was an order to get busy.   It all had to do with that open book I saw in my half dream, which was blank, but it wasn't intended to stay that way.   I had been given a task so to speak but didn't recognize it at the time. Or maybe I did but I just couldn't get myself into gear.   Now I was being told in ancient Syriac to get busy and get on with reviving what Jesus had given to the world. The closest I think the translation gets in English was something like, 'Why are you hesitating, you are to revive what Jesus had been given.'   Like I said, it doesn't translate easily into English but the meaning is quite clear.   Those empty pages in that book are to be filled and will be myself and my descendants are empowered with the task of trying to steer the people back to God and to take up where Jesus had left off in his failed task to do the same."

Pearce just sat there open mouthed and wide eyed staring at me as if I had fallen into the deep end.   Again, why is it that people that pray and talk to God are considered pious and normal and as soon as we even intimate that we've received an answer back we must be insane?   It doesn't make a lot of sense. Pearce was obviously lost for words, so I figured I better fill in the silence.

"And that's why I can assure you there are times that only faith can provide an answer and science has nothing to offer."

"But you're a scientist," he finally sputtered.

"You're right and that's why you don't' see me standing on a corner in a monk's robe holding a sign up that says 'the end is nigh' or 'John 3:16'. So don't get too worried John. Just because I told you this story doesn't mean that I've gone all religious on you. I still believe my primary role is to tell a good story!"

"But you're not even a Christian."

"You seem to forget John, neither was Jesus. He was just another Jew with a mission."

"I don't get it. Why would you be instructed to revive anything Jesus had to say? Makes no sense!"

"Sure it does John. As a Karaite, I believe Jesus had a lot to say. In fact his teachings were so much in tune with Karaite beliefs that I have no doubt he was one of us, or at that time called a Boethian."

"Can't be Doc. They say he was likely an Essene, not a Sadducee. You're claiming him to be something he wasn't then."

"Remember *Caiaphas Letters* John. Which part in that book do you recall not seeing Jesus following the scriptural laws. Personally, I only recall him arguing against the Pharisee's interpretation of those laws. That sounds like a Karaite to me. We've been doing the same thing for two thousand years, first with the Pharisee and then with the Rabbanites."

"But you didn't have Karaites back then," Pearce was still insisting I must be wrong, holding on dearly to his Christian beliefs.

"So he was a Boethian, as I just told you, or perhaps a Zadokite," I rebutted. "Same difference, just one became the other and eventually both became Karaite."

"Now you've got me really confused!"

"Don't worry about it. It will all become very clear."

---

# THE MEDITERRANEAN: 63 AD

There was a slight difficulty arranging for another berth on board ship for Osirah, but it only lasted as long as it took Joseph to come to the realization that a gold aureus in the purser's hand would be sufficient to find a name that could be crossed off the manifest and then replaced with a new passenger. Of course it was a matter of providing a few more denari to cover the passage and then several more for insurance sake before they found themselves safely on board ship.

"So where do we bed down?" Joseph inquired of Michael as they stepped on deck.

"It's simple, find a spot on top deck that no one's taken with a little shelter and that's it. Trust me it's far preferable to the berths below deck. You wouldn't want to go below deck on a scow like this. At least the air is breathable up on top."

"Is that concern I detect?" Joseph flashed a sly smile at his guardian.

"Only for myself," Corvasus was quick to defend his position. "If you choose to go below, it would be my responsibility to do likewise in order to safe-guard your welfare. And I would not appreciate being forced to berth below."

"You two are going to be a joy to be traveling with," Osirah interjected into their exchange.

"No one asked you," Corvasus retaliated. "In fact, you're not even supposed to be here. So your enjoyment is a non issue."

"Take it easy," Joseph cautioned. "She's with us now and I've already told you, she is my responsibility. You don't have to trouble yourself with Osirah at all. If there's a problem, let's keep it between you and I, okay?"

"Definitely. As I said, her opinions are irrelevant. I'm advising you on where's best to bed down. You have to rely on my opinion because it's based on knowledge that I've learned through experience. But I must admit, thus far you have not impressed me at all with your ability to follow instructions."

"Then let me surprise you now. We'll bed down in that spot over there by the tiller house. We can drape a tarp over the top and use the barrels and the racks as shelter when necessary."

"Good choice," Corvasus confirmed Joseph's suggestion somewhat tongue in cheek. "No really, it is a spot I would have selected as well. I just happen to have a tarp that we can string between the two racks and that will help keep the rain and the spray off our heads." Without hesitation, Corvasus rushed to the spot carrying everyone's bags which he distributed across the area, setting the perimeter boundaries as he did so, for everyone else on board to see.

"That was unexpected. He agreed with you. So what's the story between you two?" Osirah inquired with Michael well out of hearing range.

"No story. Just a difference of opinion. We don't actually know each other."

"That sounds... ah...I don't know....strange," Osirah struggled to find the right words.

"Not really. We Jews seem to spend a lot of time in disagreement. In fact, it's all we seem to do."

"I'm still not certain I understand."

"It's a long voyage. I'll try to explain it to you along the way. Look! He's waving to us to come over there. I guess we better do as he says. After all, we wouldn't want to ignore his superior knowledge."

"You don't strike me as being overly diplomatic for an envoy. In fact, you have a bit of a nasty streak yourself," Osirah commented in a teasing manner.

"Well, you don't strike me as being your typical palace servant either. Firstly, you're too outspoken and secondly, you have an unnerving manner of staring straight into my eyes. I would have thought slaves were trained to always look down at their own feet when talking."

"Once you tell me your story, I may take the opportunity to tell you mine."

Tedium over time became the common denominator for the majority of passengers on board. A farina paste was watered down and boiled into a thick, unappetizing porridge every morning, only to be followed mid afternoon, using the very same pots to prepare what was called a lamb stew that was virtually tasteless having been boiled for several hours. But it mattered little to those that had been standing in lines for so long, since after the usual hardtack or stale piece of bread, the stew was an epicurean delight. Even after several days at sea, for some it would still be several days before they could even think about food as their stomach churned with every cresting wave. They could be seen locking their fingers tightly around the top rails, their necks craned well over the sides of the ship while they dry retched, their empty stomachs groaning in rhythm with the waves that crashed against the hull below.

Very few verbal exchanges took place between Joseph and his body guard over the intervening days, which not surprisingly tended to suit them both just fine. Through their silence they actually learned to tolerate each others presence. The act of merely acknowledging the existence of one another and the knowledge that they had struck an unvoiced but obvious mutual agreement not to cross paths, managed to thaw the wall of ice that had been erected between them since their first meeting. Within the little cozy warren that they had created between the racks supporting the water barrels, a modicum of comfort had even been created through the efforts of Osirah.

The hospitality of their little tent-like abode did not go unnoticed by others making the voyage, creating a situation that when Michael was occupied elsewhere on deck, a small group of youngsters sailing to the Italian peninsula encouraged by their parents, would come and sit for hours on end listening and questioning Joseph on the Torah and teachings of the Tannim. It was evident that some on board had recognized Joseph from Jerusalem and had heard him speak at the Temple. Osirah found this attraction by the youngsters at first quite charming but as its frequency and spontaneity increased, it became not only mystifying but in some ways annoying. "Why is it that they come to you? Are you their teacher or do the parents just recognize an opportunity to be free of their children for a while?" Osirah questioned him.

"Is it bothering you?" Joseph inquired.

"We did have some peace and quiet for a while," she complained. "It wasn't so bad when there were a just a few for a short time when we first left Joppa but have you noticed that lately the older ones are becoming more prevalent and I even see a few adults showing up now to listen to your teachings. It makes me nervous to have so many strangers gathered around. I'm surprised that Michael hasn't chased them all away by now perceiving them as a threat."

"He know the effort would be futile. He knows enough about

my past to realize that they have always come to me. When I was growing up, they said it was a gift and that it was my lot in life," Joseph tried to explain.

"Your lot in life is to have strangers invade your privacy and throng around you until you suffocate?" Osirah mocked Joseph's answer.

"I never questioned the how or the why, only God has that answer," Joseph pontificated. "My father referred to it as 'natural affinity'. Very few men have it but it tends to make them great leaders. I think it is part of the reason that Michael detests me. He thinks it is a quality wasted on someone like myself. He probably considers himself to be far more deserving of this gift. Maybe he's right. I never asked for it and I think many back in Judea are disappointed that I never made effective use of it."

"Effective use?" Osirah sounded confused.

Joseph tried to explain. "Those advocating a revolt against Rome think I should be using it to unite the population into a massive army that will take our homeland back. Others, like the religious leaders think I should take my place in the priesthood and serve in the Temple from where I could sermonize all day and fill the coffers with gifts of gold and silver. But the common people, they just want answers to every day matters. They want to know that their lives will become easier and they will be rewarded for their piety. Like those on this voyage. They just want to hear that their lives will be easier once they arrive in Italy. If I can ease their burden, then why should I not oblige?"

"But why you?" Osirah was still struggling with his explanation.

"It started on the day I was first brought to the Temple by my father to join the congregation of Israel. The Tannim, the wise men that sat in the outer courts and taught their classes had heard that I was a child prodigy when it came to the laws of the Torah. So they challenged me but I turned the tables and challenged them in return and the rumor of that day said that I had debated the elders and won. Though there was never any issue of winning. There are always two or more sides to every law. I just pointed it out and since then everyone has labeled me according to their needs."

"But why do they come is what I would like to know?" she scratched her head. "I understand they believe you have some sort of gift but why do they feel they need you? Is our voyage not going well? Do they feel threatened in some way? Why are they constantly asking for things when they are not necessary?"

"Perhaps they are seeking that which they believe only I can provide to them. Something they cannot obtain elsewhere but do not know precisely what it is. Ask yourself, why did the High Priest hand pick me for this mission? What did he see that I can't regarding myself? This is how it has always been. All of them obviously see something that neither you or I are able to see."

"Do not place me so quickly into the same category as yourself, Joseph," Osirah excused herself from his broad statement of inclusion. I asked you this in the first place only because I wondered if others perceive what I can see."

"So what is it that you see," Joseph was curious.

"At first I thought it was this overwhelming feeling of trust that you effuse. I noticed it when you first rescued me. Why else do you think I was able to board this ship with a complete stranger without any doubt that you would protect me?"

"As I recall, you feared the alternative to find your way home on your own more. That would be reason enough."

"True but it was far more than that. An aura of comfort tempered with kindness, which provided me with trust. That is what I see. But that doesn't explain why they come to you. They do not need your protection.".

"They don't want protection from me," Joseph explained. "They want salvation from God. They believe that in some way I am a conduit to the Lord and I can give them the answers they seek."

"And are you?"

"They think so and that is enough for them," he responded.

"I think it is something more," Osirah shrugged her shoulders. "I'm not sure what it is but definitely something more."

"Too bad Michael isn't able to see it," Joseph commented. "It would definitely ease some of the tensions aboard this ship."

"Perhaps he does," she commented. "I think that he might see it very clearly and that may be the reason he resents you. Whereas he continually strives hard to lead, only to meet constant resistance, for you, as you said, this ability to draw followers comes so naturally. I believe he is jealous."

"Rest assured there are many things I possess in my character that I do not share in common with Michael Corvasus, which would explain why people don't exactly run to him."

"Perhaps you should be more tolerant of him then?" she criticized Joseph for his negative attitude. "You also seem to have a problem with him?"

"You have that completely wrong. The only problem is the one he has with me."

"No I don't. You most certainly also have a problem with him?" she insisted. "You can't even say his name without curling up your lip and sneering. I've noticed you draw any conversation we have back to your dislike of him repeatedly. That suggests you most definitely have a problem as well."

"That is where you are mistaken," Joseph corrected her. "I don't have a problem with him. I have a problem with what he represents."

"That's ridiculous. What does that even mean? What could he possibly represent other than what he is? They are one and the same."

"For someone that is supposedly a slave girl, you're a little too wise and a little too perceptive," Joseph reprimanded her gently. "But you will never completely understand the reason why I cannot appreciate what he represents. Because to do so would invite the end of my world as I know it. And I will do anything to ensure that never happens."

"That also doesn't make any sense," she analyzed Joseph's words. "Do you not think you're exaggerating his significance," she cautioned. "After all, he is only one man. How does he threaten your world?"

"I assure you I have not. He may be one man to you, but to me he is like the disease that enters through the roots and then causes the entire tree to rot from within. To understand, you would need to know how Jewish society functions, so it serves little meaning for me to say that it is unique in this world. It is neither a subculture nor an isolated island to itself. It co-exists whether here or in a community a thousand miles away from Judea. History has proven that it cannot be destroyed from the outside. It can only be destroyed from inside. Corvasus and those like him represent the first stage of that rot that will eventually destroy us. If left unimpeded, his brand of assimilation will spread like a fungus in a vineyard until the vines wither and die. To co-exist would be no longer possible. For his chosen path to thrive, his kind feel it is necessary to completely erase anything that might remind the world from whence he stemmed."

"If one man could so easily achieve that end, then perhaps your world was not meant to survive in the first place," Osirah commented, not realizing it would only fuel Joseph's anger. She retreated as soon as she saw the look of fury that rolled over his face. Backing herself against the barrels she was fearful that he might lash out.

"That is what all the nations that have tried to destroy us in the past have said," he barked at her. "Even you Parthians have said as much. But here we are and those that came before you have all crumbled into dust! The path to follow in God's footsteps is not an easy one. That is why all those other nations have failed to survive, yet we are still here."

Seeing the terrified look on her face, Joseph immediately calmed down, ashamed of his behavior. "I am sorry," he apologized, bowing his head and looking embarrassed by the fact that she had seen a side of himself that had always remained hidden.

"No, forgive me Joseph. I did not mean to imply that your society should be destroyed. Believe me when I say that I would not want that for any people."

Staring into her eyes, Joseph could see that she was telling him the truth, and he reached out to hold her hand so that she was comforted.

"If we ever start thinking like they do, then we will cease to exist!" he acknowledged.

Feeling more at ease, Osirah crawled out of the corner where she had taken refuge and kept hold of Joseph's trembling hand safely between her own. "If adopting the ways of the other nations means an end to your own culture, then why should Michael wish to do such a thing? It makes no sense to destroy your own people."

"Only because he cannot co-exist," Joseph shook his head. "As long as my world is intact, he will be constantly reminded that he is nothing more than one of us with the pretense to be much more. To everyone else he will be nothing more than 'that Jew.' As such he'll never be allowed to rise as high or go as far as he believes he should. Therefore he must destroy that which he considers to be his greatest obstacle; his heritage."

"That in many ways is sad," she reflected on what Joseph had said.

"More than sad," Joseph advised. "Many of our greatest enemies have come from those that thought exactly the same way. That if only they could find a way to erase their Jewishness by eliminating any trace of their own people, then they would be given the opportunities they have been denied. They would sacrifice their entire race in order to satisfy their own greed."

"If what you say is true then neither of you will be able to bridge your differences. You will always be at odds with each other. Now even I am sad."

"His kind, through their lies will promote the other nations to go to war against us. It is the way it has always been. Even now I feel that the time is coming when our respective worlds will clash. On my oath it will be a battle to the death and I will gladly do so to preserve all that I hold dear. Those like me will never let those others that wish to eradicate our religious beliefs and ancestry to prevail."

Osirah tried to be sympathetic but she still could not fully comprehend what Joseph was describing, the concept too foreign to a culture that had been Babylonian, Persian, and Parthian without any apparent conflict in making the adjustments to change. "I know you believe in what you are saying," Osirah lightly rebuffed his argument, "but I think you may be demonizing Michael and his kind far more in your mind than they ever truly could be. Do not misunderstand me. I know you honestly consider them to be a threat, and I cannot ever claim to even understand a mote of your world because from the little you've told me so far it seems preoccupied with fighting every civilization on earth that exists in order preserve your differences, but in reality, aren't we all different. Don't we all have our own cultures and beliefs that we choose to believe are superior to all others? But what is also true is that all civilizations, in order to survive, must evolve. I'm not saying one abandons all of their customs and rituals but just the natural progression of time cannot prevent change from happening."

"Perhaps not in your world but in mine, the issue is about trying to stop it; insuring the preservation of one's beliefs at any cost. Preserving the past for the present and the future. I know this may never make sense to you, but the difference that you cannot comprehend is that to me and those like me, it makes perfect sense."

"I'm not going to change your mind about Michael, am I" she admitted defeat.

"Never," he reassured her. "But I appreciate the fact that you try to see the good in everyone."

"Then let's talk about other matters. Let's talk about me.," she said coquettishly.

"You?" Joseph was surprised that Osirah was finally ready to reveal some of her secrets.

"You have been trying for days to have me talk about my self, so why act surprised now?"

"Because I didn't expect you to oblige," Joseph admitted. "So what is there about you that you wish so badly to tell me suddenly?"

"I said I was going to tell you about who I really am when the time was right."

"So now is the right time?"

"If it can take your mind off your issues with Michael for the moment, then I think it is definitely the right time," she confirmed.

Finally appearing relaxed, Joseph crossed his legs into a sitting position and prepared to listen to her story.

"So, you were right. I'm not exactly what I appear to be. I'm not a princess of Parthia, if that's what you're thinking. In that respect Michael was correct. And it is true, I was being used as a decoy, just as he said, but I'm not a slave."

"But Michael showed me your slave brand," Joseph interrupted.

"Only because I am part of the House of Mithridates but what he didn't realize is that the royal tattoo is more than a mere indicator of ownership. For those of us connected to the royal household, it serves as vital protection for safe passage anywhere within the Parthian Empire. Who would dare to touch or threaten someone bearing the royal seal upon their palm? And anyone that dared knew full well the level of retribution they would suffer."

"Well, from my perspective, it was obvious the raiders didn't care about this brand of yours," Joseph challenged her theory of ultimate protection.

"They were nothing more than barbaric savages but then again, they were still smart enough to sell me as far away from the Parthian sphere of influence as they could get. But once I return home, they will be made to suffer for their crimes. I will see to it!"

"So if you're not the princess, what makes you think Mithridates cares at all in having your returned?"

"Because I am a princess", she informed him, "Just not the daughter of Mithridates. I am the daughter of Tigranes, King of Armenia. As a Satrap of Parthia, he was compelled to have his children raised in the House of Mithridates. In that way the Satrap assures his loyalty to the King of Kings. I was raised like a daughter of the Great King and he will certainly avenge the insult that was done to me."

"So that really was your bridal caravan, wasn't it?"

"I was to be married to the son of the King of Pontus, while another caravan bearing the true daughter of Mithridates was on its way to Commagene."

"Your betrothed in Pontus must be worried sick about you."

"The prince is an idiot but it is my duty to do as the Great King says. If he's worried, it will be only because he did not receive my dowry."

"And what happens now regarding your wedding plans?"

"They probably think I am dead or worse by now, and have called off the wedding and should I manage to return to Parthia, they will likely see the attack as a bad omen and call off the betrothal. I can only pray that they don't try to enforce the contract and make me go through with it."

Joseph thought carefully about Osirah's revelation, weighing out all of the repercussions carefully as he saw them. "We must not say anything of this to anyone else, especially not to Michael," he cautioned her. Politically, you are too valuable as a hostage if the Romans find out. Criminally, you are just too valuable to anyone seeking a reward. It will place us all in danger but especially you. Once in Puteoli I will find a means of returning you to your homeland without too many questions being asked. I promise."

"I had no intention of letting anyone know."

"But you did tell me."

"That is what I was trying to explain to you Joseph. People want to tell you things. It's almost as if we're compelled to tell you our innermost secrets. For what ever reason, we feel safe with you. That is the gift I was trying to describe for you."

"Then I am honored by your trust. I will not betray you. For the rest of the trip we keep it our little secret."

"The Great King will repay you handsomely. Your name will be extolled among our people as a trusted friend of the royal family."

"I'm appreciative of the kindness that will be extended but I need neither the gifts nor the accolades. Neither is not the motivator that makes me want to help you."

"I know that Joseph. I see that very well. You're doing it for the same reason that you take the time to help all these other people with their issues when they come to you. That is who you are!"

"Only because of God's instruction to do so," Joseph attempted to explain his behavior.

"You are wrong," she admonished him. "You are who you are because that is who you choose to be. God did not make you choose that path."

"Ahh, but that's where you're wrong. You are Zorastrian, I presume?" She nodded affirmatively. "Then in that case, your god guides but does not actively take part in your life. You believe entirely in free will. Whereas, my God interacts in everything we do. In his hands I am like the clay on a potter's wheel. I am that which he has made me. If people are drawn to me it is because they see His light through me. They aren't seeing me. We only have free will in the sense that we can attempt to defy his instruction but by doing so, eventually we will be made to suffer the consequences."

"And there you are wrong again," she now debated him. They come to you.

It is your voice that they wish to hear, not the words of your god. It is your wisdom and understanding they seek. Perhaps these are both gifts from your god but they certainly aren't the sounds of his voice. It is your heart, your mind that they hear."

"But it's God's words that go from my mouth to their ears. I am just the deliverer of his messages.."

"Or so you choose to believe," she was still not willing to agree. Is it your god that adds the compassion to the words? No! When you listen and become concerned, is it his heart that feels the tearing as they tell their tale of woe? No! When they smile as you give them hope, was it his shoulders that carried their burden? No! Your god may have given you the tools with which to perform your work, but you are the craftsman that shapes the final work Joseph."

Joseph cracked his lips into a broad smile. "Remind me not to engage in debates with you. You make too much sense for me to challenge. But still, I was born to the priesthood Osirah, even though my family no longer serves in that function being too many generations distant from the primary families. But it doesn't mean that I don't hear the voice of God any less than my more illustrious relatives. That it my path, one which was laid out from the day I was born. The Lord has instilled that in to me and nothing can change that. He instructs and I serve."

"Or so you choose to believe. I think it is more the case that he instructs, but he leaves it to you to best decide how to serve his needs. You are still the master of your own destiny Joseph ben Matthias."

"I doubt I will ever have the chance to prove that," Joseph replied.

"We shall see, Joseph," Osirah replied as if she knew better.

---

Five days out from Joppa, the morning bore witness to a brilliant sunrise cascading like diamonds through a cloudless sky but more seriously, this was now the second day in a row without a significant wind and the vessel's progress had slowed practically to a crawl. Fitted originally as a unireme, over the interceding years numerous modifications had been made by which another half bank of oars had been fitted by means of an outrigger on either side of the hull. Placing the half banks astern, provided an advantage when the prevailing winds blew from the opposite direction to which the ship was bearing. This small addition provided enough oar-power to neutralize the wind's opposing force, while the full banks of lower oars propelled the ship through the water. But without any wind, the additional weight only served to submerge the keel further below the crest of the waves and leave the ship almost totally at the mercy of prevailing currents. The sails fell slack and the leisurely roll of the drum beat only mimicked the stroke of the oars passing through the mirror-like surface of the sea.

Normally the captain would be seen intermingling freely with the passengers but this particular morning he appeared to be slightly agitated and remained aloof. Most would have failed to perceive this mild alteration to his character but it was Michael's talent as a body guard to sense anything out of the ordinary and his senses this time were alerting him to something definitely being amiss.

"Something is wrong," Corvasus leaned over towards Joseph, whom was still spooning the thick porridge into his mouth. "He's looking nervous!"

"What are you talking about?" Joseph had just finished the last spoonful and laid the bowl to one side as he wiped his mouth with his sleeve. He was most surprised by the fact that Corvasus had even bothered to use him for his sounding board. Therefore, the situation must indeed be serious he concluded.

"Captain's not acting right. I'm guessing we must be too close to Cyprus. The current must have carried us off course during the night."

"What's that got to do with anything?" Joseph asked, having no idea of what Corvasus was talking about.

"That puts us in dangerous waters. The pirates use the coves on Cyprus to keep their ships hidden. Without the prevailing winds, there's a good chance we drifted too far north. Should that be the case, then he's got good reason to be nervous."

"So you think we might be attacked? That's what you're suggesting?"

"If I'm right, then we're in big trouble. All I'm telling you is to be prepared. You might have to prove to me shortly that you have some fighting skills after all."

"And what do you think that's going to achieve? Take a good look at these people around us; children, youths, old men and a scattering of women. Barely a fighter to be found among them."

"I guarantee they'll fight. With no other choice, they'll have to! Pirates are only interested in one thing. What they can keep or sell. Anything else goes over the side. Since most of them are destined to be shark food, they're going to have to fight if they want to live."

"Then we better start informing everyone of the situation."

"No! It would only cause a panic. That could prove to be more devastating than the pirates themselves. I just wanted you to know that I'm already putting a plan into motion. I'm off to see the captain to get his cooperation."

"So why bother even telling me?"

"Because I might need some help and you're the only one that I have available. Not my choice really. Just be ready if I need your help." Without even waiting for his acknowledgement, Michael took off in the direction of the Captain's quarters, leaving Joseph standing alone at the rail mulling over what he had just been told.

Waiting for the opportunity once Michael had disappeared behind a wall of travelers, Osirah strolled up beside Joseph and curled into his shoulder, shielding herself from the fine spray that was constantly being churned by the rotation of the oars.   "So what were you two discussing in such earnest if you don't mind me asking?"

"I don't think it was a discussion at all, more a case of Michael being Michael."

"Oh, that's perfectly clear," she mused.

"No, it wasn't, but it's too absurd to even try to explain."

"Try me.   You know I'm a good listener."

"He's worked himself into a frenzy of us being attacked by pirates or something like that. So to counteract the possibility, I think he's on a tangent of seeking to have himself declared as captain, or first mate, or something like that.   He's preparing to take over control of this vessel should we be attacked.   At least that's what I think he said."

"He's anticipating that we're going to be attacked!"   Her face bore traces of panic.

"Don't give it more credence than it deserves," Joseph attempted to dispel the entire suggestion.   "Just take a look at the water.   Everything is so calm. Just like it has been every other day."

"And don't you dismiss it as nothing more than hysteria," she warned him. "I told you Joseph; give him his respect where it's deserved.   He has skills that are well suited to the nature of work he performs. He deals constantly in the world of threats and hostilities.   If he's concerned then I think we should take it very seriously."

"We have to remain calm.   There are ships traveling back and forth across the Mediterranean every single day.   You don't hear about those ships coming under attack other than the occasional one.   Rome has eliminated most of the pirates."

"Or so they tell you," she fired back.

"What is that supposed to mean."

"Oh, please!   Governments lie to the public all the time. If they ever told the truth, they wouldn't remain in power for long.   Trust me on this.   I've lived in the palace of one of the most powerful men in the world. There were so many lies circulating among his ministers you didn't know what to believe.   So just remember you never hear a contradiction from anyone that was on one of those ships now sitting on the bottom of the sea either.   I'm scared and I think you should be too.   If Michael has a sense of danger, then I fear we are in trouble."

"Even if he should be right, there's no reason to think they'll attack this ship.   After all, there's nothing of any value for pirates aboard this ship."

"How do you know what's in the hold," she questioned.   "We have no idea what this ship is carrying."

"It's a big sea," Joseph searched for his next excuse.   "Finding this one ship in the Mediterranean is not going to be easy."

"But what if they do, Joseph?"

"I promised to protect you.   I will keep that promise to you.   I swear it."

"I have no doubt that's your intention but both you and I know that you're not a fighter. It's not what you've been raised to be. There's no shame in that but I think my chances of survival are much better remaining around Michael."

Joseph stared at her awkwardly. "I don't know why you don't think I'm capable of fighting? I may not like confrontation but I will fight to protect that which I hold dear! I promise you!"

"Just hold me," she instructed him. "I'm actually shivering just thinking about pirates."

Joseph fumbled about with his hands, not exactly certain how to place his arms around her tiny waist without offending. He fought hard against the impulses that suddenly sprung to life and coursed through his body at the merest touch of her skin, reminding himself constantly that this certainly was not the right time. He knew that his mind was bent on confusing her desire to be comforted with the store of emotions that he had kept suppressed for so long during the voyage. In fact, admittedly, they were twinges that he had not felt since he was a teenager. Though he had only known Osirah for a week, he had convinced himself that she had been part of his life for much longer. She was beautiful and the attraction was both natural and obvious but he was convinced there was much more. Twenty-seven years old and he had never taken the opportunity to explore even a fraction of his emotional palette. But then, he was also lucky enough to have a father that was willing to let him find his own life partner rather than barter his future as a financial arrangement of security between two patrician families. Now he realized just how difficult that decision was going to be.

'Damn it,' he thought to himself. 'I don't' have a clue what it is I'm supposed to do.' Rather than try to resolve all his issues at once he held her comfortably, his arms remaining frozen in their original position, ensuring that his hands remained firmly on the flat of her back and didn't wander with a mind of their own, while he stared blankly beyond the plume of water that jettisoned behind the rudder until it was no more than a white cap that faded into the distance.

---

"Ship off the starboard horizon", the watch's cry rained down from the top yard.

"What's her distance?" the Captain shouted back into the clouds.

"I place her at about a thousand leagues and she's closing rapidly."

"Tell me her sail man! Give me a report!" The Captain's voice was sounding desperate.

"Tyrian. It looks Tyrian. No, no! She's maybe Bithynian!" the crew-man screamed as the main sail's emblem came into full view.

"Well, which is it man? Tyrian or Bithynian? There's a world of difference you know!"

"She's a Bithynian war galley!"

"Bithynian here?   Can't be." the Captain muttered loudly as he tried to rationalize how a Bithynian vessel could be closing on them in this part of the Mare Nostrum.   Not unless it wasn't Bithynian at all but only using it as a disguise he concluded.   "Bloody Pirates!" he screamed to his crew. "Prepare for a battle," his voice burst above the terrified din being made by the frightened passengers.  No sooner had they heard those words, they whipped themselves into a frenzied panic.   "Crastus, god damn it, Crastus where are you?" the Captain shouted frantically.

"I'm right here, Majorian.   I'm on it."

"Where's that Corvasus fellow?   He said he'd be helping us deal with these people."

Almost on cue, Michael Corvasus charged into the midst of the crowd of passengers.   Barking out orders as if he was born to command, he separated all of the male passengers, lining them along the port rail of the main deck. Moving up and down the line he separated out those that were too old or too young and instructed them to return to their families or wherever they had bunked down but those of the right age and in good health he drafted immediately into action.   "You have been selected for a very important purpose.   All these people," Michael pointed a finger swinging it in a wide arc, "are depending on us.   If we are going to make it through this, it will be because we are willing to do whatever it takes in order to survive.   Now the Captain has instructions for us.   I want you all to listen carefully to what he has to say.   Your life, our lives depend on it. You listen and you listen well!   Do I make myself clear?"

The selected passengers responded affirmatively if not reluctantly.

Stepping on cue into the centre stage, the Captain cleared his throat loudly.   "My thanks to you, Michael," he said in a deep resounding voice that was proportionate to his girth.   "I will not try to conceal the truth from you.   It's too late for that any way, so I won't insult your intelligence.   At this very moment there is another vessel bearing down on us.   According to her sails, she's Bithynian.   Bithynian ships are confined to the Pontus Sea by the Roman navy through current trade agreements. But one of their war galleys appears to be sailing south from Cyprus and that can only mean that she's being manned by brigands that have gone rogue and have no desire to honor the Pax Romana.   Do not mistake these pirates as sharing even a nuance of civilized behavior.   Far from it! Men who are hunted behave no differently from any other animal. Mark my words, they are animals and they will show you no mercy.   Crastus, here, is my first mate," he brought his hand down on Crastus's shoulder, "and I'll be placing him in charge of all of you.   He will ensure that you man our top deck of oars properly.   He will call out the beat and you will all learn very quickly how to be sailors.   Some of my crew will be rowing right alongside of you.   Rely on their experience as your instructors.   I'm afraid that is all the training you are going to receive.   If there are any questions, I suggest you ask them now because once you're in the hold the grate will be locked as a precaution. No one moves off the rowing bench until this threat is over. Have I made myself clear?"

"What about the men on the lower deck. Why can't they do this on their own?" The rest of the men grumbled in agreement to the question raised by one of their fellow passengers.

"We have twenty oars a side on the lower deck, manned by three galley slaves on each. That's one hundred and twenty slaves which aren't much compared to seasoned sailors on a crewed warship. We're out-manned two to one in oars alone. So once you're all positioned on the top bank, we will have added another twenty oars to the water. With three men a piece that gives us a little more of a chance to escape with our lives. Take a good look at her crew, that's a full bireme in pursuit, so keep in mind that it's lighter and it's faster than this old barge. Maybe that will make you row harder because even galley slaves have their limitations. We haven't had a lot of wind over the past few days, so my guess is the slaves below will be growing tired very quickly. I can only hope our pursuers are equally as tired having journeyed far from their port of hiding. Crastus will make certain that we milk every ounce of strength you can muster. Whatever gods you pray to, I suggest now's the time to start praying."

The Captain's disheartening remarks did little to calm anyone on board and in turn triggered a heavily pessimistic response from Joseph who quickly calculated the odds. "I have a question Captain. If they're lighter and faster, do we even have of escaping them?"

The Captain glanced over at Michael, obviously peeved by the question. "This is the one you travel with, right? The one you told me about."

"He's not a military man," Michael apologized, "so he doesn't think like one. Ignore whatever he has to say."

"But you told me the people listen to him. That makes him a complication, so I'll answer his question."

"It's a simple question that deserves a straight answer," Joseph ignored their dismissive tone. Can we elude them or not?"

"Our only chance relies on time. We're three bells past noon. They still have a fair distance to make up before they're alongside us. If we give it everything we got, then there's a good chance the sun will set before they are actually upon us. And once it's dark, without our lanterns lit, and the fact that it's a new moon, they won't be able to find us. So unless you have a better suggestion, then I suggest you tell that to all these people that seem to want to listen to you instead."

"That's all we need to know," Joseph answered on behalf of the passengers. "If we have chance then we will do whatever it takes to survive."

The passengers understood that their fate lay in their own hands and having no alternatives to suggest either, they grew eerily quiet. They were resigned to whatever fate that awaited them, knowing that the appearance of being in control of their own destinies was ethereal at best.

"Crastus, let's get them below and start making sailors out of this bunch of greenhorns!" the Captain bellowed. "Michael, you're now in charge of seeing that this vessel is made lighter. She's riding too low. Get the rest of those passengers into work units and anything that's not nailed down and non-essential, I want tossed over the rail. Do we understand each other?"

"Yes sir," Michael snapped his approval. "Alright, everybody up," he shouted to all the travelers that weren't selected and led down into the hold to man the oars. "You may not be suitable for manning the oars but you're certainly fit enough to toss things into the water. Let's get moving, we have a job to do." Without a moment's hesitation he began allocating the men women and children into work parties. "If it's not nailed to the hull, I want it over the side," he shouted. "The lighter we make the vessel, the easier it will be to row. The easier to row, the faster she'll slice through the water. Let's do it people!" Scrambling over every inch of the deck, the passengers picked over every item that they could find. Some were obviously non-essential and over the side they went, but the remainder of items were unknown to them and, making it necessary to have a crew member confirm every container, serving only to slow substantially the entire process.

All eyes watched the Captain closely. They wanted to see his reactions, monitor every nuance of emotion. From even his simplest expressions they would gain comfort or possibly sense doubt and fear. The Captain was well aware of the eyes that were upon him and he clenched his teeth, determined to show not a shred of fear if he could help it. He knew that panic sunk more ships than pirates ever did.

The pursuing Bithynian bireme was in full flight, loosening her sail from the top-gallant and catching whatever winds laid further east.

"Curse their stinking gods boys," the Captain hollered, "she's caught a half sail and she's taking whatever wind may have been left over for us. Point that rudder south," he yelled to the helmsman, we've got to catch the Cretan currents!"

The vessel responded with a slight hop upon the water as she turned to the south. The Captain knew that the pirates would be on him within the hour unless he was able to maneuver to a position where he could steal the same breeze the pirates had managed to trap.

"Crastus, where are those oars, man? We need them now!"

As if in response to his question, all of oars came to life, carving into the water but with nothing close to the precision movements required. The drum beat desperately tried to harmonize the newly recruited oarsmen, but no matter how hard it sounded the stroke, there were those that had no sense of rhythm at all. Still, against the odds, the passenger ship managed to surge ahead, gaining a valuable measure or two on the brigands that followed in pursuit.

"Crastus, I don't know what in hell's name you think you're doing down there, but whatever it is, speed it up!" the Captain yelled down into the hold.

Joseph found himself seated on the rough bench between two strangers in their long gray cloaks and hoods that everyone had noticed on board but no one conversed with as they avoided all contact and kept strictly to themselves thus far during the voyage. Even now he could only catch brief glances of partial faces beneath their cowls as they were cast in shadows and remained unrecognizable. Some on board had said they were a religious order, but Joseph thought that they had to be mistaken. He knew most of the sects and he had not seen the likes of their dress before. The one to his right, on the inboard side was a giant of a man. Four cubits easily, Joseph estimated. And though he couldn't see the man's build beneath his robe, he knew he was as strong as the legendary Samson as well. How the two of them could continue to wear their heavy woolen cloaks was as much a mystery as to whom they were. The air on the outrigger was hot and humid, as the angled construction behaved more like an exhaust vent from the interior of the vessel rather than an inlet for any cool sea air. But neither the giant, nor his much smaller companion sitting to Joseph's left seemed to suffer from the heat at all. With every aching muscle in his arms and back, Joseph matched the pull of the giant until his mind had grown numb from the physical exertion.

Positioned on the starboard outrigger, they could view the Bithynian vessel clearly. Though their efforts to match the Bithynians stroke for stroke were valiant they were ultimately futile. Not being seasoned oarsmen, exhaustion was over-taking them quickly, and no matter how much Crastus urged and cursed, they could not find a further wellspring of inner strength to maintain the pace. It was all Joseph could do to refrain from collapsing under the strain, but just when he felt compelled to do so, he looked to his right and focused on the horned prow, with its iron toothed boarding hook readying itself to tear into the planks of their ship and that gave him the necessary strength to carry on well past the point of exhaustion.

Watching as their pursuers gained steadily, the Captain bellowed even more orders to everyone on board. "We need to be lighter. If it's not nailed down, I want it over the side," he commanded. "Corvasus, where are you? I need you now!"

Michael was front and centre as soon as the words rolled off the captain's tongue.

"You said you were an ex military man," the captain said to him, "So give me something military to do to these bastards to slow them down!"

Thinking for a moment, he tilted his head slightly as the kernel of an idea began to germinate. "Have you reviewed your manifest yet to see if there's anything useful we can use to fight?"

"Of course I have," the captain scowled, insulted by the suggestion that perhaps he had been derelict in his duties or not smart enough to think of that first. "Is that the best you can come up with?" he challenged.

"Then do you recall anything in the hold that's combustible?"

"It's all wood, everything down there burns. Are you going to pester me with stupid questions or do you actually have a worthwhile suggestion?" the Captain responded furiously.

"No, I mean combustible as in material you would use to start a fire and keep it burning."

"You mean something like that shipment of sacred oil for the Jews in Rome that was loaded on board? There's quite a lot of it down there since the Jerusalem Council has discouraged the Jews in the Diasporas from using their own oil for their festivals. Thirty barrels in total as I recall."

"Excellent," Michael responded. "That will do nicely. What about some pitch and fenugreek?"

"This is a ship. Of course I have those on board. They don't stay water tight; you got to keep after it. What do you have in mind?"

"We're going to set some traps for our pirate friends. I need your men to get those barrels up on deck. Then we tar and grease the outside of the barrels, and just before we toss them off the stern rail, we set them alight. That will leave the pirates with two choices, either steer around the flaming barrels, or sail through them. And if they crash in to them, then they run the risk that the oil gets all over their bow and not even an ocean is going to keep the flames spreading across their hull."

A large coarse hand slapped Michael Corvasus across his back. "Brilliant, Corvasus. About time you started thinking. At last we finally have a plan." The captain set his crew into motion to carry out the strategy as explained. Within the half hour the barrels were on deck, being brushed with the thick coating of the pitch and fenugreek mixture and lined up against the stern rail. Standing on the rear half deck, Michael could make out the faces of his adversaries as they perched themselves on their mast head, swords raised in anxious anticipation. It wouldn't be long now he thought until this hunt would be over if his plan didn't work. He shook his head to dismiss the gory image. There was no time to think about such things. Ordering three of the crew to raise the first barrel onto the rail, he touched the fiery brand to it uppermost rim and instantaneously it was ringed by a corona of green and orange flames. "Now!" he shouted and the men released the first burning barrel into the frothing water so that it trailed backwards behind their vessel. Turning the rudder right and then left repeatedly, the helmsmen made certain that their boat continued to zigzag through the waters so that each barrel dumped into the the sea was set upon a different path towards the Bithynian bireme. Over and over Michael repeated the actions until all thirty barrels were floating atop the mirror like surface of the sea, each with a halo of flames consuming the coating of tar but not yet penetrating through the wood slats of the barrels beneath.

"That's all of them! Now, we wait and see what they think of our little surprise," he said to the captain as he turned from the rail, raising his thumb up as a sign of anticipated success.

"By all the gods, may they grant us this mercy," the Captain prayed in response.

From their position at the stern, they could make out the expressions of shock and surprise on the faces of their pursuers. They had successfully mined the waters, barrels bobbing up and down on the waves, weaving to and fro as they caught the crest of one wave only to sink in the trough of another. They danced upon a complex weave that was completely random and unpredictable.

It took a combination of all their years of acquired skill and sailing prowess for the pirates to practically steer their vessel clear of the flaming flotsam. It was a trick they had heard had been used by the Greeks a long time ago and from those same histories, they knew exactly what would happen should they crash into any of the barrels in their path. But no matter how well they sailed between the flaming projectiles, they could not avoid them all unless they were to break off completely to the right or left, thereby effectively ending the chase and abandoning their prey.

With every wide berth the pirates were forced to give a barrel, the greater the distance that separated the two ships became. As tired as the rowers on the transport ship were, they could see that they were gaining not only several dozen chains in length, but most importantly precious time as well, and it stirred their inner strength for survival that they could call upon. Miraculously, they even managed to find their rhythm and were matching the horatator's beat, stroke for stroke as the separation between the two vessels grew even greater.

Joseph sensed that the giant of a man seated beside him on the bench had p hysically awaken. It was not that the man had not been pulling his weight on the oar all along, but now there Joseph hardly felt any resistance to his pull, as the hooded stranger was practically managing the oar all on his own. It was as if he and the third man on the oar didn't exist at all, merely holding on passively, in order to guide the great arc of the oar as it swung through the air.

One of the barrels broke against the prow of the pirate's vessel and a great cry went up from the passengers as balls of flame shot up into the air like missiles, raining down on their pursuer's bow with heavenly ordained hell-fire. Though celebrated enthusiastically by the frightened passengers, the damage proved not too serious for the pirates as they swarmed like ants over honey, scrubbing every inch of the prow and hull with wet rags that they had secured to long poles. Within a very short time they had scrubbed the burning oil free from the planks it clung to. But more importantly, the burst of flames had bought the passenger ship precious time and with every added minute, it rejuvenated the faint hope they still clung to that they would be saved by the approaching darkness.

By the time the pirates had navigated through the entire obstacle course, they found themselves several leagues behind. Earlier in the day it would not have been an insurmountable distance but at this late hour they must have been concerned that the hunt was practically over as the waning light of the afternoon sun was beginning to drop lower towards the horizon.

"I think they're turning," the Captain remarked to Michael, whom was standing next to him, delighted with the success of his plan. "They're breaking off, I'm certain of it. We've beaten them!" he exclaimed, slapping Corvasus along the back as he made up his mind that they had succeeded.

"They still out man us and have more oars in the water than we do. They also have a westerly at their tail that is picking up and isn't at our backs yet." Michael began to doubt his own success.

"Take credit when I give it to you," the Captain insisted. "Take a good look Corvasus," he insisted that Michael re-examine the situation, as a broad smile stretched across his face. "They're falling back further and further. They are turning, I'm certain of it. I can see more of their port hull than I could a few seconds ago. They're turning," he shouted loudly so that all the passengers could hear him and as soon as they did, they all began to cheer and shout jubilantly. "They're turning, they're turning," the chorus was repeated over and over again.

# CHAPTER SIX

## WHANGAREI; PRESENT

By this time Pearce had found his voice once more and the stupefaction of what I had to say had worn off somewhat. "So, let me see if I've got this straight. They're rowing like crazy, tired, exhausted, and as good as dead. This pirate ship is gaining on them steadily. Everyone's screaming. The women on board are already being eyed up by the pirates as to whom they're going to rape first. These pirates even get past this trap that was set for them and have nothing else in their path. This passenger ship is totally helpless and all of a sudden the pirates break off and sail in the other direction." With each point Pearce was hammering his pen against the air attempting to drive home his skepticism. "You want me to buy this."

"Exactly!"

"Exactly? Exactly what? It doesn't make sense Doc. They were sitting ducks. There's no way in the world they should have escaped like that. Doesn't make any sense."

"Oh, I don't know about that John. Miracles do happen. Don't you believe in miracles?"

Pearce shook his head in denial. "Not when they don't seem possible and especially when they're not believable."

"That's why they're called miracles John. They wouldn't be miracles if you expected them to happen. They're not supposed to be rational."

"So you really expect me...no, forget that, you actually expect all the readers to buy that this ship is helpless in the middle of the Mediterranean, about to be boarded by a shipload of blood thirsty scoundrels and God sends them a miracle? Come on now! You got to do better than that."

"That's not exactly what I said or what happened. God had actually nothing to do with it, unless you consider the coincidence of a Roman patrol boat as a miracle sent by God. I'd prefer to believe that they just happened to have an amazing stroke of good luck. But that's my opinion. If you choose to believe it was a miracle sent by God, I'm not about to stop you."

"Hey, you never said anything about a patrol boat," Pearce challenged.

"I didn't, but Flavius Josephus did. You need to remember that he wrote an autobiography of his adventures, John. I'm just adding the details he failed to provide since he was only giving the reader skeletal outline of what happened. So perhaps you should be telling him that you don't find his own story plausible. I'm certain he would disagree with you!"

"Even so, you didn't say anything about a patrol boat," Pearce objected.

"I hadn't gotten to that point yet. You interrupted me, but if you had been a little more patient, I would have reached that point in the storyline. But you should be aware that at first, no one on the passenger vessel knew why the pirate ship had turned and fled, either. As far as they were concerned it was a miracle. Even when they finally realized they had been frightened off by the first appearance of the senatorial flag of Rome rising above the horizon, they still considered it a miracle. It's a pretty big sea. What were the chances of a Roman ship showing up just in the nick of time, in that same quadrant of water, in the middle of nowhere? I'm not a gambling man but I'd say the odds were somewhere between slim and none. So no matter how you slice it, they were pretty damn lucky!"

"Exactly!"

"Oh, so now you're doing it to me."

"Doing what?"

"You know, that exactly stuff," I challenged back.

"I guess I am. Yeah, I like it. Sort of like when other people say 'whatever' but even better." Pearce was throwing back my own mocking words back in my face.

"Well don't get too comfortable using it— its mine! You have to get your own expression. My point is, if you're really following me, life is full of coincidences. Sometimes big fat coincidences and as much as you try to rationalize them, you can't. Take a look at my own life. I'm the ninety-eighth generation from Aaron and if my hunch is right, I certainly cannot be the only one in the long line of descent that has GLEEM in abundance. So why does it seem to be just me? Why haven't any of my ancestors tried writing it down before? I'm not saying they should have gone public as they probably would have been locked away or worse as most of those prior centuries were a little draconian. That is if they weren't burned at the stake first, but surely they could have written something down and kept it within the family. Their failure to do so has always been a mystery to me."

"Maybe they did and the notes just got buried with time. Or maybe they tried to say something and others in their family threatened them into silence. Perhaps they just didn't have the gift to the same degree as you?" Peace provided several suggestions

"Perhaps you're right," I agreed.

"On which one," Pearce was surprised that I had agreed with him.

"On all three of course. Any one of them is a possibility. But I still find it interesting that we've reached a point where I am only two generations away from the hundredth generation from Aaron and all these things that are world changing are expected to happen, yet I'm the only one that see it. You have to admit, that is definitely curious."

"I don't know Doc. Seems like par for the course the way this world is heading. Seems we don't know what's happening, good or bad, until the last minute."

"You really have to do better in studying your bible legends, John. The bad stuff is not unexpected at all. God was taking a hands off position for a hundred generations when it came to the family of Aaron, my ancestry. Part of the punishment for molding that golden calf in the desert, I'm guessing. He wasn't actually abandoning us, but He certainly wasn't going out of his way to bless us either. We had our hereditary position of power but when you look at everything that happened to my family afterwards you recognize that God had taken a back seat and was letting us drive the car towards oblivion. But in the end, no matter how much we messed things up, there was always that promise of the hundredth generation that He dangled like the proverbial carrot in front of eyes, suggesting that we'd be rescued at the last minute. Everything would start to be restored when it rolled around and I'm guessing the world is in such a mess as it is now because those of my hundredth generation are only infants at this time. Going to be a good twenty or thirty years before the correction takes place."

"You say you were let to suffer, but Doc, I have to disagree with you because your family was never cursed or anything like that," Pearce was quick to contradict what I had to say. "Let's be serious, even when you tell your stories, like **Blood Royale** and **Caiaphas Letters**, or **Zutra**, your family was living better than most. In fact you were literally kings within the spheres you lived in. How can you say that God abandoned you? He may have abandoned the remaining ninety-nine percent in this world but your family didn't suffer like the rest of us."

"Well, from your perspective it wasn't so bad, but in my own context, it certainly has not been a joyride. Growing up in single parent family, having a deprived childhood, living on hand-me-downs and food parcels left at the door, that wasn't any picnic."

"Yet you were able to climb out of that hole, Doc. Opportunities were presented to you that others didn't get. It was as if you had an angel sitting on your shoulder telling you what to do and when to do it and each time you threw yourself down a hole, somehow you were pulled right back up, doing better each time."

"You've been reading my bio," I commented, recognizing some of these stories I had never even told Pearce.

"Yours and several other Goldenthals," he informed me. "Seems like your family, no matter where they are, Hartford, New York, California, they all seem to do well. There are so many of you in medical and governmental positions that you have to wonder why they haven't named a hospital after you."

"Actually, now that you mention it, I think one of the hospitals in Hartford was built by the Goldenthal family there but they settled for a plaque rather than having the hospital named after them."

"And you still want to say God came down hard on your family? Certainly doesn't sound like it."

"Well, it still doesn't dismiss the fact I was born into poverty and a broken home."

"No... you can't pin that one on God.     People are people, no matter what their hereditary birth.     They love, hate, marry, divorce and do all the things that emotional human beings do without any interference from God.  If they want to beat their spouses, gamble away their money, drink themselves into oblivion, abuse their children, or practice another hundred and one criminal behaviors, that's got nothing to do with God. That's just people being people. But as bad as things may have gotten for you, He still lifted you out of that hole.   How I see it, is your family always had that blessing, just that it ended up spoiling you because you never had to live like real people.   You were always living among the treetops while everyone else was scrounging around on the ground.   The few times you tumbled down from the trees, you still found a way to climb back to the treetops."

"How exactly did we end up on a discussion about me," I interjected.   "I do recall we were talking about the pirates suddenly turning away from their attack.   Hardly had anything to do with me, John."

"Just hold on there, Doc.   You asked me and I'm telling you."

"That's the problem, John, I don't exactly remember asking you anything."

"My turn to talk," Pearce countered, obviously having a lot to get off his chest.   "I've listened to a lot of your stories over the past few years and I have to tell you, that as much as these may be the memories of your ancestors, none of you could see the forest for the trees.   You guys haven't suffered.   Where in the two thousand years of your family history have you ever had to lick the gravel off the road?   When was your family ever on the verge of extinction because you were destitute, or starving, or afflicted with plague?   The only time it seems you were ever in trouble is when you were playing power games and trying to control some country.   That's not cursed, that's an abuse of power, nothing more.   A power that was likely given to you in the first place because of a promise that God made to Aaron!"

"Licked the gravel off the road?" I questioned somewhat stupefied."

"Yeah, licked the gravel," Pearce chuckled. "I think I heard it once on Monty Python.

"Well I bet you're glad you got that you found an opportunity to use that line at some point in your life."

"You bet I am," Pearce agreed.   "And you know what's more?"

"No what?" I urged him to continue.

"If there is something special about this hundredth generation of yours, hopefully it has something to do with one of your family learning to deal with this awesome burden of responsibility that is placed on their shoulders with some humility!"

"Humility is not a word intended for use within my family," I challenged. "When I think of humility I think of people afraid to stand up and fulfill their destiny."

"And what's wrong with that? What's wrong with a little humility?"

"Now you sound like one of these never Trumpers, John. And you know what their problem is? None of them ever had the guts to stand up on their own two feet and go out and change the world. Trump may blow his own horn but I learned a long time ago if you don't blow it, no one else is going to do it for you. But people can't stand seeing someone raise themselves above the crowd and make change. So they hate that person when in reality they hate their own weakness for not taking a chance, not seizing an opportunity, failing to announce to the world, 'Hey I did that!', while someone else takes all the credit which only makes them more miserable and hateful of everything around them. To disguise their own self-loathing, they spend all their effort trying to tear down people that have risen above the rest. Rather than say to themselves, 'if he can do that, then I can do something special as well. I can make a difference and people should know what I accomplished,' instead they cower in the shadows, make anonymous insults and threats, because they're nothing but scared little rabbits that are afraid to have an independent thought and make a unilateral action, but are willing at the drop of a hat to condemn anyone else that has the courage to stand on the mountain top. So before we go any further, John, are you the man climbing the mountain, or are you that little rabbit hiding in that hole in the ground?"

"Doc, I wasn't suggesting you shouldn't take credit for all you've done. I was only trying to say you should stop trying to sell that how shtick on family suffering. You are standing on the mountain top and shouting down at everyone else and I don't think you should ever stop. The world needs a wake up call and I'm in full support. I was just saying that your family had the opportunity to do so time and time again and you always seem to fail to complete the task."

"Not through any fault of our own," I advised him. "Every time we got close, there were always those individuals that went out of their way to thwart our success. Those were our never Trumpers and they seem to be there since the dawn of time."

"So what are you exactly saying? That all those people against Trump are wrong and he is right?"

"Of course not, Pearce. Trump is his own worst enemy. I just caution people not to tear something down unless you have something better to replace it with. Right now I think America is faced with the decision on the lesser of two evils. And from my perspective, I'm not sure which one is worse. But that is for them to decide and I wish them luck in doing so."

"And in your case, what are you expecting, for God to clear out all those people that stood in your family's way? Are you saying He abandoned you because he didn't provide a clear path each time he asked someone in your family to do something? I don't think it works that way Doc."

Pearce lectured me. "I think you have to clear your own obstacles out of the way."

"You know, John, I think you're absolutely right. If you have a cancer, you cut it out. Like God said, 'If my right eye offends me, pluck it out.' Time for me to stop thinking about how many times my family failed to succeed in their missions and focus on removing the obstacles."

"Wait Doc, I didn't mean for you to do anything drastic," Pearce became fearful of my tone.

"Don't worry John, it's not up to me. By the time one of my grandchildren adopts the mantle of the hundredth generation, I'll probably be dead and buried. But at least now when he or she reads this, they can see that there's a road map to try and change the repetition of failure in my family. The key is to eliminate any obstacle, decimate any dissent, eradicate all that will stand in the way of the Lord's intentions."

"I was intending for you to go all Rambo, Doc. You can't just blow away anything or anyone standing in your way," Pearce was gravely concerned.

"Sure you can," I disagreed. "Think about it. Think about how much better this world would have been if my ancestors had succeeded in their mission but the one failure they all committed was they never eliminated those that opposed them. Those that stood against God and the world He intended. The greatest enemy to God is man and unless we remove the evil from this world, we will never have the peace that has been promised."

"That wasn't the point I was making," Pearce attempted to change course.

"Sure it was John, you just didn't know it." I grinned and winked at him.

"Ahh... you're just pulling my leg, aren't you?"

"Perhaps," I laughed, "But you'll never know." I laughed again.

# MARE NOSTRUM 63 A.D.

It took almost an hour before the patrol crafts were anchored safely along-side the transport vessel; close enough that they were able to lower a small rowboat over the side capable of transferring their boarding party. One by one the Romans ascended the ladder until they stood on the main deck before the Captain, whom greeted each one enthusiastically, a contagious grin on his lips and a vigorous shake of their hands. There was no difficulty in identifying which one was the commander of the Roman fleet. He was a most impressive sight; tall and stately, wearing a bronze helmet crested by a luxurious plume of red dyed horse hair high above his brow. Across his cuirass breastplate was embossed Sol Invictus, the deity he obviously pledged his allegiance to.

He pointed his short baton at the captain, raising it and lowering it in rhythm to his own voice. "What is your supposed destination Captain? Are you even aware that you're not on any of the demarcated trade routes? Unless you are trying to hide something in your cargo, you shouldn't be here and sailing outside the trade routes is a violation of maritime law. Do you have any idea captain of the trouble you are in?" the Commander's tone of questioning obviously an indication that he was not impressed by the Captain's exuberant welcome.

The Captain didn't take much notice of the Roman's displeasure, simply thrilled that they had escaped from the jaws of death, "I think as far as we are all concerned Commander, we know this route simply as survival. It's certainly not one that we would have taken intentionally, but that fact that we are alive only supports that it is the right route. And to be honest with you, I don't have a damn clue as to where we might be and I'm certain if you discuss it with anyone aboard this ship, they don't really care either. Praise Neptune that we're alive. So you want to go ahead and charge me with some violation of Maritime law, then be my guest!"

The ship's crew broke into a chorus of rowdy praise upon hearing their Captain's invocation of Great Sea King Neptune, much to the Commander's surprise.

He stepped menacingly towards the ship's captain, the baton still gripped tightly in his hand. "I don't appreciate the humor in your being lost at sea, Captain," he bellowed. "There are rules that are imposed upon the traversing of this sea. Rules that have been in force since Pompey rid these waters of the pirates that infested them.

No sooner had he mentioned the now over-stated and obviously false story of Pompey the Great ridding the Mare Nostrum of pirates, the crew of the transport vessel showered the Roman Commander with a tirade of angry shouts that indicated they no longer believed the Roman lies.

The clamor only served to irritate the Commander further. "Unless you provide me with your manifest and your original sailing plan, you will be found in serious violation of those rules. So captain, let me make this perfectly clear to you, you're going to find yourself in serious trouble unless you can provide me with a good reason to avoid me seizing this ship," the commander threatened, throwing a stern warning glance to all on board that still abused him with their howls of disdain. "In order to maintain order from chaos, we have rules on this sea. And one of those rules is that you sail in the sea lanes only!"

"Forgive my bluntness Commander, but may I formally suggest that you tell that to the pirates that had been pursuing us for the past few hours," the Captain stated both respectfully and condescendingly simultaneously. Certainly not an easy feat to accomplish when dealing with those in authority but he managed to do so and the Commander clearly recognized the somewhat mocking tone. The Captain then signaled for his cabin boy to retrieve the necessary paperwork.

The Commander's mind was still swirling from the statement that there were brigands nearby. "You are suggesting that there are pirates on these waters," he repeated somewhat dumbfounded and disbelieving.

"I believe that is what I said to you Commander. I agree, I should have had the paperwork ready as soon as you set foot on my deck but surely you can appreciate how overwhelmed we all are, knowing that there is a Bithynian pirate ship sailing hastily to the east with an empty hold. Looking at the fine cut of your own ship's bow, I'm certain that if you made the effort, you wouldn't have too much trouble catching up to them. After the race that we gave them, I doubt very much their arms could propel them very fast if you gave pursuit."

The Commander was still unwilling to acknowledge his own failure to rid the sea of pirates and relinquish his autocratic tone. "Even if it's true that you narrowly escaped from being preyed upon by the few pirates that may still remain on these waters, I cannot allow you to sail as you have done in total disregard of the demarcated sea lanes."

"You want to fine me, then fine me," the Captain stood his ground. "But the longer you remain here, the greater the chance those pirates will elude you. And when we do finally make safe harbour at our destination, I will file my log of our journey and it will make mention of how we narrowly escaped being boarded by pirates but instead were boarded by a Roman patrol ship that appears to have no interest at all in apprehending the brigands."

It was a point that finally registered with the commander. "As soon as I review your paperwork you can be on our way but don't let me catch your ship violating our laws again. Consider yourself most fortuitous this time but you won't be so lucky the next time." No sooner had the Commander performed his required duty his demeanor changed completely as he clasped the Captain's forearm. "And may the rest of your journey be a pleasant one and may Neptune send you a gentle wind to safe shores." The change in his attitude caught the Captain by surprise but he was more than happy to return the clasp with a firm shake.

The cabin boy reappeared with all the necessary charts and logs and handed them over to the Commander. The Roman only gave them a furtive glance, not actually concerned any longer with the Captain's documentation. He was now preoccupied with other matters, having failed to spot the Bithynian pirates within his own patrol zone and knowing the Captain's log once filed could result in his being disciplined. Word of such an occurrence would be far more than just a major embarrassment and he preferred that it did not get reported back to his admirals. "Now I will see if we can send those cursed brigands to the bottom of the sea. Farewell Captain. Hail Caesar!" The Commander crossed his arm over his chest and shot forward a stiff armed salute. Then he turned and waved his boarding party to descend back into their small boat that nestled against the hull.

As he watched them leave, the urgency of their current situation dawned upon the ship's captain. "Sir, a moment please," he shouted to the Commander. The Roman turned his head to hear the request. "We have put most of our vital supplies overboard in our effort to avoid being captured and now I fear our biggest problem will be a shortage of water. We would greatly appreciate your generosity in providing us with any supplies you could possibly spare."

"Captain, in case you haven't noticed, we are a patrol craft, not a floating supply depot. Set your bearing northeast along the approved routes and make for land there. You'll be able to replenish whatever you need on shore."

"Thank you, Commander," he replied bowing his head slightly in deference. "For nothing," he completed his sentence as soon as the Commander was over the side railing and far enough out of ear shot. "Bastards, think just because they have a fleet of ships that they somehow own the world. I got news for them. They're just one more empire to be buried by time. Just wait until I file my report! Let's get the men back to work Crastus!" he blasted an order. "Don't think we can sit in the middle of this sea all day. Get me a bearing on the route to the north east and set sail. We have some supplies to replenish."

---

Dusk crept over the ship by the time the Captain stepped out of his cabin and walked over to the towering mast. The crew and passengers assembled around him in anticipation of his words. He bore a solemn expression, rarely lifting his eyes from the acacia boards that ribbed the main deck. He cleared his throat loudly, then began to speak. "You are a very lucky people; extremely lucky to be exact. Your lives have been spared from what most certainly appeared to be death at the hands of those bastards. We all owe a great debt of gratitude to Michael Corvasus, whose quick thinking saved us from certain death. We all shall be forever in his debt. To all, this would probably appear to be a time to rejoice. I know that you are tired and you would just like some time to reflect on your good fortune. We have sailed a long distance from whence we started, but we must still sail another long distance as well. That I'm afraid is not to say that the rest of our voyage will be without danger. I know, you are saying to yourselves that we've already had our share of misfortune and are not deserving of any more. Honestly, it should be otherwise but we have not passed unscathed from our recent ordeal. My oarsmen are tired and are unable to endure the four hour shifts that are required of them. This will undoubtedly slow our progress and therein lays our greatest problem, for we are already short on supplies, much of which were thrown over the side and lost to the sea. And let it be known, the sea does not return any of the gifts it is given. To be more precise as to our exact dilemma, it would appear that in all our efforts to escape by lightening our cargo, unbeknownst to you good people, inadvertently we tossed our fresh water overboard along with a fair portion of our food supplies. Food we can survive a while without, water we cannot. It has now become necessary to ration our water until we can obtain more."

"And how long will that be," a voice surfaced from among the passengers.

"The Commander has advised us to sail northeast in order to secure more supplies and that is what we are doing."

Another voice was raised from among that particular group of men concealed beneath their long robes and shadowed cowls which Joseph had shared an oar with. It was the towering giant that raised his voice to ask a question. "Captain, I beg an explanation if you please. If we are in such great need of water, then why don't we simply sail directly north and obtain what we need from the shores we already sail past? Or why not from Rhodes? If we follow the course the Commander instructed we'll be on a course to Crete, which is much farther than either of those other destinations."

"So, you consider yourself somewhat of a navigator do you? Had some sailing experience, I see," the Captain scoffed. "And you probably think you've made a good point, but only if this was a lifetime ago. That land to the north that you'd like us to sail to is under control of the worst scum you can find in Ephesus. That's a well known fact to all of us that plow these seas backwards and forwards. They would make the pirates seem tame in comparison. Any scavenging party we'd set upon that shore wouldn't last the morning before they were seeing the insides of a slaver's caravan. The Romans may claim to own this sea but it is a most hollow boast. As for Rhodes, it too has become extremely dangerous, since the rest of us that sail these waters know that the pirates are now sailing unobstructed from the inland sea through the straits, and use the island as a port almost exclusively for their own vessels. Even the Romans give it a wide berth, though they won't admit it. We are far better sailing the extra day and making land on the north coast of Crete. It's only another day at most. Does that answer your question?"

"It does sir," the reply was sincere and respectful.

"And is there anything else you wish to know?"

"Not at the moment. You're correct, I am a sailing man myself, but I freely admit that I was not aware that the pirates had taken hold of so much territory. No one speaks of it."

"Roman dominance of the land and the seas is definitely not what it used to be," the Captain replied, "Though they pretend otherwise. Once upon a time it was unconquerable. No empire or country could stand in its way. It would have been blasphemy to even think that it could fall. And now it would appear to take nothing more than a band of privateers to shake it to its core. So once you all finally reach your destination in Rome, remember it is not the paradise you think it might be. Rome's days are numbered.

---

What was only a matter of days felt like months to the exhausted and parched passengers. Idle minds fed on the fear that in some manner this particular voyage had been cursed. Whatever little bit of food that was received by Joseph, he would carefully portion and offer at least half to Osirah, most times without her knowledge but as she witnessed his strength gradually ebbing she grew suspicious of his decline.    And when Osirah finally realized what Joseph had been doing she became furious.

"No wonder you appear so gaunt," she scolded him.    How long have you been sharing your meals with me?    I'm not starving you know.    It's not as if I needed your food."

"I'm fine.    Do not concern yourself with how much I have been eating.    I eat enough and that's all that is important."

"You think you're so smart, Joseph ben Matthias.    You've told me so much about yourself and I'm amazed by how little you really know.    The real world has very little to do with the fantasies you dwell upon.    You talk of deliverers and your great messiahs, and yet you can't even acknowledge when this world is spitting in your face.    Do you really believe that the majority of people you show kindness to even appreciate what you offer them?    Do you think some one like Michael would have even considered offering his food portion to someone else?    When will you open your eyes and see how things really are?"

"Do you?"

"Do I what?"

"Do you appreciate what I offer you?"

"What's that got to do with anything?"

"You brought it up.    You said people don't appreciate the kindness I show towards them and I'm asking, do you?"

"This isn't about me."

"Yes it is.    I offered my food to you and now I'm asking if you appreciate it."

"That's not fair."    Osirah's face flushed with embarrassment, not understanding the true nature of Joseph's question.

"If you appreciate it, then my sacrifice was well worth it."    Joseph stared deeply into her eyes looking for any evidence that she did truly appreciate his generosity.

"It's a kind gesture when people do those things" she explained carefully avoiding a direct response to his question.

"And some people do it for certain other people because they want to demonstrate how much they care."

"Joseph, an act of kindness should not be performed with the expectation that it should harvest a response.    Why can't it just be an act of kindness and nothing more?"

Now it was Joseph's turn to interpret Osirah's unspoken message.    She seemed to be suggesting that they were to remain only friends and any expectations greater than that were premature.    But these feelings he was experiencing were all new to him and he was having trouble dealing with them.    Having spent so many years in learning the laws and instructions of the sages, he had never given female companionship much consideration and now Osirah had roused a series of dormant emotions of which he had little understanding. He struggled with the knowledge that he must now he had to contend with a full range of conflicting feelings and inexplicably, it was making him angry. "Do you see Michael offering any of his food to you?" he challenged her, the rawness of his emotions surfacing to the forefront.

Osirah stared coldly into his eyes, the blackness of her pupils seething with her own emotions. "I'm not certain what you're trying to imply Joseph or where you think you are going with it but whatever it is, I do not like the sound of it."

"I see the way Michael talks to you. And then I watch how he swaggers around everyone else. How if it wasn't for him none of us would be alive today. I know that he's inferred how I wouldn't stand a chance of succeeding in my mission without him. And does anyone object to his prancing around like he's the emperor, himself? Does anyone try to set him straight? Noooo! You just accept it. All of you!"

She shook her head in total disbelief. "I can't believe you're turning a discussion about sharing your food with me into an attack on Michael. In my opinion, you are struggling with a whole lot of issues that you just don't know how to express but this certainly isn't the way to do it. It's probably best that that you stop now before you say something you are going to regret. And about him saving our lives, he's right. He did! I can't believe you're trying to argue against the facts."

"How can you agree with them? He struts around this ship like an overstuffed peacock and everyone croons at his passing. His flaming barrels bought us some time, nothing more. Had it not been for the Roman vessel approaching from the   south, the pirates would have caught up with us and we would have all been finished. We didn't have any new tricks, no weapons, not even prayers would have saved us. We were nothing more than fowl ready to have our bones picked clean. His clever idea didn't stop them! Or was I just hallucinating about the Roman patrol ship?"

"Whatever this is all about, Joseph, I don't want to argue with you. You are better than this to sound like a jealous schoolboy. I am no great fan of Michael's but I do know when honors are deserved, and that was one of those times. If you somehow think his   moment of glory makes you less of a man in my eyes, then I'm sorry. We needed time   in order to survive and he bought us some. Let him have his glory. Can't you grant him that?"

"It's not his moment of glory I mind   It's his vainglorious attitude that bothers me. It's the fact that I don't really know whose side he's on."

"You're beginning to sound ridiculous. What sides are you talking about? You can be so frustrating sometimes. The only sides to this issue were either being dead or being alive. And if you chose to be alive, then he was on that same side as you."

"I'm talking about sides on a much higher scale," Joseph tried to explain.

"I'm talking about two civilizations each being a side and the gulf that lies between them. The only way to bridge that divide is for everyone to find the common ground. No decent person sacrifices one for the sake of the other. Michael Corvasus has turned his back on tradition, law and history."

"You are rambling. What are you talking about?" she blew out in an exasperated breath. "You're jumping from one topic to another without any sense!"

"He cares nothing for Judea."

She shook her head, more from confusion than disagreement. "Are we having the same discussion? I'm talking about his saving our lives, and all you can think about is how Roman the cut of his clothes are. Guess what, Joseph? This may come as a surprise to you but I care nothing for Judea either. Does that make me your enemy too? I'm sorry Joseph, but if anyone needs to find that common ground, I think it may be you."

"You don't understand," he whined petulantly which only made her angrier.

"What is wrong with you? What is there to understand?" she fired back but as she gazed into the baleful look filtering through his eyes she understood immediately. She had completely misread the situation. Breaking into a consoling smile, Osirah suddenly hugged Joseph, catching him completely by surprise.

"What was that for?"

"For my being such a fool," she answered. "Why can't you just get past your inability to come out and say what's really on your mind. Why do you have to disguise everything about how you feel? And by the way, I do appreciate your sharing your food with me. You're a good man, Joseph ben Matthias and I do care for you very much if that's what you want to hear. And maybe there can be something more but don't rush me."

# CHAPTER SEVEN

## WHANGAREI; PRESENT

Pearce was ready to spar a few more rounds. I could see it etched clearly in his face. His eyes had narrowed into a menacing squint that equated to his thoughts being mired in disbelief. He still couldn't connect the dots to see how any of the events being revealed related to any of my ancestors.

"I've got it now! This relationship between Joseph and Osirah turns into something later and it's her offspring that you're descended from. Right Doc?"

"Wrong!" I shook my head in denial. "If that was the case then Joseph would have still been my ancestor and I've already told you that he wasn't."

Tossing his pad and pencil into the air, in an act of total frustration, Pearce admitted his failure to resolve the lineage. He felt stumped. "Then this makes absolutely no sense! I can't understand how you can be sitting here telling me about this very private moment unfolding between these two people and neither of them has anything to do with your ancestry. If it's not part of GLEEM, then the only other option you leave me with is to assume that you're making this up."

"That's your problem Pearce, you think in only one direction; father to son, and so on. Well, I'm telling you, he wasn't an ancestor and neither was she, but someone that was watching them quite closely was in a manner of speaking, and that's the part you haven't figured out. I'm actually surprised at you. I thought you would have caught on to this a long time ago."

"Well if it was someone else, then why would these memories watching two other people be that important that he's going to incorporate them into his ever-lasting memories. Tell me that!"

Sometimes Pearce can be so frustrating. "I am telling you why. If you just listen it will become very clear to you. Why are you making such a big issue over this? I'm not trying to make you believe that I can recall every word verbatim that they spoke that day. I am a writer after all. I take the essentials and I spin a story around them. That's what writers do. And you've been with me long enough to know that's not the way GLEEM worked anyway. But I can describe events and how they led to other events, and the filling in of the dialogue is what carries you from point A to point B. So give me some leeway as an author and stop trying to throw a wrench into the machinery all the time!"

"I guess I'm just a little cranky today," Pearce somewhat apologized, I think. "It's just that you ask people like me, and all the readers to accept what you have to say as gospel, and in cases like this, it's very hard to do so on blind faith, no matter how well I know that the other material you've provided in the past has turned out to be true."

"Now, I believe you're beginning to understand the dilemma I constantly face as well. So much of what I see in my head has to be taken on blind faith too. I don't know what's real. I have to just believe that it's there as a thought, a memory, whatever, because it did happen. And in most cases, ninety-nine out of a hundred times it turns out to be correct when someone digs up corroborating evidence. I've had to learn to just accept many of the things I write too as reality, because I have no other explanation. So if one of my ancestors saw Joseph spending an excessive amount of time with Osirah, then it's up to me to fill in the possible reasons for it. Yes, it is called being creative, but if it makes sense, then just go with it."

"I guess I've just got to be more patient and wait for the who, what, where and how. You have to appreciate that part of my journalistic training wants to know immediately. I am sorry Doc for giving you a hard time. My bad." Pearce was now scrambling along the ground on all fours, looking for his pad and pencil after he had thrown them blindly into the air.

"I'll give you an example if it helps," I offered. "I told you about how I found out that I was Kahana. How no one told me and in fact my mother never said a word either. After my father had left, she tried to expunge every trace of him from our lives. So even if he had told her, there was no way she was going to pass it on. So I had that episode where I was half asleep and heard myself being called. But I was being called by the name Kahana, which I had never encountered before from anyone."

"Yeah, I remember that part Doc. And you dreamt you followed this guy down a stairwell in the desert that led to an underground temple or something and you found a book with empty pages. You've told me all that!"

"Yes, that's the story I'm referring to," I confirmed and even though I told him not too long ago that I wasn't going to tell him much more, I knew it was necessary if he was ever going to understand me at all. "But that wasn't the only time things like that occurred."

"You had this cloaked guy lead you down more paths," Pearce postulated.

"No! Nothing like that," I corrected him. "This was different. Once I was reading the book of Judges and something occurred that changed my entire focus on my beliefs as a young Jewish boy."

"I didn't think young boys read that kind of book even in your younger days."

"They probably didn't, I did. But then again I wasn't exactly your average young boy."

"And why in heavens would you say something like that," Pearce mocked me as if to say I wasn't anywhere close to average now either.

I snapped him a look of utter contempt. "Let's not get snarky," I warned him. "Just remember that is is because of GLEEM, John, that you even have a writing career to speak of. You best remember, Genetically Linked Enzyme

Enhanced Memories is the reason why we're here! The reason why you're always here! So if you want to suggest that not being average somehow deserves ridicule then I'd think again before you piss me off and snuff out your paycheck."

"Being a tad touchy yourself, aren't we!" Pearce rebounded from my outburst. Oh, yeah..I wasn't thinking Doc in my choice of words. GLEEM is very important and I wasn't meaning to put you down at all for it."

"Well, you better not have been because in case you forgot, GLEEM is all we've been talking about all these years. But back to where I was heading with this. Just think about it. You're a kid, and you don't know whether you have an over active imagination or living with virtual nightmares. Things happen and you can't explain them, and it doesn't take long before you get labeled as being strange or weird by other kids. So yes, I liked to read the Old Testament books, in both English and Hebrew. Let's just say it provided me with entertainment."

"So, what did you see?" Pearce deftly moved me back on to the topic and realigned my initial focus.

"I saw a mistake. A story line that wasn't right. That had been changed."

"Changed?"

"Yes, changed. Changed from the actual events."

"And you know this because....?"

"Because I knew what had actually happened. And I knew whom it had actually happened to. So I knew what was written wasn't right."

"And this is most likely because you had these memories of what really transpired through GLEEM."

"Except back then, I hadn't even thought about GLEEM at all. Back then I only understood it as a gut feeling. An instinct! But it was strong, and I knew it was one hundred percent correct. It was this story about a traveling priest. A priest with a servant girl and he goes into a Benjaminite town for the night. The girl is sexually assaulted by the townsfolk and killed during their gang rape."

"That was in the bible?"

Obviously one of the stories that Pearce's Sunday school teacher had overlooked. "Yeah, that story is in there," I reassured him. Book of Judges."

"But why?"

"Ahh! That's the sixty-four million dollar question. Not the type of story one would expect to find in a holy book. Especially since the outcome was the priest summoning a council of all the tribal leaders and forcing them to exact revenge against the Benjaminites. By the time they were finished, there was virtually nothing left of the tribe of Benjamin. Pretty harsh when you consider it was over the death of a slave girl."

"I don't follow," Pearce commented to me.

"Slaves were nothing more than property. Destruction of property had an entire set of rules for legal enforcement and the wholesale slaughter of a tribe wasn't considered one of them."

"So, you're saying that there was a lot more going on here than meets the eye."

"You should know me by now, John. I wouldn't bring this up unless there was definitely a lot more to this story."

Pearce began tapping his pencil impatiently against his pad.

"I'm getting there. Just hold on. If you read the story, you'll find that the priest is referred to as Jonathan ben Gershom the grandson of Manasseh. There's a problem with that. By this time, the only priestly tribe was Levi. If Manasseh had any earlier priestly ties, they had forfeited them by this time. So either the Bible is wrong or someone purposely altered the story!"

"But why couldn't this have been some guy named Manasseh that was from the tribe of Levi," Pearce asked quite innocently.

"Oh, that was a possibility, but the story definitely indicates that this Manasseh was a big player and his name carried some weight. The only Manasseh we know of with any significance back then was Joseph's son. So that's where being able to read the same story in Hebrew is an advantage. And it was definitely inferring much more than someone with the name belonging to the tribe of Levi or at least perceived as a Levite."

"So, you're saying there's a mistake in the Book."

"No, the Book doesn't record mistakes. You can't have mistakes in the Bible. As soon as the Bible has mistakes than it's just not acceptable! Editors would have removed it a long time ago because you can't build a faith on mistakes."

"I don't get it. If it's not a mistake, then what is it?"

"The truth. This was never about the rape and killing of a female slave. This was about an insult to a very powerful man, this one called Jonathan, a priest. And what might even be more important but overlooked, he was the son of Gershom. So this Gershom had to be really important as well and respected enough that any affront to either of them would unite all eleven tribes against one single tribe. But the only Jonathan son of Gershom that was also a priest as far as we know of from the Bible just happened to be the grandson of Moses."

"Now you've really lost me. How can he be the grandson of Moses and from the tribe of Manasseh at the same time? That just doesn't make any sense. Does it?"

"All the sense in the world if you know Hebrew," I informed him. "They only implied he was from the tribe of Manasseh because they said Gershom was the son of Manasseh. So this Manasseh was the grandfather of Jonathan, in the same way that Moses was grandfather to someone named Jonathan. Now pay attention as this is very important; there's only one letter difference in Hebrew between the name Moses and Manasseh. Add the letter 'nun' to Moses and you have successfully made the change."

"So you're saying the name was deliberately altered. How can than not be a mistake or at least a deliberate error? You're implying that the Bible has misleading information in it." Pearce was getting that crazed look about him once again. Any time I imply that there may be religious fallibility he tends to get a little irritated and very defensive.

"You have to appreciate that the religious scribes would never dare tamper with the Bible blatantly. So even though they added this letter to the name Moses, they had to make certain that other scribes new it was an intentional alteration. So they wrote the 'nun' slightly elevated above the rest of the letters in the name. They did that so it would always be known that they added this letter."

"And you can still look me in the eye and state that they didn't tamper with the Holy Scriptures?"

"Most definitely. Because at the time they were writing this, they still knew the full name of Moses. One day I'll tell you about it but he was probably known as Nunmose as one of his royal names. So theoretically, they weren't altering anything that wasn't true as they perceived it in their own minds. Instead, they were merely providing additional information. And as I intend to write in a new book called ***Once A God***, Moses was probably from the tribe of Joseph."

"Hey, everyone knows that Moses was the brother of Aaron and that makes him a Levite too. Doesn't it? How could he be a Levite and from Joseph's tribe? That's getting as bad as suggesting that what the scribes did wasn't a crime. They knowingly altered the story no matter how you try to exonerate them."

"I promise you. At the same time I explain his actual name, I'll explain the ties between Moses and the tribe of Joseph and Manasseh as well. You just have to wait for that book to be written. Perhaps it will be my next story. Let's wait and see. But more importantly is for you to recognize that these scribes didn't tell any lies. They just didn't tell it exactly the way it was. And that's where GLEEM kicked in. And because of it, I confronted the rabbis at the school I attended."

"They must have been horrified," Pearce suggested.

"Actually, they were impressed. They wanted to know how I knew. How I knew what they had always known."

"They knew?"

"Turned out there are a lot of secrets that have been protected over the millennia. Some of them pretty big secrets. This was something that they had always known but just never bothered to share with anyone else."

"So what did they do next?"

"They were really impressed when I suggested that there was a tie of Moses to Manasseh. Since I knew that they were also aware that no scribe would dare change anything in the Torah that would be construed as a lie, then it meant the alteration was still making a true statement. They didn't deny it. But were still very insistent on my telling them how I came to this revelation."

"Did you tell them about GLEEM, Doc?"

"Like I said, I didn't really comprehend what GLEEM was at that time. All I told them was that I just knew. That something inside my head told me that this was what was the truth. You see, GLEEM would suggest that I was also exposed to this privileged information that the rabbis were in possession of. Not such a great surprise considering that Jakob Goldenthal was the offspring of a rabbi that came from a long line of chief rabbis. There would have had to have been a lot of guilt in knowing what they knew and keeping it concealed from the common people all those generations. This corresponds well with the theory behind GLEEM, but I didn't know any of this at that time. And I certainly knew even less about my ancestry at that time. Picture this though; they're impressed by what I had to say. So much so that not only do I become the valedictorian for my graduating class at Eitz Chaim for that year, but the head of the school approaches my mother about allowing them to take care of my future by enrolling me in the yeshiva at their expense."

"Yeshiva? What's that all about Doc?"

"Just another name for rabbinical school. I guess they figured if I was aware of some of their most carefully concealed secrets, then I must be getting word from above. And if that was true, then they had an obligation to ensure that I was brought in to the fold. The old, 'better have him with us than against us theory.'"

"But you didn't do that," Pearce stated what was obvious knowledge. "Wouldn't that have been some big thing in your community?"

"Probably would have been. I think my ancestral memories had a major role in my rejecting their offer. After that, the revelations started coming fast and furious. It wasn't long after that I realized that I was more Karaite than Rabbanite. And that pretty much put a kibosh on their plans for bringing me into the fold."

"Any regrets?"

"None at all. With my Karaite beliefs, I wouldn't have lasted long in that environment. I'd be asking too many questions and would have caused them a lot of grief!"

"But getting back to the point...."

"Yes, that's right. I was making a point about how I know what I know, even if as in the case of Joseph ben Matthias, he wasn't my ancestor. "

"Precisely!" Pearce re-emphasized.

"Easy, everything he did left a deep impression on my ancestors that were close to him. As you'll see from the rest of the story, not even he was aware of how close they were at all times. My family was on a mission, and that was to see that events turned out exactly as they wanted."

"Okay," Pearce capitulated. "I'll wait and see how it all develops but if you want me to continue in being a believer, then this has to be good."

"Oh, it will be good. I can definitely tell you, it will be good!"

# AEGEAN SEA; 63 A.D.

There were still almost two days sailing to the Isle of Crete when the giant that had remained secluded among the enclave of robed and hooded travelers sat down uninvited beside Joseph during the morning meal.    Extending an extremely large right hand he introduced himself. "I am called Jacob ben Simon."

"You were the one I rowed with," Joseph responded, clasping the man's hand in greeting only to find his own hand dwarfed by comparison.    "I have noticed that you travel quite inauspiciously with your comrades, but I should warn you, in reality you're tending to draw far more attention to yourselves than I think you desire."    Joseph pointed over in the direction of the tiller housing where Jacob's associates all remained huddled.

"An unfortunate hazard with the number of people travelling the seas these days.  The opportunity to remain practically invisible is no longer a viable option.  But I will come straight to the point Joseph, I...we need your help."

"Without knowing who you and your friends are, I cannot promise you anything.    I can only say that I appreciate what they all did on the rowing deck when we escaped the pirates.    The momentum we gained to elude the Bithynians was provided by all of your combined efforts.    I saw that.    I was there.    I know who deserves the credit for our escape."

"Men on a mission have a reason to row harder," Jacob explained.    "A mission that I cannot explain fully to you at this time," he replied discretely, "but I can assure you we are on a mission of great importance.  When we arrive at Crete I will tell you more."

"Why not tell me now?" Joseph insisted on knowing.

"Because the man you travel with would not take kindly to what I have to say if he should overhear us.    I must go now, but I promise that I will search you out once we reach Crete."

Joseph nodded, agreeing to meet despite his knowing nothing of these men, but his curiosity had been aroused.    Osirah was returning from the wash cupboard, which overhung the stern rail when she saw the giant leaving.

"What was that all about?" she questioned as soon as she returned to her seat beside Joseph.

"I can't say that I really know.   He just asked me to wait for him to make contact in Crete" Joseph replied in all honesty.    "He never told me anything."

"Well I must admit that it did appear as if you two had something serious to converse about considering it was nothing."

"Honestly, he didn't tell me anything other than we'll talk further and that was it."

"Be wary of them Joseph," she cautioned.  "Of all the passengers, they are the most peculiar in the way they keep to themselves and cover their faces in shadow all the time. I don't like it. I'm certain that Michael would have his concerns as well."

"Only if you told him Osirah, and you must promise me, not a word about this to him. Promise!"

"It could be dangerous, Joseph. What about your mission? It's his job to keep you out of trouble."

"I need you to promise me!"

"Alright, I promise but I still don't like it. Did you ever think that they might have been hired by people that wish to see your mission fail?

"Why would anyone wish to interfere with secluring the release of a bunch of old priests whom have far outlived any political influence they once may have had?"

"Why do people do any of the things they do? Because they can and because they do!"

"That even makes less sense than my meeting these people," Joseph snickered at her comment.

Osirah stared at Joseph in frustration. "Why do I even try to reason with you? You are as stubborn as a mule! If you're content to walk headlong into trouble then why should I even try to stop you?"

"Don't worry. I can take care of myself. There is this tendency for everyone to underestimate my ability to protect myself. Rest assured I can."

Osirah found it suddenly very difficult to speak. "You can be so stupid sometimes. I've been trying to say that I care about you, Joseph. I know I told you several days ago that we are just friends but I was lying to myself as much as I was to you. That's what women do when they try not to let themselves be hurt. But it's all a lie. I think I'm finding myself caring deeply for you."

"And you already know that I have similar feelings towards you," Joseph reaffirmed. "I told you that already."

"I know that is what you have said but your actions have never shown any actual signs of your affection?" Her stare burrowed deep into his eyes as she hunted for an answer.

Joseph could not avoid revealing his dark, haunting secret any longer. "I'm not very good around women. I'm not even certain what I'm supposed to do in fact."

Osirah drew a deep breath cupping her left hand over her mouth. "Are you saying that you've never been with a woman," she gasped in disbelief.

"Of course I've been around women before," he protested. "That would be ridiculous that I've never been around a woman."

"That's not what I'm asking, Joseph," she quickly reasserted her position. "I mean you have never been intimate with a woman before. You've never had sex." She immediately reached out and gently stroked Joseph's upper arm knowing the answer.

Joseph looked around furtively to make certain no one had overheard her question, his face reddened with embarrassment. "Why do you make it sound like it's a bad thing," he sounded annoyed. "It's not that unusual. In my world we are instructed to wait until it is the right time. Expressing self control is essential to separate ourselves from the animal world beneath us. We must concentrate only on the spiritual world and only partake in the physical world for procreation once a marriage has been arranged."

Before Osirah even had the opportunity to respond to Joseph's explanation their conversation was rudely interrupted.

"And that is why I have as little to do with the world of my birth as possible," Michael ridiculed the practice, having overheard Joseph's feeble attempt to explain his obvious absence of a single romantic bone in his body.

Joseph could only cringe at the thought that Michael had overheard their conversation. He searched for the words with which to retaliate but he couldn't find any.

"Do you really want to know the truth Osirah?" Corvasus continued uninterrupted. "It's a world of hypocrisy. They all feel one way and do another. Sooner than admit to the truth they will lie to each other in order to convince them -selves that they're somehow better than the rest of the world. Truth is they secretly covet the Hellenistic world and all it has to offer, including its assorted hedonistic pleasures, but they are even too afraid to admit it. Then they go and give a lame excuse that they would be betraying their precious heritage; a heritage which has offered them nothing but servitude to one empire after another. Don't waste your time trying to find any evidence of manhood among his kind," Michael waved his finger in front of Osirah's face. "It doesn't exist. Joseph is a freak but not for the reason you might think. Normally they'd marry their boys off by the time they're eighteen just so they can get...what was that word you used ...Oh, yes, procreation...so they can get all their procreation done with at an early age and then get back to their studies. The fact that he's in his late twenties does make him an unacceptable oddity even to his own kind! If you ask me, it is my suspicion that any man hasn't desired the pleasures of a woman underneath him by the time they reach his age, then they aren't interested in women at all, if you catch my drift."

"That is a foul and insulting lie," Joseph shouted furiously as he moved towards   Corvasus, his fists tightly balled.

"And what are you going to to about it," Michael taunted him. "You going to defend yourself by threatening me perhaps? Or you simply going to talk me to death. I'm certain that will really impress your lady love here."

"Why don't you go elsewhere, Michael. Neither of us want you here. So leave!" Osirah stepped between them.

"That's the way it is now, isn't it Joseph. Let your woman do your fighting. You Jews in Judea make a lot of noise about fighting Rome but the truth is you are all nothing but scared little boys. Running to the Temple to pray to God to come fight the big bad battle for you because none of you have the balls to do it yourself.    You all lost your manhood the day they cut off your foreskin as babies. Put a sword in his hand and it would be about as useless as the one between his legs.   Isn't that right Joseph?   Osirah's not going to find much in the way of manhood under your tunic, is she?    Take my advice girl and get yourself a real man and stop wasting your time on the likes of him."

Joseph could not decide if he felt more wounded by Michael's ridicule or by the fact that Osirah thought it was necessary for her to come to his rescue. Whichever the reason, he felt both emasculated and immobilized, unable to respond in his own defense.

"You asked once, what I have against my own people, well the answer should be pretty obvious to you by now, Joseph.   You're all pathetic!"

Finally finding the will to brush Osirah to the side, Joseph stood toe to toe with his more muscular framed adversary but the thought that Corvasus could easily dispatch him was no longer a concern.    "You know what Michael, you'll never be a Roman no matter how hard you try to rub the Jewish stench from your skin.    I think that is the reason you resent me most. Because to you I represent something that exists within yourself that you find repugnant but it can't be removed, no matter how hard you try.    How sad that you can only exist by still earning your wages in servitude to the same people that sicken you. You're a hypocrite as long as you still suckle at the teat of your Jewish parentage and you know it! You will never find acceptance into the Roman world you yearn for Michael because you will never be able to disembowel that part of you which is Judean.    To the Romans you will always be a dirty, filthy, little Jew and you know it!"

Unexpectedly, Michael turned away angrily, walking towards the ship's prow without ushering another word.    Joseph had struck the raw exposed nerve that fueled Michael's self-loathing.    Corvasus resented that he was dependent on the very people he despised.    No matter how Romanized he would become, he would never be allowed to escape his Jewish heritage which haunted him.

Placing her hand against Joseph's cheek, Osirah caressed him gently, attempting to calm the rage that still burned within, only to have Joseph push it away brusquely.    "What did I do?" she sounded wounded by his action.

"I didn't need you to rush to my defense," he stated angrily.    "I am capable of defending myself.    I'm not a little child!"

"I never said that you were, Joseph ben Matthias," she responded angrily.    "But if you're going to behave in this manner, then I might have to reconsider.    Don't make yourself out to be as big a fool as he is. Do you understand me?"

Joseph recoiled from her threatening demeanour.    He knew that this time he may have bitten off more than he could chew.    An enraged Osirah was a force of nature that he had no desire to oppose. "I'm sorry," he apologized.    "I'm just so mad at myself and I feel so helpless.    I think Michael my have been right."

"Don't you go and play the 'woe is me' game either, Joseph ben Matthias. And certainly don't you pay Michael Corvaus any heed. He has his own problems because a man cannot have his feet on both sides of a fence at the same time."

Joseph lowered his head between his hands as he felt a wave of remorse crash over him. "It's more than that Osirah. He said things that are true. Something has happened to me and I'm afraid that I am unable to share myself with a woman. I don't have a clue as to what I should do. One part of me aches to pull you into my arms and do things I cannot even comprehend. While the other part of me wants to flagellate the flesh from my bones for daring to even think in this way and offending God. I fear I am broken."

Osirah wrapped her hands about his face and nestled his head upon her waist. "Is there no room for love in this religion of yours? Can your god be so cruel that he denies you the pleasures that he can never bring to you? Is the inter -twining of a man and a woman something so vile that you must reject all that it offers? I am reaching out to you with my heart and you make me feel as if I am an abomination because I come from a different set of beliefs. Will your god not let you find any place in your heart for me, Joseph ben Matthias?"

"I...I...am so confused," was all that Joseph could sputter at that moment.

"Your eyes say that you want me but you can't even permit yourself the words to tell me that it is so. What has this god of yours done to you?"

"I am my own man," Joseph protested towards heaven as he reached out and took Osirah's arm gently then pulled her slowly towards him. "Do you hear me Lord? I will decide what is best for me," he railed against the cloudless sky. As if the weight of several tons had been lifted from his shoulders, Joseph suddenly permitted his hands roam freely across her waist as he pulled her into his lap. The message he delivered next was clear as soon as their lips touched; a message far greater than any words could convey. The flood of sensations rocked him as if he had been struck by a bolt of lightning.

In a world where raw emotion was constantly suppressed and every urge extinguished almost as soon as the desire arose, Joseph found himself breaking free of the psychological constraints that had bound him since his youth, and the thought of that freedom suddenly terrified him. In unleashing the ravenous beast, his new fear was that he'd be unable to control his desires, and that would be far worse than living the pretense that he had no desires at all. Osirah could sense the conflict that still raged within Joseph's tortured mind and immediately swayed the battle in her favour by pressing her lips more firmly against his, permitting their souls to merge for what seemed to last a life time. Joseph's arms encircled her petite frame as he pressed their bodies together so that their hearts beat in unison through the fabric of their clothing. Her breathing spontaneously quickened, at which point she felt compelled to finally force her mouth apart from his. "I'm sorry but I have to stop this now or I'm afraid I won't be able to stop at all. We will become a shocking spectacle to the other passengers," she said apologetically as she withdrew.

Similarly, not wishing to release her but fearing too that he would cross the point of no return, Joseph reluctantly released his grip from around her waist. "Nor I," he panted regrettably. "I only wish that this moment could have remained forever," Joseph admitted. "I have been a fool, haven't I? I condemn Michael for what I considered the sins of this world, yet here I am wishing I could carry you off to some private place where I can ravage you like all those that I have condemned as nothing more than animals. How could I have been so blind not to see that his was the real world, and mine was the fabrication of lies.?"

"The only fool I have encountered was the one who believed for so long that he was anything other than a normal man, with normal needs and desires. What I can't understand is why would anyone do such a thing to themselves? Deny themselves the very pleasures that render us human, not animals. How cruel for a society to impose such restraints on young men, teaching you that to love is wrong, and that men and women are distinct and should be separate, rather than being two halves of a whole. "

"Now I am more confused than ever," Joseph confessed. "What was said to be wrong now seems to be so right. But if it is so right, then why do I still feel so guilty for having these feelings?"

"I am truly sorry Joseph if I've caused your mind to be embroiled in turmoil, but I have no regrets in finally telling you how I feel about you. As long as both of us were dancing around, avoiding our true feelings, we were just lying to ourselves and that is far worse than being truthful to oneself."

At that moment Joseph found some clarity amid all his confusion. "What I do know is that a woman should never apologize for being so beautiful and kind that she was able to actually make me want to find my true self."

"Do you really think I'm beautiful?"

"Why would I ever lie to a princess," he displayed his most beguiling smile as he looked deeply into her eyes.

"Even a princess is only a woman," she quickly reminded him. "A woman no different from any other and with exactly the same needs. A man needs to love the woman not the title."

At that moment Joseph's expression became dour and Osirah sensed that his mind once again began to fill with doubt. "Who am I to kid myself?" he questioned. "As much as I feel for you, we both know it cannot come to anything. You will always be a royal princess and daughter of Tigranes," Joseph lamented. "However I might feel for you and you feel for me, your station in life will always prevent us from being together. When this voyage is over and I find you safe passage home, I will cease to exist in your world. I am not worthy enough to exist in your world," Joseph sighed with a forlorn look.

"There is one fact that I did hear about your world," she snapped at him angrily, "And that is they say you Jews play upon guilt your entire lives; your guilt, your mother's guilt, even the guilt of the world. True, I am a princess, but that does not mean I do not have my own mind and the fact that you were chosen as an emissary for this mission means that you are far more than just a commoner. You don't have to try and win me over through guilt. I am yours if you want me. Just say the words, Joseph."

"Don't promise what can never be." Joseph countered by placing his index finger across her lips as if to tell her not to tease him with the impossible. "I am not a prince, I have no title and I certainly have no great personal wealth to speak of. They haven't even told me why I was chosen for this mission other than to say I will know soon enough when I arrive in Rome. I don't even have my own home for us to live in. I have nothing to offer for a princess."

"You can be such a fool, Joseph ben Matthias. There is nothing that my father can't resolve," she grinned back, "Trust me. After all, I am his favorite daughter."

---

Joseph and Osirah woke in each others arms to the sound of the voyagers shouting jubilantly, overcome with excitement after so many days at sea, as they could now clearly see the outline of the island from the rails. They sang, cheered and some even danced with joy, their voices parched by the salty air. The jagged rocky isle jutted from the     Mediterranean like a spear rising above the crests of the waves. The Captain ascended from the depths of the lower deck, followed closely by Crastus. As he walked towards his cabin, he spoke loudly to his first mate intentionally so that everyone would overhear their conversation.

"At last Crastus we have come to the end of our problems. We'll get our fresh supplies from the Cretans and then set sail for Rome as quickly as possible." Crastus nodded his head in agreement. "Tell the crew to find us safe harbor along the northern coastline."

"Aye Captain. The north shore it is." Crastus was across the deck in a flash in spite of his age and crooked body. Once the instructions were passed on to the helmsman, it was only a matter of hours until the vessel was moored safely alongside two other ships that had arrived earlier in the day. One was a Roman galley, proud and immaculate as it bobbed upon the surf, the other a tall masted Cyrene trader, as dark and foreboding as its people were known to be fearsome.

As Joseph strolled across the ramp bridge extending to the dock, he glanced over his shoulder and saw Jacob watching him closely from the deck of the ship. Joseph continued to walk along the weathered boards until he found himself on the shore with its rocky, uninviting terrain.

The Captain and his first mate had proceeded to the nearby town to secure the necessary provisions to replenish their lost supplies. Arriving in town, there was not as much available to purchase as the Captain had hoped.    Apparently the Cyrenian vessel was forced to sail to Crete for similar reasons and they had already purchased most of what was available.

The storekeeper scratched his balding pate as he proposed what was at best a feeble suggestion.    "The Cyrenians are renowned traders.    If you should be carrying anything of value, I'm pretty certain that they'd be willing to trade you the rest of the supplies you require."

The Captain laughed heartily.    "Good sir, if I had any cargo of value, do you think I would be serving as a passenger ship for such a motley lot as is now walking on your beaches?    Besides, anything that may have had any value is likely feeding the fish now."

"Perhaps some of your passengers are carrying sufficient funds with them. Cyrenians are also known to love a quick profit.

"I'm sure there are quite a few of them carrying a bundle of gold and silver," the Captain rsponded, "But I doubt very much that they'd part with it on their own accord and certainly not for the purpose of feeding anyone but themselves."

"I can't think of anything else," the store keeper replied.    "But if I could make another suggestion then; fill as many barrels as you can with water and forego some of the food that you're trying to purchase.    You can make another docking before you reach Italy.    Sail to the Grecian mainland and you'll be able to acquire the provisions you need there. Dyrrachium is flush with food from what I hear.    Generally, I'd tell you it would be a safe port of call, but so much has changed in the last few months, I can't guarantee anywhere can be considered safe any longer.    So be careful."

"A    good    suggestion    mate    but    I    have    a    sneaking    suspicion you're not telling me everything you know," the Captain insinuated.

The shopkeeper leaned closer so as not to be overheard, "The Romans don't want it known but it's nothing that you haven't already experienced.    Do you think you're the only one that had a tale of Bithynian pirates to tell me?    Almost every nunidae I'm hearing of such an event. The imperial navy has even lost several ships.    It cannot offer you any protection.    There are pirates practically everywhere.    Coming from the African coast, the Adriatic, and even Cilicia.    They already control much of the Sea.    Do not sail out into the trade routes as the Roman's tell you.    They are completely out manned by the raiders and can't even protect themselves.    Hug the coast if you can. It will take you much longer but it will provide you with a far safer passage."

"But what about the pirate coves along the banks," the Captain challenged the advice. "Surely they are as much of a concern as the pirates sailing on the water."

"At least from the shore they will see you're nothing but a passenger ship of little value.    Most of them aren't slavers, so they aren't interested in human cargo."

"Things have gotten that bad?"

"Worse," the shopkeeper replied.   "If you've never prayed to mighty Poseidon, then now would be a good time to start."

"I've tried it a few times but he just doesn't listen to me. Pretty bad, eh? To be a sea captain that is despised by the Lord of the seven seas.   I'll hug the coast like you have suggested.   It will take a lot longer than my passengers are prepared to suffer, but they'll have to understand and live with it."

"And 'live' might be the key word for them to remember," the shopkeeper emphasized..

"And what do I owe you?"

"That will be two hundred sesterces."

"Merde!" the Captain explained.   "For what?   I see that not all the pirates are on the seas!"

---

As he knelt by the pool of clear water, cupping the cool and refreshing liquid to his lips, Joseph felt a heavy hand fall upon his left shoulder.   He turned to see the broad face of Jacob hovering well above him. Without saying a word, the stranger crooked a finger urging Joseph to follow him under the cover of a nearby outcropping of trees.

Joseph rose and trailed but only for a short distance before he suddenly stopped, as a wave of apprehension stirred from within.   "I will not go further. Where are you intending on taking me?"

"Only to where our words can have some privacy," the tall, burly giant reassured him.

"I'll be forthright with you Jacob, if what you want from me is in violation of any laws, I will have no part in it.   I don't even want to hear about it, so don't waste your breath trying to tell me about it."

The giant chuckled softly, not a hint of malice in his laughter.   "What I have to say is not wrong, at least not in any way that one should think as being wrong.  Let us go sit in the shelter of those trees and I will elaborate for you."

Jacob marched the short distance to the outcropping of cedars and found a comfortable rock to sit upon, waiting for Joseph who followed reluctantly. "I take you to be a man that would not break a confidence," Jacob stared sharply into Joseph's eyes.   "As you have obviously seen on board our ship, the men I am traveling with prefer to remain sequestered and aloof.   Like yourself, we have been sent on a mission. Not by the high priest of course, but by those that move around in similar circles."

"You know of my mission," Joseph blurted, caught completely by surprise when Jacob revealed he knew the purpose of his voyage. "How is that possible?"

"As I was about to say to you, we have been sent by some that would be considered associates of Damneus.   They are well aware of the purpose of your trip, and saw an opportunity for you to do far more than just seek an audience with the Emperor in order to gain the release of several priests."

"More? What does more mean exactly?"

"An opportunity to discover information in regards to Rome's true intentions for the near east."

"Then you are spies! Who sent you?"

"Does it really matter? It could be Damneus himself if that would make a difference to you? You realize there are many other sources of power in Judea that have nothing to do with the priests. I'm certain you could think of a long list of names that could easily serve as my employer. What matters is that we have an opportunity to achieve several goals rather than just one."

"And how exactly would I fit into this plan of yours?"

"You have in your possession a document that will gain you access through many portals once you land. It will introduce you to all the right people and provide you with immediate recognition. Some of those doors will take you right into the palace but probably no further. On the other hand, my benefactors though are quite powerful in their own right and very well connected. They could provide you with the leverage to open more doors within the city that would be impossible to open otherwise. Under the diplomatic security of your letter, you would be able to bring us inside of some of those places that we cannot access on our own because we do not represent any official government officials in Judea."

"So let me see if I have this straight. You're benefactors are supposedly powerful but they can't open the doors you need to open. Only I can do that with the letter I'm carrying. How is it you even know about this letter I'm supposedly carrying?" Joseph demanded to know, both alarmed and intrigued by the level of knowledge that Jacob appeared to have but certainly was not entitled to.

Once again Jacob laughed with the same soft chuckle that betrayed a man of his size. "Let's just say a little bird told us and leave it at that. Your mission for the Sanhedrin provides you with enough authority that you could easily open those doors among Rome's officialdom without even breaking a sweat. That's all we ask. An introduction here, a suggestion there, nothing more is required. In return, we will serve as you official entourage and make certain that you meet the right people that govern Rome. Did you not think it strange that a mission of this nature, which is befitting an ambassadorial party, was not given the appropriate level of security and dignity that befitted it? Normally there'd be half a dozen people just to provide a suitable appearance when entering the imperial court. All you have is Corvasus and he'll abandon you as soon as he has his money."

"To be honest, I did think it a bit strange, but I presumed that the rest of my party would consist of the delegates I'd be meeting once I reach Rome. I wasn't too worried about it until now."

"No, it isn't going to happen that way. That again was my employer's handiwork. He was able to convince the Sanhedrin that making an understatement would be less threatening to Nero, when all along he planned to have my party join yours so that when we did make port, it would appear to everyone that you headed a fairly sizable delegation."

"I don't believe you!    I'm certain that there are preset arrangements once I meet the appropriate agents in Puteoli.    Damneus told me so."

"It's true," Jacob insisted.    "There is no one waiting there for you. Only the Sanhedrin's banker to provide you with money and a guide that would take you to Rome and introduce you to the more prominent members of Jewish-Roman society.    You see, in order for you to make any impression at all, you would be forced to seek us out."

"Us, us, who's us that you keep referring to?    I see nothing but a group of men in cowls and cloaks.    How any of you might be connected to the Sanhedrin is a mystery and one I'm certain that I do not wish to know!"

"In time you will be made aware of whose faces lie beneath the cowls. That is when you will willingly accept our offer.    Which you will, even if it means you arrive in Rome and find that Damneus has not arranged for you to have an official entourage."

"This is all bullshit. Michael Corvasus knows who I'll be meeting.    There are members to my party that he will be arranging to join me once we've landed in Puteoli."

"Seriously?" Jacob snorted.    "Has he given you any names?"

"It's a secret.    Only he knows whom I'm to see."

"Well that's convenient. We already know that he's to introduce you to the money man because after all, he wants to be paid.    But after that, what would be his obligation to take you around and introduce you to anyone?"

"Stop playing games with me," Joseph started to grow nervous about Jacob's true intentions, suspecting far more was involved..

"You never stopped to consider the situation, have you?    Here you are representing the Sanhedrin and there's only you and one other man.    Oops, make that you, one other man, and a dark haired beauty whom I don't think was part of the original plan," Jacob flashed Joseph a churlish grin upon saying that.    "You'd pick up a few more, a banker, a guide and perhaps even an old man or two from the Jewish community in Rome, but that would be about it.    I guarantee that Corvasus is leaving as soon as he drops you off at his contact point.    This was all prearranged because that's where we were intended to step in.    I just thought it is better you know now. I swear to you, this is true."

"But how could anyone be so certain that I would entertain your proposal, let alone accept it."    The tone in Joseph's voice was beginning to sound desperate.

"There are no certainties but I think you will find our offer to be your entourage in Rome most inviting once you meet the rest of my comrades.    And the absence of anyone of significance in your party will make you realize that all along it was my group that were the intended ones to join with you in Rome."

"So why tell me all this now if you're going to make your proposal in Rome any way? Why bother to reveal this supposed master plan now?"

"As I said, I reconsidered and thought it best now than later. Because when we do meet up again in Rome, you will be able to reflect back upon our little conversation that we're having right now and you will know for certain that I have told you the truth."

"So if it was always Damneus's intention to have you join with me, then why not just bring it out in the open and introduce yourselves the first day we stepped aboard this ship?"

"You assuming that Damneus is the one that gives us orders. I will tell you this, that we are not taking any orders from Damneus. Not now and not ever.

"Because your mission has nothing really to do with mine, does it?" Joseph questioned him.

"That is not entirely correct. They are connected but our mission primarily is to aid our country. In so doing, you benefit as well, perhaps indirectly."

"Indirect benefits! I've heard people try to justify espionage before, but this is the first time that I've ever heard it being proposed as 'indirect benefits'. I don't want you and your companions to be offended and take this the wrong way, but it should have been obvious to your employer that I cannot and I will not be involved in espionage. I am bound to my responsibilities to the Sanhedrin. If you were to accrue any suspicion, I would be the one to be accused and my mission would become doomed to failure. I don't want to say whatever you are doing is wrong, but my character must be scrupulous and anything that places me under scrutiny would jeopardize my success. I hope I have made myself clear."

"We all want the same thing; a free Judea. The Sanhedrin is made up of seventy of our leaders. Do you really think Joseph that all of them are of a single mind with Damneus? Do you really believe that they would all agreed to send you here for only one purpose of freeing a bunch of old priests that no one even remembers after a decade of being sent to Rome? That was the pretense, we are the reality. We are here to change our destiny and you are key to making that happen."

"Perhaps twenty or thirty years from now when the Romans have become a much weaker force in the world, then your mission would outweigh mine in importance, but to prepare for war now...."

"Who said anything of war?" Jacob interrupted him before Joseph could say anything further.

"It needed not to be said. You all seem to know about my mission, so I can probably guess who it was that has sent you on this voyage. There are a lot of people speaking of the coming confrontation. You can hear it being whispered along any street in Judea or Galilee and I know the ones in the Sanhedrin that fuel such passions. But I regret to inform you, I am not the man you require to help you. Your quest is but a dream at this moment, mine is the reality!"

"I beg to differ with you Joseph, but you are entitled to your opinion. I assure you, it is far from being the dream of madmen. I am truly sorry that you cannot see it at this time, but that time will come shortly, so I need not press you further. It will all become clear to you when you reach Rome. Until Rome I will not trouble you again.I promise."

"Do not bother to waste your time in Rome either, Jacob. Damneus is no fool. If there were those in the Sanhedrin undermining his authority he will have known about it and already counteracted their plans. For your information, it is probably why he gave me two letters to carry, not just the one you speak of. There obviously will be people waiting for me when I arrive."

"We shall see Joseph, all in due time," the giant shot back his parting remark.

Brushing the leaves and dirt from their clothes, the two of them surfaced from behind the outcropping of trees and mingled among the returning passengers, each going his separate way. By early evening the vessel was ready to sail. Acting upon the merchant's advice, the Captain had a number of the food barrels scoured and refilled with precious water from the fresh running springs of the island. The passengers were rounded up and returned to the ship, their names checked against the manifest to ensure that they left no one behind. Before the moonless night had cloaked the island entirely, the craft navigated its way out of the secure harbor towards the coastline of the mainland.

# CHAPTER EIGHT

## WHANGAREI; PRESENT

"Why don't we head back into the house? It's actually getting a little too cool and breezy out here for my liking," I suggested. Pearce looked reluctant to leave the park like setting of my farm. "There's coffee waiting for us there." That was enough to get him walking alongside of me.

"So this Jacob is the connection." Pearce was still searching for a way that I could have had any of these memories.

"In more ways than one," I suggested. "But he isn't in any way related to my family if that's what you're trying to surmise. But this meeting is critical to why I am in possession of so many memories. So I guess in a way, you're right."

"As are you..., it is getting a bit windy out here. Where'd this wind suddenly come from?"

"This is the Northland, John. A relatively narrow stretch of land into the Pacific. What do you expect?"

It wasn't long until we were sitting across from each other inside my living room.

"So what research have you been working on lately?" Pearce inquired.

"Oh, I could probably tell you John, but then I'd have to kill you."

The look of shock and disbelief was worth every bit of consternation it had caused him. It wasn't until I lowered my stern expression and cracked a smile that Pearce realized I had been teasing but at the same time I was still very serious. There would be no discussion of the research. We had a book we had to finish.

---

## AEGEAN SEA; 63 A.D.

The sun rose only to find the vessel still feeling its way along the Cretan coastline. The lack of wind had slowed the voyage to a snail's pace but the security of seeing a familiar coastline relieved the travelers of any anxiety they might have felt. Except for Osirah for on that particular morning as she dipped her fingers into the all too familiar gruel that passed for their breakfast, she felt a cold shiver run the length of her spine.

"Something disturbed me about that Cyrene ship, Joseph," she shuddered as she tried to shake the dark thoughts that gripped her mind without success.

"I don't understand," Joseph replied calmly, trying to help Osirah relax.

"Yes, let me hear too," Michael interrupted callously. "Let us hear what one such as you has to say about such matters." Corvasus still did not know that she was not merely the servant of a princess. "Shall we tremble at the thought of your miraculous powers of intuition? Are we to panic because you had a bad dream?"

Osirah's black eyes flashed with a fierce intensity that even caused Michael to immediately take a step back and silence his babbling. "Do not take me for some uneducated female that you've become accustomed to in the brothels you visit. I have been well tutored at the palace. I know that if I was sailing from Cyrene to Rome, I would have set my course almost due north. Crete would not have been anywhere near to the route I'd be taking. So why would it be moored in Crete? Why would they be taking on supplies if they were only making a direct crossing? These are questions you should have been asking."

"But you are making the assumption," Joseph carefully pointed out, "that the vessel had set sail from Cyrene. Perhaps it had not. Perhaps it set out from Alexandria. Then it would make sense."

"That is possible," she agreed, "but the Cyrenians are not on good terms with the Egyptians at this time. I am still bothered by its presence. You may think of me like Michael does that this is merely the foolishness of a young woman, but there is a dark cloud present in my thoughts, as if it were an omen. Somehow that Cyrene vessel is to play a role in our destinies."

"You know I would never accuse you of being foolish, Osirah. And I certainly would never come to Michael's defense over any matter but there are times that we all think that we have felt a premonition only for it never to come to fruition. I just want to make certain you don't worry yourself needlessly. But if you believe there is something we should fear about that ship then we best keep a look out for it."

Barely audible, Osirah faintly whispered, "But we have not even reached Greece as yet."

"What was that," Joseph asked but Osirah waved the question away indicating that it was of little importance.

"And what will become of me once we reach Rome and you aren't there to protect me," she inquired of Joseph.

"What are you talking about?" Joseph tried to dismiss her question but knew it stemmed from whatever premonition she had foreseen.

"That's not a problem," Michael answered. "I'll ransom you back to your Princess. I'm certain she'll be more than pleased to pay anything we ask to have her precious servant back." His tone was filled with sarcasm, knowing full well that a servant girl would never earn a ransom. "Then again, if she doesn't, I can always sell you to some rich Senator in Rome. What a prize you would be. His very own Eastern princess," he laughed, not knowing how close to the truth he really was.

This time it was Joseph's turn to glare angrily at Corvasus. It was a look that made it perfectly clear that he would never have the opportunity to make such arrangements as long as he was alive. Joseph quickly wrapped his arms around Osirah, providing a reassuring hug. "Have no fear. I will protect you. I will see to it that you get back to your family. I will keep you safe. You have my word on it."

"I know you will," but her voice trembled as she spoke.

---

It was late afternoon on the third day since leaving the isle of Crete that the vessel nestled into the eastern shore of the Grecian mainland, in the region known as Dyrrachium. A flock of hungry gulls circled noisily overhead, occasionally breaking formation to strafe the water and capture what few morsels were carelessly dropped over the rail into the sea. Crastus announced that the time had come for those passengers destined for Greece to prepare to disembark shortly after arriving at the harbor port of Pilos. It may have not been their original port of call on the Grecian mainland, but under the circumstances it would serve. Too much time had been lost already to start sailing through the Aegean. Two hundred and fifty travelers went ashore, leaving only around fifty to undertake the final leg of the voyage to Rome. Some of those that left had booked passage to Rome but by this time they had enough of sailing and preferred to take a land route to their final destination.

With their departure, the deck had become practically empty with so many leaving, much to the delight for the remaining passengers. From the port town, the provisions required for the last segment of the voyage were procured. In fact a surplus of supplies was brought on board because the Captain had decided that the remaining voyagers had endured enough sacrifices and deserved a little celebration at his own expense.

As soon as those continuing on the voyage had rearranged their belongings, laying claim to some of the more luxurious locations scattered across the main deck, the ship set sail, using the fading light of dusk to steer a course through the island channels that embroidered the mainland. Winter meant that there would be a gentle mist rising from the sea at night, but the Captain feared sailing with poor visibility far less than he feared laying at anchor in unknown waters. Sailing at night became the norm.

By morning the sea had become ink-black with algae, another common indicator of winter sailing in the Aegean. These were clear signs that an colds spell was preparing to settle in, with the wind out of the northeast dropping the temperature dramatically, and the gentle mist at times giving way to a heavier precipitation. Nothing to worry about as far as the Captain was concerned. It may have only been a couple of days out of Pilos but the crested waves now traversing the Adriatic were churning the sea into very different waters from the calm straits they had left behind.

Keeping warm became the priority as the passengers all huddled beneath several layers of blankets. Joseph pressed Osirah tightly against his body, shielding her from the wind's icy fingers; neither minded terribly as the bonds between them grew considerably stronger with each passing moment. It wasn't even necessary to exchange words any longer, the closeness of their bodies saying it all; they had become inseparable.

Though the passengers were oblivious to any of the lore borne by the inclement conditions, there were murmurings among the crew that the voyage had definitely been cursed by the gods. They could not deduce the reason why, but it was becoming clearly evident to these superstitious mariners that their troubles were far from over. Not even the oldest among them could recall such a bitter chill in the air so early in the season. It may have been the start of winter but that was not enough of an explanation for the weather turning so foul so early. After another three days at sea, the winds had grown even stronger and more violent. With each passing hour they became more furious, until they were practically gale force, tearing at the sail and shaking the mast vigorously. By this time the passengers too recognized that they were in imminent danger but they convinced themselves that the Captain's luck would hold out. They were helpless, with nothing more to do than watch the clouds race across the skies, while at the same time avoiding the cold waters splashing across the deck as huge waves whipped wildly against the hull and then washed over the rail.

Crastus barked the Captain's orders to the busy crew. The men furled the sail before the storm had a chance to tear it to shreds, and all oars were pulled inside before the crashing waves snapped them like twigs. But once successfully performing those tasks, the crew had no other choice but to stand prepared and ride out the weather until the gods saw fit to restore a reasonable calm. They prayed loudly in the hopes that Poseidon would be listening to their offerings.

The storm showed no intention to abate or to relinquish its pent up fury. Instead, with a terrifying intensity, the waves became mountains of black water, pounding at the mast's weakening supports. This mighty tree, standing midship, creaked and groaned as if in pain. Crastus' mariner intuition immediately set off alarm bells and he ordered his crew members to lash the mast to the side rails as quickly as possible. With massively thick ropes in hand they crawled and staggered to the centre of the main deck but before they even had the opportunity to throw the first loop around the base of the mast, a rogue wave hurdled over the top-rail, tossing four of the sailors like so much flotsam into the jaws of the yawning sea. The remaining crew members stood dumbfounded as they scrambled back on to their feet. And that's when they all heard it; a sound so surreal that no one could accurately describe it. To some it resembled a high pitched squeal of a wild boar, to others the grinding of stones in a gristmill, whichever, it resounded throughout the hold and spread the fear of the inevitable. The winds seized the furled sail and drew it back upon the mast like a gargantuan bow. Moments later the halyard snapped, sending the heavy wooden blocks crashing the thirty feet from their perch beneath the cross-tree to the deck below.

There was definitely no doubt now in anyone's mind that the gods had cursed this voyage, nothing remaining except for the crew and passengers to submit to their cruel and omnipotent will. Not long afterwards the top-gallant followed the identical path of the halyard as the winds tore it from its bindings, let ting it fall with devastating accuracy upon the scampering crew. Then the bunt lines slackened and the sail unfurled, causing the ship to catapult and convulse wildly on the crests of the waves. It took only one more wave to seal their fate. By comparison it could not even be called a massive wave. A fraction of the size that cracked the halyard. Under normal circumstances it would have been considered insignificant, unable to do any real harm. But this was not normal circumstances. The ship's structures and frame had been battered and suffered far beyond their endurance points. So now even this not so threatening wave proved to be enough to split the mast at its base. Like a falling tree, the mast tumbled and rolled, crashing through the deck boards as if they were carved from balsa leaving a cavernous wound that completely exposed the interior of the hull to the raging sea; nothing but an empty space where once the rudder house had been.

As white froth flooded the inner decks, panic spread among the passengers and the horror intensified beyond measure. People ran frantically between the splintered boards, desperately searching and grabbing for their earthly possessions a mere step away from being swallowed into the murky depths. The Captain ordered the two small boats on board to be lowered over the side but Crastus had already put that plan in motion long before the command was ever issued. Just as one of the rowboats was about to touch the surface of the sea, a rising wall of water hammered it against the hull of the vessel, shattering it into nothing more than useless fragments. Now there was only one small boat left; far too small to ferry so many.

The ship pitched towards its gaping wound, rolling almost thirty degrees, and thus causing the barrels in the hold to break free and hurtle with enough force to splinter the already damaged hull further. Within seconds the waters flooded the lower compartments, forever silencing the hysterical screams of the trapped oarsmen. Soon the sea swirled about the middle deck, where the Captain stood bravely at the wheelhouse, still commanding the survivors to abandon ship. Desperately holding on to anything that proved buoyant, the last of the passengers and crew scampered to the top deck and dove headlong into the churning sea.

Joseph, Osirah and Michael pushed their way past the debris that rimmed the rail but they were too late as they watched the remaining rowboat push away from the mother ship with its over laden burden. Running over to one of the few intact crates still on deck, Joseph and Michael pried its top off using the metal rods that had broken away from the mast supports as crowbars. Dragging the lid over to the rail they tossed it into the black water and the three prepared to dive in afterwards, swimming to their makeshift raft before it drifted off on its own accord.

"Wait a second," Joseph shouted as he slapped his forehead in disgust. "I forgot my bag. I'll be right back! Get on the raft and I'll join you shortly."

"Forget your bag, you idiot," Corvasus shouted only to be drowned out by the howling wind.

"I'll wait for you here," Osirah responded, refusing to jump into the water until Joseph returned.

"No! Into the water you go!" Joseph picked up Osirah and tossed her over the side not providing her with an opportunity to protest. Michael was already up and over, having one look back at Joseph before he leaped as if to say, "you stupid fool." As far as he was concerned his obligation to protect his charge was over. Suicide was not one of the clauses in his contract.

Osirah balanced herself unsteadily on the raft as she screamed for Joseph to forget his bag and rejoin them but it was too late. He was already on the far side of the dying vessel, searching among the floating debris for his precious bag that contained the letters Damneus had provided to him. It was an impossible task, and finding himself knee high in the circling waters he was forced to abandon his search. He managed to return safely to the near side where he had parted from Osirah and Michael but the raft was no longer in view. The waves had carried everything far from the floundering vessel and the storm's engulfing darkness had swallowed every bit of light beyond thirty feet from the rail. Joseph shouted out their names into the mocking wind, but he could hear nothing but the gale laughing cruelly with its hollow echo at his dire predicament. Then suddenly, he thought he could hear Osirah calling his name. Running along the rail towards sounds he could scarcely isolate from the crescendoing cacophony, it was as if he could feel Osirah's panicked screams and whatever the nature of the force that bound him to the Parthian beauty, he could now sense exactly where she was. As he mounted the rail preparing to dive into the sea, a colossal wave shot across the bow striking him from behind and submerging him into the darkness of the cold, angry waters.

# CHAPTER NINE

## WHANGAREI; PRESENT

Rising from the chair, where he had made himself extremely comfortable, Pearce began to pace about my home office, looking at all the certificates and diplomas that I had displayed across the wall. "You don't know when to quit, do you Doc?"

"If you're referring to my degrees, then no, I don't. You know, I even thought about doing a fifth degree after I finished my MBA. I guess my way of thinking is that if I was to stop learning, then it must mean I'm dead. Because until then, I'll just keep absorbing everything I can."

"So what was this other course of studies you had in the works?"

"I thought about doing a Masters in Toxicology or perhaps even another PhD."

"So what stopped you...?"

"Life," I answered simply. "There comes a time when you have to just live rather than study. At least that is what the ex-wives kept claiming. I'm not to sure if they were right because each degree I earned had a purpose, a level of achievement in moving towards a goal in life, and they certainly didn't object to the money earned based on those achievements."

"Well, I don't know about that, Doc. The Missus, she'd probably say if it was me, then it's a case of not knowing where you're trying to get to. And I'd just be taking the long way around in trying to find that I'm going no where."

"She might have a point there...that is if it were you! But with me it's a personal journey and at the end of it all, I'll have fulfilled a dream."

Pearce looked at me peculiarly, as if trying to decide whether I was sincere or not. "Doc, I would think with all the dreams you've already described in your books, you really don't have a need in having any more."

"There's always that one elusive dream," I reminded him. "Not a fantasy, not an impossible task, but one you were actually meant to achieve in this life."

"So what does that mean? Are you going to do another degree or not?"

"Think so. I'm looking at another Masters in Epidemiology from the University of Edinburgh. Three year online course."

"And that is going to fulfill your purpose in life, this elusive dream you mentioned?"

"Heck no!" I laughed at his suggestion. "I just need it to keep my mind functioning in retirement. Our purpose in life is something completely different. I don't haven any control over that. Getting a degree is completely under my control."

"So you think that there's a purpose to everything that happens to us, especially to you. And that would mean there was a purpose in everything that happened to your ancestors as well. Is that what you're trying to say? We don't have free will, we're just fulfilling some predetermined destiny?"

"I didn't say there wasn't free will. I believe I told you earlier that you can still refuse or ignore the destiny you are supposed to accept. Millions of people do, but they all feel there is some emptiness in their lives and they don't actually know why. I think you'll agree with me that in almost every case, which I have revealed to you, there has always been more than mere coincidence involved in these people lives. Why should mine be any different? Perhaps it's not my purpose to become historically significant but that is not to say that what I do is without impact somewhere down the line of my descendants. And remember this, as I tell you about this story, and the next, and the one after that one, it was only a couple of decades earlier, when you came looking for me and the world had neither the inkling nor even the slightest interest in the matters concerning the Kahana, and now genetically linked memories is a hot item. It's in our research, our movies, our books, practically everywhere. So perhaps it was your destiny to bring that all to light even though you didn't know it at the time."

"I still go with the coincidence angle," Pearce refused to accept the idea that there was no free will.

"Object all you want but that's what is so remarkable about my family's place in history. Everything had to be absolutely perfect for them to have had their impact and for that perfect moment to have taken place over and over again meant that there had to be an unseen force behind it all. Coincidence? Providence? Those don't even come close to doing it justice. I believe it has to have been much more!"

Pearce squinted his eyes with a degree of skepticism. "You're implying an omnipotent power. As a scientist you can't really believe that? Sounds like something more that I would say."

"We've been through this once before, John. Just because I've dedicated my life to science doesn't mean that I don't believe in the hand of God. How could I possibly not with all that I've seen and done? He's had a hand in everything my family has achieved. It would actually be impossible for me not to believe that he still continues to do so! Just perhaps without the same intensity he did hundreds or thousands of years ago."

"You're suggesting that God is losing his power?"

"No, I'm suggesting the further we move away from the center of his power, the weaker it becomes in intensity."

"What? That's crazy. What do you mean moving away from the centre of his power."

"I have my theories John, but let's not go into them now. Let's just say the further blood moves away from the heart, the slower its movement and the less intense the pulse that is generated by it. If we think of God's heart as the center of the universe, then we experience the same thing."

"But that would mean at some point we move far away from the source of His power and he no longer exists in our world," Pearce sounded concerned.

"Only if the universe is infinite in its expansion. I don't think so. I believe it is curved and eventually turns back on itself."

"A curved universe," Pearce pondered the idea.

"Not so outrageous a concept," I advised. "Einstein thought the same thing. Many others do now as well."

"And therefore your perpetual quest for degrees is somehow related to this circular universe and has been ordained by God?" Pearce's voice was still tinged with disbelief.

"Don't be ridiculous! I do that for me. But my desire to do it has been handed down to me over the generations. I know exactly how Jakob Kahana Goldenthal saw his role in academia because in many ways his memories are mine. His driving forces are my driving forces. And when I finally get around to telling his story, you'll see exactly how his pursuit of further education brought him into historical focus. "

"Now don't get me wrong Doc, I'm not about to say this to piss you off but does your family actually evolve in any way, or are you just all doomed to repeat over and over again the past. Making the same choices, doing the same things, living the same lives?"

"You make that sound as if it were terrible thing, John. I don't think it's terrible at all. It's reassuring in some ways if you were to ask me. Anyway, who said evolution was all it's cracked up to be?"

Waving his pencil frantically, Pearce shouted out an "Aha." He looked at me menacingly. "Now I've got you. You know and I know all things must evolve; survival of the fittest and all that stuff. So whether you want to admit it or not, you're family has to evolve and change must happen!"

"I think that you are misquoting Darwin Theory quite badly there, John" I cautioned him. "I believe Darwin had confined his theory to physical evolution only. He was not making reference to the psychological makeup within a species. For that you're best to refer to Freud."

"But you have to admit Doc, over time, even within a family they're going to change the way they think and behave in order to keep up with the changing times. And as soon as you adapt to your social environment, then you're no longer able to live exactly as your ancestors did. Everything around you, whether it is technical, behavioral, even the your social attitudes are going to be different with each adaptation."

"What, you've become a social anthropologist somewhere along the way? Yes, those things do evolve too, but Darwin wasn't concerned about that. Survival of the fittest was his calling card. That's how he viewed the world. The problem is that he failed to recognize that long term survival was more likely among those least adapted to their current environment because change is often cataclysmic."

"Huh? What are you talking about?"

"Just what I said," I instructed him. "The less suitable an organism is to a particular environment, the more likely it is to survive when there's a sudden change to the habitat. It's often better suited to whatever follows."

"I'm not certain I'm following you, Doc."

"Darwin's theory is fine as long as everything is static and you're a cockroach, but that's not the way things are. Dinosaurs grow big, and thereby dominate everything, but they are best adapted to their tropical environment, and bang, it all changes over night and they're extinct. Why, because some little lizard that grew hair and had its young live, while all the time running between the toes of some Tyrannosaurus Rex was better suited to the environment when the climate got cold and all the eggs in nests were eaten. Darwin overlooked the cataclysmic changes that happen constantly on the earth. His survival of the fittest model is limited and applied best to a world without change or one with a very slow progressive change. Whereas those animals on the fringe, not only survive in the environment they're not well adapted to, but can do very well when the climate changes and they happen to be ideally suited to the dramatic change."

"Survival of the fringe! I like it. It has a good ring to it." Pearce hurriedly scribbled down this latest theory as if he was on to something unique. "So how does that ascribe to your family?"

"I'd say my family history is about as far as one can go out on a fringe without being locked away. Just take a look at some of the characters. Most didn't fit at all in their own environment. They certainly couldn't be considered mainstream. They were just too different in their beliefs from anyone else. And yet, because of that ostracism, displacement, banishment, and a host of other dilemmas they faced, they were able to survive for three millennia and have impacted on an awful lot of history in the process."

"That may be true, but it still meant that in order to have survived that long, they must have evolved in their thinking. They had to cope with each new situation, so how could they possibly have repeated the lives of their ancestors if some of those situations didn't even exist in their time?"

"It is on the surface a thorny issue, alright. But don't be fooled into thinking that just because something looks different, therefore that must be the case. That's why we have more than one sense to rely upon. It's those other parameters that have to guide us through our blindness.'

Pearce dotted the end of his sentence and looked up from the page. "I think we can keep spinning around and around and never coming up with the answer. Perhaps we should just agree to disagree."

"Splendid idea," I reassured him. "Now let me get back to the story because I   never told you how I know any of this happened to Josephus and I know you've been dying to find out and I'm about to come to that part."

"Right, splendid idea!"

---

# ADRIATIC SEA; 63 A.D.

Spitting up saltwater, Joseph regained consciousness in an unfamiliar, ill-lit, damp cabin. From the swirling sensation in which his mind reeled and the general pangs of nausea in the pit of his stomach, he knew immediately that he had to be back on board a ship, but that was impossible and he began to doubt his senses.   As he opened his eyes, he found himself lying on a floor littered with sprawling bodies.   All he could think was that if this was heaven, it was pretty damn disappointing. It took several minutes before he could focus his senses, but once his vision had cleared he was able to discern the tall figure of Jacob towering over him.

"Where are we?" his voice croaked.

"You had the good fortune of landing on me when you fell in the water. I'm a good swimmer and managed to keep both of us afloat until we got picked up."

"Yes, but where are we?" Joseph repeated.

"On the Cyrene vessel, the same one we were moored beside in Crete. How's that for coincidence?"

"How many of us were saved?" Joseph sputtered, clearing the last of the water from his lungs.

"Only twenty-nine," Jacob replied solemnly.

"Were Osirah and Michael amongst them?"   Joseph sounded desperate as he awaited the answer.

"If you're speaking of the two that traveled with you then I'm afraid that they weren't among those rescued."   But before Joseph could even register his grief, Jacob pinned him down so that he would have to listen. "We looked Joseph! I assure you, anyone that was visible was rescued.   The Cyrenians even used nets to dredge just below the surface just in case some had sunk below the waterline.   But as for your friends, they weren't found.

"They   were   floating   on   top   of   a   crate,"   Joseph   moaned as he buried his face in the palms of his hands.   "They were using it like a raft."

"Then there's a very good chance they made it to the shore.   We didn't find the little boat either so I have to assume they made it safely to the beach.   If either hadn't made it to shore then surely we would have found them adrift.   And we didn't, so that's in the favor of all those people. Boats may sink but rafts don't. The reality was that it wouldn't have taken any of us much effort to make it ashore.    We were closer to land than you'd think, while we were floundering aro und.    Because of the storm and the darkness of night we didn't even know what direction to swim. If it had been daylight, most of us could have probably swum to the beach safely; it was that close.    Unfortunately, without a sense of direction, some actually swam in the opposite direction and went further out to sea.  But a boat or a raft, they naturally drift on the waves and the waves would take them towards shore."

"I appreciate what you're doing.   I know you're trying to make me feel better. And after all, you did save my life and for that I am eternally grateful.    I won't forget that but right now I think I need to be alone."

"You look tired," Jacob responded.    "You should rest now.    I will leave you." Jacob rose and started to leave.

"Jacob, wait!"    The giant of a man stopped in his tracks. "I'm sorry, I'm not thinking properly. That was rude of me.    I should have asked how many of your party survived. It was wrong of me not to have done so."

"Just one other.   He's lying over there."    Jacob pointed across the cabin. "I believe you know him."

Looking to where Jacob pointed, Joseph squinted in the dim light at the young man lying on the other side of the cabin. It took a moment before he could fully register his identity.    "Yoni, is that him?    What in God's name is he doing here?"

"I told you that we had the support of some very highly placed people."

"But this makes no sense at all.    That's the nephew of Damneus.    His father is Elioneiai, who is chief patriarch in Antioch.    I'm certain that there's no way that Damneus's and his brother would approve of this. I mean, Damneus sent me on this excursion in the first place."

"Why do you automatically assume that the High Priest had anything to do with Jonathias' presence here?    You know that as far as families go, the house of Caiaphas is not exactly what you'd call close."

"But I know Elioneiai isn't about to support rebels, at least not openly. We may only be distant cousins but there are certain things you do know about your family."

"There you go again making assumptions. Why assume that we are rebels. Patriots would be more appropriate. Brothers are no longer close and parents today know very little of what their children do.    It's a sign of the times.    The children are far more rebellious and even if the parents do know, and don't approve, what could they do to stop it? Turn their own son in to the authorities?    I   think not!"

"So his cousin Jonathan is he somehow involved as well," Joseph deduced from Jacob's answer.

"Do   you   really   need   to   know   more?"   Jacob   asked while he nodded his head..

"I need to know a lot more," Joseph commented.    "I've lost my only connection to anyone that was awaiting me in Puteoli.    My only letter of introduction and my banker's letter are now at the bottom of the sea. I'm almost afraid to say this, and probably will regret it, but I think I need your help. So, please Jacob, try not to make me regret this decision!"

"You need assistance to complete your mission and we need a traveling companion to replace some of the more prominent members of our group that were lost. I think that it is highly probable that we can help each other. Simply put, what other options do any of us have?"

"Right now I agree the options are limited," Joseph replied.

Jacob grasped Joseph's weakened body and hugged him to his massive chest. "Do not worry Joseph. I will see to it that we cause you no trouble and Jonathias carries documents of his own that should help you in your mission."

"I don't understand. He was given letters of introduction as well."

"You could say that...."

"Do I want to know?"

"No, I don't think so."

---

A Cyrenian crew member entered the cabin carrying a large cistern of broth which he set down gingerly in the centre of the room. Joseph seized the man's still outstretched arms as soon as he had laid the baked red clay bowl on the boards. The Cyrenian jolted backwards, freeing himself from Joseph's grasp and then fled from the cabin screaming.

"What's wrong with him?" Joseph inquired of Jacob. "All I wanted to do was ask him when we'd arrive in port."

"There is nothing wrong with him," an incorporeal voice floated from the corridor outside and into the room. It was soon followed by the entrance of a rather thin man wearing a white skirt, arm greaves and a large curved dagger that protruded ominously from his sword belt. There was little doubt that this was the Cyrenian captain. "You are merely strange to him. He doesn't know your language and you bronzed skin people of the Mediterranean are extremely foreign to us. In fact when we want our children to behave, we use tales of the bad Asiatic, who come in the night to steal them away into slavery. Sometimes we say if they are really bad then the desert people will eat them. I'm afraid my cabin boy has a very fertile imagination. As for when we land, it is only a matter of a day or two. We are actually sailing around the heel of the peninsula as we speak. The winds will determine exactly how long. Surely you can be patient a little bit longer."

"Patience!" Joseph sputtered, "We have suffered the horrors of the voyage of the damned. Patience is something I have so very little remaining. Would it be at least permissible to go topside? The air down here is stale."

"I'm afraid that won't be possible. It is for your own safety. I think you can appreciate that some of my men may already have an abnormal fear of strangers like yourself. You can imagine the stir from devils such as yourselves walking freely among them. They may even try to harm you. I wouldn't want that to happen. I know you can appreciate my concern and cooperate with me a little longer."

Joseph merely nodded his acceptance.

"Then enjoy what will be the last one or two days of your voyage and dream of setting your feet on dry land. Until then, I'm afraid you will see very little except this room. I will take leave of you until then." Without waiting for their questions the captain left the cabin and posted guards at the door to see that none of the passengers made an effort to leave.

"Are we prisoners now," Joseph turned to Jacob for an answer.

"I don't think so. This isn't a slaver ship and the Captain did seem genuinely concerned for our safety."

"And did you see what our Captain was doing before the ship capsized?" Joseph asked Jacob. "Now that was concern," he commented.

"Yes, I agree," Jacob replied as he attempted to recall the events of the last few days. "When I last spied him, he was below deck trying to free the galley slaves."

"He cared more about those slaves than he did for his own life." Shaking his head, Joseph felt himself drowning once more with grief. "So many lost. I pray that Osirah was not one of them. May God protect her wherever she may be? There was so much I wanted to tell her." He felt his throat choking back the tears. "And now I fear I will never be given the chance."

Jacob held Joseph's shoulder, dwarfed by his hand as he began patting it in a comforting manner. "Say it anyway," he advised. "Wherever she may be I'm certain she will hear you."

That night Joseph's thoughts were only of Osirah. He would awaken, shaking in terror from the nightmare of seeing Osirah's shimmering blue dress floating directionless upon the cold murky water. So many things that he now could only tell her in his dreams. So many feelings that he kept suppressed and shielded from view only to see them unveil in his visions. Closing his eyes, he silently cried himself back to sleep

At daybreak he awoke to find Jacob and Jonathias sitting at his side and staring down at him. He shot upwards, quite startled by their presence. "Is there something wrong?" He then looked directly at his cousin, "I didn't expect to see you here," he mentioned as he caught his breath.

"Well where else would you expect us to be?" Jonathias snapped. "It's not like we have too many places besides this cabin where we can go."

"That's not what I meant," Joseph explained. "What are you doing here. I didn't expect to find you on my voyage Rome."

"Some things are never what they seem," Jonathias teased without actually replying.

"There's a lot to discuss," Jacob interrupted. "We were waiting for you to wake up so we could get started."

"If it's about helping you, as I told you, I lost everything when the ship went down. I have no letters of introduction, no knowledge of whom I was even to meet when I landed. Michael kept that all to himself. I don't even have a way to find out who these people were. They will have to make themselves known to me."

"Do I look worried," Jonathias quipped. "Listen cousin, none of that is a problem."

"Oh yes, I forgot. You have your own letters, don't you?" Joseph's tone was clearly condemning Jonathias' letters which Joseph could only assume were counterfeit..

"And why is that so hard to believe? They'll be enough? You should know that all of us among the Kohanim have access to the scribal libraries. It's not as if it would be too difficult to obtain a letter of introduction if it was necessary," Jonathias explained.

"It would be, if it was to have the signature of head of the Sanhedrin," Joseph was quick to refute. "Or did you find a way to add that too?"

"Do you think someone in Rome really cares if it is signed by the head of the Sanhedrin, or the secretary, or the chief judge? It's a name. That's all they're concerned with. They wouldn't even know who the signature belonged to if we didn't tell them. They just look to see if it is on the official paper."

"You have this all worked out, don't you?

"If you mean, did I have any doubt about you assisting us, and us assisting you, no," he responded coolly to Joseph's question.

"I don't understand. I was given this assignment by your uncle. I can't believe he'd have selected me thinking that I would permit myself to be lured into some kind of conspiracy and obviously there must have been some indication that there was a second mission being conducted. He wouldn't overlook something like that. Which makes me wonder why you would think it was possible that I would cooperate, knowing that Damneus is known to be quite unforgiving if he feels he's been betrayed."

"That might be so, but this has nothing to do with my uncle and everything to do with my grandfather."

"Caiaphas has been dead for some time now. Unless you're communing with the dead, which is a sin by the way, I don't believe he somehow has arranged all this," Joseph mused. "So what's the real story?"

"As you know, I had the opportunity to spend a considerable amount of time with my grandfather. I think I knew him like no one else. Not my father, not my uncle, no one. He was wise beyond this world. He saw things that no one else saw. He could see a man and know everything about him without a word being spoken. There's a lot being said about what he did and what he didn't do. But there's one thing he told me that I have never forgotten!"

"Am I supposed to guess what that was?" the doubt of his cousin's true purpose continued to find its way upon Joseph's lips.

"He told me that messiahs weren't born, they were made. He said, find the one gifted with the aura of leadership, that special charisma, the ability to persuade others, and with the proper guidance they will become a messiah."

"So what does that have to do with me?"

"Everything," Jonathias answered. "My grandfather felt he had found that man. He envisioned salvation was possible through a spiritual unification that would sway our occupiers through sheer force of numbers. He was wrong. Violence can only be overcome with violence. But even though he knew that he had failed, he assured me that every generation had its deliverer. I just had to pay attention to the signs and I'd find the one marked to be that man. My uncle saw that you were different but never saw that aura my grandfather spoke about. Others did. They spread the word and we knew the time had come."

"Others?"

"Damneus rules the Sanhedrin but he does not control their minds."

"And so these others, they obtained a copy of the letter of introduction and then set this all up with your little group that you'd set sail with one directive and that was to get me to join your little band of men." Shaking his head in disbelief, Joseph didn't know whether he was disgusted or flattered.

"Though you may not recognize it yet, you have an innate ability to lead. You are not one to abide injustice. And though you may not agree with everything we stand for, you will do what's best for your people, no matter what personal sacrifices that means you must undertake."

Jacob nodded in agreement as his companion spoke.

"Even if I was to agree to go along with this entire façade that you're proposing, it is still my one and only intent to get the priests released and then sail back home."

"And it is our intent to see that you do exactly that," Jonathias confirmed.

"But once I'm back home I'm just going to live a nice quiet little life and I can't see how you're going to make me change that."

"We will not change anything. Fate will do that for us. If I am wrong about whom you are, then you lose nothing. If I'm proven right, then your life will never be the same once you return to Judea."

Still shaking his head, it was difficult for Joseph to accept what Jonathias had insinuated. "So you expect nothing from me? I just do what I have to do, and that's that. I guess I can live with that. But I have to tell you, I see one major failing in the entire scenario you've painted…"

"And what's that?" both Jonathias and Jacob inquired simultaneously.

"Even if somehow fate did decide that my life was never going to be the same, the only way someone could be accepted as being the messiah would require that they be anointed by the High Priest. And there's no way that Damneus would ever consider being a part of that."

"You're assuming that somehow my uncle is going to be the High Priest forever.    Rest assured, that will not happen.    He's certainly not going to in the position like my grandfather for seventeen years."

"How can you be so certain?"

"There are others in the family to see that it doesn't," was all that Jonathias would say on that matter.

# CHAPTER TEN

## WHANGAREI; PRESENT

Pearce was wearing his Cheshire smile spread broadly across his face, as I looked up.

"So, what do you find so funny, John?"

"I knew all along how this whole memory thing came about.    I always knew that Joseph Caiaphas would be involved in some way.    And I was right, wasn't I?"

"Yes, you were right," I relented. Of course it's only the case If being right meant that I had to practically spoon feed him the answer, then he was right. I kept thinking, what if I hadn't mentioned Jonathias's relationship with Caiaphas? Would he have been able to put the pieces together himself? "Caiaphas may have only had a short feature presentation in the New Testament, but his influence was felt well beyond the little information provided in the Christian Bible."

"I kept thinking to myself that if this Josephus wasn't an ancestor of yours, then there had to be a connection through your only family line that I knew about," Pearce snapped back his response. "And now it will make sense to all the readers as well since they're the critical judges of your work, constantly dissecting every little piece of information you throw at them."

"I did tell you that I would eventually explain the connection.  Sometimes the best little family secrets are the most revealing.    Who would think that for the next hundred years after Caiaphas, his family would keep trying to apply this Messiah Formula over and over again in order to liberate their nation?"

"What do you mean over and over again," Pearce questioned.

"Ah, there's the real mystery.   Because now that you're aware of this intricacy going on behind the events of Judean politics of that time, you'll have to do your homework and try to determine which the events over that one hundred year period could be attributed to this secret plan to create a messiah."

"Why don't you just tell me, Doc and save me all that time."

"That would take all the fun out of it John.   I wouldn't be doing anyone a service if I just gave them the answer. They'd never remember it let alone believe it.    But when you or anyone else has to actually dig out the information for yourself, that's when you come to realize that it is true, and then you never forget!"

# PUTEOLI 63 A.D.

It was late on the second day following their rescue and the survivors were growing increasingly restless, knowing that they were soon to be disembarking. The not too distant sounds of the waves crashing against the rocky coast could be easily distinguished from the creaking of the boat as it moved through the shallow waters. Not long afterwards the Cyrenian captain stepped into their secured cabin.

"Your journey with us is now at an end. Rome is directly north from here. This port that you are going to set ashore at is known as Puteoli. I believe it was where you were intending to sail to. I am sorry if you have lost everything and are unable to journey onwards from here, but I am unable to help you further. My responsibilities for you end here. Whatever gods you may worship, may they watch over you and protect you. I bid you all farewell."

Escorted from the cabin, the passengers were led along the length of the main deck towards the stern aperture where they were lowered by ropes into the chest deep water. The twenty-nine survivors waded towards the beckoning shore. One father was seen carrying his young daughter upon his shoulders, one of the few children that managed to cheat death during the shipwreck. Those few passengers still in shock from the entire ordeal were carried gingerly by others until they were laid on the cream colored sands of the shore and left to await the hospitality of the people of Puteoli should it happen to be forthcoming.

Jonathias and Jacob sketched their future plans in the fine grained sands while Joseph paced nervously along the beach, staring angrily out towards the cruel sea. "I can't believe they just left us here like so much driftwood. Why couldn't they dock in the port like a normal ship and let us walk onto the platforms as if we were more than just bilge waste?"

"Relax Joseph," advised Jacob. "The Cyrenians are a strange lot. I don't think they wanted to be questioned as to what they were doing sailing so close to our floundering ship in the first place. This way they can pretend that nothing ever happened, they never saw a ship and we didn't even exist. After all, you need to remember that relations between the Romans and the Cyrenians are dicey at best."

"How is it you know so much about the politics of these sea raiders," Joseph was curious. "For a Galilean sailor, you seem to know a lot more than any one would expect."

"I don't know if you meant that as an insult or a compliment. Best I take it as a compliment," the giant replied then returned to sketching in the sand.

"But you're not going to answer my question, are you?"

"No," Jacob shook his head.

All the while that he paced, Joseph paid no attention to the survivors that had slowly encircled him. It wasn't until they began to plead with him to provide them with guidance as to what they should do next that he realized he had become completely surrounded. Even so, he refused to raise his head to acknowledge their presence. Their lamentations grew louder but still he refused to acknowledge them. As far as he was concerned, he had his own problems; determined to prove to Jonathias that he was not this supposed savior that he and his organization suspected. A messiah would bear their burdens but he refused to shoulder them any longer. Why were others always seeking him out for help? Couldn't they see that he was barely capable of helping himself? He grew angry by the thought that he had to be what others wanted him to be.

"Joseph!" Jonathias yelled. "Joseph! Snap out of it. What is wrong with you?" Tearing himself away from his drawing in the sand, he moved towards Joseph and grasped him by the shoulder. "Can't you hear these people? Can't you give them at least a minute of your time? They have lost so much. Ease their torment; give them a glimmer of hope. That's all they seek!"

"No, that's what you seek," he shouted at Jonathias. "That's what you want me to do!" Joseph turned and gazed into the anxious faces that encircled him. "What do you want from me?" he shouted at the people. "Why do you think that I have answers for everything? Do not expect simple answers and solutions for all that has happened to us. There are none. When all is lost, then it is time to start over. God gives us two choices in times of distress. You can choose to surrender yourself to your anguish and perish in doing so. Or you can rise above your sorrow, prove that you are more than some insignificant beast of the field subject to the mercies and torments of the universe, and regain that which is most important; your dignity as human beings. What you have achieved before, you can do once more. Your dead are gone and buried at the bottom of the sea. Grieve for them, mourn for them, and then live for the living. You owe them that much. For some of you, this place is nothing more than a stop along a journey that will take you back from whence you came. If so, then you are lucky because you will be able to return to a fairly normal life. For others, that voyage was the end of a dream that was supposed to take you to a better life. Now that dream has become a total nightmare. If that be the case then look around you. Puteoli is a thriving place. It was the intended place of your disembarking though it may not have been your final destination. There is the chance to forge a new life here if you seek it. For the rest of you, Rome is where you must find the answers to your questions. Rome is where your journey begins. Think of this as a new beginning and a chance to erase the past. May God bless you and protect you on your journeys wherever they take you and thank the Almighty that at least unlike those that have been lost to the sea, we have been given this opportunity to begin anew."

Jonathias nudged Jacob in the ribs and whispered, "See, I told you. He's the one. Even when he doesn't want to do it, he still ends up raising their spirits because he knows no other way to talk to them. As much as he wants to yell and scream at them to go away, he can't bring himself to do it."

Jacob nodded his agreement. "Even when he really wants to tell them all to get lost, he still manages to give them hope."

Whatever magic Joseph weaved into his words, it had the desired effect on the bone-weary travelers. He had spoken in Aramaic so that the majority would understand him.    They picked up what few belongings they had and started along the road to Rome.  Though few had any idea of where they were going or how they would succeed having lost all their personal belongings, they found comfort in his words and a belief that there was an answer awaiting them in the great city.

"On to Rome," Jacob bellowed as the people departed, encouraging every one to begin their long march.    Taking the other direction, the three traveling companions followed the Via Puteoli until it forked just outside of the town. Joseph permitted the other two to steer him in the direction of their choosing with out question.    As he followed them he could not help but notice that Puteoli was a hive of new construction with building projects underway in practically every direction he looked.    Tall buildings separated by wide streets that were thronging with people, especially in the market place even at this late hour in the afternoon. He could not help but wonder why they had not sought a refuge inside the town while they sorted their next move.    Jacob who seemed determined to move on a set path of his own making and this troubled Joseph.

"So what are we to do now?" Joseph questioned. "I can speak their language, so we don't have a problem there, but I have no idea what I was supposed to do once we arrived? I presume there were people waiting for me but they probably think I went down with our ship and left. Only Michael knew where and when I was meeting someone in Puteoli.   So, perhaps we would be better off seeking council inside the city rather than pass it by. Someone there might recognize my name and set us in the right direction."

"Rome is our true destination and it is several days away." Jacob then pointed a finger in the direction of a three story building at the intersection of the crossroads. "But for now I suggest that we begin over there and avoid entering the heart of the town.    Trust me, there is nothing there for you now! Whomever was awaiting you is most certainly gone, along with the Sanhedrin's money."

"How can you be so certain?"

"Because it's what I would do if I got news that the ship I was waiting for had sunk at sea.    No way I'd wait around until someone started asking questions about where I got all the money that I was suddenly spreading around. Money that you no longer needed, being dead."

"But that's you," Joseph refuted his large and cynical companion.

"No.    That's what anyone would do.    Take it as a given.    Now it's best we go over there," he pointed. "The crossroad inns are far more enlightening and a mine of information," he winked mischievously which did not go unnoticed by

Joseph.

"Why do I have this overwhelming suspicion that you didn't pick this inn by chance?" Joseph hesitated while squinting his eyes as he surveyed Jacob's expression. "Perhaps you've been here before? Or perhaps this inn is one of your meeting places?"

"Yes."

"Yes what?" Joseph wanted to know. "That you've been here before or that there is someone waiting there for you?"

"Yes, yes then," Jacob grinned.

"So that's yes to both questions."

"Just learn to trust us, Joseph. Unlike those other people, we do have a plan." Together they crossed the building's threshold. Spreading before them was the large main room filled with long woken tables and heavily worn benches.

"There's hardly anyone here," Joseph commented on the surroundings. "Is this your welcoming committee according to your master plan?"

"Yes," replied Jacob once again. "And I suggest we all sit down and get some real food while we have the opportunity." Jacob banged his hammer like fist against the table summoning the innkeeper.

A rotund, jolly man with a moon-like face stepped from the back room answering the summons. The white apron he wore was soiled with grease and hops, clearly marking him as both the cook and server in this establishment. He asked in the Latin tongue how he could be of service but before Joseph even could catch his breath to make a response, Jonathias was already speaking but what he was saying made no sense.

"If one seeks a singer, then find King David, if one seeks a poet then find King Solomon, but if one seeks an actor, then find the King of Actors, Aliturius."

Joseph looked at his companion with astonishment. "I thought you said you couldn't speak Latin?"

Turning toward him and smiling, Jonathias answered with a ripple of laughter, "I can't. That's all I know."

But it was enough. The innkeeper bowed his head graciously and bounded up the staircase with ease. Quite an accomplishment for a man of his girth.

The sudden disappearance of the man left Joseph even more confused and suspicious of exactly he hadn't been told. "So it's true, you were intending to come to this place all along."

"I already told you it was," Jacob responded. "Isn't that what yes means?"

"What exactly is going on here? You say you know this place well and that coded phrase was some kind of password! For what purpose?"

"Patience cousin," Jonathias advised. "Soon everything will be clear."

"May I be of assistance to you gentlemen?" A new voice had entered the current conversation, emanating from someone standing halfway up the wooden staircase. The three turned their heads to stare upwards at the richly dressed tall stranger. His distinguished appearance was handsomely striking, a radiance shining from his face, which could easily be mistaken for that of a king or eastern potentate. The stranger smiled at his newly arrived friends as he ran the fingers of his left hand through the silver curls of his tidily coiffed hair.

"Wait a second," Joseph spurted out the words, clearly astonished by the gentlemen. "You just spoke perfect Aramaic. How would you even know we'd understand that language? Who are you? I demand to know what's going on here?"

The stranger beamed a broad smile back at his inquisitor. "I can speak numerous other languages as well," he replied as he descended the stairs. " Would you like to hear them? Name one and I'd more than pleased to impress you."

"I demand to know immediately what's going on here! I don't like being played for the fool!" Joseph hammered a fist angrily against the table top, consumed by a suspicion that he was being constantly deceived by everyone.

"Please, cousin!" Jonathias interrupted, "May I introduce to you Aliturius."

Joseph hovered over his cousin menacingly. "And just who is Aliturius? I want to know everything now. Enough of this toying with me!"

"Alright, alright. There's nothing devious in the slightest, I assure you. This is Aliturius, the most famous actor in all of Rome. He is our first contact on our mission. He has been expecting us."

"Actually I was expecting you days ago. You're late! I could have been gone by now. Actually, I should have been gone by now," he corrected himself. "Am I to presume correctly that this angry one is the one you spoke about?" He pointed directly at Joseph.

"How is any of this possible? I wasn't supposed to be here with you, I was to be elsewhere in Puteoli with Michael. Not to mention all the days lost with the storm. None of this makes any sense. How could this perfect stranger have been told that I would be here?"

"You're right," Jacob agreed. "We were supposed to make land, make initial contact with Aliturius and then wait here while Aliturius performed in a theatre in Puteoli for the week. Then he would return and we would all travel to Rome where you would have been by then to meet you."

"But you had no way of knowing that I'd agree to join with you on your mission. In fact Michael Corvasus would have made certain that never happened . Why would you have even bothered to try and meet me in Rome? It would have been a waste of time."

"Ahh! So he is the chosen one," Aliturius piped in. "He still has no idea how this works."

"I really wish everyone would stop referring to me as that. And what do you mean by how this works?"

"Yes, Aside from his angry demeanor, I can see it," Aliturius continued as he looked Joseph up and down. "Abadeus," he commanded in Latin to the inn keeper whom had followed him down the steps. "My friends will need rooms for the night. They are the ones we were expecting. And some food and drink, if you please." Then switching smoothly into Aramaic once more without the slightest betrayal of incorrect accent, "I thought there was going to be more of you."

Jonathias cleared his throat. "We had an accident along the way. Our ship went down. We lost the rest of our comrades."

Aliturius tutted with sincere remorse. "How horrible. There was talk of a ship wreck. I had no idea it was yours. The seas are an unforgiving force of nature. Once it takes, it never gives back. But at least you have survived, as well as my good friend Jacob. Who was it that was lost?"

"Marcus, Simeon, Judah and Banneus."

"Oh dear, the poor lads. So young. Such a terrible waste," Aliturius sighed. "We must send word to their families. We must not let their deaths be in vain."

"Excuse me," Joseph interrupted, "I am sorry for your friends and I know it must be a terrible tragedy to you all, but I'm afraid I still haven't been told exactly who you are and how your involved in all of this."

"Jonathias, I'm surprised at you," Aliturius scolded his young compatriot. "There is no reason for secrets among us. Why haven't you told our new friend Joseph about me?"

Jonathias hung his head like a young child being scolded by his parents. "It's not like Joseph has been exactly enthused with allying himself with us. It was more a matter of circumstance that we have joined together. I did not wish to overload him with information at this point. I thought it better to feed it to him slowly. That way it would be much easier to digest."

"But you knew all along that he would be joining our cause. It was written in his destiny. You should have told him everything."

"Can everyone stop talking as if I have no choice in my life choices," Joseph still objected to all their references to destiny.

"We all must do what the Lord intends us to do," Aliturius lectured Joseph, "Well, I might as well do things myself. I am Aliturius as you may have already heard," the older gentleman extended his hand to Joseph in greeting. Joseph stretched out his hand in return and the two men shook hands and then sat side by side at the table. "Do not let these clothes confuse you, good friend Joseph. I dress like a Roman, look like a Roman, because for all intents and purposes, I am a Roman. But originally my home was in Galilee. I am as Jewish as any of you." Aliturius paused for a moment and reflected. "Well..., perhaps not as Jewish, but I am still a Jew at heart. I lived in the city of Tiberias and came to Rome when I was still a young lad. And as you may have guessed from the elaborate code words your companions used to summon me, I am an excellent actor. Wait, let me correct that statement, I am Rome's greatest actor!"

"An actor?" Joseph questioned with a mixed attitude of dismay and suspicion as he looked Aliturius up and down.

"Typical Judean thinking," the senior gentleman quipped. "Actors couldn't possibly afford to live as actors because Judea ranks them right up there with carrion eaters and bottom feeders.    This is Rome, dear friend.    And in Rome, acting is an exalted profession which pays quite handsomely.    The Emperor is both benefactor and patron of the fine arts.    And when you happen to be Nero's most beloved player, then one can dress in such finery every day of their life."

"You are familiar with Nero?" Joseph's voice rose several octaves as he asked the question.

"Did I not just say that," Aliturius turned and questioned the two other travelers.    "I could have sworn I said that. Tell me I didn't say that."    Aliturius donned an air of bravado.    "I have been both guest and celebrant many times in the Emperor's palace.    Whenever I am in Rome, the Theatre Marcellus is cleared of any other performances, just so the Emperor can watch me perform.    When I do the tragedies of the great Greek play writes even the god's weep in response to my performance."

"A letter of introduction gets you through the gates, Joseph," Jonathias explained, but it does not get you an audience with the Emperor. For that you will need Aliturius.    You would have stood in a long line of ambassadors, only to be heard by some low level magistrate, that is if you bribed well enough, then perhaps you might have had an audience with Nero.    But it would have cost you a lot of gold coins."

"That would explain the heavy purse I was intended to carry," Joseph thought out loud.

"Yes, it would have got you a little further than most," Aliturius took command of the conversation again, "But still no guarantee. Hence, I am your guarantee of success.    That's why we knew that eventually you would welcome our assistance.    Understand Joseph, your problems are my problems.    Are we not kindred spirits, sharing the same ancestry?    It would be my privilege to assist you, and in return, your presence will greatly assist the rest of us."

Joseph placed his chin onto his folded hands and spoke to all three men. "So you knew all along that I would need your help?"

"Let's say we suspected so.  Other delegations have failed miserably but we were aware that Damneus thought you would get further based on your persona.    We weren't going to approach you until you had sat in Rome for several weeks awaiting an audience with absolutely no response.  We already had an idea whom Damneus had instructed your guide to seek out once you landed. Believe me when I say that he most certainly would have annoyed the Emperor more than anything.    Rich Jews are vital to the well-being of the economy, but it doesn't mean Nero likes doing them any favors. He tolerates them because the machinery that runs this empire stays greased."

"Why not take him to me now," Joseph questioned. "You obviously know whom he is, so you have an obligation to take me to him."

"I might have considered it, but he left the city as soon as your ship failed to arrive on schedule.    Probably heard that it went down," Aliturius suggested.

"And why would he have done that?" Joseph sounded even more skeptical.

"Because now he is even a richer Jew!    He is the same man that was supposed to give you your money upon arrival and pay Corvasus."

"You knew Corvasus as well?"

"I did, and believe me when I say you are lucky to be rid of the man.    He is a leech on our Jewish backside. Never trusted him."

"You're implying that both of them were thieves.    Why would Damneus trust my success to thieves? You have to do better than that to convince me."

"Both men are not only a thieves but a slave holders as well," Aliturius sounded irritated.    "Did Corvasus not brag to you about this villa estate that he owns?"

"Ahh..actually he did," Joseph reminded himself.

"Who do you think runs his estate while he's gone? Slaves of course!    As for the other, he's one of Rome's biggest slave merchants. So is that enough to convince you of their character?    Do you know what slave holders are like, Joseph?    Do you have any idea?"

At that moment Joseph thought back to his first encountering the slave peddler in Joppa and what he had done to Osirah and then he knew exactly what Aliturius was inferring.    "Yes, I do," he admitted.

"Good, then you understand now the kind of men you were dealing with."

Joseph winced at the thought of what would happen to Osirah if both she and Michael had made it to shore.    "And do you know whom the one that was meeting us would have introduced me to?" Joseph asked.

"Probably the Empress," Aliturius mused.

"I don't understand.    Why her?" Joseph was curious to know.

"Firstly because as I said, he has a tendency to annoy the Emperor and secondly, because as a slave seller, he has endeared himself in the past by selling the Empress a certain kind of slave that met her requirements.    Therefore, he would have found it far easier to arrange an individual hearing with the Empress than with Nero," he snickered as he concluded his reasoning. Both Jacob and Jonathias quickly suppressed a stifled laughs as well, obviously sharing a private joke with Aliturius.

"I'm missing something here, aren't I?" Their winks and nods between themselves did not go unnoticed by Joseph.

Without taking the time to respond, Aliturius shouted into the void of the tavern, "Abadeus, where's that wine already?    A toast to our new friend!"

# CHAPTER ELEVEN

## WHANGAREI: PRESENT

Taking a deep breath, Pearce released it slowly in a long, excruciating sigh. "You're also carrying on some private little joke that you're not willing to share with me yet, aren't you?"

"I've always warned you John, stop personalizing everything my characters have to say. It's not my joke, it's theirs. So in good time I'm certain they will share their little joke with you but for now it stays hidden because history was made from those things they didn't reveal."

"You know it's this penchant for secrets that got you in trouble in the first place," Pearce warned me.

"If you're referring to those agents trying to find me a while back, then I was better off having kept my secrets all to myself in the first place. If you hadn't run that expose on me, none of those events would have happened."

"Sooner or later you would have slipped up Doc and they would have been coming for you."

"Perhaps you're right, but more importantly, we agree that those days are over and now the entire subject of GLEEM is off the cutting board, no pun intended. They're too busy trying to build their little contraptions to turn brain cells into X-Box machines."

Pearce sighed at the thought. "Do you think they'll get very far with it?"

"Doesn't stand a chance," I offered my opinion. "At least not yet. I believe they're looking in the wrong direction."

"What d'ya mean?"

"Everyone has their own little theory on GLEEM now. Right? It's out of the box and now everyone's talking how memories can be encoded and transferred from generation to the next. So, what I had to originally say isn't very unique any longer. They wouldn't need to dissect my brain to see what makes it different, because they know now, it isn't any different. It's not wired any differently, it's not producing anything in excess or abnormally, and whatever they have to look for can be found in any old Joe Blog's brain. They already know that when they took out Einstein's brain and studied it. It's not what it looks like but how you use it. So it is pretty obvious that they don't have a clue about what it is they're looking for. We've become a video dominated society. Our entertainment, our games, even our work has become visual imaging to the max! So of course, the geniuses that they are can only comprehend GLEEM in a visual context. That somehow we record images as memories and therefore you only need the proper player-recorder and anyone else can see those images too."

"Yeah," Pearce nodded, "that's sort of what all the sci-fi movies are suggesting. Go as far as even suggesting memories will all be put on a disk."

"Right, because they can't imagine how it could be present in any other format. Everything they believe breaks down to a digital code, even our memories, perhaps our entire existence."

"Pretty much Star Trek, Doc. Digitalize you and then they can transport you."

"But what if our brain doesn't work like that? What if it works on an entirely different algorithm? After all, it's using the same amino acid building blocks to make a memory as it does to make anything else in the body. You only have so many nucleic acid base pairs before you run out of combinations. Millions of memories and there has to be a foul up somewhere."

"So what are you suggesting then?"

"There's got to be another block of code that tells the cells that this is the recipe for a hormone, or this is for building body parts, or this is a memory. A segment of base pairs at the terminal ends of the proteins that clearly identifies the purpose for this particular combination, saying read this as a memory, and nothing else."

"How's that any different from their interpretation of some kind of video player mechanism?"

"It's not a player, it's a processor. It interprets and immediately the full memory comes into existence. It's not visual, audible, or any of the other senses. It's virtual in existence. Another sense entirely that we don't even have a name for. It tricks the mind into thinking it sees or hears things but it's not real. Sort of like what happens when you smell an odour that reminds you of a favourite food you had as a child and suddenly that childhood memory of when and where and what you were doing at the time pops into your head. So there was no visual player involved. Your sense of smell acted as a processor that in turn triggered another mechanism that released a memory."

"Okay then," Pearce sighed somewhat exasperated, "so you build a machine that can do that."

"No," I shouted at his failure to grasp my explanation. "You can't build a machine! That's what I'm trying to tell you. It works completely on a non-mechanical level. No machine, no computer is ever going to have that level of sophistication that it will be able to translate what's not existent into reality. It's not going to happen by current technological thinking."

"Then you're saying that it's impossible," Pearce tried to put his words into my mouth.

"I didn't say impossible, just not possible as long as they're trying to achieve it with the technology at hand. As long as they're visually impaired, so to speak, they won't be able to crack it!"

"What then?"

"Organics!" I screamed much in the way that Euripides must have shouted his famous phrase "Eureka."

"Organics, like in fruit?"

"No," I corrected him.    "Don't be ridiculous. A whole new kind of technology.    Machines from living organic matter."

"Now you're beginning to scare me Doc.    This is beginning to sound a bit like Frankenstein.    Perhaps you should settle down there a bit."

"Sometimes I wonder why I put up with you John," I tutted.

"Because I'm cute and cuddly and my printing house sells your books like hotcakes."

"I guess so," I huffed.    "But it isn't pretty having to do so!    So if you're planning to write this down, you better get it accurate because if I see any reference to Frankenstein or the sorts, I'll be after your head for misquoting me. Frankenstein was about stealing body parts and giving them an electric jolt to get them working again. Coincidentally, that was what they did for the initial cloning projects! But I'm not talking about that at all. I'm proposing a new concept of culturing, growing, and shaping an organism into something alive yet for all intents and purposes not sentient, but merely functioning in a capacity similar to a machine.    That's an entirely different concept from Mary Shelly's. Who knows, it could be a hundred years down the road, perhaps even a thousand.    Then again, it could happen tomorrow. It's hard to say any more. But it starts out looking at the simplest of nervous systems and seeing it as nothing more than a device that functions through cellular kinetics.  And therein lays the beauty of this technology.    A brain is a brain so to speak.    Lowest order animal to highest order, they all have the same essential areas of function and motor senses. So as long as you can create a cellular mass of neurological tissue that resembles a brain it will serve the purpose of acting as the processor."

"What then," Pearce asked now intrigued by the concept.

"That's when we really appreciate the simplicity of the construct.    We cross-wire it, so that we plug the memory areas into the visual cortex.    So instead of a memory, it actually sees the event as a physical occurrence.    And if we're clever enough, we'll be able to map the signals occurring within the visual cortex to optical imaging.    Just like watching digital images on a screen even though your computer is doing nothing more than crunching a binary code."

The expression on Pearce's face became overly concerned.    "Let me back up for a sec, Doc.    I can grasp this, I think.    Build a brain out of living cells, wire it all up so that it can transfer what it's doing onto a screen of some sort, that's all fine, but what I haven't come to grips with is where this memory came from in the first place.    How do they get hold of it to put it into this organic whatchamacallit?"

"That part they have to work on first. If they have any intention of using this as a regular procedure, then they're going to have to find a way to extract the memories as chemical proteins without leaving behind Swiss cheese for a brain in the person donating the memories. Of course if the person was already dead, then this wouldn't present a problem at all but you'd have to collect them while the brain is still kept oxygenated following the death."

"Getting a little morbid there Doc, aren't we?"

"Much rather have them work on a dead guinea pig than go after something live for a change."

"Meaning yourself."

"Exactly!"

# THE ROAD TO ROME; 63 A.D.

Aliturius had long since departed to his scheduled performance at the local amphitheatre of the Three Medusas, leaving the three travelers behind to finish the cask of wine on their own. Jacob was doing his best to empty the flagon but before he could do so, he was laying sprawled across the table snoring so loudly that the walls practically vibrated.

"Joseph...I was just thinking about what Aliturius had to say about the Emperor, and I know you probably don't understand at this moment, but I want to reemphasize that the Empress is definitely the key."

"I know that you're all trying to conceal some piece of knowledge that you all share without coming right out and saying it...and I honestly don't know why but I'll play along...you don't have to tell me. The Emperor as everyone knows is a tyrant. There has to be a truth to all the stories circulating about him, so I'll treat him as one. So, I'm already aware that he's too resistant to make an attempt to ingratiate, at least by someone like me. So I always intended to measure my words carefully. But why you all think the Empress is any easier to convince, considering it's well rumored that she was the one responsible for Nero killing his mother and mistress doesn't make any sense to me either. Don't think me overly naïve but she could very well be the one we have to fear most if she can treat murder so lightly."

"She can be cold blooded," Jonathias agreed, "But she can also be very generous to those she considers as a friend."

"Becoming friends with the Empress sounds like a more difficult task than doing so with Nero. Joseph peered over at Jacob who was still snoring noisily. "Now, if there's really a task that worries me then that's it right there. Somehow we must carry our sleeping giant up to his room. God give us the strength."

That night when Aliturius returned, he narrated for hours without end about their destination; the fabled city that had been built on the seven hills. Rome was an enchanted land where any man could have his dreams fulfilled.

Neither of his guests    could remember exactly how they made it to their beds. Perhaps they had drifted off during the storytelling and had been carried to their rooms much in the same way they had steered Jacob to his cot but it mattered little once they closed their eyes.    Tomorrow would be the beginning of a brand new adventure.

---

Jacob's brow was furled and his fists clenched the arms of the high backed chair as he sat blankly staring at the doorway to the inn. No sooner had Jonathias swung through the inn's doorway, Jacob set upon him with a verbal barrage. There was one thing he could not tolerate and that was apparent insubordination from anyone, including a close companion.    "Do you think you can do as you please?  Just wander off without a concern for how you might be jeopardizing our mission?   What do you think you were doing?"

"Actually, I was just taking a walk," Jonathias replied in a matter of fact tone of voice.

"I don't care if you were out kissing Nero's gold plated ass!   As long as we're obvious foreigners in this place, we are not to be separated.    Is that understood?"

"And when did Jeshua appoint you lord and master of us all.   If I recall correctly, I'm the one that happens to be his brother-in-law, not you!"

"At least he had the common sense to put me in charge of this mission because he knows you're not the one to measure out the risks.   And putting your self in unnecessary danger by venturing out alone is a risk!"

"Me? I'm not the one to weigh out risks?   Hah!"

"Wait a minute," Joseph interrupted as he was descending the stairs and stopped in order to listen to their conversation.    "Let's go back a bit to what you said.   Your brother-in-law is behind this?"

Jonathias was relieved by the intercession that Joseph provided.   He had been through enough arguments with Jacob in the past and wasn't looking forward to another of his pig-headed lectures on responsibility. "I told you Joseph that you'd be surprised by the people that were supporting us."

"But your brother-in-law is none other than Jeshua ben Gamaliel.   He's what… second or third in line to the high priesthood now. It doesn't make sense. Why would he risk everything on some mission that could jeopardize his obtaining a position that offered him real power to change our future? I don't see the logic."

"Oh, now you've done it," Jacob hissed at his companion contemptuously.   "You know that Jeshua wanted his name kept out of any of our discussions.   Wait till he hears about this!"

"What? You think that Joseph wouldn't have figured it out at some point.   There were enough clues there.    Sanhedrin documents, official seals, not to mention my own presence on this mission.    All the writing was on the wall.   So I don't think it really matters about keeping our secret benefactor hidden any longer."

"Jeshua ben Gamaliel," Joseph repeated. "Wow, if he's the motivating force behind your endeavor then things must be far more serious than I thought. After all, he's not to be considered anyone's fool. I personally have the utmost respect for him. If the House of Phiabi is willing to lay all they have on the line for your mission, then how could I possibly refuse your offer to act as my intended entourage?"

"See," Jonathias hissed back at the giant.

"You still didn't have the authority to breach confidence," Jacob glared back. "While in Rome, I'm still to be considered the one in charge."

"Well, you big dumb ox, in case you haven't noticed this town isn't Rome!"

"Enough!" Joseph shouted above the rising din. "Get ready to leave. Aliturius will be coming back any minute with his wagon and he will be expecting us to be ready to leave immediately."

"So?" they both responded simultaneously, instantly ending their little argument. "It's not like we got a lot to get together before we leave," Jonathias quipped. "In fact, let me look. Still have the same clothes on from the ship wreck? Yep, we're ready."

No sooner had Jonathias completed his sentence they all heard the lilting voice of Aliturius summoning them to come outside. "Climb in anywhere," he instructed when they made their appearance. Aliturius was comfortably in his spot beside the wagon's driver. As for the rest of the troupe, they were piled on top of each other with barely an inch of breathing space between them.

Before the three new members of the party had an opportunity to even find a spot to squeeze into, there was a sudden jerk of the reins and the horse drawn cart jolted along the uneven road heading north. Leaning back in his seat, Aliturius turned his head so he could speak to his guests. "Allow me to introduce everyone. This one," he pointed at a handsome blonde haired youth, "is named Vacillius. He is the young hero in all of our plays. Not too surprising. And this old man over here," Aliturius chuckled as he patted the man's shoulder, "is Sindorius, a portrayer of kings, wise men and magi. That one is Bindus, blessed with a phenomenal beauty that ideally suits him to play both gods and goddesses. Don't you think he's just absolutely gorgeous?" Aliturius gave Bindus a subtle wink as he turned away. "Our driver here is Macherus. Custodian, body guard and generally plays soldiers, villains, and the likes. He is excellent no matter what role he plays. And finally that leaves Carbo, that fellow over there. Our narrator. His stentorian voice is the finest anyone has ever heard. Say something to our new friends Carbo."

"Pleased to meet you," Carbo responded in a deep melodious voice.

"Wasn't that tremendous?" Aliturius accentuated. "Did you hear the quality of that voice? Fabulous!"

The three looked at each other and then nodded. Personally they couldn't tell a great actor from a tailor but for Aliturius's sake they decided to agree.

"Meet our new companions," he announced to his fellow thespians. "The big man is Jacob, and this smaller one is Yoni.    And that serious looking fellow over there is Joseph."

"Greetings," the actors responded in unison.

"Oh, you really are a big fellow, aren't you," Bindus smiled at Jacob.

Not knowing how to react, Jacob blushed, then harrumphed as he cleared his throat and then eyed his feet conspicuously, trying not to look at Bindus directly. He understood enough Latin to comprehend the nuance behind Bindus's words immediately.

"And a shy one too," Bindus giggled.    "Oh we will have to get to know each other. And we have so many days cramped in this little wagon to do so. I am so excited!"

"Bindus, please try to behave yourself!" Aliturius commanded in a voice possibly tinged with jealousy.

Both Joseph and Jonathias flashed cutting grins at their companion, which silenced him for the next few hours, as he was afraid to say anything that Bindus might deem as encouragement.

The harnesses rattled to a steady beat as the horses churned the stoned road beneath their feet. The country side, a combination of green rolling hills and shaded valleys filed continuously past the wagon.    It wasn't long until the sounds of the white capped waves crashing against the rocky coastline were lost in the distance.    All the time Aliturius kept spewing fact after monotonous fact about the history of battles that had taken place during the Italian wars with Rome associated with each landmark they passed.    Joseph nodded acknowledging each statement, half listening, half oblivious, but what he did realize was that Aliturius had never said a word further about the mission which obviously meant that none of his acting troupe was involved in the plan.

As the cooler air of the evening settled upon the travelers, Macherus pulled on the reins, bring the horses to a halt, and then attached their feedbags to their halters.    "Might as well set up camp here," he advised Aliturius.

"Why not?" the troupe leader agreed.    "Here's as good a place as any."

"Where's here?"    Joseph inquired of his host.

"Here  is  neither  there  nor  where," Aliturius  riddled,  "But merely here.    Here is a place in the middle of nowhere if we choose wisely and make certain we're away from    the road.    Otherwise we'll get no sleep at all.    The road at times is heavily traveled, so I think its best we retire a good distance away from it; too many travelers, too many    bandits for us to encounter them all.    In a few days we'll be in Rome as long as we can continue to set a good pace.    What more do you need to know."    Aliturius ended with what was more a statement than a question as if to say to Joseph he had said all that he was going to say on the issue.    After all, he was in charge.

At the first light of dawn, the horses were rehitched to the wagon and Macherus climbed atop the board that served as his seat. Shouting a wake-up call, he summoned everyone to resume their positions in the carriage immediately. It was Aliturius's duty to remove the feed bags that still swung from the horse's halters from the evening before and tossing them into the back of cart, barely missing Carbo's head as he did so. "Time for us to get on with our plans if we don't wish to squander away this fine day."

"Exactly how long will it take us to reach Rome?" Joseph asked, the question sounding innocent enough but being more concerned of whether he could withstand several more days of a historical monologue from Aliturius concerning what he considered inconsequential political issues that happened a long time ago in a country that was so very far away from his reality.

Scratching his head as if to suggest that the answer was going to be far more difficult than the question, Aliturius rolled his head from side to side before responding. "Now if we are to have the good fortune of making good speed as we did this last day, then I would reckon five days to reach Rome. Now that's only if we should make the required forty miles a day. But then I doubt we can continue at that pace. It's a fine team of horses, but they're pulling a considerable amount of weight. I would think that thirty miles a day might be our actual pace. If that should be the case, then it could take six or even seven days to reach Rome."

Joseph took a deep breath and released it slowly. This was a trip that he was not looking forward to. "Aliturius? Can I ask a favor?" he spoke in Hebrew.

"Certainly my friend. I would be pleased if you would," answering in the same language.

"I think we should be discussing the matter of our mission while we have this time together."

"And how do you propose we do that with so many ears in attendance?"

"Now that is an interesting dilemma I admit. I've determined that other than yourself, no one else from among your little troupe of players appears to be of Judean origin. That would limit their involvement. But it also readily resolves the dilemma. I doubt very much that they speak anything other than Latin or Greek. If that's true then we have an option to continue to speak either Hebrew or Aramaic, which I doubt they would know."

Holding up his hand, Aliturius signaled Joseph to stop. "Don't you think they would find it somewhat suspicious if we started speaking in a language they couldn't understand for days on end? Not to mention extremely rude. I think we're best waiting until we reach Rome before we discuss the issues."

"I think it would be a big mistake to waste all of this precious time that we've been afforded," Joseph quickly reiterated.

"Perhaps there's a compromise," the very intuitive thespian suggested.

"A compromise?"

"Yes, a compromise. I promise to not fill your day with a litany on Rome's history and tourist sites, and you promise to be patient with me and understand why we can't discuss anything quite as serious in such an open forum." Aliturius flashed a smile showing that he knew exactly what was bothering Joseph.

"Was I that obvious," Joseph winced at the cutting barb that he had just been jabbed with.

"Let us just say that you aren't the first person that has been bored to tears with the Historia Romana. Probably every school child in this country has felt that way at some time.

Sensing that he may have offended his host, Joseph felt he had to repair the damage quickly. "I'm sorry." He felt foolish having found himself at a loss for words except for that childish phrase which everyone uses but so very few truly mean.

With a slap on the back and a wink of his eye, Aliturius swept the entire matter under the carpet. "There's so much more that we can discuss which will be of value and interest to you. I'll spend today telling you all about the Emperor and his Empress. After all, you're going to have to know exactly how to deal with both of them at the appropriate time."

"Either piss in the pot or get off!" Macherus bellowed to his master.

"So eloquently put," Aliturius smiled back. "I believe he'd like us all to get on the wagon or he'll shove off without us," he translated for Joseph's sake.

"He wouldn't dare do that."

"Oh yes he would," Aliturius advised. "It wouldn't be the first time he's made me chase after that wagon."

"You must have been furious with him at the time?"

"At the time, yes. But it's hard to stay mad at my dear Macherus. Let's climb onto the wagon before he makes fools of us both."

---

Several days into the journey, Joseph found himself entranced with every word that Aliturius had to say about life within the Imperial court. Any of the stories that Joseph thought he knew about the old days of the Herodian court paled in comparison to the extremes to which the Roman ruling class would indulge their impulses. Matricide, patricide, fratricide, almost every kind of murder possible; in the several days that Joseph listened to the tales he learned more about the different ways one killed members of their own family than he ever dreamt possible. The path to the Emperor's ivory curule chair was bathed in blood. He could not even conceive of how or why the Senate, the equestrian order, or for that fact, the common people, could bear the touch of the hand that squeezed the life from the republic in its vile grasp. What was it that so fascinated people that they were willing to worship evil so whole heartedly, even if it was to their personal disadvantage? Contemplating this mystery kept

Joseph spellbound for the remainder of the journey. For the first time since he left Jerusalem he began to understand why Damneus had picked him for this mission. Too many times in the past the envoys sent to Rome to plead for the safe return of the hostages had failed simply because they did not understand the terms of negotiation based on an ideology so foreign to them. You could not negotiate using eastern logic. It had no place in this cradle of decadence. In order to successfully fulfill his mission, Joseph realized he could only do so if he played the game according to Roman rules. Not the way that a Michael Corvasus thought was necessary but in the manner that someone like Aliturius had done. Patiently, cooperatively, but most of all sublimely. Being there when necessary as a willing participant but never staying too long and wearing out one's welcome.

On the sixth day that the cart rattled towards its destination, the roads were already thronging with people before the sun had fully risen in the east.

"Well my friends, here we are," Aliturius exclaimed, "the heart and soul of the world. Whatever you thought you knew about Rome, be prepared to forget it all!"

"Don't you think that might be somewhat of an over statement," Joseph dismissed the comment after having spend days listening to Aliturius tell all his stories.

"Not at all, dear boy," the wily and wizened thespian quickly responded. "See, therein lies the difference between our two worlds. As Jews, we tend to think we know all the answers. But here in Rome, they know all the questions. And that is a significant difference. Whereas we feel all there is to be learned has already been learned, but these Romans, they continue to learn and absorb, and are never content with the present. That is their heart and soul which you're about to see it for yourself."

"There are times Aliturius that you're sounding very much like someone else I used to know. He also was a Jew trying to straddle two different worlds."

"You're referring to Corvasus. Straddling is hardly the word I would use to describe my accomplishment. I tend to think of myself having a foot firmly planted in both worlds unlike Michael Corvasus who could never master that trick. Take a look about you my friends. Where would you ever find another city that so self assured in its power that it doesn't even surround itself with walls for protection? Can Jerusalem, dear Jerusalem, city protected by God, even make a similar boast? I'm afraid not. With all our faith, we still rely on massive stones to keep our enemies at bay. But here, they have built the most effective wall of all; an invisible wall of fear. When we learn how to build a similar wall, then we will have the right to boast like Rome does."

"Yes," Joseph confirmed, "you are definitely beginning to sound more like him," he laughed.

The wagon weaved through extremely narrow streets, shielded overhead by leaning tenements that blocked out the sky. The white stuccoed apartments stood in closely packed rows, mostly three stories high, but every so often one would stretch upwards a towering five stories. Red tiled roofs and painted shutters contrasted sharply with the austere whiteness of the city. This was the area known as the Subura, Aliturius explained, and once they reach the cross-roads they would be into the corda, the essence of Rome itself. Once past the crossroads the streets widened into cobblestone causeways, crisscrossing in a never ending pattern as far as the eye could see.

In every direction that Joseph looked, there were amphitheaters and circuses overshadowing the stately municipal buildings with their fountain dotted gardens haloed by columned porches. The aqueduct that interlaced the city transported the water from the distant highlands to the open mouthed fountains spouting their streams into lily frond ponds.

Turning right on Tuscan Boulevard, Macherus steered the wagon into the forum between the Capitoline and Esquiline Hills. Aliturius dismounted, waving for Joseph, Jacob and Jonathias to follow. "Macherus, my good man, continue on to the theatre. We'll join up with you later. I'm going to give our guests a tour of this magnificent city that they won't forget."

Taking the lead, the four men from Judea strolled through the famed gardens of Tiberius. "Over there is the temple of Castor and Pollux," Aliturius pointed. "Or as the Greeks called them, the Discouri. That building on the left is the Basilica Julia. The gardens there are even more beautiful. Not a single stone out of place. An architectural example of what can only be described as perfection. This causeway we're now on is known as the New Way. That building is the Temple of Caesar and the arch beside it commemorates Augustus Caesar."

All along their route the statues stood in noble expression and heavenly posture. Aliturius patiently tried to explain the purpose of the Vestals and why girls as young as seven were brought to their temple by their parents only to be left in the care of the pontifex until they were thirty years old. At that time they would be released from their vow of chastity and free to pursue a normal life, as normal as possible for a woman already considered to be a spinster. The explanation was lost upon the three travelers; the entire concept was too foreign to their Mideastern minds.

Onward they were led, past the great palaces of Augustus and Tiberius, bricked entirely with marble and trimmed with gold. By late afternoon they had meandered their way across several bridges and numerous valleys into the new district built upon the Janiculum Hill. Aliturius had them follow into a small building that was situated at the end of a narrow street. He spoke softly. "This isn't comparable to what you've grown used to seeing back in Judea," he apologized, "but this is it."

"This is what?" Joseph questioned.

"My synagogue, of course! I haven't entirely abandoned my birthright, you know. I needed a place to worship that was more in line with my, how would you say... more enlightened perspective. So when I couldn't find a congregation that exactly suited my beliefs, I built one that did. There are perhaps only fifty of us in total that meet here but we consider it our second home. Come in, you'll see."

Looking around the structure, Joseph purposely held back from commenting immediately. Now that he had had several days to know his host a little better, it was no great surprise that the so-called synagogue appeared to be nothing more than an assimilated version of a Roman temple. Much in the way that Aliturius had absorbed the culture of his adopted homeland, the furnishings, or lack of them had influenced his sanctuary. Almost Spartan in its décor, the congregation had nothing more than a few tables and several wooden platforms on which to place the scrolls. But for what it lacked in furnishings it made up for entirely in columns and mosaics. Still adhering to the Hebrew ban on graven images, the mosaics consisted entirely of brilliant masses of flowers and scenes of nature. Beautiful, Joseph readily acknowledged, but definitely not suitable for a synagogue he thought to himself. Even the coloured glass in the windows, a very expensive item that would have set back Aliturius thousands of denarii, was so foreign to Joseph that he was certain it would never become widespread in its use. Stained glass he felt had not place in a house of worship.

"Elias...Elias, are you here?" Aliturius's voice echoed through the room.

A frail and withered voice responded from the back chamber. "Hold on, hold on. I'm not a young man you know. I'm coming. No reason to shout. I'm not young, but I'm not deaf either." From behind the exquisitely designed blue drapery that hung over the doorway, the bent over graybeard emerged, leaning heavily upon a gnarled staff. His thinning hair was concealed by a low peaked turban, the whites of his robe stretching to the floor and sweeping the dust as he moved. Holding out his wrinkled hand, he greeted his distinguished friend. "It is so good to see you once again my brother. Peace and the Mercy of God be with you. You have brought us some guests. These must be brothers too," his face lit up. "And Judean from the looks of them."

"These are the very important men I spoke of to you, Elias. They are the ones on the mission for the Sanhedrin."

"Oh, you mean the ones that were sent to gain the release of the priests," the old man clarified as he recollected their conversation.

"Does everyone know of my supposedly secret mission?" Joseph questioned half rhetorically. "It would appear that secrecy is something the Sanhedrin handles very poorly."

Elias laughed. "My young brother, when have you ever known of a secret remaining a secret in all our history? We Jews are notoriously bad for keeping anything in private. Perhaps that's why God chose us to deliver his message. He knew we'd tell everyone about it! But come, sit!" Elias led them over to the few chairs that were centered in the hall. "Come, tell me about Jerusalem. I have heard so little of late. Is this talk of war true?"

"You've heard of that too," Jacob piped in.

"Yes, yes, no secrets remain secrets for long in Rome either."

"Things are not going well", Jonathias replied. "The situation is very tense. It will only take a single spark to light the inferno."

"Or a single man," the old graybeard's eyes sparkled.

"You're right as usual, Elias. This is the one." Aliturius sounded exuberant.

"I knew it, I knew it," he slapped his knees. "The moment I laid these tired eyes upon him, I knew he was the one!"

Joseph withdrew his chair slightly, distancing himself from the old man. "Why does everyone keep saying that? I have no intention of being anyone's messiah. Since coming on shore people have been laying this burden upon me. I do not know what any of you are all talking about. I have a mission, I will do it successfully, and then I will return home to my very peaceful and quiet life thank you!"

Jonathias snickered, then raised the back of his hand to his face in order to conceal the laugh.

Quickly turning in his seat, Joseph flashed a menacing stare at his cousin.

"Do not try to fool an old man," Elias cautioned, "especially one who can see the evidence before his very own eyes. We are all men playing roles in a play written long ago by the Almighty. Some of us learn our lines well, others merely fumble through our parts. But nonetheless, the play must go on until the finish."

"Elias is a Phiabite," Aliturius explained, "just like Jeshua ben Gamaliel. Are you beginning to understand a little better now?"

The realization was dawning rapidly and Joseph nodded his head very slightly at first and then a little more deliberately as the comment sunk in. "Then it's true. The house of Phiabi still possesses the power of the urim and thummim. You see things that no others can see."

"Yes," the old man smiled. "Now you understand. That which the Pharisees condemn us for possessing will ultimately lead to our freedom. They are a jealous rabble that will do anything to take God's gift from us, even if it means thwarting all of our efforts."

Turning towards Jonathias, Joseph continued the vein of thought. "And your brother-in-law, he too has seen something about to happen and that's why he's sent you on your mission as well?"

Nodding, Jonathias bore an expression of guilty as charged. "We have learned not to doubt his visions. You are the man we seek. You are the one that was born to lead."

"But that's not exactly right," Joseph objected. "It is said that many are called by God but only one is chosen. That means there are others as well. I'm not necessarily the one. I can simply refuse. There are others that can take my place."

"No one can refuse the will of God," Elias shook his finger angrily at his guest.    I know who you are Joseph ben Matthias.    I know what flames burn inside your chest and you will not refuse.  I have seen it and you will not refuse!"

Joseph's head was swirling and as he rose from his chair his legs were numb and barely able to hold him upright.  Somehow the words of old Elias had triggered a fog within his brain.    He stumbled from the synagogue and out into the street.    Aliturius quickly ran to his side to support him as did Jacob and Jonathias.

"We will meet again Joseph ben Matthias," the old man called out after therm.

There were more people in the street at this hour and Joseph was not unaware of the suspicious glances they all seemed to be casting in his direction. "I know you are all thinking ill of me at this moment.    But I truly do not want this mission that everyone appears to be obsessed in charging me with."

"Be quiet now," Aliturius whispered as he helped the other companions swing Joseph's arms over their shoulders.    "There will be no talk of this in the streets.    While in Rome we must appear to be nothing more than Romans, as difficult as that may seem.    To do or say anything otherwise could spell our deaths.    They already suspect us all to be in league with the followers of Jesus of Nazareth. In Rome that can be a very dangerous situation.  Let's not give them any reason to believe they are right.    Not a word of what Elias or any of you said until we are safely away from the streets."

# CHAPTER TWELVE

## WHANGAREI; PRESENT

Pouring himself another cup of coffee from the pot Pearce took a moment to reassess the storyline. "Another name I saw on your family tree. This Phiabi character. Is he important?"

"Quite. My family are Phiabites."

"Documented?"

"As well as anything can be fully documented for just over two thousand years if that's what you're asking. The Kahana are said to be Phiabites, and a relative in Israel repeated that claim to me forty years ago, so he was somehow aware of it. No one has disagreed to the family claim over the centuries, ergo we must therefore be Phiabites. It's simple arithmetic."

"And what does it mean?"

"There are a couple of interesting stories. As far as I can enlighten you, it means, 'the face of my father.' A peculiar sort of family title, don't you think?"

"But what does it really mean?"

"I think it has a double meaning. The first being a reference to whatever my father may look like, the son always bears a strong resemblance. Which holds true in my case because if you saw my father, you'd swear I was a clone. The second meaning is a reference to our original ancestor's presence before God in which he saw the face of the Almighty, hence the face of the supreme Father and that image was burnt upon our souls in the form of the gift of urim and thummim."

Pearce took a sip of his coffee and was deep in thought. In his eyes, I could see that he was cogitating a question that would be a humdinger. "So, correct me if I'm wrong, but you're describing the origin of GLEEM here. Seeing what you father could see, the urim, thummim, and practically being a genetic clone of your father as you said, was in fact probably their only way of explaining GLEEM back then. Correct?"

"A definite possibility," I congratulated him on his flash of insight. "Face of my father has a genetic reference no matter how you slice it. It not only smacks of visualization but also definitely refers somewhat to a continuity."

"Did they understand?"

"For those that could deal with it, it was simply seen as a gift from God. For those that couldn't, it was a curse from hell!"

"No in between?"

"I don't know. Guess it depends what day of the week you catch me.

One foot in heaven one foot in hell seems to reasonably describe most days.

"I didn't expect that."

"Why not? I always told you that I wouldn't wish it on anyone else and spoke of how much a curse it could be."

"I don't know. I guess I just thought that over the years we've been discussing it, you had come to grips with it. Wasn't that the idea? You talk it out and it frees you from the burden. Sort of like therapy."

"That's probably true in most cases, but there are some images that I just can't escape. Some things which make me realize that I'm a prisoner of GLEEM in the same way some of my ancestors must have felt."

"But you know where the line is drawn between your own thoughts, don't you?"

"Do you even know? How does one know where the line is actually drawn between imagination and reality? I've been struggling with that all my life and still I don't know if anyone can really make that delineation one hundred percent of the time. "I'll let you in on a secret John…" I leaned forward forcing him to do likewise as I spoke in nothing more than a whisper. "I don't know! Most of the time I don't have a problem, but when it comes to some of the images from someone like Jakob Goldenthal, who's life I appear to be paralleling, then I can't make that distinction. As I told you before, just take a look at his life and mine. He spoke German, Russian, Italian, Hebrew, Arabic, Romanian and a little bit of French and English. I speak German, Hebrew, French, English and a little bit of Spanish and Chinese. He liked languages and it's obvious I must like languages too. He was a philosopher and writer that dabbled in science. I'm a scientist that dabbles in writing and philosophy. He was supposed to go for Rabbinical training and told them to stuff it. I was supposed to go to the Yeshiva courtesy of Eitz Chaim for rabbinical training and I told them to stuff it. He worked at a university and so too, I've worked at a couple of universities. The parallels go on ad-infinitum."

"So you have some similarities. Not that big an issue." Pearce was able to reduce all my concerns to nothing. But that's only because he didn't see exactly what I was trying to point out.

"It's worse than that, John. It's not a case of similarities; it's a case of merging. Do you know that I can close my eyes and I can see the Empress Elisabeth standing in front of me?"

"Hey, I can close my eyes and see Nicole Kidman standing in front of me, and not necessarily clothed," Pearce quipped. "So what's your point?"

"It's not just seeing her, it's feeling my heart race, my palms sweat, my head spin. It's his eyes looking at her but it's me feeling the effects."

"And who says I don't go through exactly the same thing when I think of Nicole Kidman."

"You're not exactly picking up on what I'm trying to say, John," I said scathingly. "Elisabeth has been dead for over a hundred years. I can see her as a young beautiful, vibrant woman and it's not a case of yearning for her, it's a case of missing her."

"As in knowing her?" He was finally beginning to understand.

"Yes," I replied. "As in the biblical sense of knowing her. Geez, you can be such a prude at times. I can still smell her, feel her, taste her. The smoothness of her skin. The warmth of her touch. She had this essence of rose water about her. The little girlish laugh that always made me melt. Except not me, him! Her skin was so pale, like a glazed porcelain doll. You know, they all write about her as being a blonde. The only time she was blonde was when she was still a young girl, the same way that most youngsters are a dark blonde before their hair turns auburn. I would like to say that these are his thoughts, his feelings, his visions, but they're not. I've come to realize they are actually mine. It's me with her. It's me laying with her. The madness is rooted in the fact that I cannot make a distinction between my life and his when it comes to her."

"I guess that could be a problem," Pearce once again made an understatement in that manner that I had grown accustomed to.

"You might say that. I don't want to live his life. I want to live my own but in order to do that you have to know where the separation lies."

Pearce rolled back into his seat. "We are definitely going to have to do that story soon."

"I don't think it's going to help clear out those memories even if we do write it down on paper"

"Then we have nothing to lose and you have everything to gain, as I see it Doc," he enlightened me.

---

# ROME; 63 A.D.

"Wait!" Jonathias cautioned, cocking an ear towards the blackness. "Did you hear that?"

"I heard nothing," Aliturius replied.

"Probably nothing," Jonathias tried to convince himself. "I can't believe how dark these streets are. I can barely see my own feet. We should have started out earlier in order to avoid nightfall."

"It's not the night," Aliturius corrected him, "It's the overhang from all these buildings."

Contending with the total lack of visibility, they groped and probed their way through the shadows, moving slowly along the sheltered streets. From just in front of them there resonated a sound like a hard substance clapping against the cobblestones. Aliturius jumped backwards with a fright as he bumped into the hooded figure of a man standing purposely in his path. If not for Jonathias standing behind to steady him, he may have fallen to the ground. They could see the glint from the blade of the polished knife catching the single thread of moonlight that momentarily struck a raised right hand.

"You two!" a voice surfaced from the darkness, "Do you not know that it is not safe to walk the streets at night. No way of telling what kind of unsavory characters you might encounter."

"I can assure you that there will be no reward this night if you insist on perpetrating this crime," Aliturius warned the man. "And it is two of us against one," Aliturius reminded the stranger.

"Hey," the thief responded, "In case you haven't noticed, I'm the one with the knife. So make sure neither of you start getting stupid on me."

Aliturius watched anxiously as the blade flicked nervously in the man's hand, while extending his arm and holding Jonathias back, whom he could sense was ready to attack.

Suddenly the man jumped to his right side and reached for his ass. "Hey, who did that?!" he called out into the darkness. He rubbed the sore spot that now bore the imprint of a large sandal. Another kick from the opposite side jolted the thief backwards, "Come out and show yourself!" That was shortly followed by another kick leaving the thief scurrying into the darkness and running for his life from his hidden assailants.

"And don't you come back," Jacob yelled after him, his voice emanating from the shadows. "Now I enjoyed that!" Jacob exclaimed. One needs to be more careful when they select their victims."

"So did I" Joseph agreed, his form just as invisible in the blackness as was Jacob's.

"Not fair," Jonathias complained. "I was about to settle the matter myself."

"As dark as it is," Aliturius reminded his young friend, "He still was the one holding the knife. I do believe for all our sake, this was a much better ending to the threat."

"Definitely not doing that again," Aliturius sighed in relief as they finally emerged from the darkness created by the black canopy of the overhanging apartments. The four of them laughed heartily as they entered into the dull umbrella of a clouded sky that lay beyond. They continued to follow the road which guided them the rest of the way to Aliturius's home.

The visitors were astounded by the contrast between the two areas of city they had traversed. From the dark, cold, honeycombed warren where the synagogue lay to the vibrant, almost festive atmosphere catered to by shimmering lights where the house was located.

"And you called where we had just been the New City," Joseph commented, sounding somewhat confused. "You'd would think if they could light the streets in this district, then it could have been done just as easily in that part of the city they want to call 'New'?" he questioned in disbelief.

"A paradox, isn't it?" Aliturius riddled. "How is it that the new city is so dark and uninviting, whereas the old part of the city is much more alive and vibrant, illuminated by hundreds of naphtha lamps throughout the night.    But I would have thought that you would have noted the obvious reason?  The Janiculum Hill with its New City is nothing more than a haven for refugees and foreigners. Why do you think our synagogue is built there?    As far as Rome is concerned, it is where all of its poor and undesirables reside."

"Considering we were almost attacked there, they may not be wrong," Jacob commented.    "When it comes to the undesirables part, that is."

"I admit that we were in the wrong place at the wrong time," Aliturius confessed.    "I should have known better.  It is no secret that Rome cares little for those    squatters    that    have    come    uninvited    and    refused    to    leave. Without proper legislation, the civic authorities have allowed them to construct their homes wherever they please.    As you may have seen, even in the dark, the workmanship is appalling and the awnings and overhangs are so close that they actually touch forming the dark tunnel we experienced that prevents any light from penetrating.    As much as I would have liked to avoid that route, unfortunately, in order to reach my house that was the fastest way of traversing the city.    And more unfortunately, you run the risk of meeting a few of the vile criminals along the way. But all said and done, gentlemen, we are here!"

Stopping in front of a four storied structure, Aliturius winked at them.

"Which floor is yours?" Joseph inquired.

"Don't be ridiculous my dear boy, all of it is mine.  This was a gift from the Emperor, himself.    It is provided to me and my troupe for as long as I live and now it will be your home while you're in Rome as my guest."

"You are most gracious," Joseph bowed, "but do you think it wise to have us stay at your home.    You heard Elias, most people seem to know about me and that Rome cannot keep a secret.    It wouldn't be long until my mission draws the wrong kind of attention to you."

"Do you think I have been able to weave my way through life without the hint of scandal in the past?    A bit of intrigue makes life worth living.    Besides, you're on a mission by one government to another.  That automatically grants you a degree of diplomatic immunity that cries out for attention.    What good is being a celebrity without a hint of notoriety?    Now come inside all of you. You will need a change of clothing and a bath before I take you to the palace."

Scaling the winding stairs to the fourth floor, Aliturius led his guests into one of the several unoccupied rooms of his apartment building.    Lighting the oil lamps that ringed the walls, the flood of light revealed a lacework of cobwebs covering the furniture, and extending from the wooden chests to the acting props and forgotten relics of past performances.    "My apologies, I've been away from my    home    for    quite    some    time    now    and    it    doesn't    appear    that Macherus has been tending to his house dusting duties.    He complains bitterly whenever he has to do any house cleaning."    Aliturius turned a key in the lock of one of the chests and raised the lid.

"I have just the thing for you," he said to Joseph.   He then handed Joseph a fine white tunic with a belt of braided gold threads, followed by a purple cloak that fastened about the neck by means of a red jeweled clasp.

"Purple," Joseph emphasized in shocked embarrassment.  "Isn't that a little too presumptuous.   It's usually reserved for one of royal standing.   What if Nero takes it as an insult, or as my mocking him, if he sees me in it?"

"My dear boy, if you want to be worthy of standing before the Emperor of the world, then you better have some regal bearing.   Otherwise you won't stand a chance of being heard.   Either meet Nero as a peer, or don't meet at all!   I will introduce you as your country's ambassador.   As I understand it, you have some Hasmonean blood in you, don't you?"

"A little," Joseph acknowledged.

"Royal blood is royal blood.   As far as he's concerned, you're a prince. Leave it to me.   Jacob, this one is for you."

Aliturius unfolded a scarlet tunic with pleated skirt and then laid on top of it a bronze embossed cuirass.   "This will do fine." As a finishing touch, Aliturius dug deep into the bottom of the chest and extracted a white cape bordered with a pair of red stripes.

"Am I a general?" Jacob inquired as his fingers traced the outline of the chariot of Apollo on the breast plate.

"I think we last used this in the Aeneid, but yes, tomorrow you will be a general."

Jonathias leaned over and peered into the wooden chest.   "What do you have in there for me?"

"Yes...let me see."   Aliturius scratched his scalp while he pondered the question. "I still have an Ajax costume, an Oedipus outfit, and, ..oh, yes...this will do nicely...Prince Perseus.   A blue tunic with an exquisite jeweled belt. You'll look absolutely fetching in this. It's definitely you! This is good. You'll all make quite the impression tomorrow.   I just pray he doesn't remember seeing these outfits worn during any of my plays."   Aliturius   laughed at the thought.   "That would be so embarrassing, wouldn't it?   Nero has such a terrible memory though, so I doubt we need to worry."

"How will we suddenly get an audience tomorrow?" Joseph asked, seriously doubting it was even possible.   Everyone said it took weeks to get an audience with anyone of high ranking."

"I'll think of something to get you in.   Don't worry. After all, what would be the use of being one of Nero's favorites if I couldn't pull a few strings? By the way, there's a bath on the first floor. I suggest you all use it. Your long journey hasn't exactly kept you smelling like roses. I will have the house servants draw and heat some water and afterwards they will show you to your sleeping chambers.   I hope they at least have been keeping up with their cleaning duties and kept the bedrooms tidy. You'll need your rest.   Trust me, we will have a busy day tomorrow."

In the morning, Joseph donned his costume and while standing before the full-length polished brass mirror, he shamelessly admired his own reflection. There in all his glory stood Priam, King of Troy, and for the moment Joseph's imagination reveled in the ecstasy of kingship.

While at the same time, Jacob regaled himself in the raiment of command, a leader of men, a commander of thousands and he felt himself infused with power. He then hurtled himself down the staircase hoping to be the first to the main floor but both Aliturius and Jonathias were already waiting. Jonathias, draped in the unmistakable searing vitality of the hero Perseus, slayer of the Gorgon, Medusa. And Aliturius, flowing in luxuriant silk robes and looking positively brilliant as no one other than Aliturius could do.

Joseph was soon to join them and once assembled they began the short walk to the palace, passing the rows of Praetorian guardsmen that uttered not a single word, letting them pass unobstructed as soon as they saw Aliturius. Upon climbing the steps of the palace, Aliturius was approached only once by a single palace official, whom immediately assigned them an escort upon recognizing the Emperor's very close friend.

"Is it usually this unprotected that a group of strangers like us can walk unmolested into the heart of the Imperial palace?" Joseph inquired. "I find this most unusual."

"Do not be fooled my young friend. We have been watched by hundreds of pairs of eyes as soon as we entered the court yard. Had they not clearly recognized me, they would have fallen upon us long ago. No, what you've seen today is the level of power that can be manifested, merely through being a friend of those that are mighty."

Joseph detected something in Aliturius's tone that indicated that without him, Joseph's mission never would have succeeded. "Are you suggesting that any success I might have on my mission was only possible as a result of our chance meeting?"

"No, because my dear boy, there was nothing chance about our meeting," Aliturius stated. "Haven't you realized that yet?"

Led through the back corridors of the palace, they bypassed the waiting lines of bureaucrats that awaited their imperial audiences. Chaperoned directly into one of the throne room's antechambers, their attendant left them standing in a room of marbled tiles and shimmering agate walls.

"Where did he go?"

"Do not worry, Jonathias," Aliturius commented. "It's whom he returns with that is far more important."

A few minutes after Aliturius had finished his words, the official was back and waving Aliturius and his companions forward into the next room. Entering cautiously, there upon the raised dais sat Nero and Poppea in matching gold and silver inlaid ivory curule chairs, surrounded by a bevy of advisors, all whom were then ringed by the fierce looking praetorian guards in their black armor.

Joseph looked at Aliturius in amazement. He had not heard a sound, seen any motion and yet the chamber was now suddenly filled with the mass of royalty's entourage, comprising guests and senators. It was as if they had appeared magically, wished into existence by Nero. Aliturius motioned to him to remain silent. Now was not the time to ask questions.

"Aliturius, patron of the arts, shining light of Rome, and his companions," the herald announced solemnly grunting somewhat unapprovingly as he referred to the three Judeans without names.

Rising from his chair, Nero propped himself on the first step of the dais. His torso was stocky and the thickness between his head and shoulders passed for a neck. He looked liked he could have been a wrestler, rather than a ruler, but nonetheless, there was an unmistakable air of regality about him. A ring of laurel leaves flaked in gold rested upon his tightly curled head of hair. Looking very much the the part, he was the king of kings, the Emperor of the western world.

Poppea remained seated, smiling politely at her visiting friend. She was attired elegantly in fine silk, sporting a multi-jeweled necklace that matched an equally elegant tiara. Her dark brown hair was coiled in several braids that sat atop her head leaving her beauty fully visible.

Nero outstretched his hands. "My good friend, how long has it been? Three months, perhaps four? I have missed you! Imagine my surprise when my servant told me you were waiting in the back hallways. If filled my heart with gladness and gave me the excuse I needed to dismiss some dreary and boring entourage from Cappodocia that was beseeching me as usual for more troops to protect them from the Armenians. How many more men must I place in the Pontus Region before these annoying people learn that they might actually need to defend themselves when attacked?

"It is a troubled area of the world, your Majesty. They look to you as a father, always there to protect his children."

"Yes, it is true," Nero agreed, "But this father has other children that also require his attention."

"And you will always do your utmost to protect all your children as is your legacy, Excellency."

"And you must not leave Rome without your presence for such long periods, Aliturius," Nero quickly glided back to the original topic. "There have been no others worthy of playing in the theatre Marcellus since you left."

"None but you of course, my Lord," Aliturius hastily interjected, "As if he had rehearsed this particular line many times before.

"So true but my modesty prevents me from mentioning such a thing. Perhaps you have a part for me in your next play?" Nero waited patiently for the reply.

"Great Caesar, you above all know how flattered and honored I would be to have you perform in one of my plays but you are also certainly aware of what a tremendous problem that would create for me.   You are too great an actor to be surrounded by mediocrity.   You would put me and my fellow thespians to shame.   The audience would cry out, "Aliturius is a sham.   He cannot act!" And they would boo and hiss me from the stage.   I would not be allowed to show my face in Rome again.   Such would be my fate."

Basking in the superfluous flattery of his friend, Nero barked a hearty laugh.   "Well put Aliturius.   I would not have it said that Nero damaged your reputation as a fine actor.   Perhaps a play where I was the only actor, then no one else's reputation would be damaged.   What do you think Aliturius?   A play with only one actor!"

"A brilliant idea, Excellency. Truly, unparalleled. No one has ever thought of it."

"What say you, Poppea?   Aliturius thinks it to be an excellent idea."

Poppea failed to respond, too preoccupied with the precious beads around her neck that she rolled between her fingers while she stared into the sun baked face of one of the three foreigners that stood before her.

"Is that not so, my dear?" Nero asked impatiently.

Awakening from her trance she cleared her throat.   "Is what not so, Majesty?"

"I asked what you thought of my starring in a one man performance.  It has never been done before."

"The people would be absolutely delighted, Majesty.   It would be an occasion that they would never forget.   History would remember it with accolades.   But that is for a future time.  Do you not think we should inquire of Aliturius whom these other gentlemen that he brought with him are? After all, he did obviously bring them here to meet with us.   Perhaps they have come on urgent and pressing business?"

"Forgive me Aliturius, my wife is absolutely right.   Please state your business with these gentlemen."

"These men…" Aliturius paused to clear his throat, "are emissaries from the province of Judea.   I have extended our Roman hospitality to them as is deserving since one whom hails from the Hasmonean household. As none of them speak any Latin, I have undertaken the task of being their spokesperson."   Aliturius motioned to Joseph to play along with the ruse and not let it be known that he understood perfectly what was being said.

"Why do they look like they've just stepped out of one of your plays?" Nero asked curiously.

"Nonsense," the Empress Poppea interceded quickly and dismissed her husband's concern.   "I believe they look just fine, Majesty.   Can you not recognize the elegant Hellenistic dress of our Eastern provinces?"

"Yes. Most certainly I do." Nero tried to cover up his lack of worldliness. "I merely was teasing my old friend."

"Do they speak Aramaic then, Aliturius?" Poppea asked excitedly.

Aliturius winced slightly before answering. "Yes, they do, Majesty."

The expression on Nero's face indicated that he was annoyed by his Empress once again upstaging him and playing games of which he could not take part.

Practicing a broken Aramaic, Poppea began to converse. "Welcome to our country. I hope that you will find Rome to your liking."

Upon hearing the Empress utter a familiar language, the three immediately began to chatter among themselves.

"We have found the city much to our liking and having met you this day has only made our journey far more pleasant," Joseph replied. "When they talk of your beauty back home, they cannot do you justice. Your eyes are of a green that only comes from the glittering stars that shine in the sea of night."

"What did he say, Aliturius? I could not make out everything he said. Something about my eyes, I think."

"Well, I couldn't understand any of it," Nero sounded disgruntled.

"This one is named Joseph ben Matthias, of the royal house of the Hasmoneans, my Lady. He has taken the liberty to say that your eyes sparkle like the stars of the night. I beg your indulgence, my lady, and hope you will forgive him his transgression of being so forward. It is just that in Judea they speak of your beauty but he was overwhelmed by the reality."

"Tell him that I am greatly flattered," Poppea shivered with delight. "I will forgive him his transgression. No, wait, I'll tell him myself."

"Can we get on with the order of business!" shouted Nero. "If all they wished to come to Rome for was a glimpse of my wife, then this audience is over with!"

Descending the short flight of steps, Aliturius conversed momentarily with Joseph, who in turn handed over a scroll that he kept concealed beneath his tunic. Aliturius had a replacement letter written in Greek and Hebrew when he learned that Joseph had lost all of his worldly goods during the shipwreck, including the letters from Damneus. As Jonathias had mentioned to Joseph, no one in Rome's officialdom actually cared who signed the documents as long as they had one on what appeared to be official paper. "This document," Aliturius began, "is the reason that these august men have come to Rome."

Joseph recounted the statements written within the scroll while Aliturius translated. "More than fifteen years ago, when Felix was procurator of Judea, he transported many of our most acclaimed men to Rome to be placed in custody. He did so to subdue the masses which had grown agitated by the denial of their civil rights. That time has long since passed and those prisoners whom were priests and not revolutionaries are still confined under house arrest here in Rome."

Nero stifled a loud yawn. "Tell this Joseph fellow, that if putting them under arrest the first time stopped the dissension within his country, then keeping them confined to these homes will only serve to continue the suppression of the agitators. Think of it as a precautionary measure."

Joseph already knew what Nero had said and was growing quite agitated while Aliturius translated, continuing the pretense that these Joseph knew no Latin at all. Joseph fought hard to keep his emotions in check, knowing that any display of emotion would eliminate any chance of success his mission had. So he bit his lip hard and forced himself to remain calm. Once more he pleaded for their release but this time trying a different angle. "These are old men, who do not have much longer to live. Let them die in the land of their birth. Let them touch again the soil of their youth so they can feel it once more before they lie buried beneath it. I beseech thee, great Nero, ruler of the mightiest empire in the world, show these men just a bit of the clemency for which you are renowned. Let men who are of no danger, find mercy in your justice."

His brow furled, Nero cast a penetrating look at his old friend that searched for an answer far below the veneer of the actor but he could not find any. "I don't know why you have become involved in these affairs, Aliturius? Is there some hidden aspect of your life that has drawn you to this fool's errand? I love you like a brother, but you are wasting my time with such trivial matters, especially for some group of silly foreigners that I still insist appear to be in costume. There are times you truly surprise me. Why not leave these men to their own kind. Honestly Aliturius, did they think they could simply ask and I would quake in my sandals and comply with their request. Please Aliturius…they haven't even brought me any gifts to try and win my favor. What were they thinking? More than that, what were you thinking?"

"If I may take liberty of speaking again on their behalf, Excellency? That wasn't an oversight. There are gifts awaiting their delivery to you, but there was a mishap along their voyage and the only person among their entourage that knew of which individuals were arranging the tribute was lost at sea. It will take them some time to identify through the community whom those people were, but there will be tribute, of that I can assure you."

The Emperor lowered himself back into his chair releasing a sigh of exasperation. "This entire episode tires me," he conceded. "Now these silly men must search through the Jewish population of Rome in order to find the gifts that were supposedly intended for me. You probably don't know that community Aliturius, but I do. If there was any tribute to be paid, I'm sure it is long gone by now. They thieve from their own kind. It is in their blood. I swear, Aliturius, if I did not know this was for real, I think this would be some outlandish comedy written by Vintinius that you were all playing as a prank upon me. Be done with them and don't get involved with these Jews. Trust me when I tell you that they are nothing but trouble."

Joseph was seething just beneath the surface but he continued the fight to subdue any trace of anger. He could not let his feelings escape, as he clenched his fists, digging his nails into the heel of his palms as he did so.

"I'm certain, Excellency that once they speak with the elders of their community they will be able to return with the tribute most swiftly.

"Don't be so gullible my friend. As I already told you, I have dealt with these Jews a long time. They are all the same, Aliturius. Heaven help us, there are a hundred thousand of them in this city, so I think I know them quite well. I'm telling you, right now there is one of them sitting smugly on a king's ransom somewhere in this city, knowing that the only lead to him is lost at the bottom of the sea and none will be the wiser that he has taken their treasure. Do you really think he's going to step forward and say to these three, 'here it is! I'm so glad you were able to find me!' No, I tell you, it will not happen. He will squirrel away that treasure so none will find it and take a long trip away from Rome so that none will find him either for a very long time. That is the nature of these people. As I said, it is in their blood. Much in the way that insurrection is second nature to them as well. Be rid of them while you can."

"My Lord, please, for my sake, will you not at least give these men the opportunity to plead their case further and present you with whatever gifts they can raise from the community in the near future. I gave them my word that I shall aid them." Aliturius humbled himself before the Emperor, bowing his head as he pleaded. "It will be myself that bears the shame of this entire episode because I will admit that in my haste, and perhaps in my foolishness as you have advised, I befriended these people because my heart is filled with Roman hospitality no matter who it is that seeks my aid. And in so doing I gave them my word that I would help them with their supplication to you, so that all men, no matter where they hail from will say Rome is generous and benevolent and as Rome is Nero, so too does the Emperor's kindness embrace all men."

"And so you did," Nero commented. "You said you would aid them and that you have done. They have had their meeting with the Emperor. You owe them nothing further."

"But it is my honour, your Majesty that is at jeopardy. My Roman pride as a man of my word. Who will ever trust Aliturius in the future, if I can't even keep a simple promise to a group of weary travelers?"

Nero's heart softened as his friend continued to plead on behalf of the Judeans. Whatever was the mysterious link between Emperor and actor, Joseph saw that Nero was wavering and retreating from his initial stance.

"Because it is you that has chosen to speak on their behalf I will think about their petition. I make no promises, Aliturius, but a man like yourself should not have his reputation damaged simply because you found it in your heart to show them mercy. But go now, this audience is over!"

"Wait," Poppea shouted to everyone's surprise. "Where are they to stay?"

Aliturius admitted that he had also provided them with lodging, another sign interpreted by Nero as his friend being too soft-hearted for his own good.

"That will not do!" Poppea scolded. "Tribute or no tribute, they are still foreign envoys and must be treated as such." Turning to Nero she explained, "One is even of the royal household of Judea. We have often given lodging to his kin. How could we ever explain that we turned a Hasmonean prince away? I insist that they have rooms provided in the palace. I will have my servants see to their care. But I also insist that you must remain in the palace as well, Aliturius. I will need your skills as an interpreter since you are familiar with their Aramaic tongue."

Nero began to object but upon seeing the determined expression upon the Empress's face he thought better of it and said nothing. "I've always been meaning to ask you Aliturius as to how you became so well versed in Aramaic." It was the first time that Nero raised suspicions regarding his favorite actor.

"It is no secret you Majesty. Your empire is so vast that it is now a must that anyone travelling to its eastern provinces speaks in the common tongues if they are intending to practice their trades. As much as it pleases me to perform in Rome for you Excellency, it is necessary that I perform everywhere in order to remain relevant."

"Yes, yes…of course," Nero agreed. Hand in hand the imperial couple descended from the dais and departed to another of the anterooms where they would entertain the cases of those bureaucrats whom were still waiting in long lines outside the chambers to have their grievances and petitions heard. The royal entourage followed close behind and when all had passed through the heavy brass doors, then the last of the Praetorian guards pulled them shut leaving Aliturius and his small party alone with a few of Poppea's palace servants. The chamberlain ushered the four of them to the living quarters of the palace, providing each with their own state room. Spacious and luxuriant, each room was the mirror image of the other, down to the minutest detail. Red velvet drapes hung heavily from gold plated rods. Small marble statues were evenly spaced along the mantle which bordered the four white plastered walls at roughly shoulder height. Aliturius was familiar with the history of these rooms. They were partly the legacy left behind by the Emperor Claudius. He liked repetitiveness. He was comfortable only when his surroundings were familiar. Some thought of him as being mentally slow in this regard, but those that understood him knew that his mind actually worked more efficiently than most, finding patterns by which to solve most problems. Patterns that most others overlooked and thereby condemned themselves to repeat their mistakes over and over again.

Entering into Aliturius's suite which was adjacent to his own, Joseph sat on the corner of the square bed frame. "That didn't go exactly as planned," he commented with a huge sigh of disappointment. "What do you think are my chances of obtaining release of the priests? Nero doesn't appear to be over eager to comply."

Sitting in a high backed chair that was positioned half way between the bed and the balcony, Aliturius gave the question a brief moment of contemplation prior to his answering. "I must admit, that Nero might actually be right. We may never find that money now, if it becomes known that your traveling companion was the only one given the identity of which men were responsible for its safekeeping, even though we are pretty certain of who it is. But if our involvement becomes known, then it will get back to Damneus and jeopardize both our missions. Even if you raised it separately, without our involvement, it would likely become an issue of the money already being spent, and that being the case the Sanhedrin would be too embarrassed to pursue it. They would never expose themselves in a Roman civil court to decide iniquities among our own people. So, if we're looking for success through Nero, I would have to say your chances are not favorable."

"So what you're saying is that the mission is doomed then," Joseph sighed again.

"I didn't say that," Aliturius corrected him quickly. "I just said that Nero would not likely be too quick in releasing the priests. The Empress, on the other hand, just as we had said earlier, will be far easier to deal with."

"Again you refer to matters I do not understand."

Slapping his knees in frustration, Aliturius proceeded to explain. "I swear by the Almighty, you are thick sometimes. You may be the Chosen One, but you're not too swift when the choosing happens to be done by the women of this world, are you boy!"

"What are you implying?"

"Egad boy, have you ever taken a good look at yourself in a mirror."

"I try not to concern myself with appearances," Joseph responded. "It would be a sin if one loses sight of what is important and only focuses on their own petty issues."

"Who told you that crap," Aliturius challenged him. "Obviously someone worried that you'd be spending all your time beating off the women. I'd be after you myself if I knew you were of that persuasion."

"You're actually suggesting that I can influence the Empress based on my appearance?"

"I guarantee that if you looked in a mirror, you would see the same thing Poppea saw when you stood in front of her. She was practically undressing you with her eyes all the time you were standing there. Have you given any thought why you were selected for this mission, at all?"

"If I'm to believe you, it's because I'm your so-called Chosen One. But you didn't do the selecting. The Sanhedrin and Damnesus did, and they picked me because of my ability to speak Latin fluently and the fact that I had a good knowledge of the workings of Rome."

"Pardon my use of Greek but bullshit! You and a hundred

other people that come to mind in Jerusalem can speak fluent Latin and know Rome far better than you do because they've been here a dozen times. Trust me when I say, you are half way down the list in that case. Perhaps Damneus believes that you top the list, but the reality is that you still haven't realized it was Jeshua ben Gamaliel who proposed you in the first place and then made certain that you got selected."

"But why?"

"You're still not listening Joseph. Because Jeshua is the leader of our group and he had deduced that you are the Chosen One. Jeshua has followed your career to date. He's convinced you're the one to deliver us in our time of need, and so are many other influential people back in Jerusalem. All the signs are there. Even old Elias knew that you were the one. But there was more. We had discussed how best to succeed in achieving the release of the priests long ago and knew it would have to be through the Empress. Nero was never going to budge on the matter. Keeping the priests under house arrest provided him with a sense of security and control when it came to managing Judea. But Poppea, she is a creature with certain tastes one might say; specifically a taste for the budding fruits from the East. And guess what. You're that fruit!"

"No, you have that all wrong. I'm no one's budding fruit as you call it."

"Jeshua ben Gamaliel tends to disagree. He did enough polling of the young girls in Jerusalem to know that they're absolutely wild about you boy. If only you took your head out of your books you would have seen it too. So, if he says you're a budding fruit, yet to ripen, then I for one believe him. And seeing you in person, I have no doubts."

"This is insane! You have all gone mad! Are you all in on this together? I'm some fruit to be harvested? I'm surrounded by insanity!"

"Not insane! Enlightened! This is a different world we now live in. Women increasingly have an enormous amount of power and influence. Perhaps not yet in Jerusalem, but certainly here!"

"So what now," Joseph asked incredulously, "the Empress of Rome just suddenly summons for me and then picks my proverbial fruit. Is this what you all imagine? Is that how you expect it to happen? If it is, then I think you have all lost your way completely and aren't worthy to call yourself leaders. This is absolute lunacy!"

Joseph was growing steadily angrier with each passing comment. To even suggest that his only qualifications for this mission was the fact that among all the young legal minds of Judaea, his was the only one that combined beauty of body and had still remained untainted by sexual pleasure was too much to even contemplate.

"Mark my words, she will come for you. She hunts down virgins like a fox does chickens."

"I'm not a virgin!" Joseph lied in his defense.

"Jeshua ben Gamaliel says that you are. He should know!"

"How would he know? In fact, don't answer that, I don't really care. It's a matter of my going along with this and I realize this has been all one big joke to all of you. No wonder you were all so smug back at the inn. You all have been planning to offer my body to the Empress since the beginning of this entire mission like a piece of meat. Even when I think back to Damneus's words to me before I departed, I'm now certain he was in on this too in some way, even if he didn't know the full plan. Give me a good reason why I just don't leave Rome and wash my hands of all of you!"

Aliturius folded his arms across his chest and through some theatrical means that Joseph could only guess at, appeared to grow in size and stature before his very eyes. "If you want one word, then 'pride'. If I was to give you two words, they'd be 'pride and destiny'. It is not in your nature to accept failure and whether you're willing to admit it or not, you know that you're destined for greatness. The only obstacle in your way is yourself. You can either think of what might occur as you're being sullied and taken advantage of by a woman of insatiable lust and greed, or you can view it as one of the greater conquests you will make during your passage through life. You, a mere mortal from an insignificant corner of the empire, climbing atop the most powerful woman in this world and striking a blow for every citizen in Judea. Think of it! For over a hundred years they've had us bend over and rammed us up our backsides. Now you can do it to them at the highest pinnacle of their echelon. If you can't take pleasure in that, then at least let the rest of us take pleasure in the thought."

"I don't know how you did that?"

"Did what?"

"Make me feel guilty for not wishing to let myself be used as a sex toy." Joseph shook his head in disbelief that he was even considering going through with it. "But mark my words, I have no intention of having this turn into some long standing relationship."

Aliturius laughed heartily, resuming the appearance of the doting grand-father that Joseph had first been introduced to. "I can assure you that certainly will not happen. Don't believe any of this has a serious vein. It never has, it never will. This is Rome after all. Morality has an entirely new definition in this city. Nero is always drunk, bedding women or young boys, and don't for a minute think that Poppea is any different. She has all the morals of an alley cat. The worry my boy, is you. Make certain that you don't start taking all of this too seriously because she certainly won't. When she summons you, you just have to keep her happy for the moment. Knowing her, there probably won't be a second opportunity."

"I can't believe that any of you can believe that God would sanction such a liaison."

"Perhaps it would be better if you think more of what God would have to say if you return to Jerusalem without his priests!"

"You don't understand," pleaded Joseph.

"Far better than you think. Even one of my persuasion has had to entertain the Empress from time to time. Not so easy for me but it has its rewards. Now that's acting!"

Joseph rose from the corner of the bed and began to pace around the room monotonously. He wondered why he was having such difficulty accepting the matchmaking that had gone on before he had even left Jerusalem. It wasn't even the fact that he was now required to perform like some trained monkey on the end of a leash. No, it wasn't that at all, he realized. It was the worry as to whether he could perform at all. Jeshua ben Gamaliel had been right all along. This was unknown territory, even to someone like himself that always felt he had the answers to everything. Look at Aliturius the voice in his head commanded. Take a look at Aliturius! Joseph convinced himself that if he could do it with Poppea, then anyone could.

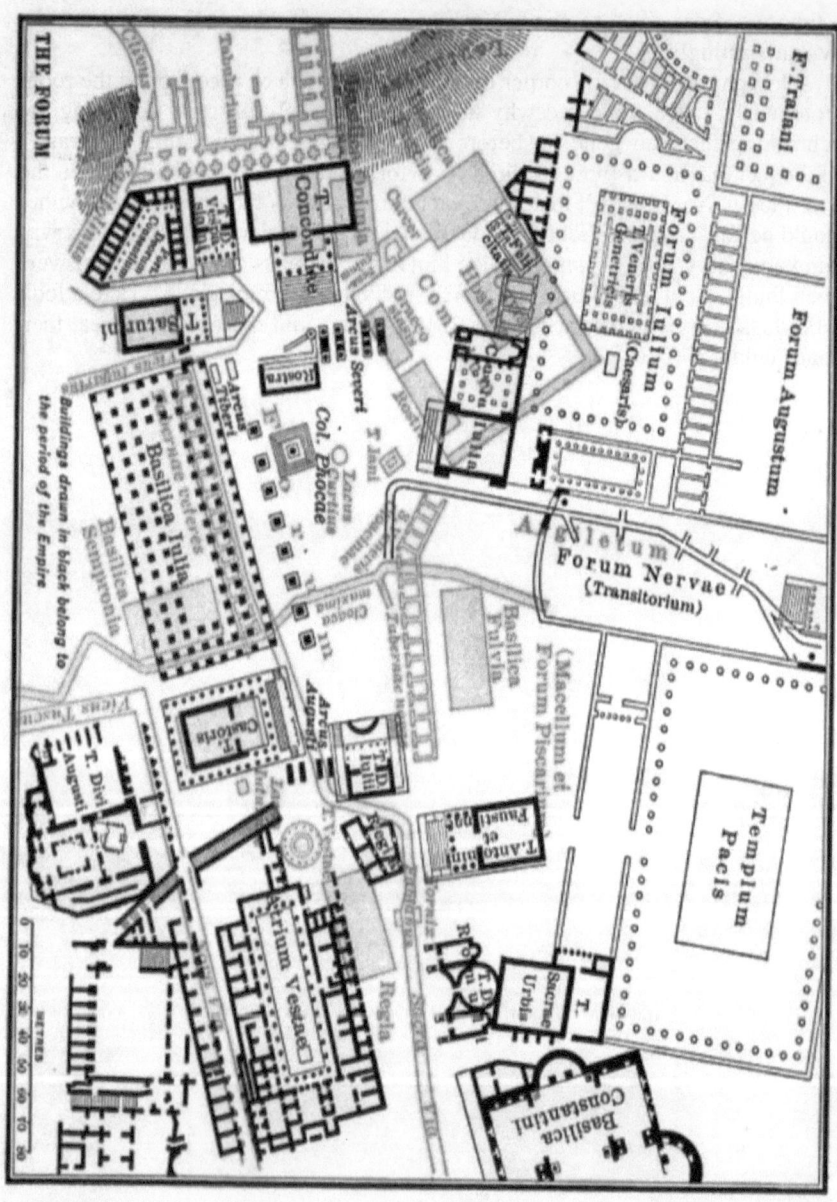

# CHAPTER THIRTEEN

## CAESAR'S PALACE; 63 A.D.

The four of them met in Joseph's suite later that afternoon to discuss their strategy. As they stood on the balcony with its panoramic view of the city, Aliturius tried desperately to talk about relevant issues but it was clearly evident that Joseph's mind was already a thousand miles away. He stared blankly at the crowds that filled the six forums that lay to the west of the palace. The din from each forum thundered like a thousand kettle drums beating beneath the stroke-master's club. He could feel his temples pulsating with each blow, the sound of blood rushing through his veins and ringing in his ears. The clamour of Rome was overwhelming his senses until he felt as if his head was about to explode.

In the streets below the peddlers hocked their wares and the shopkeepers kept a stern eye on their merchandise, careful to guard their produce from the swift hands of the street urchins that buzzed about everywhere like flies around a dung heap.

Aliturius put his arm around Joseph's shoulder and attempted to console his young companion. "Yes, it is a lot to take in and I don't think one ever really grows accustomed to it." He pointed towards the basilica where there were hordes of people seemingly milling about aimlessly with no actual purpose, explaining to his Judean friends that Hurlian, the people's favorite barrister was defending a very prominent client that belonged to the publicans and that's why they had gathered. The trial hadn't yet started but the word on the street was that it would end in yet another acquittal for Hurlian. "Look over there," Aliturius diverted their attention to the north. At the furthest end of the imperial forum, the people were gathering to watch a young man dressed in full battle armor race from the city in his quadriga, a chariot pulled by four coal black stallions. "See that man," he continued. "That is the tribune, Titus. I can tell you now that that name will one day be echoed throughout the empire. Right now he's about to return to Germania, where he's to assume total control of the provincial government. Meanwhile, his father Vespasian is in charge of the forces mopping up in Britannia. You won't find two more capable commanders anywhere, not to mention two more powerful men when they combine their forces. Nero is well aware of that. That is why he continues to send them both as far away as possible from Rome. When it comes to self preservation, the Emperor is no man's fool."

"I take it that the army doesn't love their Emperor," Jacob postulated.

"It works the other way as well. With Nero it certainly can be said that he doesn't love his army. That's why he relies so heavily on his Praetorians, and forbids any other standing armies within the confines of the city. He's learned his lessons well from those that came before him. Armies will make an Emperor, or they'll bring about his downfall. Best to keep them as far away as possible."

"So who does love him, then?" Joseph finally broke his silence.

"The people," Aliturius advised. "Nero's popularity stems from the very people he rules over. He gives them what they want. Bread, games, baths; especially the baths. You'll see that soon. By late afternoon the streets will be empty and everyone will have gone to the public baths. Nero has been responsible for some of the finest bath houses in Rome. Even more luxuriant than the ones that Tiberius built. The people marvel at the baths. Halls paved with marble. Walls of creamy alabaster, brought all the way from the deserts of Arabia. Orange marble with green veining from North Africa. Lucullan marble from Melos and the polished glass-like marble from the islands off the coast. They are the most extraordinary buildings you can lay your eyes upon and he gifted them to the people. And the people know that they have been given a gift of unparalleled value. They love their baths, with hot and cold water flowing from the mouths of silver cows and clay molded virgins. Rich, poor, they all come together in one place and the words upon their lips are ones of praise for Nero. That is where the Emperor's strength lays."

Jacob was awed by what Aliturius had to say but still remained focused on the military. "So, he's got an army he doesn't trust, but an entire population of citizenry that adores him. I'd sooner have the army behind me than the unruly masses."

"Nero considers himself to be a patron of the arts, and architecture, and all things urbane. His strength is grounded in the Subura, the area of the common man. He knows he will never have the support of the military. Even Julius Caesar appreciated the strength of the Subura even though he did have the love of his soldiers under Marc Antony. But in the end, just remember that didn't keep him from being assassinated."

At that moment there was a gentle rapping upon Joseph's door. Still withdrawn into his own thoughts Joseph ignored the gentle tapping but Aliturius responded and let the three men enter. Each servant carried a full wardrobe of clothes that they spread out across the bed. "From the Empress Poppea," stated the chief steward, "to the Judean envoy, Josephus Matthias, gifts for you while you stay in Rome." Without even looking at Joseph, the three men wheeled about and were gone from the room.

Finally Joseph's attention was drawn away from the balcony and was now focused on the delivered gifts as he began to finger through the pile of clothing. "I've never seen so many outfits of such quality. There must be at least a dozen outfits here."

Not in the least bit surprised, Aliturius offered Joseph with his assessment. "I would consider it a possibility that your stay in Rome will be longer than we may have anticipated, judging by the amount of clothes Poppea has sent you. The Empress has    definitely made it clear that she expects to see you more than once."

Ignoring the insinuation, Joseph continued to flick through the vast mountain of clothes. Before he could even comment further, there was another rap upon the door and this time Jacob proceeded to open it.

"Must be driving the guard outside crazy that he can't see what we are doing in here," Jacob hinted.    "Probably wants to insist again that we keep the door open."    But when he opened the door, it was not the posted sentry at all, but instead    one    of    the    maid    servants    to    the    Empress.    They    all waited patiently for her to say something but not a single word was forthcoming.

"Well girl, spit it out!," Aliturius ordered.    "Do you have something to say or not?    Get on with it!"

She stepped inside the room, sealing the door from prying ears behind her. "I beg your pardon, Master Aliturius, but the message I am bearing is for the one called Joseph alone."

"I'm his translator girl. If you have a message for him then you better tell me.    Let's hear it!"

The maidservant appeared nervous.    She did not want to disobey a direct order from her mistress but what Aliturius said made sense. "The Empress Poppea has requested the presence of the one called Joseph within her chambers within an hour's time.    She has something of grave importance to discuss with him."

"But he'll need his translator there as well if that is the case," Aliturius insisted.

"No," she replied bluntly.    "Only the one called Joseph is to attend.    She was very clear on that."

"Return to your mistress," Aliturius commanded.    "You have delivered your message and it has been received.    He will attend her shortly."

The girl bowed and exited from the room almost as quickly as she had entered.

The old thespian smirked at his colleagues, especially at Joseph.    "Most impressive.    The    Empress    has    requested    that    she    see    you    in    her chambers.    She's not wasting any time. Very impressive indeed!    Not even here a full day and already she's requested you for a private audience.    I believe that must be a new record as far as I'm aware.  You better pick one of these tunics she sent you and get ready. Come on boys; let's give Joseph here some privacy to get himself together.    He has a very important mission ahead of him."    With one last wink and Aliturius was out the door followed immediately by the others, leaving Joseph to wait pensively for the next knock upon the door.

---

The path through the corridors to Poppea's chambers seemed endless as Joseph followed closely behind the same maidservant that had now returned to retrieve him.   Not a single word exchanged between the two as they walked together as Joseph maintained the facade that he spoke no Latin.   As he moved through the labyrinth, he tried vainly to convince himself that his journey would soon be coming to an end, in spite of what Aliturius had to say to the contrary regarding his alluding to multiple visits with the Empress.   But each time he'd attempt to convince himself it would be so, he was haunted by Aliturius's taunting smile telling him that it would be a long, long time before he ever laid eyes on Judea again.

Upon arriving at the Empress's quarters, he was left standing alone at the center of a huge hallway that ran between two immense, richly decorated rooms that were practically mirror images of each other.   At the farthest end of the hall he could just make out the distant image of Poppea in her salon, surrounded by three maidservants.   She lay on a low couch wearing a blue gown held by a single shoulder strap snugly belted about her exceedingly tiny waist. He watched, quite fascinated, while two of her servants washed and pedicured her toes.   The third servant's role appeared to involve continuously scenting her body with fragrant perfumes.   The girls giggled as she waved them away with a flick of her hand.   Joseph had not even realized that he had been moving steadily closer the entire time that he had been watching, drawn by an invisible magnet.   As soon as the girls had disappeared from view, she looked at him and inhaled slowly.

"I am so glad that you came," she stumbled over the words in Aramaic; correcting herself each time when she recognized she made an error in pronunciation.   "You are probably wondering why you are here."

"I am honored that one so worthy has actually bothered to make time for one like myself of so little significance."

"Oh that is good!   Humility!   You have been schooled well.   I'm certain that Aliturius has had a hand in your education.   He can be such a gossip at times!"

"Your highness…?"

"Oh, let's be forthright with each other," she protested.   "Ever since Aliturius brought you into the throne room, I have thought of little else.   I'm a very straightforward woman, no?" she laughed enticingly.   She didn't wait for an answer.   "Why shouldn't I be?   I'm the Empress of Rome.   Anything I want, I get.   Do you understand?   For the time being, you have captivated my interest."

"I am honored," Joseph responded, pretending that he did not comprehend the full meaning and intimation of her words.

"Most others wouldn't even have dared appear before us offering us not a single gift.   And with such great demands too!   Such audacity!   Unheard of!   But when I saw your face, the noble contour of your nose and mouth, the light that shone from your eyes, I actually understood how you could be so brazen.   There really was a gift being offered and that gift was you.   I want to open that gift. I want to peel back the layers of wrapping and revel in the surprise concealed within. I want to explore why it is that you seem so different from the others. I want to help you."

"I am flattered by the attention that the Empress has extended towards my cause," Joseph found his voice faltering as he tried to speak.

"How flattered are you?"

"I don't understand," Joseph excused himself.

"You said you are flattered by my attention, so tell me why," she demanded to know.

Clearing his throat, Joseph attempted to answer. "Having gazed upon your indescribable beauty, I find that it has given me all the encouragement I need so that I will not falter in my mission." Joseph tried desperately to sound official in his answers while still letting Poppea know that he fully understood why he was there.

Poppea purred softly. "I believe the gift of flattery is all yours. How beautiful am I, Josephus? I will call you Josephus from now on. It sounds so much more Roman." She knew from his obvious discomfort that she had found a flower in its first bloom, succulent, fragrant, never before basking in the rays of the sun. She was enjoying herself devilishly well. "I'm sorry, I didn't quite hear you."

"If beauty be the rose colored clouds of the sunset, or the laughter of a young child running through the tall grass, then by far you exceed all these in the name of beauty."

"My, my… you do have the gift of the poet. You do know how to flatter a woman. And I love to be flattered. Why is it you men from the east seem to innately know the right things to say? I must make it a point of finding out how you do that. You must tell me everything there is to know about your land."

"I would not know where to begin. There would be so much to tell. It would require a lifetime…" Now he had done it, he realized his comment could be taken out of context. He tried to suppress his final words, but it was too late. They had already left his lips before he had a chance to retract what he was saying. He had just given Poppea an excuse for detaining him in Rome for as long as she pleased.

"Oh, I am so glad that you will try," she smiled pleasantly. "I have always harbored a fascination for your part of the world. So harsh, so brutal, and yet you appear so civilized!" Almost as if in response, she began rubbing her hand up and down the length of her body as she imagined how alluring the East could be. "That is why I have made such an effort to learn Aramaic. It is more than a passing interest." She pursed her lips to emphasize her commitment. "Aliturius knows. And I know all about his origins as well. It is our little secret. My husband still believes him to be Athenian."

Closing his eyes, Joseph wondered what he was to do now. He was trapped in her little game of cat and mouse and Poppea most certainly was a very hungry cat.    He thought about what Aliturius had to say to him, advising not only to play the game but to win.    To play on behalf of everyone in Judea that was now dependent upon him.

It was then that Poppea motioned for him to sit beside her, patting the couch invitingly.    He sat down somewhat awkwardly, twisting his body so that he was half on, half off of the cushions.    There was the slightest hint of a scowl, fleeting as it may have been across Poppea's face as she watched his attempt to try and maintain a safe distance between the two of them.

"Tell me about yourself," she inquired.

"A man, like most others," he answered    "Nothing special."

"Even Aliturius is a man," she frowned.    "Not much of one but he's still able to perform when necessary, despite his inadequacies.    Are you suggesting that all men from your country are similar?"    She sighed with an air of disappointment.    "How disheartening."

Joseph shook his head in denial.    He wasn't certain what he should say at that moment, only that the thought of himself and Aliturius being cut from the same cloth made him shudder.

"Good!" she exclaimed with a robust enthusiasm. "I was positive that my intuition about you wasn't wrong."    Sliding across the couch she forced herself up against Joseph's quivering body.    "Now isn't that much better?" she cooed. "I want you to treat me like a woman from Judaea.    Ravage me like a hungry sheikh wanting to taste the pleasures of his harem."

Joseph failed to move, his limbs had grown rigid, which only served to render Poppea even more excited as she realized she had been right about his being a virgin as well.

"Am I not appealing to you?" she drew her lips into a heart rendering pout.

"Too much I'm afraid." He felt panic stricken but there was nowhere to run.    "I shouldn't be feeling this way about you.    It is wrong.    You are the Empress of Rome!"

Reaching through the cloth of his tunic, she felt the imprint of his member and then squeezed it gently.    It came alive in her hand, forcing itself fully into the cup of her fingers until it began prying them apart through the sheer size of its swelling.    Poppea licked her lips, excited by the enormity of his penis.

"Your body betrays you Josephus," she smiled devilishly. "It says this is very right!"

"No! This isn't right!    You are the Empress of Rome.    You are the wife of Nero," he bleated knowing that any refusal on his part could result in his death.

Poppea gave a wicked laugh.    "It is a marriage in name only.    And even so, it is an institution of man's invention."    She gripped his member more tightly as if punishing him for even mentioning Nero at that moment."I am still a free woman, to do as I please.    You wouldn't want to upset me now while I hold your manhood within my power, now would you?"

Joseph found her argument most persuasive, especially since he desired to return to Judea with all his appendages intact.     She licked away the cold sweat that beaded on his brow.

"Do you fear me so?" she asked with childlike innocence.

"You are everything a man could desire and more.     But you are also an Empress.     Even if it is only a marriage in name only, if caught, I would still most certainly be served up to your lions in the arena."

Poppea laughed delightedly.     "Is that all that is bothering you?     Don't worry.     My chambers are always locked from within.     They were locked the moment you set foot in the corridor.     No one comes in and no one goes out unless I say so.     I assure you, this room is sealed from prying eyes and wagging tongues.     Does that make you feel better?"

Joseph nodded silently as the sweat still beaded on his forehead.

Sensing his capitulation, Poppea pulled her dress down to her waist, exposing her silken flawless torso.     Joseph's eyes were transfixed upon her glowing body.     She cupped her hands about her firm, round breasts and lightly squeezed her dark, erect nipples.     "Are these the breasts of an Empress, or are they merely the tender white breasts of a woman filled with passion?" Placing his limp hands upon her firm bosom, she began moving them seductively across her soft, pale flesh.     Closing her eyes, an alluring smile upon her lips, she moaned softly at his caress, encouraging him to gently tantalize her engorged nipples until it was no longer necessary to support his hands any longer. The gown fell from her waist, allowing the delicately scented essence of her being to flow freely down the inside of her thighs.     He inhaled the sweetness of her flesh and his hands strengthened in their resolve, as they lay side by side, filling the full length of the sofa.     Everywhere he looked, he found the thinnest of gold bands, about her wrists, her ankles, neck and waist.     They shimmered brightly in the soft light from the oil lamps, accentuating her nakedness.     She kissed him firmly upon his lips as her one hand pulled up the hem of his tunic so that she could release the full length of his member.     She laughed excitedly as she kneaded it towards its maximum potential.     Any trace of resistance was now long suppressed and the fingers of Joseph's right hand explored excitedly between Poppea's legs, searching,     circling     and     continually     moving     into     new     recesses     of unexpected pleasure.

Joseph felt as if he had been reborn.     A dimension now added to his life that he was not even aware had existed previously but from which he could no longer restrain himself. Poppea was certainly aware of this metamorphosis in her sexual partner and allowed her body to respond freely to the touch of his hands. Pulling herself on top of his prone body, her pelvis rubbed enticingly against his as her body swayed with ritual precision. Her limbs shook to his every thrust, her hips expanded upwards to meet his.     She felt his passion released within her, his years of self restraint cast into purgatory as he drove forward.     Riding upon a whirlwind of     insurmountable     fury,     she     laughed     and     chattered     feverishly, uncontrollably, unintelligibly.     This was hers, all hers; a vein of untapped pure energy that she personally had discovered and unleashed. She wanted to possess it, control it, keep it forever! She rode upon the swell of the storm until they both fell frantically into the oblivion of wild ecstasy.

# CHAPTER FOURTEEN

## WHANGAREI; PRESENT

"Nothing to say?" I prodded Pearce.

"Geez, it's hot in here."

"Your right, I'll open the window." I went over to the window and slid it back. The cooler air hit my face and had an immediate effect.

"So?" I pressed him.

"What do you want me to say?" he responded peevishly.

"How about, I guess I can understand how he might have a chance to secure the release of the priests, when no one was able to do it for twelve years prior," I suggested.

"So he does get the priests released?"

"I didn't say that. I just suggested he had a better chance of doing it."

"Using this different type of diplomacy?"

"I think that kind of diplomacy has been going on since the dawn of time. Who's to say how much of history has been shaped by the woman behind the man or on top of the man, depending on the perspective. Helen of Troy was more than just a pretty face."

Pearce thought about it for a moment. "End justifies the means type stuff."

"I think that's how Josephus ultimately saw it. It wasn't going to happen any other way. Even he admits in his memoirs, that when his ship went down he pretty much lost any chance of freeing the priests. After all, he lost all his documents, friends and most of all, his connections. He describes his success as depending on his wiles. I guess that was just a polite way of covering up what really happened. The term wiles can be interpreted in a lot of different ways. So Josephus wasn't covering up as much as he was playing with words."

Pearce thought that was quite amusing as I detected a little chuckle on his part. I guess he had a different view of what Josephus was doing.

"You know, Doc, that's what I love about your family's history. No matter what century you're talking about, nothing's really different from right now. It's like your entire family is caught on instant replay. There's always something to do with a male-female relationship that determines the outcome of history."

"And that is why most say that history repeats itself," I reminded him. "It really does!"

"Yeah, I guess you're right. But you would know, with GLEEM and all."

"It's true. I'm telling you, we think we're unique, but in reality, we're merely repeating what has gone on before. It's unavoidable. We're hardwired and you can't change the programming. Personally, I think we only delude ourselves by thinking we can."

"That's pretty fatalistic."

"Listen John, it's a difficult pill to swallow that history is cyclic. After all, everything we learn tells us that it's progressive, but think about it," I raised my hands in an open gesture of supplication to him. "You remember what I told you about evolution?"

"About survival of the weirdest rather than the strongest," he recalled.

"I don't think I described it exactly in that way. But that was the basic principle."

"What about it?"

"Well, there was more. Evolution is an accelerator. It allows a species to speed up its development by making quantum leaps. So a species like man can go from a tree swinging orangutan like creature five million years ago, to Homo sapiens a mere hundred thousand years ago."

"Four million, nine hundred thousand years doesn't seem to be a major quantum leap in my books," Pearce scoffed thinking he had the better of me.

"Take a better look," I advised him. Five million years ago, an orangutan. Three million years ago an Australopithecus. One million years ago a Hominid or what we'd call a man-ape. Five hundred thousand years ago, Homo *erectus*. Three hundred thousand, Homo *habilus*. Two hundred thousand, Neanderthal. One hundred thousand, Homo *sapiens*. Do you see what's happening, the changes are coming faster and faster. Evolution is making these huge leaps as I mentioned. And the time period between these changes is getting shorter and shorter. So why then, does it take ninety thousand years for Homo *sapiens* to go from a forager to creating his first civilization? Something doesn't add up. The interval is too long, considering how fast we were developing as a species. Civilization should have taken place long before the ice age. After all, we know Neanderthal already practiced primitive religious rites. To have a concept of religion necessitates a well developed imagination. It requires the ability to think ultra-dimensionally. And as soon as you can do that, you have the heart and soul required for civilization building."

"But everyone knows that didn't happen until mankind was able to harvest crops and domesticate animals around five thousand B.C.," Pearce reminded me, pulling out the typical Grade School fact sheet that everyone stores in their mind from their Grade 8 social studies class.

"Well, if that's so, then how do you explain that the city of Jericho has been calculated to be ten thousand years old? Or that the sphinx shows water marks from a flood that occurred nine thousand years ago. Then again, there are the man made pylons at Baalbek that are determined to be over ten thousand years old. The list goes on and on. Sure, we may date our history from 5000 B.C.E., but what if that's only because whatever had come before had been wiped out and mankind had to start all over again?"

"That theory has been done to death," Pearce commented. "No one has been able to show any tangible proof of an earlier civilization. We would have dug up some evidence of it by now."

"Oh, what I just mentioned doesn't send off any alarm bells. We're already talking about a three or four thousand year discrepancy. Who says it can't even be more? Maybe we have dug up the facts," I hinted, "but we just don't realize it. You know how the human mind works. If we're told that nothing existed before seven thousand years ago, then in all likelihood, anything that was dug up would be placed within that existing time frame because to do otherwise would invite ridicule. No one wants to be ridiculed for their findings and we even know now that Kathleen Kenyon intentionally lied about the dating of her excavations."

"Perhaps?" was all that Pearce could say.

"Probably would be a better answer, but then what else is new. Some of mankind's greatest discoveries were founded in the face of ridicule and adversity."

"But without scientific proof, you're not about to change anyone's way of thinking," Pearce argued.

"Proof is always the difficult part," I admitted. "Long in coming, but once it's here, stand back because there will be a heck of a lot of changes made. But here's an interesting tidbit of information. Not so long ago they did some tests on those Jews that claimed to have descended from the twenty-four houses that served the position of High Priesthood. Particular attention was paid to the Y chromosome since the priesthood is based on a male to male descent. And you know what they found...?"

"I'm certain you're going to tell me," Pearce said unabashedly.

"Of course! They found a particular set of genes that were unique to the descendants of the high priesthood. There really was a remarkable correlation between the test results and the word-of-mouth from father to son over the years. Almost two thousand years since the destruction of the Temple and yet the oral traditions have been preserved with practically no hint of falsification by any other families."

Pearce didn't appear overly impressed. "There's more to this, isn't there?" he guessed correctly.

"Yes, much more," I advised. "Hey, it's no big deal for a Mideastern culture to preserve its history through oral tradition. After all, the bible went unwritten for half a millennium and it survived. And in families like mine, the descent issue has been preserved from time immemorial. So obviously, that's not the point I'm trying to make here. How long do you think it takes to develop a distinct gene locus on a chromosome?"

"I don't know", Pearce shrugged. "A long time, I guess."

"Try a little harder," I urged.

"Ten thousand years," he stabbed at an answer.

"Wrong! Try a quarter of a million."

"Okay, a quarter of a million. So what does that mean?"

"That means our concept of civilization's time line is incorrect," I told him. Because the Y chromosome is passed on intact from father to son, no exchange of material with the maternal side, it in fact is a living museum of the first ancestral male parent."

"Okay..." John leaned forward a little more interested now.

"So if it takes a quarter of a million years going backwards to see where there was a divergence of a gene set, then it means that we priests, those like myself, have a direct uninterrupted male lineage all the way back to this ancestral parent that by our understanding of history was or should have been nothing more than a Neanderthal or other primitive type cave man."

"I still don't see the point."

"If my family lines were created only three thousand years ago, during the Exodus, then my Y chromosome should be no different from anyone else's that left Egypt at that time. We would have been just a typical Joe Blogs that happened to attain a high quality job that we passed down to our children. But the fact was we were already genetically different from the average person when we took on the job of Israelite High Priest. So different in fact, that for the couple of hundred thousand years prior, we were keeping ourselves distinct from the mainstream populations and didn't allow ourselves to diffuse among them, nor go a generation without male offspring. So that by the time 1200 BCE rolled around, everyone already knew that Aaron and his relatives were of a different order of magnitude."

"Which meant that he wasn't the start of something new, but at that time the end of something that had already been going on for tens of thousands of years," Pearce processed my statements.

"Exactly," I shouted. "Everyone gets these chromosome kits and from it they can say you're a distinct haplotype, or have a unique set of SNPs which they link with other people having similar results and say you're a family. So for example, you take the Kohenim, and they'll report perhaps two dozen different lines that they say represent all the Aaronic families. But we know those differentiations happened long after Aaron lived. And if we were to suggest that every mutation only occurred after several generations, then for even a simple change to show up as a divergence, it would require a couple of hundred years to occur. Now imagine all those mutations over twenty-four different distinct lines and try to trace them back to a singularity before even the first mutation occurred. That takes you back tens of thousands of years, exactly as you just said."

"SNPs?"

"Single nucleotide polymorphism," I explained. "So you understand that our DNA strands consist of nucleotides which are assembled in a specific order. And we've given these nucleotides letters like G, C, T, A or U for the amino acid they consist of. So as soon as one of these nucleotides is replaced by a different letter, we have a mutation and a branching from the original genotype. If most of your SNPs match to the original bloodline, so to speak, then you are descended from that family."

"Aha, I think I've got it," Pearce had a Eureka moment. "You're saying that there are too many of these mutations to among all the families identified as High Priests to have descended directly from Aaron. And if that's true, then the original genetic sequence had to have begun much earlier, and Aaron was just one of the many branches on the original family tree."

"Now you got it!" I exclaimed. "Aaron and his children may have been the Chief High Priests of the Tabernacle, but there were already other related families that were still considered as High Priests but not in the top position. They may have assisted Aaron's family or else they served in conducting religious services in town and village temples. But the bottom line was that they were still High Priests and they all descended from the same common ancestor that Aaron descended from and that ancestor was thousands of years before any of them. But we already knew that since the Bible mentions that Korah considered himself to be on an equal standing with Aaron and wanted the Chief High Priest position for his own family. So our view of civilization being only this short period of seven thousand years does not take into account that we already had families that existed at this so-called 'Dawn of Civilization' time with predetermined and designated hereditary functions.

Aaron was the culmination of some form of primitive hierarchy and order that had existed for eons. Then again, maybe it was not so primitive. And it had to have been set up when there were very few people in existence, otherwise there would have been no way that the order could have keyed in on a single gene profile. It would have been diluted right from the onset had they picked a few people at random to fill whatever position it may have been those tens of thousands of years earlier."

"Which means...?"

"Which means John that what they taught you in school was someone's best guess that got turned into gospel. But rather than correct the error they just continued teaching it and piling more and more layers on top of it."

Pearce tapped the side of his head with his forefinger. "I get it now. You're saying human history had a reset button pressed maybe five thousand years ago and we have forgotten everything that came before it."

"I wouldn't go as far as saying everything, but certainly what we think is our history is full of error and incorrect conjecture."

"So what's this all got to do with sex as diplomacy?"

"In case you haven't noticed, history is all about sex! How else could I even be be referring to genetic lines?"

---

# CAESAR'S PALACE: 63 A.D.

Slipping quietly into his chamber in the early hours of the morning, Joseph swore that he would never say a single word to his companions about what had occurred, even if they had waited anxiously throughout the night to hear of his encounter with the Empress. Fortunately, they had finally given up and went to sleep when he failed to return even in the latter hours of the evening. Without taking the time to remove his tunic, he lunged into his bed and buried his face within the tasseled pillow exhausted.

He awoke the next morning to find his companions standing beside his bed side, hovering over him like vultures over a carcass.

"Well?" Jacob let the question linger as they eagerly awaited an answer.

"Well, what?" Joseph replied groggily, still not fully awake.

"Did you achieve anything?" Jacob demanded to know, though the question was more an appeal to know the details rather than the results. There was no answer forthcoming. "Hello...? I asked you a question!"

"Go away," Joseph's muffled voice surfaced through the duck down of the pillow.

"No, we will not go away!" Jacob refused to comply. "We will stay here and bellow all morning long in your ears until they're ringing unless you tell us what we want to hear."

"I am very tired, and feeling drained, and all I ask of you is that you let me sleep away the morning," Joseph complained. "Is that too much to ask for?"

"Tell us what we want to hear and we'll let you sleep," Jacob bargained.

Pulling himself into a sitting position, Joseph acknowledged the presence of his companions for the first time since his return to the room. "You're not going to go away, are you?" They shook their heads in reply. "Well then, I'll tell you what happened. So here it is. Listen carefully as I'm only going to say this once. The Empress has decided to make Josephus my official name while I stay in Rome. She thinks it is more befitting for a friend of the Empress to have a Roman sounding name.

"And...?

"And what? That's it! Now let me sleep."

"You know what we want to hear," Jacob insisted that there was more to the story.

"If you mean about the priests, she promised to look into it!?"

"That's not it either," Jacob shook his head but it was obvious to the others that Joseph was not going to say another word.

Sensing that prodding Joseph any further was only going to create a conflict, Aliturius interrupted in order to calm the situation. "Do not worry my friends. The Empress is as good as her word. When Poppea says she will look in to the matter, then I can assure you that she will. She never forgets to repay a favor," Aliturius winked slyly at Joseph, knowing full well that the Empress only made promises if she was totally satisfied..

"But what about the favor?" Jonathias jumped on the mention of the word, disappointed that Aliturius wished to draw the conversation away from what really mattered, as far as both he and Jacob were concerned.

Joseph stared into Jonathias's inquisitive eyes with a countenance that quickly froze any thoughts by the others of having fun at his expense.

"Well, I think a little celebration is due here. I can't say for certain how Poppea will do it, but I do know she will deliver them at some point in the future . And I know it's still the morning but I believe we deserve a little celebration on Joseph's success. I just happened to have two magnificent bottles of sacred wine, directly from my cellar in the synagogue waiting for us in my chambers. I suggest you drag yourself out of that bed Joseph, or should I say Josephus, and come to my room.

All of them followed Aliturius into his chambers where he uncorked the bottles, one at a time. He then raised the wide rimmed spout to his lips and took a swig. Passing the bottle into Jacob's outstretched hands, he invited him to do likewise. "There's nothing like a little consecrated wine to celebrate with, eh fellows?"

"Not my usual breakfast," Joseph was not too sure about drinking this early in the day.

As the sun continued to climb overhead, the four of them sang and drank themselves into a drunken afternoon slumber. Any work of value on their parts that day would have to wait until the evening at the earliest.

---

With their heads feeling like mill stones, weighing heavily upon stiff and aching necks, their temples pounding to the point that they were ready burst, the four of them struggled valiantly to rise from wherever they had fallen during their drunken stupor.

"What the hell," Jacob complained. "What kind of sacred wine was that?"

"Elias may have let it age a little too long," Aliturius guessed.

"You think?" Jacob responded incredulously.

"Good thing you never got a chance to serve that to your congregation or you'd all be stumbling through the streets and getting arrested," Joseph warned.

"Yes, I believe it would have been a bit of an embarrassment," Aliturius admitted.

Pulling himself off the divan on which he sat, Jonathias dragged himself over to where Joseph lay. "Joseph, we need to talk," he said fairly quietly, more so because the sound of his own voice made him wince in pain.

"I think we are talking, cousin," Joseph was suspicious of what would come next.

"There is the matter which I need to discuss with you urgently."

"Surely, it can wait until late morning," Joseph attempted to delay their conversation.

"What do you mean?  It's already the late afternoon," Jonathias sounded confused.

"I meant tomorrow morning!"

"No, now!" Jonathias insisted. "We need to talk about it now!  We had an agreement.  Your aid in exchange for our having gotten you an audience before Nero."

"You want my aid right now!  As in this instant?"

"No, I just wanted to discuss the issues with you."

"If that's the case, then why don't we wait until we're both a little more clear headed." Joseph rubbed the sides of his head, indicating to Jonathias that he was not in any condition for a serious talk..

"We agreed that when you succeeded, you promised that you would help us with our little mission.  Those were the terms."

"Yes, I did agree but I don't see any high priests sitting in this room.  Do you?  You can't say I succeeded if there's no proof as yet.  I don't even recall being able to plead my case fully in front of Nero. I do though think I remember him dismissing us rather abruptly before I had the opportunity."

"Well, according to Aliturius, your success is only a matter of time; days or weeks perhaps. Approval from the Empress Poppea far outweighs that of her husband. And it's pretty clear that you have her approval, even if you don't want to provide all the details.   But our mission is a little more delicate and that's why I need you to work quickly on our behalf."

"Other than knowing you are spies working for Jeshua ben Gamaliel, I don't know anything about your mission. And I can't let your mission jeopardize the return of the priests in any way. So why don't we wait until I actually have the priests until we do anything that could ruin my chances for success."

"What Jacob and I need from you will take time to obtain.  If we don't start immediately it will be too late."

"Don't you think you need to tell me what it is you need first," Joseph advised.

Jonathias inhaled forcefully as he prepared to explain.  "We need you to gain us access to the training fields."

"What do you mean exactly by training fields," Joseph was already afraid to ask.

"Where they do their military training," Jonathias explained somewhat sheepishly, expecting a backlash from Joseph.

"What! Their military fields!  As in their army camp? Are you serious!," Joseph did not take it well at all.

"It's not as difficult as you think," Jonathias defended his plan.

"And how do you propose I do that? Am I just to ask for permission for us to go observe their military in all its glory?"

"I wouldn't have asked if I didn't think you had it within your ability to achieve this for us. It is not unusual for them to take foreign ambassadors and dignitaries through the training fields, in order to impress them with the might of Rome. It's intended to make all the other nations think twice before doing anything stupid such as going to war with Rome."

"So all you want is a tour?"

"Not exactly."

"I didn't think so," Joseph knew instinctively that there was far more involved.

"We intend to explore those areas of the camp that are usually off limits to foreigners."

"You are insane. The Empress perhaps can appreciate and understand my connection to a bunch of imprisoned priests, but how in the world do you expect her to give permission on my behalf to let spies, and that's what you are, ransack the military encampments? Why don't you have me ask her to open up the armories for you as well, so that you can select a few weapons to take back with you? All you're going to do is ensure we all have a nice cozy prison cell to share together."

"That's why we need to be thinking about it now. It will take time to find a way. But Jacob and I have faith in you Joseph that you won't fail us."

"Go ahead and keep your faith but I am not as insane as you two might very well be."

"Let me intercede on their behalf, Joseph," Aliturius cut off Jonathias from speaking any further, "All they ask is you see if there is an opportunity. A possible way in which it can be achieved. Nothing more. No further involvement on your part. If it can be done, then I will do the rest. And should they find themselves in trouble, I will see to it that you are insulated from anything they have done. Is that fair?"

Reluctantly, Joseph nodded his head to agree. "I'll look into it. Now let the conversation drop for now." He dismissed any further talk about their mission with a wave of his hand.

---

Later that evening Joseph moved quietly along the corridor, returning to Aliturius's chambers. Knocking gently on the door, he ensured that he would not disturb either Jonathias or Jacob, who were in their own rooms. As the door swung open, Aliturius greeted Joseph warmly, ushering him inside and then closing the door quietly.

"We have to talk," Joseph said as soon as the door was closed.

"Yes, I know," was all Aliturius had to say, well aware of what troubled Joseph.

"You ask too much of me."

"We haven't asked any more than what should be expected."

"That is not entirely true.    Your purpose is entirely at odds with my mission. I'm here as an envoy of peace, yet you want to camouflage your own aggressive intentions under the shadow I cast. I was willing to let you pretend to be my entourage, thinking that all you wanted was access to the Emperor yourself, but now you have exposed your mission as being pure espionage and that jeopardizes everything."

"Which we already told you would be the nature of our business but you didn't seem to be overtly troubled by it when you still needed our help," Aliturius presented the facts calmly.

"I thought you needed access to people. You understand, a few bribes here, some favors there, and you'd obtain a few governmental secrets to make everyone happy. That was the extent I expected.    I had no idea you were intending to break into a highly restricted area that will be heavily guarded and if caught then it wouldn't be just them, we'd all be executed as spies."

"Are we not in this together, Joseph?    Do you truly believe that your interests differ so greatly from those of your people?"

Joseph sighed.    "I am a man of peace.    What you are intending to do is only useful to those planning to go to war."

"To every thing there is a season and a time and purpose under the heaven. A time to rend and a time to sew, a time to keep silence and a time to speak, a time to love and a time to hate, a time for war and a time for peace."

"Quoting Ecclesiastes to me isn't going to change my mind," Joseph countered.

"No, but I hoped it would make you think about how your people are oppressed and cry out for help.    If you have the opportunity to relieve their suffering, can you so easily turn your back on them. Are we not all bound by a common thread that makes us willing to sacrifice our own life if it means the salvation of our people?"

"I did not think you'd try to use the old guilt trip scenario so soon to sway me.    My mother always waited until she had run out of options."

Aliturius laughed heartily.    "I'm not your mother and I don't believe we have that much time to entertain the usual customs.    If I could do this without you Joseph, I would, but for me to make a request to attend the training fields would raise numerous questions that would be difficult to answer. Especially since I have worked hard over my lifetime to convince them all that I am a pacifist and abhor the sight of bloodshed.    But for a foreign envoy to ask such a request, as Jonathias mentioned, it's quite common place.    The Mars Field is actually an open area that people can watch the training maneuvers daily from a distance on the sidelines."

"So why do they need me if they can go there themselves?"

"Aliturius motioned for Joseph to follow him out on to the balcony.

Pointing across the Tiber River, he focused Joseph's attention to a specific location. "That over there is the plain known as the Mars Field. From dawn to dusk the army conducts its maneuvers on that very field. Even from this distance we can see them going through their motions."

"But you don't want to just watch them go through their motions," Joseph guessed.

"I will be honest with you Joseph, our need is far greater than that. If you look carefully, you will see several low constructed buildings at the far end of the plain." Aliturius had Joseph crane his neck well beyond the railing. "You can just make them out from here. Those are the offices of the high command. Access to the perimeter of the plain is not difficult. Roman citizens can go there freely and foreigners can obtain the pass of which we speak. But access to those offices is forbidden for anyone outside the military."

"You mean impossible"

"Not impossible, just difficult."

"So how do you expect me to do the near impossible?" Joseph refused to admit that it could be done.

"If you are not in the military, then you have to have in your possession an imperial edict or seal. And imperial signet ring will do."

"Oh, is that all," Joseph replied sarcastically. "I'm guessing that the scribes back in Jerusalem were busy writing counterfeit documents for Jonathias and weren't able to make a counterfeit Imperial ring."

"Not for lack of trying," Aliturius admitted much to Joseph's surprise.

"Seriously? You tried to make one?"

"I have seen the rings worn by Nero and Poppea so many times that I would sketch them for our artisans to recreate but they were never to the same quality of design. A single flaw would result in immediate execution."

"And somehow what you're going to suggest to me right now is less risky," Joseph remained skeptical.

"Get Poppea to give you one of her signet rings and it will open doors that are usually locked to everyone. Add to that an imperial letter of introduction, and I will bet the officers would fight for the opportunity to show you around their secret offices personally. "

"You make it sound easy," Joseph scoffed. "As if she's going to simply hand me a ring without questioning my intentions."

"Keep her satisfied and she will give you whatever you wish for," Aliturius spoke as if from personal knowledge. "Just remember that pesky foreign ambassadors are well tolerated, whereas spies are killed. Once you have provided a means of access to Jonathias and Jacob into the buildings, then they are on their own. You needn't even know what they're up to."

"Oh I see. Just let them do their thing and when all of us find ourselves in the Coliseum about to be fed to the lions, I can then turn to them and say, 'what in the name of God did you do to get us into this mess?' No, I'd think I'd rather know in advance what I'm risking my life for."

"For God and country, dear boy. Isn't that enough?"

"No," Joseph responded abruptly. "I need a little more convincing. You want me to risk everything and you're telling me nothing."

"Get Poppea to provide you with a signet ring and a letter and I'll tell you exactly what is happening. Things are about to change drastically in Judea and you will be pivotal to our success or failure."

"Is this some sort of messianic prophecy that you're all holding on to?" The thought that they still considered him to be a fulfillment of some delusional belief made him angry.

"You scoff at it now but if you could see it from our perspective, you'd see all the pieces coming together."

"Then what happens next in this grand vision of yours," Joseph challenged Aliturius to provide some proof of what they believed.

"You will see for yourself when you next meet with the Empress. She will be calling for you late this evening. It is her habit or doting on a new paramour until she tires of you."

"Are you suggesting that I'm now a paramour?"

"You certainly no longer a toy for casual pleasure, dear boy. You must have impressed her greatly."

"And what if she tires of me tonight and I don't have the opportunity to persuade her to provide me with a ring and a letter?"

"She won't," was all that Aliturius had to say.

"And what makes you so certain," Joseph remained unconvinced.

Aliturius smiled knowingly. "As much as you may detest the idea of being her sexual partner, the fact is you will do whatever it takes to complete your mission because you fear failure most of all. She is as much a challenge to you as you are to her. You will soon discover that she is very generous with her lovers. She'll give you everything you desire. Even a ring and a letter if you ask for them in the correct manner."

"And what exactly is the correct manner that you're referring to?" Joseph wanted to know.

"That my boy is part of your awakening. You will know it when the time is right. So as I mentioned, getting access to the training fields shouldn't be too difficult, and if you mention to her how much you'd like to see the maps held in the general office, I'm certain she'll arrange that to happen as well."

"Wouldn't a request of that nature sound a little too obvious that I'm up to something treacherous?"

"Not at all! The maps are quite a conversation piece among those that have seen them. Exquisite works of art in fact! They have been viewed quite often over the years by dignitaries from foreign countries because of their detail but I must admit it has been a rarity. But I'm certain it wouldn't surprise her at all that you've heard of them and would like to have a look. I've even heard that for the right price they might give you a copy!" Aliturius winked at Joseph, suggesting that he should know exactly what price he was talking about.

Joseph still doubted the accuracy of Aliturius's evaluation of how easy this would be. "So even if I do get you a signet ring and a letter of introduction, neither Jonathias or Jacob are going to be able to go off on their own unescorted. The ring will be in my possession. They're wasting their time if they think somehow they will be permitted to sneak around and enter prohibited areas.

"If that is the case then you have absolutely nothing to worry about. But we can worry about those details later. Right?"

"Right," Joseph nodded in affirmation but Aliturius's willingness to accept failure so readily made him even more wary. If other dignitaries could visit the Mars Field and gain access to the map room as Aliturius had indicated, and it was highly unlikely that any of them were bedding the Empress or Rome in order to do so, then what wasn't he being told about this mission?

---

Jacob was jubilant when he met with Joseph on the morning almost two weeks after their arrival at the palace and saw the ring upon Joseph's little finger. "Is that it?"

"Yes, that is one of the Empress's signet rings. She was finally willing to trust me with privileges it provides," Joseph explained to his colleague. "Apparently these rings are capable of opening far more doors in this city than we realized."

"And the letter....?"

"All in due time. I think the Empress was hesitant in taking on any more than she had to."

"What does that mean?"

"That means we'll be chaperoned all the time that we're on the Mars Field. She is no man's fool. I have earned her trust as long as we stay on a leash. No venturing on our own and that way she doesn't anticipating having any complications. The letter was viewed as an unnecessary complication."

"As Aliturius told you, we need that letter," Jacob showed that he was extremely disappointed.

"I got you the ring," Joseph protested. "Maybe it won't provide the access or freedom to move about you expected but that's what you have, so make due with it!"

"We needed that letter," Jacob repeated.

Joseph stared at his companion as if he had seen him for the first time. "I did ask for a letter but then she asked me what I'd like her to write in it. But I didn't exactly know. So I told her that Aliturius mentioned that we'd be really impressed by things like the map room and similar locations that Nero would use to impress his foreign visitors. Since I couldn't be specific, she couldn't exactly write a letter but she said instead she would arrange to have us escorted by a high level officer or administrator so that if there was a particular place or event we wanted to see they'd be able to gain us access at the time of our request."

"We don't want an escort," Jacob vented his frustration. "There are things we need to do unobserved. This isn't what we expected."

"And that's why you wanted a letter. I got that understanding when she explained that the ring will open doors as I mentioned but its an official letter that will get you inside the rooms if they're listed."

"How can we find anything if we've got some Roman clinging to us as all time?"

"I have an idea. Why don't you tell the sentries when we arrive that you don't want an escort and then see how they react. You might as well say tell them up front that you can't really conduct you're spying to steal their secrets as long as they're watching. I'm certain they will understand and they'll say, by all means, go ahead. Feel free to do whatever you please."

"You're mocking me."

"How can you tell?" Joseph asked facetiously. "Which part gave it away?"

"I don't like to be mocked."

"And I don't like to be tricked into doing things which endangers myself and anyone I care about. If the Romans ever find out that I'm helping you steal their military secrets, they won't hesitate in seeking out and destroying my family or anyone else I'm associated with. And I've worked out most of the details as to why you wanted this letter. It struck me odd when I was speaking with Aliturius a while back. When he told me lots of foreign dignitaries request to see the military training fields and are even taken into the map room, I started to wonder why did he need me. He could have asked Poppea for her ring any time that he pleased. But the letter, that was a different kettle of fish. That would have taken a level of persuasion he didn't have in him. That's why you needed me."

"But you didn't get it," Jacob reminded him.

"That's true, I didn't.

"So what do you suggest then? How should we proceed?"

"I suggest you accept that this is what we have for now and you and Yoni can see just how many doors this ring can open without breaking any laws. I'm not certain exactly what you and my cousin actually have planned, but I can only advise caution whatever it is and don't do anything stupid. I haven't quite figured out your need for the letter but I'm assuming it somehow provided you with an alibi if you should get yourself into trouble. So that means we take it slowly and proceed with caution. Don't force your way into any confrontations. If you're thinking about doing anything that is a high risk then I ask you to reconsider and don't place any of us in danger. Are we in agreement?"

"Do you want to know?" Jacob suggested he was prepared to tell all.

Placing his hands over his ears, Joseph shook his head. "At one point I thought I did but now I think it's best that I can deny any part of whatever you're considering. So don't tell me. I don't want to know anything!"

"So did the Empress say when we can go looking around the Mars Field?"

"Anytime. Apparently she has already informed all of the sentries to be expecting us soon and suggested we'd be visiting frequently." Turning his head sideways to look out the balcony, Joseph continued to speak, "As if that's not going to make them suspicious," Joseph muttered under his breath

"What was that?"

"Nothing," Joseph responded. "I just said be careful not to make yourself too suspicious."

"I'll be right back."

True to his word, Jacob snatched Jonathias from his room and returned in a flash. "Okay, let's go!"

"You mean as in now?" Joseph was taken totally by surprise.

"Yes now!" Jacob insisted. "You said anytime."

"But I didn't actually mean that I wanted us to go right now. Aliturius isn't even around."

"We don't need Aliturius. Now's good," Jacob affirmed.

Reluctantly Joseph acquiesced.

---

It took a substantial amount of time to weave their way through the winding corridors of the palace, past all the inquiring looks of sentries and suspicious palace officials, but eventually they charged into the streets beneath a cloudless sky. Walking by way of the forum, they avoided the crush of the morning crowds that pressed relentlessly along the Via De L'Agora. It was the most indirect of routes, but one which Aliturius had carefully and purposely laid out for them to follow to avoid as the city's network of Praetorian spies. Upon reaching the plain across the Tiber, they found that the entire area was demarcated by a series of red painted posts, each bearing a simple message written in a multitude of languages:

## NO TRESSPASSING BEYOND THIS POINT

Ignoring the warning, Joseph and his party continued to march along the worn cobblestones, periodically waving Poppea's ring in front of the eyes of any overzealous guards that were victims of their own xenophobia. No sooner did the sentries identify the ring, they immediately stood aside, clearing a path and giving leave to the three companions to continue on their way. Jogging across the field in their direction at a steady pace while bearing full armor an officer rapidly approached the visitors. Pulling up before the three Judeans, he blocked them from moving further. Joseph waved the ring once again, but the officer did not shy away this time.

"I know who you are," the Roman commented seemingly oblivious to any authority invested in the ring. "I have been expecting you."

Joseph feigned to not understand the soldier but the Roman merely laughed, stating, "The Empress has made me aware that you are fluent in Latin."

"I wasn't trying to create a problem for you," Joseph quickly apologized.

"Do not worry. The Empress trusts me explicitly. She let me know that you are able to converse fully in our language and even predicted you might try to hide that fact."

"I had my reasons," Joseph quickly defended himself.

"I'm certain you did," the officer didn't seem to care. "I am Marcus Aemelius Lepidus, tribune of the 1st Roma Legion, and I am here to serve you."

"I know that name. Your career is quite renowned," Joseph sounded impressed.

"The name is quite renowned," the tribune was quick to correct him. "Since my illustrious ancestors all bore the same name. Sadly, I cannot compare myself to any of them. These are different times. The Aemilius Lepidii are consigned to the past, this is the age of Julians and Claudians."

"I wouldn't be too sure of that," Joseph smiled. "This is a rapidly changing world. Those in power don't seem to last too long. I wouldn't lose faith yet that you will bring glory to your name some day."

"I thank you for your supportive words, Ambassador Josephus. Just don't proclaim them too loudly or the Emperor might see me as a threat. Shall I take you for your tour now?"

"Wait a moment. Let me just explain to my companions that you are our escort. They, unfortunately, don't speak Latin that well."

From the look on Lepidus's face it was evident that this was not the first time he had to escort what he obviously considered a group of illiterate foreigners. "Of course," he acknowledged Joseph's request. "I will try to speak slowly as we tour the grounds," he exhaled deeply. "That should give you time to translate everything I will say during your visit." Leading his guests directly onto the parade grounds, Lepidus carefully explained the coded signals transferred through the use of banners and the sounding of the trumpets.

Jacob and Jonathias attentively awaited the translations that Joseph provided. "All I have to do is memorize the phonetic sounds of the commands and the corresponding movement of the ensigns," Jacob surmised.

"I wouldn't bother," Joseph commented. "He just said that they change the code regularly so that it is different for every encounter." Joseph thought he had poured cold water on Jacob's suggestion but Jacob disagreed.

"I'm a military man, Joseph. I know all about changing codes. There are only so many combinations, and the entire set is changed, not just a singular command. Once I associate the maneuver with the signal, I can crack any code change they throw at me. Do me a favor; ask this over-decorated fellow a few questions for me.    Ask him if he can confirm that this is the 10th Legion.    The same one that is due to be commissioned in the East after it completes its fifth year of training."

Lepidus confirmed Jacob's inquiry, intrigued that this foreigner would have knowledge of which legions were dispatched across the Empire.

"He is curious as to how you knew that," Joseph translated.

"Merely a rumor that was mentioned in Jerusalem and a coincidence that it just so happened that we are here to watch them," Jonathias attempted to smooth the situation.

"Coincidence my ass," Joseph retorted.    "You knew all along that the 10th Legion was training here.    What are you plotting?    To somehow destroy this legion before it reaches our shores!"

"Don't be ridiculous Joseph," Jacob laughed at the accusation.    "No two people could possibly do that.    Don't ascribe to us more ability than we actually have.    I serve my country no differently than you do.    But like I said, I'm a military man, and the army is the only life that I know.    My father was Agrippa's master of the horse during the short span he ruled as king of Judea, and I am every inch my father's son.    Of all the things my father taught me, he emphasized this point most of all, 'Know your enemies'.    So, I am here to learn everything there is about my enemy."

"You speak of enemy as if we were at war."

"We are at war, Joseph.    You're the only one in Judea that hasn't realized it yet!"

"Is there some sort of a problem," Lepidus interrupted Joseph, overhearing the rising timbre of their voices, an indication that the discussion had turned a bit ugly.

"A simple disagreement on the strength of this legion," Joseph lied. "I was saying that this was a full legion and my friend was arguing that he was certain it was not."

"It is most definitely a full legion," Lepidus puffed up his chest. "If you examine them carefully, you will notice how their strength lies in their formation, which gives the illusion of having gaps between the units, thereby giving the false impression it is under-manned.    Divided into ten cohorts, there are four in the front line, three in the second and three in the third.    That is what we refer to as the offensive formation."

Lepidus sketched a checkerboard pattern in the dirt. "Each cohort has six hundred men it; ten rows deep and sixty men across.    The cohort is then subdivided into six centuries, each having one hundred men."    Lepidus drew a line behind the fifth row of    the cohort in his diagram.    He then divided each row of sixty men into three groups of    twenty.    "See, each century is made up of five rows of twenty men.    You can identify their commanding officers by their helmets.    Either ringed or plumed depending on their rank.    See that one there," he pointed, "that's the commander of the legion. His helmet is different from the others.   It's all comes down to basic arithmetic."

"Do you always tell foreigners exactly how your army is organized?"

"Always!" Lepidus grinned. "We want our allies and our enemies to know just how strong and efficient we are as a killing machine.   Tends to unsettle them when they see how simple and effective it is.   And if they had any thoughts of rebelling, it makes them think twice."

"What's the point he's making," Jacob tugged at Joseph. "He's grinning at me like a fool."

"He's saying he doesn't care if you're a spy because they even bring their enemies here to show them the strength of the Roman armies.   As far as he's concerned, they are unstoppable and just like a juggernaut the army is designed to roll over an enemy regardless of numbers due to their reliance on organization."

"Oh, is that all?   I thought he was telling us something we didn't' know," Jacob laughed, smiling at Lepidus, who in turn returned the same Cheshire smile. "What he is too stupid to realize is that if we can understand their signals, then we'd be able to disrupt that infamous organizational strategy they rely on."

"But as he told you, they're changing the code constantly," Joseph reminded his large colleague.

"And as I told you, there are only so many combinations that can be selected.   We know the commands are first received by the standard bearers of each cohort and then by the tribune of each unit.   This is then passed on to the centurions and they in turn shout the orders to the men under their command.   So the key is identifying that first command because that will tell us which combination they are using. Now imagine if we were able to understand these commands.    Not only understand them but be able to slip our own standards into the fray and start cross signaling contradictory orders."

"To what end…"

"Their strength is also their weakness.   They are so disciplined, that they will automatically follow the signals before they realize they have been deceived."

"So how do you intend to identify that first command?" Joseph inquired.

"We watch," was Jacob's simple answer.   "We watch today, we watch tomorrow.   We keep watching until they begin to repeat a sequence and that's when we know they've exhausted all their combinations."

"Clever," Joseph nodded admittedly. "But that could go on for days, weeks even."

"Unlikely," Jacob smiled and nodded toward Lepidus who smiled whimsically, not knowing what the Judeans were saying.

"Why would you say that," Joseph wanted to know.

"Because they're simple soldiers, not philosophers or educators," Jacob snapped back.   "Soldiers probably have as much memory as a mule.   I'd guess ten combinations would exceed their ability to recall the signals. More like seven at most. Isn't that right?" Jacob addressed the question towards the Roman officer while nodding his head.

Lepidus nodded his head in return automatically, having no idea what he had been asked.

At that moment the trumpets rang out, standards waved in the air, and the legion advanced towards the army of standing hay bales that opposed them. The leather straps of their cingulum slapped against bare thighs creating an entrancing rhythm. Twelve thousand feet pounded in unison against the brown broken sod. Once more the trumpets and horns resounded as they advanced. Three hundred feet distant from the bales, a blistering sound of coronets brought the legion to a sudden halt. Jacob etched every sound, every sight into his memory. Once more the horns barked out a set of orders and the banners waved correspondingly in a dance all their own. The brisk movements signaled the front four cohorts to begin their approach. The distance to the straw opponents decreased rapidly; two hundred and fifty feet, two hundred and thirty, two-ten. At a distance of two hundred feet the first and second rows of each of the four cohorts broke formation and charged in unison. A hail of javelins sank deeply into the bellies of the straw soldiers, and immediately after their release, the soldiers drew their short swords from the scabbards and rushed forward to impale the imagined enemy in hand to hand combat.

Then the next three rows of the cohorts raced forward, hurling their javelins to the rear of the immobile enemy cutting off any attempt to escape. Drawing their swords, they then charged into the skirmish.

Advancing one third the distance to the front line, the remaining twelve centuries dug into their positions, readying themselves for any subsequent commands. Fifteen minutes later the horns sounded and the rear guard flung their javelins to the rear of the enemy and joined the conflict. Simultaneous, the first twelve hundred men into the melee were relieved and retired from the fray. Another fifteen minutes passed and then the horns sounded once more. This was the signal for cohorts five, six and seven to rush forward and secure a decisive victory, while the original twelve hundred reassembled their formation and prepared to join the battle at the next sound of the horns.

"Impressive, isn't it," Lepidus commented to Joseph. "Notice how every quarter of an hour fresh troops are sent in to relieve the previous attackers. Battle strength can be maintained for almost ten hours continuously in this manner."

Turning towards Jacob, it was Lepidus's turn to smile and nod, knowing full well that the Judean giant had to be impressed by what he saw and guessing that his purpose in coming was more than being a mere observer.

"If they're as good as he says, how do you even expect your little ruse with the fake standards to have any success?" Joseph nattered at Jacob. "It's obvious that they're too well disciplined to follow any misleading instructions. They'd know something was wrong right away. There's a natural sequence to what they do and they repeat it consistently. No way they're going to fall for a signal that contradicts the sequence."

"They are good, but not invincible," Jonathias finally inserted himself into the conversation. "Just remember it was nothing but a Thracian slave that handed them their worst defeats simply because he knew enough of their signals to confuse them in a similar ruse."

"Spartacus was over a hundred years ago," Joseph reminded them. "They would have made improvements to ensure that wouldn't ever happen again!"

"Spartacus?" Lepidus caught the word in their conversation and wanted to know what was being discussed. It was a word that was rarely spoken in Rome, always fearing that one day another slave revolt would bring Rome to the edge of destruction.

Joseph knew that he had to respond both quickly and innocently to throw Lepidus off the scent of any suspicious behavior on their part. "We are wondering how someone like Spartacus was able to even score one victory against troops trained as efficiently as these. He shouldn't have had a chance to strike fear into the heart of Rome."

Lepidus appeared more than happy to answer the question. "He never had a victory against troops like these Pompey was out west with his army, young Julius Caesar was out east. And Crassus refused to use his army unless the Senate handed him the Imperium without any threat of retribution. So until the Senate was prepared to make Crassus dictator of Rome, all that Spartacus had to contend himself with was the home guard under the ineffective command of a couple of senators. Against a legion like you see before you, Spartacus found his rebellion quickly snuffed out before the flame even had a chance to burn brightly. Crassus dispatched him easily."

Joseph translated for Jacob's and Jonathias's sake.

"So he would like us to believe," Jacob huffed.

"Now, if you will be so kind," Lepidus urged, "I will start you back on your way to the palace. There is a meeting of the chief military council scheduled for this afternoon and that is a very serious matter. Any non-military personnel, especially foreigners, found within the confines of these grounds after the all clear warning is given, will be considered as spies. You wouldn't want to be here if that were the case. Not even that ring you're wearing would save you. But I promise that if you come again tomorrow, you will see some very interesting maneuvers The siege equipment will be in operation tomorrow. I guarantee it is a most impressive sight."

"And you're not bothered by our constant presence," Joseph still found it incredibly difficult to accept the openness of the Roman military displays.

"Not at all," Lepidus assured him. "We prefer our provincial leaders know full well the consequences of a revolt. It is my responsibility to make you think twice about any insurrection. I am guessing that I have done so today, and therefore I have succeeded in my duty. My Empress will be most pleased."

"You do your job well, Commander Aemilius Lepidus," Joseph assured him, while at the same time wondering what other jobs he's performed for

Poppea.

"What did the pompous fool say this time?" Jacob wanted to know.

"He wanted you to know that the rebellion you're planning doesn't stand a chance," Joseph responded.

"He did not," Jacob was certain Joseph had made that up.

"He invites you back tomorrow to see the siege engines in action, just in case you still think you can rebel against the Empire."

"Arrogant asshole," Jacob muttered while still smiling at Lepidus. "Tell him we will definitely be here tomorrow."

Escorting the foreigners to the edge of the Mars Field, Lepidus bid them farewell, snapping a sharp military salute.

The walk back to the palace was a highly animated discussion, as they deliberated the merits and weaknesses of the Roman formations well beyond what they had seen on the Mars Field. Jacob still insisted that the formations were flawed and exposed to counter attacks, insisting that all the straw men in the world weren't going to reproduce the real life events of an actual battle. By the time they reached the forum, it was practically desolate, the shops closed as was custom at that time of day, so that the proprietors could attend the baths. The deserted marketplace was a sharp contrast to the constant hammering they experienced on the military field. The almost serene quietness of the forum betrayed the soul of the city. This was a Rome rarely seen; caught in the transition between its hectic, overpowering pace and a transcending, lazy, tranquility. It was a sensation they remembered well but which none of them had encountered for weeks since they began their journeys, and it made them long for the peaceful serenity of home.

# CHAPTER FIFTEEN

## WHANGAREI; PRESENT

"Spartacus was a bigger issue than that!"

"Of course he was, but no Roman worth his salt would admit to the truth, especially when the lie was far more convincing," I stated stoically. "Rebellion is ruthless. Any rebellion! The situation they faced, with a Thracian gladiator leading a rebel force of seventy-five thousand men, fully armed, was threatening to the very existence of Rome. The probability of a slave king sitting in the ivory curule chair of the senate was looking like a good bet."

Pearce walked over to the coffee pot, lifted it, and then shook it to indicate that it was empty. That was one of his favorite moves I had grown accustomed to over the years. He never asked for a cup of coffee when there was none. Merely shook the pot with the expectation that it would magically appear. I wonder how his wife reacted to that. If I behaved that way my wife would know exactly what to do with that pot.

"Let's go to the kitchen" I relented. "I'll fix up another pot and see if we have anything in the fridge for you."

"Sounds good to me." Pearce grabbed his tape recorder, pad of paper, and dogged my footsteps. "Honestly, Doc, was he really that much of a threat as you think?"

"Bigger!"

"How so?"

"Did you ever watch the four seasons of Spartucus on TV that was shot by Starz?"

"Yea, I did," Pearce reponded. "Really good show," he added.

"My youngest son worked on the sets and costumes for that show. We'd talk endlessly about it. They tried to make it as historically accurate as possible and overall, I think they did an incredible job."

"Wow, your son did that? You must be pretty proud of him."

"Proud of all my kids, John, but must admit that James did a great job. But one of the things we discussed was that Spartacus could have taken the city of Rome any time he pleased."

"So why didn't he?" Pearce asked quite legitimately.

"Because of that same thing Aliturius alluded to. The fear of Rome. It was a city without walls that protected itself though the fierce image it projected around the globe and none would dare to challenge it."

"But you're suggesting it was all imagined."

"Picture this; he had just defeated the combined senatorial armies. Pompey was off in Nearest Spain and Crassus, like Lepidus said was no military man. He wanted power and he wasn't going to move a muscle until he had it. Even when he did go against Spartacus, it wasn't a case of his army being superior but the case of Spartacus making a couple of strategic errors that cut his army in half and left himself with no escape route.    Prior to that, all Spartacus had to do was make a bee line to Rome and it would have fallen to him.    The slaves of the city would have swelled his ranks to a size that not even Pompey could have taken him when he returned.

"So Crassus didn't have the resources to beat him?"

"In their first encounter, Spartacus defeated one of Crassus' legions. You have to remember it took Crassus a decimation and a good deal of time before he could even get his army into a fighting mode."

"Decimation?"

"Something they used to do to weed out cowardice.    If they had a cohort or legion that turned tail, they would line them up and every tenth man would have to die, beaten to death by the men of his own legion.    In Crassus's case it was effective but it could have just as been equally demoralizing.    He got lucky on that one."

"And    this    unfathomable    fear    was    the    only    thing    that kept Spartacus from razing Rome?" Pearce quizzed.

"He's a hard man to understand.    You'd think being a slave turned gladiator he'd think nothing would be better than burning Rome to the ground and squashing it under his heal.    But all he seemed to care about was getting his people out of Italy and living a quite life.  It's a bit of a paradox.  His nature and natural ability seem to have been entirely at odds with each other. On one hand he's a pacifist and on the other, the most ferocious enemy Rome had ever faced."

"Probably a Gemini," Pearce proposed as he took a sip from his cup of instant coffee.

"Wouldn't have surprised me if he was. Seems common. A lot of great leaders    are like that."

"Is that so?"

"Just wait and see," I answered reassuringly.    "Just wait and see."

---

# MARS FIELD; 623 A.D.

With the break of dawn, Jacob and Jonathias were well on their way towards the training grounds.    Joseph had declined the offer to tag along, having received a summons from Poppea, which had suited them both perfectly as they felt their failure to communicate with Lepidus could work to their advantage if he became frustrated and decided to leave them to be watched by a more junior officer. As long as they had Poppea's ring, they felt as if they were invincible, able to do as they pleased, without having Joseph weighing them down like an anchor stone, discouraging them from doing anything that he considered foolish or impetuous. Jacob wore that ring over the first knuckle of his little finger. For a little ring, it wielded tremendous power and Jacob both respected and was in awe of it.

The artillery and siege equipment was rolled out onto the plains in several wagons. As Lepidus had promised, this was going to be a most interesting day. They purposely limited their presence to the outside perimeter of the field, not wishing to be readily visible nor recognizable, assuming that it might be a means by which they thought they could avoid sharing Lepidus's company for the day, but much to their disappointment, they were wrong. Marcus Aemilus Lepidus was able to see them at the periphery, and as soon as he did so, he strode out to greet them and then immediately began to provide them with the details of the day's events, even though they could not understand a single word he said.

In the hands of skilled craftsmen, the siege equipment was assembled into their massive structures within minutes. By the time they had finished, the engineers had assembled over forty weapons of various sizes and shapes. A few minutes later and the artillery was already in use. There were a few non-torsion weapons mixed among the equipment being trialed, such as a composite bow mounted on a sliding arm. The soldier operating the bow would use his body weight to slide the arm back, thus arcing the bow, at which time it would be strung with a missile almost five feet long. Not very efficient Jacob concluded based on the amount of force required to lock the bowstring.

Almost all the other weapons were of the torsion variety, ballistae, catapults and the dreaded scorpio. The ballistae were horrific inventions, precise and accurate in the art of obliteration, capable of tossing fifty to sixty pound stones with ease. With a maximum range of four hundred yards, they spread fear and panic whenever and wherever they were deployed. Within one hundred and fifty yards, they could tear holes through the heaviest stone fortifications.

Between the scorpio and the catapult, it was difficult to say which incited the most terror among the enemy. The sound of their coils snapping, the bow strings twang, and the whir of the arrows as they sliced through the air, brought with them an incredible rain a fear on most opposing forces. But today they were deployed against an empty field, permitting the troops to learn or refine their skills as the field was strewn with litter as oak splinters sprayed across the field wherever the projectiles landed.

The troops performed their magnificent spectacle of fire power long into the afternoon. Neither Jacob nor Jonathias could tear themselves away from the action, waiting to the very end so as not to overlook a single operation. When it was finally over, they watched how a few of the soldiers were sent onto the field to gather any of the missiles that might still be of use. Each arrow carefully twirled, looking for any evidence of irreparable damage beneath a discerning eye. Only those that had barely perceptible imperfections were selected for reuse. The rest were discarded into a heap for burning at the close of the day. By the time the soldiers had finished their collection of material for reuse, the engineers had already dismantled their machinery and carted them from the Mars Field.

"What do you think," Jonathias asked.

"I think we can take them!"

"No, that's not what I meant. I was asking what you wanted to do now?"

"I still think we can take them."

"Maybe so, but we have a lot more intelligence to collect before we even want to explore that possibility," he reminded Jacob. "Watching them perform things we already know isn't providing us with anything of value."

"The day's still early, why don't we see just how much authority this ring actually gives us," Jacob suggested.

"Just remember what Joseph had to say about us getting caught with regard to his deniability. He'll sever any connection between us and him, and be the first to hand us over to the authorities. He's serious, I can see it in his eyes. He's still not committed to our cause."

"Don't worry about it. All in good time," Jacob nodded. "He will come to see the light. I know he will. But don't you start quivering in your sandals on me now too! Since when have you become so concerned about our being apprehended? Something like that goes with the territory! Don't be going all squirrelly on me now and becoming another Joseph. One man afraid to do what's right is enough."

"You can't ignore his warnings completely. He may be right about a few things."

"I won't say I don't have my own doubts but not this time. You know how I operate. I avoid trouble like the plague."

"It would be a lot more comfortable for both of us if we knew what we were looking for," Jonathias comment bore a twinge of agitation.

"That's wonderful, sunshine! If we knew what we were looking for then we wouldn't exactly be on a secret mission, would we? We'd all like to know. That's why they sent us. Aliturius has been working very hard to find out exactly what it is and thus far he has absolutely no idea of what the Romans have hidden in their arsenal. It's all just one big rumor but all my senses tell me it's got to be true. But there's only one way we're going to find out!"

"I recognize that but it still doesn't change the fact that we're going in blind. And that's the trouble as I see it. For all we know, there's no truth at all to the rumor."

"Oh, there's truth all right. They don't go to all the trouble of being very secretive over nothing. Aliturius has a keen sense about this. They have some secret weapon, and they've been very careful to ensure that no one outside of an elite few have seen it. And they intend to have it ready to ship east in anticipation of a revolt in Judea. If we are someday going to overcome the occupation, then we have to know what it is they have in store for us before we find out on the battlefield, when it will be too late. We won't be able to counteract some unknown. So we go slow and steady until we can locate it. We try not to act suspicious. The more they see us here as casual observers day after day, the less noticeable we become. And then we can make our move."

"We don't exactly blend in to the crowds," Jonathias cautioned. "In fact in case you haven't noticed I'd say we stand out like a sore thumb. That's going to be our first obstacle."

"Ahh, we'll get into far less trouble here than Joseph will back at the palace." Jacob tried to slough off his younger colleague's anxieties.

"What trouble could Joseph even remotely get into back at the palace?" Jonathias inquired. "He's the Empress's plaything already. What else is there to do?"

"According to Aliturius, plenty!"

---

"There's a messenger here for you," Aliturius looked smug as he passed on the invitation to Joseph, while grinning ear to ear. "It appear that the Empress is now ready to see you again." The lilt in the actor's voice was tinged with a mischievous overtone.

Having waited most of the morning, Joseph appeared excited by the possibility, springing to his feet, he crossed the room to the door in a flash. "I have a good feeling about today," he commented. "Today I believe we will hear good news about the priests?"

"Yeah, right. That definitely might be what she wants to tell you." Aliturius turned away so that Joseph couldn't see his face as he hid the fact he was stifling a burst of laughter.

"Should Jacob and Jonathias should return before I do, tell them that I am with Poppea and the success of my mission appears to be getting closer."

"Of course I will. Don't rush yourself dear boy," Aliturius instructed. "Take all the time you need."

Following the servant girl along the same maze of hallways as the previous time, Joseph wound his way to Poppea's quarters. Once they arrived at her apartments, he was taken along a different route, to the suites in the north end of the palace. The Empress's handmaidens were scattered throughout the complex, playing games and chatting incessantly among themselves. Joseph's appearance gave them a lot more to suddenly chatter about. At the centre of the complex sat Poppea, on a very ornate red cushioned throne of obvious eastern origins with its high back and heavily ornate legs. The Empress appeared to be oblivious to his arrival until one of her servants leaned over and whispered into her ear. Only then did she turn her attention to Joseph and greeted him warmly.

"Welcome Josephus. I am so glad that you came. My Aramaic is getting much better, don't you think?"

"I am actually astounded by how quickly you have mastered it."

"Almost as well as you mastered Latin in one day," she smiled devilishly.

"I never intended to mislead the Emperor into thinking that I didn't understand him when he was talking."

"But you never informed him otherwise, either. You simply let Aliturius do all the talking."

"I can explain."

"There is nothing to explain. I would have done the same thing if I was in your shoes. Oh, come to think of it, I did. I have been studying Aramaic for years. I am, as you might say, fluent."

Joseph reflected back on their first meeting and tried to remember if he had said anything to his companions that he would not have wanted overheard. As if she could read his thoughts, Poppea broke into his recollection. "Oh, don't worry, other than telling me how beautiful I was and how my eyes were like the stars in the sky, you didn't say anything that you should regret."

"I appreciate your candor, my lady."

"Just remember that there isn't anything or anyone I can't master if I put my mind to it," she commented coyly.

"Of that I have no doubt, my lady."

"Even this matter of your priests in case you're wondering. I have made a few inquiries and put into motion several legislators to obtain their release. I expect all should go well. I can't give you a specific date, but you should take heart. Until the time that day occurs, I would greatly appreciate if you would do me the favor of instructing me."

"I don't understand. As you admitted, you're fluent in Aramaic."

"Anyone can teach me a language," she giggled, "but there's so much more I want to know about your land; your ways, your people. Most of all, I want to understand you."

"Some things of our ways are not to be discussed," he apologized.

"I am very serious about this Josephus. I expect you to be tending to me every day. I will not take no for an answer."

"You really haven't given me a choice," he responded, eyes cast downward. "You are the Empress and I must obey."

"Is it really so bad having to spend your days with me? Was what we have been doing so revolting to you that you cannot tolerate it? I'd almost say that you're afraid to even speak of it! Still your body betrays you and is more than willing to fill me with your essence. This is what I must understand about you. It confuses me. It excites me! It is so un-Roman. How can your mind be saying 'no' while your body keeps screaming 'yes' ?"

At that moment one of the handmaids leaned over and whispered once again in Poppea's ear.

"My bath is ready," Poppea announced. "We will continue this discussion in the caldarium. Come now."

The Empress arose, surrounded by her fawning retinue of servants. Trailing behind, Joseph entered into the salon of the caldarium. Loosening but a single strap, Poppea's robe slipped gracefully to the ground. Reddened with embarrassment and afraid that at any moment her maidservants would notice his heightened state of arousal, Joseph began to say something but was cut short immediately by the Empress.

"NO! You may not leave if that is what you were about to ask. What are you so afraid of? Of being a man? Of not being able to live up to your previous performances because my maid servants are here? I do not know whether I should be delighted or disappointed in you! All I know is that this childlike innocence of yours intrigues me and drives me wild. It is strongest in you, though I have seen it in others from your land but none so shy as you. I have to understand it. Why are you so different?"

Joseph felt as if he was treading in deep water. If he offended Poppea, he would not have to worry about the priests, he'd be lucky if he would be able to leave Rome with his neck intact. Acquiesce to her demands and her interest might turn to boredom, also guaranteeing his mission to fail. Everything she was asking was a violation of his heritage, his upbringing, and his moral laws. But worst of all, she knew exactly what she was doing and she was still applying tremendous pressure; more than pressure, it was like a cat toying with a mouse. Joseph bowed his head. "I am sorry, my lady, if you have found fault with me. I am merely the product of an ancient culture, and standing in a lady's bath is not part of that upbringing. It does not mean that it is wrong, only that I am not accustomed to it."

Poppea laughed a sweet girlish giggle as she stepped into the steaming pool. At the very instant her foot touched the water, her handmaidens disrobed and followed her into the pool of water. Joseph's jaw dropped as he silently watched the entourage of naked feminine flesh parade around the caldarium. Poppea purred as the servants caressed her glistening body with oils and soft sponges.

"What's wrong, Josephus? Cat's got your tongue," she toyed further with him. "You may join us if you wish. You have already known the pleasure that one woman can bring you, imagine what several can do. I am certain that some of my servants have already caught your eye. I do not mind sharing you with them as long as you don't take too much pleasure in their bodies. Come on in. It is a most pleasurable and relaxing experience. Remove your shackles and let yourself enjoy the moment."

Joseph shook his head but didn't' utter a word.

"Perhaps if you sit you will regain your tongue," she teased him.

Sitting by the side of the pool, he tried not to stare too noticeably at the budding breasts of the nymphet that presented the cushion to him.

"Well, at least I know that it's just not me that makes you so hesitant," Poppea mused watching his reaction around her maidservants. "You really must try not to be so inhibited, Josephus. Why is it you people cannot see that you're God has given us these bodies to take pleasure in."

Finally catching his breath, Joseph found the acumen to speak once again. "Actually, my lady, we are taught that he has given us these bodies to trial us against temptation."

"That is ridiculous," she frowned. "How mean spirited for a deity to try and deny you from enjoying sexual pleasure. It sounds truly evil and spiteful! Why would you even follow such a belief/?"

"It teaches us discipline," Joseph tried to explain.

"And so desire is wrong?"

"It can be."

"I would suggest that instead of wrestling with temptation you try learning to live with it. It would make life so much easier for you."

Raising his hand to his lips, he tried to think of what to say next, but he failed to find a suitable argument. None of his education had prepared him for this. "Someone else told me the same thing," he finally uttered.

"She was a smart woman. You should have listened to her."

"I never had the chance," he said sadly.

"Look at you! Putting yourself through such torment! Why don't you just admit what is already on your mind. That you would love to be in here with me, sponging my body. Is that not so?" For the moment she gave her hands the freedom to roam across her breasts and between her thighs. "Look at me, Josephus!" But he continued to keep his eyes focused on the tiled floor. "I said look at me," she commanded the second time, to which he responded obediently. "I know that I fill you with desire. And you are equally well aware that I am toying with your emotions. But I will do so every day until you are honest with yourself. Until you admit that desiring me is not wrong but one of the most natural emotions a man could ever exhibit."

Joseph silently whimpered as he followed the course of her hands. "What you ask for is a man of noble character; a man that can actually be honest with himself A man that can look at your nakedness and see the beauty within harmonious union and overcome the lust and animal nature. I am afraid I am not that man."

Poppea laughed, not in ridicule but a heartwarming, sensuous laugh, her green eyes dancing with delight. "My dear Josephus, the mere fact that you haven't dived into this pool and ravaged me the moment I took off my gown is very much a testament that you are that man. You analyze, rationalize, and then try to express what you feel through words. That is no animal that does that! That is the epitome of a man. But there are times I wish that you would release your inner animal."

"The temptation is overwhelming, my lady and I fear that the animal you speak of will break loose."

"Then let it loose," she encouraged. "I have taken your virginity; it is time that I take your modesty as well and free you from your chains. There is no reason for you to deny yourself the fruit of planting your seed. Come take what you have already planted." Strangely, the metaphor made perfect sense to Joseph but he did not know the reason why. But with his ever increasing state of arousal anything Poppea had to say would make perfect sense.

Poppea's body undulated in the steaming pool as her servants lavaged her softly rounded shoulders with precious bath oils. Joseph could no longer turn away from the cascade of sexuality that flooded his eyes. The titillating giggle of Poppea's laughter echoed in his ears as she ascended from the bath and stood motionless in front of him. She handed him the large towel that was proffered by one of the servants. "Here Josephus. Towel me dry! Make certain that you don't miss a spot."

# CHAPTER SIXTEEN

## WHANGAREI; PRESENT

"I can see your point," Pearce nodded in concession to me.

"What point was that," I questioned.

"That Joseph couldn't actually write any of these events into his memoirs."

"Perhaps he could have, but I think when he wrote his memoirs he was focused on restoring his reputation among the Jewish community. I doubt very much if adultery would have gone over very well."

"But it really wasn't his fault."

"Since when is adultery about fault? If you're looking for fault, go blame Nero. It was obvious that he wasn't giving Poppea what she needed."

"Perhaps she was just insatiable?"

"You'd like me to go there wouldn't you John? Well get your mind out of the gutter because I'm not. This isn't a story about Poppea's sexual habits. It's about Josephus. Put Josephus into a world devoid of morality and men will do things that they normally wouldn't do under ordinary circumstances. It's human nature. But as you well know, once you released the genie, you can never put him back into the bottle. Any man would be changed forever. That's the danger and that's what Josephus has to deal with within his own mind."

"But Josephus never writes about any of this occurring in his own memoirs and therefore you're just surmising that his relationship with Poppea scarred him."

"Like I already said, yes and no. I know what I see from the images that GLEEM flashes into my mind. And the Josephus that emerged from Rome was never the same as the man that first arrived. I never said scarred. That's your take on his situation. Perhaps it made him a better man? Who are we to judge? The exact details I will tell you about quite succinctly. And these will be factual!"

"I will do my research," John made me aware.

"I wouldn't expect any less of you."

---

## ROME, 63 A.D.

Aliturius was quietly relaxing in his suite, rehearsing the manuscript for an upcoming play, when Jacob and Jonathias burst into his suite of rooms. "So, how did your day go?" he inquired as they surrounded him, showing their obvious eagerness to speak.

Jacob tried to mask the exhilaration that he had experienced while watching the siege equipment and after casually perusing several strategy maps that errant officers had left openly displayed on the tables that lined the plains. "We have seen no more than we have already seen before. Everything looked the same as it is in Judea. We haven't learned anything new."

But being a master of the performing arts, Aliturius easily read the glint in Jacob's eyes and knew that the military strategist of their revolution was in fact very satisfied with the day's outcome. "You mean they didn't unveil their secret weapon today." Aliturius was pleased with his manner of throwing bait to fish and both Jonathias and Jacob recognized he was holding on to a secret of his own.

"You sly old dog, you found out what it is, haven't you?" Jonathias blurted excitedly.

"Of course! I told you I would. Did I not say that trying to convince me to run with you all over the Mars Plain was a foolish idea and that the best way I could discover their plans was to work from within the palace walls?"

"Yes, you did say that," Jacob admitted, "but still, we did find out a lot of things while we were there."

"No you didn't. You just told me you didn't see anything new," Aliturius taunted him.

"I admit I downplayed it," Jacob confessed. "But what do you know?"

"It's called an onager....or that may have been onanger. Strange name either way. Doesn't really matter what they call it. There is a working model apparently. They have been testing it in secret and it works. They say it will change the face of warfare as we know it!"

"What's it look like?" Jacob inquired.

"It's a secret weapon, how would I know what it looks like? But what I did overhear was that it can shoot multiple missiles with a single loading. "

"So what's the big deal about that? Load ballistae with several rocks and you have multiple missiles in a single shot too. That's hardly novel. If that's the best they've come up with then we have nothing to worry about!"

"Oh yes you do," Aliturius warned them. "This weapon can be adjusted to send each missile to a different target. What do you think of that? It can reach those in the front lines and strike at those in the rear at the same time. Imagine an entire row of these engines doing that simultaneously. You wouldn't be able to move up fresh troops in relief as your front lines are being decimated. Your army would be wiped out before it even got close to do battle. You wouldn't even be able to predict where they were targeting so you could get out of the way."

"That would be quite serious," Jonathias interjected.

"You think!" Aliturius ridiculed his associate's understatement. "Serious?" Aliturius practically shouted. "That is the best you can come up with. How about horrific, or terrifying? Those are words that I think more accurately describe the destruction this weapon can rain down on our armies."

"You made your point," Jacob came to Jonathias's defenseNow that is a machine that we must see," Jacob suggested. When are they going to unveil it?"

"If I knew that, I wouldn't have suggested you go to the fields every day, now, would I? You're going to have to continue doing what you're doing until such time that you find out where they're keeping it. It could be days, weeks, even months before you find it. Whatever it takes. But discovering it is of little value. You must find out enough about it to identify its weaknesses. Remember, everything has a weakness."

"But we may not have enough time." Jacob lamented. "From what you tell us of how well Joseph is getting on with the Empress, we could be heading home shortly," Jacob cursed, feeling trapped by uncontrollable circumstances.

"Let's not be too hasty in making assumptions," he was quickly corrected by Aliturius. "I think the Empress will be keeping our friend Joseph on a tight rein for quite some time. She is not unlike a cat. She will want to play with her captured mouse for some time before she devours it. But nonetheless, it's your mission to find this device as soon as you can. We can't take a chance that she tires with her little mouse early."

---

After several more weeks had passed, there was still no unveiling of any new war engine soon to be deployed by the military. As could be expected, the two Judeans were growing impatient but nonetheless were present on the plain most days, until now their appearance was so commonplace that it didn't even raise an eyebrow and not even Lepidus came to greet and oversee their visits any longer with any regularity. It was almost as if they had blended into the normal military organizational apparatus. If on a particular day they failed to arrive, that would set tongues wagging as the Romans that had grown accustomed to seeing them would generate questions as to what might be wrong with their two foreign guests.

When Lepidus did show, it was obvious that his once haughty attitude had also changed. Though Lepidus had not learned to speak any Aramaic, and neither Jacob nor Jonathias let on to the extent of the Latin they had learned by this time, there was an easy communication between the tribune and his foreign friends. Through the exchange of hand signals and patiently slow speech, they made themselves understood, and there was a growing appreciation between the two military men for each others potential as an ally or possible adversary.

It was early morning in the month of Quinctillus, or Iyar by the reckoning of the Hebrew calendar, when Jacob awoke, barely sleeping the night before as he bore a lot on his mind. He silently got dressed, exiting his room without making a sound, only to enter the next room adjacent to his. He crossed the floor, making every effort not to stir his slumbering companion.

"Is it morning yet?" Jonathias groaned, still more asleep than awake and hardly aware of Jacob's brooding presence hanging over him.

"No, go back to sleep," Jacob whispered. "It's still the night. This is just a dream. I'm not really here." Turning over on his mat, Jonathias was snoring loudly once again within a matter of only a few seconds. Jacob rifled through his belongings, frantically searching for the Empress's ring that Joseph had entrusted into Jonathias's care. It was neither on top of the dresser nor on any of the tables. Only when Jacob began a quiet search beneath the bed did he find the ring with its precious imperial seal. Jonathias had rolled over, allowing his left arm to dangle over the side, and hanging there before Jacob's eyes was the glittering gold ring with its precious inscribed stone. With practically surgical dexterity that clearly defied the thick and stocky fingers of his meaty hands, Jacob was able to easily extricate the ring from Jonathias's middle finger.

Slipping from the room, Jacob turned as he passed through the door, mouthing what he knew could very well be his last farewell to his comrade. He was a soldier, going off to battle, and he was well aware that there were never any guarantees of a safe return. Too many weeks had been wasted, hoping and praying that the Romans would unveil their weapon of mass destruction. He couldn't wait any longer. Drastic action had to be taken. Within minutes he was already well outside of the palace, walking briskly along a carefully planned route which took him through a zigzag of paths and narrow streets far from the usual course of travel they had taken every day on prior visits. Only the occasional vendor or delivery wagon bothered to travel these back roads, their wooden spoked wheels rattling noisily across the age-worn cobblestones. It would still be some time before the sun rose, and he could feel the heaviness of the morning mist enveloping him within the coolness of its moist touch. Now that he had crossed the Tiber, he knew there would be no turning back, having strayed by that time too far from the security of friends and the sanctuary the palace afforded. Only when he had passed the houses on the Janiculum Hill did he even hesitate to stop. Perhaps he had second thoughts, possibly even contemplating the option of turning back. He didn't know the actual reason why himself. It may have even been a stray thought crossing his mind to enter the house of Elias and pray in the sanctuary for some last minute encouragement from a far greater power. Whatever had caused him to pause, it was lost to a wave of nervousness as he took a deep breath and steeled himself, continuing to move on past the houses lining the narrow street.

He briskly strolled past the road that ran past the main sentries post rimming the training fields, ensuring that he remained far enough distant that he would not be identified. Sweeping the circumference of the plain, he approached it from the north, where he had noted weeks ago that the field was less trafficked and the security was at its thinnest. With most of the legionnaires still sleeping in their barracks, he appreciated in the emptiness of the Mars Field, a vast, secluded patch of ground; a wasteland of crushed gravel, pounded by millions upon millions of hobnail boots over the centuries.

He rigorously scanned every movement, plotting in his mind the paths traversed by every soldier that was pulling sentry duty, carefully timing their travels as they moved along the perimeter. Counting the seconds under his breath, Jacob thought to himself that the Roman defence against intruders was both careless and good simultaneously. The carelessness came from being overly confident that no one would ever try to break into the camp and therefore they only deployed a single line of sentries. The good was that this single line of sentries may only be walking the outside perimeter but they had divided the circumference into small segments, ensuring that no single sentry had any sort of blind spot.

It would be difficult to remain unseen but Jacob knew that once beyond this single line, there would be no one left to stop him. He pawed the Imperial magic ring nervously. He knew that he had taken it not as a means to gain entry but instead as a possible escape device if everything turned into a disaster. Presenting the ring to any of the guards would place him on the site at a specific time and that would be enough to charge him with espionage. No, it couldn't be used at all if he was to succeed. Jacob knew that if he did manage to become exposed, it would be the last time he'd be able to flash Poppea's authority around in an effort to escape immediate execution but it would not likely keep him from being arrested. And certainly it would probably be the last time Poppea would ever voluntarily hand over her signet ring to anyone. He knew that whatever the outcome should he be identified at the site that particular morning, there was no way he could see himself moving about the palace as freely as he had done previously as the Empress's guest. Most likely he would be sitting in a cell with Joseph trying to win his release along with the priests. It was clear that his survival meant he could not let himself be discovered anywhere close to the Mars field, ring or no ring.

Searching for a complete line of cover stretching all the way to where the storehouses were situated at the centre of the camp was fruitless. Trying to find even a blade of grass close to the warehouses was in fact a major effort. The reality was that there was no cover. Once he was past the red warning flags that bordered the edge of the field, if caught, he'd be declared a spy. Watching the direction the flags were fluttering, Jacob determined that it was best to run headlong into the wind so that any sound he made would be carried in the direction away from the encampment. Swallowing his fear, he waited until the guards moved to the farthest ends of the patrolling circuits, and then darted towards the storehouses, all the while maintaining a crouched posture, creating a silhouetted caricature of a large ape charging across the Mars Field. At any moment he knew the turn of a sentry's head would spell his doom. All he could do was run and pray.

He actually moved quickly for a man his size, sprinting as best he could without standing erect. Miraculously, no one had seen him and as he approached the camp's center he was pleased to find God had blessed him with the presence of bushes that rimmed the military buildings. Diving behind them, he could no longer be seen by the patrolling guards or anyone else beyond the camp borders. He laughed silently to himself. Crossing the field had been easier than he first anticipated but now that he was close enough to the command structures that he could almost touch them, he saw there was nothing to laugh about. The Romans were not as careless as he had first speculated. There was a second set of sentries posted by the buildings that were not seen during his previous visits and were not visible from the perimeter of the field. The guards were ideally positioned so that from their vantage point they had no need to walk the grounds looking for any suspicious activity; they were able to visualize everything from where they stood.

Kissing the medallion about his neck, he experienced a shiver of good fortune that reassured him he would be able to creep past this last set of guards without any problem. His prayers had been answered. As much as this second pair of sentries had a full view of the field, their heads were bobbing up and down, a sure sign that they were half asleep while on duty. There would be hell to pay if they had been under his command he mused.

From behind the leafy outcropping, he peered above the crest and studied the armory buildings carefully, realizing he had a new dilemma. "Which one," he thought to himself. Pick the wrong one and he'd be searching fruitlessly, his mission ending empty handed at best. This is where the information provided by Lepidus would have to pay off. The tribune had indicated that all Roman camps, no matter where they were situated within the Empire were built following a master plan set by the Senatorial Imperium. Consistency was a highly praised concept within the Roman world. If that was the case, then all that was required was to select the same building that would have been the design engineers building back in Judea.

Feeling the warming rays slowly heating the beads of sweat on the back of his neck, Jacob became alarmed that the hour was growing late. The sun was just rising above the horizon but soon the army would be awoken by the shrill sound of blaring coronets. Time was running out. What he had to do, he had to do now. Propping himself above the concealment of the shrubbery, he snatched a final, encompassing look at the camp layout to make certain he had not forgotten anything when making his decision. Nervously, he sucked in a deep breath. Sinews tightened, while his knuckles turned white under the pressure. No second chances. He was off. Leaping past open spaces, and sprinting as fast as he could to avoid detection, within seconds he was alongside the building he had determined as being the right one.

Prying a slat loose with his vice-like fingers, Jacob peered into the interior's waning darkness, just making out the faint outlines of several war engines. He then levered a pair of loose fitting boards apart until he was able to squeeze and wriggle his massive frame through the narrow orifice he created, his tunic catching on a pair of nails that protruded from the frame but he ignored the embarrassing tear in the fabric. He suddenly found himself among weapons of all shapes and sizes that completely encircled him as he waited impatiently for his eyes to adjust to the semi-dark interior.

This was exactly what he had been searching for; a bounty of weapons of every sort and manner. Parts of ballistae, cords from catapults, everything from the small scorpio to a sixteen arrow engine that he didn't even know the name of. The design engineer's building was cluttered from one end to the other with projects in development. Glancing over at the north corner of the structure, it was packed to the ceiling with a variety of battering rams. The engraved smiles of the cast iron heads laughing in mock silence as he passed between them. Their menacing steel-gray eyes watched every move he made. Traversing from one end of the building to the other, no matter how hard he searched he could not find the fabled machine that Aliturius had spoken of. Everything he saw thus far was merely an upgrade to machinery he was already familiar with, and even then, some of these intended improvements appeared from his point of view, impractical. Perhaps Aliturius had been wrong. Maybe it wasn't ready to be unveiled as yet; possibly not even built but simply a sketch on some piece of parchment somewhere in this building. If that was the case, then he knew the plans would have to be somewhere in this building. Then again, perhaps this wasn't even the correct building, he began to doubt his selection of this particular structure. He quickly dismissed that thought. Doubt he knew could prove deadly.

The sun was now risen above the horizon, bringing with it the portent of disaster. A feeling of dread was quickly descending like a mantle upon Jacob as he was still unable to find any trace of the secret plans for the deadly device Aliturius had described. He slumped over the table in the east corner, disheartened and defeated, letting his fingers unconsciously wind about a small cord that ran inconspicuously across the table top. As he pulled his finger free of the annoying, string accidentally pulling the cord as well, only to hear somewhere beneath the table a resounding twang. Crawling under the table, he removed the covering cloth to reveal a contraption of some weird sorts he had never seen before. Small enough to pick up in his arms, he placed the scale model on the table top. It was a most curious and peculiar object not resembling any weapon that he had ever seen the likes of before. Upon closer examination, the cord became a sling, a stick, part of the propulsion unit. There was even a carriage making it possible for Jacob to roll the model along the table's surface. Like a child with his first toy, the sheer enjoyment led him from one discovery to the next. The movement of the wheels turned a set of miniature gears that automatically wound the propulsion mechanism. And then it happened again, another resounding snap of the cord and the propulsion unit released its imaginary load. Brilliant, Jacob thought to himself. 'So that's how it works!' A self winding mechanism that repeatedly releases the load at ever increasing distances because of the forward motion of the unit. Surely it had to be designed by a Greek he was convinced as no Roman could have dreamt up such a clever device. Not only was it capable of spraying the opposing force with missiles at various distances but it did so with such rapidity that their enemies would not even know where to run for safety.

Plans! He knew he'd never be able to escape carrying the model. There had to be plans! Slipping back under the table, Jacob banged the frame until he found exactly what he was looking for. The hollow ring pinpointed the table's concealed drawer. Everyone knew it was standard practice for Romans to have secret compartments in their tables for exactly this purpose. Easy enough to open now that he had found it. The papers inside were a full set of onager diagrams. Propulsion came from over the top, unlike existing war engines. There was no bowstring, the common defining characteristic of both ballistae and catapults. Somehow the set of gears and pulleys made that requirement obsolete at the same time allowing the onager to propel a missile almost twice the distance of any conventional weapon currently in existence. The Romans would be able to launch an attack even when they were still out of sight of the enemy. Towns could be taken before they even knew they were under attack! The entire face of warfare had been changed by this one siege engine. A new era of warfare was about to be spawned by this weapon of mass destruction. Jacob felt a surge of emotions flooding his consciousness; fear, horror, but most of all the excitement of discovering this truly unique and remarkable weapon.

Tucking the rolled plans securely beneath the braided belt of his tunic, Jacob began rummaging, looking for any other papers he could find. Maps were of particular interest, especially if he could find any that showed deployment of troops, but before he had the chance to find anything more of value, the doors to the armory warehouse swung open and a shower of light pierced the half darkness. Jacob struggled to regain his vision after being momentarily blinded, finding himself face to face with four equally slack-jawed soldiers. No one moved; no one flinched. Their every muscle paralyzed from the shock of encountering an intruder in their supposedly secure warehouse. Sticking to the shadows of the building, Jacob made certain they couldn't make out anything more than his hazy silhouette. He knew that after so many visitations to the Mars Field, even the common soldiers would have been able to recognize him easily. Regaining his senses and bearings, Jacob let the adrenalin fuel his body as he ran at top speed, placing his arms in front of his face and crashing through the board and batten walls opposite to the still shocked and motionless soldiers. Splinters shot explosively through the air, his forward momentum carrying him well beyond the grasp of any gawking infantrymen marching outside. Picking himself off the ground, he ran toward the open field, faster than he had ever run before. In the dull light of the early morning he knew he still had a chance of not being recognized as long as he remained low, thereby concealing his true height and massive frame.

Fully aware of the spiking crescendo of confusion emerging from behind, followed immediately afterwards by the thumping of pursuing footsteps as hobnail boots crushed the loose gravel, Jacob focused his attention on the series of bridges leading back to the heart of the city. They would be narrow enough to present an obstacle to his pursuers if only he could reach them before his pursuers caught up. Driving his legs against the trampled earth like a pair of powerful pistons, he flew across the Mars plain with uncanny swiftness. Fortune was still smiling upon him as he reached the first of the bridges that crossed the Tiber. Resting his arm against the pylon he stopped momentarily, out of breath, his heart pounding frantically. His muscles ached but after taking a quick look backwards at his pursuers, he knew this wasn't a good time to let himself enjoy a respite. Like ants, the legion was swarming over the road as far back as the warning signs on the field. "Fuck", he gasped. Too many to likely get out of this alive, Jacob assessed his situation and it did not look good. He had to rethink his strategy. He still felt he could give them the slip if he made it to the residential areas. Time to get his legs moving once more.

There was a rush of air swishing past his right ear as a spear splashed into the river beside where he stood. It had come from his blind side and that meant that they were way too close. He forced his legs to start churning with renewed vigor, crossing the bridge and along the valley roads leading to the city, sprawling before him.

Another sound just barely registered in his thoughts, it being masked by the cacophony of screams and shouts form the soldiers. "Shit, horses!" he cursed. The hoof beats possessed an almost magical enchantment that brought spectators onto the streets as they watched the unfolding drama. "Vultures," Jacob spat, as he ran past their smiling faces and pointing fingers. At least none of these street mongrels would recognize him if they were ever questioned and thus far none considered themselves brave enough to impede his path. As exhausted as he was, he led his pursuers through the narrowest of avenues, where only the breadth of a single horse could pass at one time. It was a clever tactic that only served to both infuriate and antagonize his pursuers even more.

Ascending the Palatine Hill, the alleys rose sharply, sapping what little strength he still remained in his legs. He imagined he could feel the hot air from a horse's nostrils snorting down the back of his neck. There was no time to look behind in order to confirm whether it was merely his imagination or not. "Not today," Jacob reaffirmed to himself. "I will not die today." There had to be a means of eluding them. Scanning his surrounds he searched for any hint of the Almighty's helping hand. "Now would be a good time Lord," he screamed inside his mind. "Don't abandon me now!"

Utilizing his last ounce of fleeting reserves, he leapt into the air catching an outstretched awning. It wasn't a moment too soon as the current of air created by a blade of polished iron passed beneath the bloodied souls of his feet. It was then he realized that there really was a horse breathing down the back of his neck. Swinging his massive body onto the overhang, he secured a precarious perch on a window ledge by the toes of his right foot and then stretched as far as he could in order to grasp the eve of the red tiled roof directly above.    From there he was able to flip himself on to the roof of the building, safely out of reach of the charging cavalry.    The horsemen followed as best they could from the ground below while Jacob leaped from roof top to roof top, the occasional clay tile shattering beneath his feet or sliding down to the street below where it fractured into a hundred shards, often painfully striking his pursuers.

"There he is!" shouted a citizen from his balcony three stories high. "Over there!" as he pointed the soldiers in the right direction.

"Fucking asshole!" Jacob shouted loudly at the man in the little Latin he had learned.

The chasing infantry split into small units, each division provided with the task of searching a building.    A platoon consisting of some of the more agile soldiers clambered on to the rooftops in order to give chase high above the streets of the Palatine but their hobnail boots were definitely not suited for the smooth tile surfaces, as they slid and slipped, struggling to maintain their balance. Quite a few lost their footing, plummeting with devastating effect to the cobblestone street    a    good    twenty    feet    below.    The    clash    and    clang    of    their armor reverberated like brass drums, causing those still in pursuit high above the streets to either slow their chase or stop completely, fearing for their own welfare.    It was all the diversion needed for Jacob to make good his escape.    As the foot soldiers and horsemen craned their necks in the direction towards the now brilliant morning sun, their quarry was no longer in sight.

Jacob never stopped and never looked back to see if his the Romans still followed.    Using one of the taller apartment complexes as cover, he crossed over to what appeared to be a more affluent row of buildings and then lowered himself over the side and through an open window, of one particularly richly decorated apartment, careful to ensure that he was unseen by prying eyes. Unseen except for the young woman whose morning bath he had just interrupted as his feet thudded hard against her polished wooden oak floors.

Wild eyed and stunned into silence, she remained motionless as the towering Galilean approached her. Jacob attempted to communicate in as soft and least threatening a voice as he could muster, but between his shortness of breath and the harsh guttural sounds of his Aramaic accent, it only served to frighten her further than she already was. Terrified, she placed one arm across her breasts and the other cupped protectively between her legs, thinking she was about to be raped.    She prepared to scream but before she could utter a sound, she was silenced by a half-closed fist squarely across her jaw, immediately rendering her unconsciousness.    Jacob pulled her limp body from the tub before she drowned, laying her gently upon the bed, apologizing profusely as he did so, even though he knew she could not hear him.

Understanding full well how a military operation would unfold when pursuing an enemy, he knew the soldiers were unlikely to abandon their mission until every home in the district had been searched thoroughly. Calculating on that immutable fact, a bizarre idea sprang into the Galilean's mind.

Pillaging through the woman's closets, Jacob found a long, billowy cotton dress with an attached cowl. Removing his tunic, he then forced the apparel over his torso, stopping to take an admiring look in the long polished brass mirror that stood in the room. Not very flattering, he thought as he made a wry face at his reflection. What was intended to be a loose fitting dress that wrapped around the body like a robe, was now a tight fitting bodice. The hem of the dress barely covered his crotch. Tying a cape he rummaged from the wardrobe around his waist, he fashioned it into an apron and quickly resolved that problem of anything showing between his legs. Much better, he thought. Now at least he could pass as one of those barbarian slave women from the upper reaches of the Belge, he convinced himself. Belgian slaves were all the rage that season as handmaidens by the ladies of Rome. Now it was just a matter of keeping his face completed covered at all times. The less seen the better.

"This could work!" he thought to himself as he pulled the hood up over his head. As he walked back towards the wardrobe he caught his reflection in the brass mirror and immediately put his hand to his chin. Cowl or not, no one would believe a woman with a beard. The dress also needed a bit of padding in the right places. Finding a drawer full of scarves he began rolling them into balls and placing them into the folds of the dress wherever he felt he lacked the correct proportions of the female gender. Gallic women were big thankfully. Very big in all the right places! And now for the 'piece de resistance', he thought. Finding a tightly woven scarf, he placed it over the bridge of his nose and tied it at the back of the neck beneath the cowl. Not a single strand of his beard showed now. Though the Belge women were not know for wearing veils, many a time he had overheard the stewards in the palace, with the little Latin that he understood, suggesting it would be a preferable habit if they did, and one which most of the men in Rome would applaud. Not to say that the Belge women were unattractive, not at all, but so many suffered from rotting teeth as a result of the change in their diets when they were brought to Rome, that the Romans were terrified to look upon them, fearing the Medusa's curse. Well this was one Gallic woman that would terrify them to no end, he laughed. Pity the Roman that would find this sight attractive, as he gazed one final time into the mirror.

He then glanced toward the bed and hesitated, fearing that he had caused her irreparable harm as well as drawn erotically by the curvaceous figure of the young woman lying naked on the bed. The slimmest of legs framed an inviting mound covered in thick auburn hair. For the moment he had forgotten about escaping and was standing inexplicably beside the bed. He ran his hand along the back of her calf, taking a deep breath as he did so. His breathing became heavy as he closed his eyes deep in contemplation. So young, so beautiful, so desirable, the thoughts filled his head. He felt the stirring in his loins as his hand unconsciously massaged the firm calf muscles on the back of her legs. He began to tremble nervously but then just as suddenly he recoiled in horror as if he had been bitten by a snake. What was he thinking; he shook his head vigorously, clearing his senses. 'Too long away from home,' he reminded himself. 'Not my fault. That was it! Most definitely time to leave.' And for safe measure, to ensure he did nothing stupid, he pictured Joseph remonstrating him for already being in too much trouble for one day! The image of Joseph angrily pointing a finger in his face was enough to break the trance.

His swagger in attempting to walk with an air of femininity was comedic at best, but undeterred, he hung an empty food basket over his left arm and swayed through the congested streets, as calm and collected as one could be under such circumstances. Everyone he passed along the way stared in disgust, only to receive a courteous nod from Jacob, which most found even more disturbing, causing almost all of them to turn away immediately. In fact, every man he passed tried to focus as little as possible on his appearance, lest they catch the Belgian's attention, which they feared would happen. Maintaining a serenely casual strolling pace, Jacob followed the path leading from the Palatine Hill towards the Velian slope. As soon as he was able to visualize the peaked roofs of the palace up ahead, his pace almost doubled. He looked skyward and said a short prayer. God had most certainly taken pity upon his wretched soul this day.

Stopping a short distance from the main gates of the palace, Jacob took the opportunity to dive into the shadows of a narrow alley, where he removed most of his disguise but kept the apron like cape wrapped around his lower half, which afforded him a modicum of modesty. The rolled up plans were inserted into the waistband of the apron, ensuring that they could not fall out along the way. Removing any traces, he buried the removed clothes deep into one of the passing trash wagons that rolled along the dark road. Now, his only concern was whether or not he had been identified and the palace guards were now alerted to his earlier escapades down by the Mars field. It was highly likely that the Praetorian guards at the palace would know about the theft of military intelligence, since their little secret network of spies and informants were stationed everywhere throughout the city. Even if he had not been positively identified, any sort of description released would put the constabulary of the city on alert to find a very tall, bearded man. That might be just enough to place him immediately under suspicion. Therefore, he had to find a way into the palace with -out passing any of the guards along the way. Skulking around the outer perimeter of the palace, he found the section where part of the wall ran a short distance from Joseph's balcony. During the time he had spent admiring the views from his room and the others, he noticed there never was anyone using the area of the gardens that lay just beyond their suites. For whatever reason, it was always bypassed by any of the palace security patrols. Perhaps they considered the wall to high to climb over for any man without the use of a ladder. And obviously any one carrying a ladder near the palace would be immediately under suspicion and detained. But what they had not accounted for was that Jacob was not most men. With a quick scamper, followed by a hop, and then a Herculean jump, he vaulted at least four feet into the air so that fully extended he was able to grasp the top lip of the wall that was easily thirteen feet above ground level.   Pulling himself up onto the crest of the wall, he then dropped gently into a rainbow of colorful bushes that filled the gardens and which broke his fall.     Not too many people could get over a wall that high with that sort of ease, he thought to himself as he smiled.    They wouldn't be expecting that, he reassured himself. For the first time he felt he was confident he would succeed. Once safely back in his room, he would deny ever having left the palace that morning.    Using the trellis that framed Joseph's balcony, he climbed stealthily until he was able to slide invisibly over the stone railing.  He was positive that his entry remained completely undetected.

Joseph's room was devoid of any signs of life, another stroke of unbelievable luck.     Everything was going much better than he could have ever hoped for. Making his way into the corridor that ran outside their cluster of suites, he tip-toed to his own apartment, sliding through the archway of the alcove that shielded his outer door.    Gently closing the door behind him, he let out a huge gasp of air in relief, resting his head momentarily against the door while he reflected on how fortunate he had been.    It was over. He had done it!

"Guess you think you're pretty damn smart," the voice snapped like a whip against the back of his head.    It startled him enough that he hit his forehead against the door quite harshly.

"That hurt," he moaned as he rubbed the area of contact with the fingers of his left hand.

"Not as much as I'm going to hurt you, you stupid fool!    I should crack that skull of yours open and save us all the problem of hoping you'll find a way to kill yourself and save us the bother," Joseph admonished him.

Jonathias was still too enraged to say a word as he stared at his long time companion standing practically naked before them.    When finally he did recover his voice it was none to pleasant. "I'm actually thinking of a far worse punishment," Jonathias reprimanded Jacob.    "Lop your bloody skull off. What's the big idea of taking off in the night without me?     No wonder everything's such a mess.    Without me around,    there's no way to keep you from creating a disaster.   You've put us in quite the stew!"

Joseph continued to hammer away in anger.    "Because of your absolute stupidity, my entire mission in Rome has probably been jeopardized.   How could you even conceive of such an idiotic idea?    I don't know if you realize it, but every soldier within ten miles of Rome is looking for a tall bearded man with a swarthy complexion.   Do you think they won't figure this out!"

"There are a lot of tall bearded men in Rome," Jacob defended himself.

"Not four cubits tall there isn't," Joseph screamed furiously as he hurled an empty jug in Jacob's direction only narrowly missing him as it smashed against the wall.

"Hey, you could have hit me with that!" Jacob shouted.

"I was trying to hit you, you dumb-ass! How many do you think answer to that description?   And of all places to be caught.   In an impregnable armory!   I think that's immediate crucifixion, if I'm not mistaken!"

"It wasn't that impregnable.   I did manage to get in.   And I did manage to get out too."

"And why aren't you wearing a tunic?" Joseph continued his chastisement. "I left it behind."

"You left it behind!" Joseph screamed as he smacked his own forehead with the palm of his hand.   "Why not just tell them who you are.   They get hold of that and they'll know exactly who it came from.   Might as well say Made in Judea!   I should turn you in right now and be done with you," Joseph fretted.

"It will be okay," Jacob tried to reassure the both of them.

Jonathias was still mulling over Jacob's latest comment.   "Left it behind where?"

"What's it matter?" Jacob turned on him.

"It matters," Jonathias was adamant.

"Yes, where is it? Joseph added.

"In some apartment block.   I doubt they'll make anything of it."

"And why's that," Jonathias insisted on knowing.

"Because…" Jacob sheepishly avoided answering the question.

"Oh, this is going to be good," Jonathias already knew that they were in for one stupefying explanation.

"Finish it!" Joseph demanded.

"Because the woman is going to think she's a rape victim and rape victims never talk."

There was stunned silence in the room as Joseph along with Jonathias just looked back and forth from Jacob to each other and couldn't find any words to say at the moment.

"I didn't do anything to her," Jacob found it necessary to defend himself and break their silence.

"Did   you   even   think   about   the   consequences   that might be borne by the rest of us for your little misadventure?"

"Let me be even more direct!" Jonathias shot his next question like an arrow straight through Jacob.   "Do you ever think?"

Jacob glanced at his companion with a threatening stare that stopped Jonathias from commenting any further.

"What matter of demon possessed you to commit such a foolhardy act," Joseph continued to berate him.   "Could it really have been worth the price that we all might have to pay?"

Reaching beneath the waistband of the apron, Jacob withdrew the plans he stole and handed them to Joseph.   "Judge for yourself!"

"I don't think I want to touch it," Jonathias declined the outstretched scroll forcing Jacob to unroll it himself on the table.

Jonathias   closed   in   behind   Joseph,   peering   over   his   shoulder at the blueprint.

The room grew extremely quiet as Joseph carefully perused the sketches.

"It's a unique form of propulsion, if I am not mistaken. I'm not a military man, but I would think that this design is from something we haven't witnessed on the battle field before. Am I correct?" Joseph guessed at the design.

"Damn right it hasn't been seen before," Jacob slammed his fist down on the table. "It fires further, reloads faster, and can practically win a battle all on its own. It's an automatic weapon. This device will change the face of warfare. From these plans we'll learn everything there is about it; how to exploit its weaknesses, damage it and especially how to construct our defenses to render it ineffective. From this day onward, the onager has been rendered ineffective. So yeah, the answer to your question is yes it was worth it!"

"All well said, but we still have to figure out a way to counteract it," Joseph reminded him before celebrating Jacob's discovery.

"When the time comes that we face this thing on the battlefield, it will do no more damage to us than any of the other war machines can achieve. Those back in Judea with a little more knowledge than we have will certainly figure out a way to neutralize it. The Romans will know themselves that they lost the element of surprise when the time is ripe!"

"Only if we go to war and they bring this machine out against us!" Joseph threw water on Jacob's defense.

"We will be going to war!" Jonathias surprisingly shouted in Jacob's defense. "Don't you see or understand, we already are at war? One way or another it's inevitable. What he did today was because they are our enemies! Don't delude yourself into believing otherwise."

"I'm not the one that's delusional," Joseph shot back. "The big idiot with a death wish is delusional if he believes eliminating one weapon from the battlefield will win a war. It was foolish and stupid what he did today. Nothing more than that!"

"You don't understand," Jacob shook his head. "One superior weapon can change the face of war. This weapon had that potential but not anymore? We will study it, we will break it down, and we will learn how to counter it. By taking away their advantage, we increase the odds in our favour. We have a chance."

"Do you hear yourself? A chance? You want to sacrifice hundreds of thousands of our people on a chance?"

"We cannot remain victims of Roman tyranny for another generation," Jacob argued. "We must throw off the shackles of oppression."

"What tyranny? I am tired of everyone screaming that we are living under tyranny. They've given us roads, aqueducts, they allow us freedom of religion, we have our own court system. Show me the tyranny!"

"We are not free!" Jacob reiterated.

"What the hell do you call freedom?" Joseph in turn pounded his fist against the table. "It's a dream, an illusion. Not something we should be so damn willing to die for."

"I can't agree with you Joseph," Jonathias spoke up again. "Neither can Ben Gamaliel, or all the others that support our cause. Freedom is real."

Joseph wrung his hands behind his back as he continued to pace about the room. "I can't argue with either of you any longer. If you see war as a viable solution then we will never be in agreement on this issue. I will give you this though Jacob; at least you had enough common sense in that head of yours to not use the front door of the palace. It will take a major effort on our part, but I'm certain I can convince the guards that you never left your room. We should make a point of letting the Praetorians see you walking nonchalantly about the palace once you put on some clothes. The more relaxed you look, the more it will convince them that you never left. And by process of elimination, if you never left, then the spy must be someone else. Thank God that there are enough foreigners in Rome that you aren't the only big dumb ass in the city."

"Sounds like a plan to me," Jonathias confirmed. "You know, I think we might just be able to pull this off."

Joseph immediately stopped pacing about the room. "Yes this might work but we have a few things we must do immediately. None of us will ever be allowed to go out alone into the city again. I won't permit it. I don't trust you. Any of you! And the beards have to go."

Jacob put his hands to his grizzled face with alarm. "Not my beard! Anything but that. Everyone that sees me will think that I've become assimilated! I'll be humiliated back home!"

"Not fully, I didn't mean that. Just that you can no longer wear it down to your chest. From now on we go Roman style. Just a scruff of a beard showing. Unfortunately, mine must come off too," Joseph sighed. "Just when I was finally getting it to grow in. I can't say I'm very happy about that, but the decision is out of my control. It must be done."

"But won't they even become more suspicious if suddenly we all clip our beards shorter," Jonathias raised a concern.

"If we all do it, we can claim that we were tired of being out of style with Roman society," Joseph responded.

"You'll definitely look more Roman," Jacob tried to soothe the situation. "I bet the Empress will even find you more attractive."

This time the small clay oil lamp that Joseph hurled at Jacob didn't miss. "Shut-up," Joseph warned him. "Don't ever say a word about me and the Empress again or I'll finish you off! Don't think that I'm bluffing."

The intensity of Joseph's rage was enough to convince Jacob not to pursue it further. He rubbed the trickle of blood from where the lamp creased his skull and remained silent.

"I still think if we shave off our beards, it will make us look even more suspicious, rather than less no matter how you try to spin the story?" Jonathias still questioned the logic of Joseph's suggestion.

"Well you have nothing to worry about," Jacob quipped quickly about his companion. "That little pittance of a beard you're so proud of could do with a good tidying up. Nobody would probably even notice the change!"

"Why don't you kiss my ass?"

"Okay, enough!" Joseph quashed any further comments. "Yes, at first we may look suspicious," Joseph agreed. "But in doing so, we'll become so obvious that they'll overlook us because we'll be right up their noses. No one could be that stupid to shave off their beards in order to conceal the crime while parading around the palace knowing full well they'd be looking for exactly that kind of behavior."

"That doesn't make any sense," Jonathias challenged.

"Sure it does. It's exactly what I was thinking," Jacob piped in.

"Oh, shut up," they both responded in unison.

"Trust me on this," Joseph assured his colleagues. "The more obvious something becomes, the more it tends to be overlooked. It's human nature."

"And what should we tell Aliturius," Jonathias asked next.

"In what regard," Joseph was keen to know what Jonathias was hinting at.

"You know," Jonathias replied. "In regards to our mission. Jacob's and mine. Do we tell him that we've accomplished what we set out to do and then try to get back to Judea as quickly as possible?"

"Is that it?" Joseph was even more irate. "Finished your job, so to hell with mine."

"That's not what I meant," Jonathias attempted to calm him. "Of course we won't go back before the priests are released. But now that we've achieved our primary goal, perhaps Aliturius could start using a little more of his influence to resolve your mission."

"What influence does Aliturius have that I haven't been told about?"

Both Jacob and Jonathias looked at each other with amused surprise. "You mean you haven't figured it out?"

"No, care to explain?" Joseph wasn't enjoying their little secret they shared.

"You don't become Nero's favorite actor merely by acting in the theatre," Jonathias suggested.

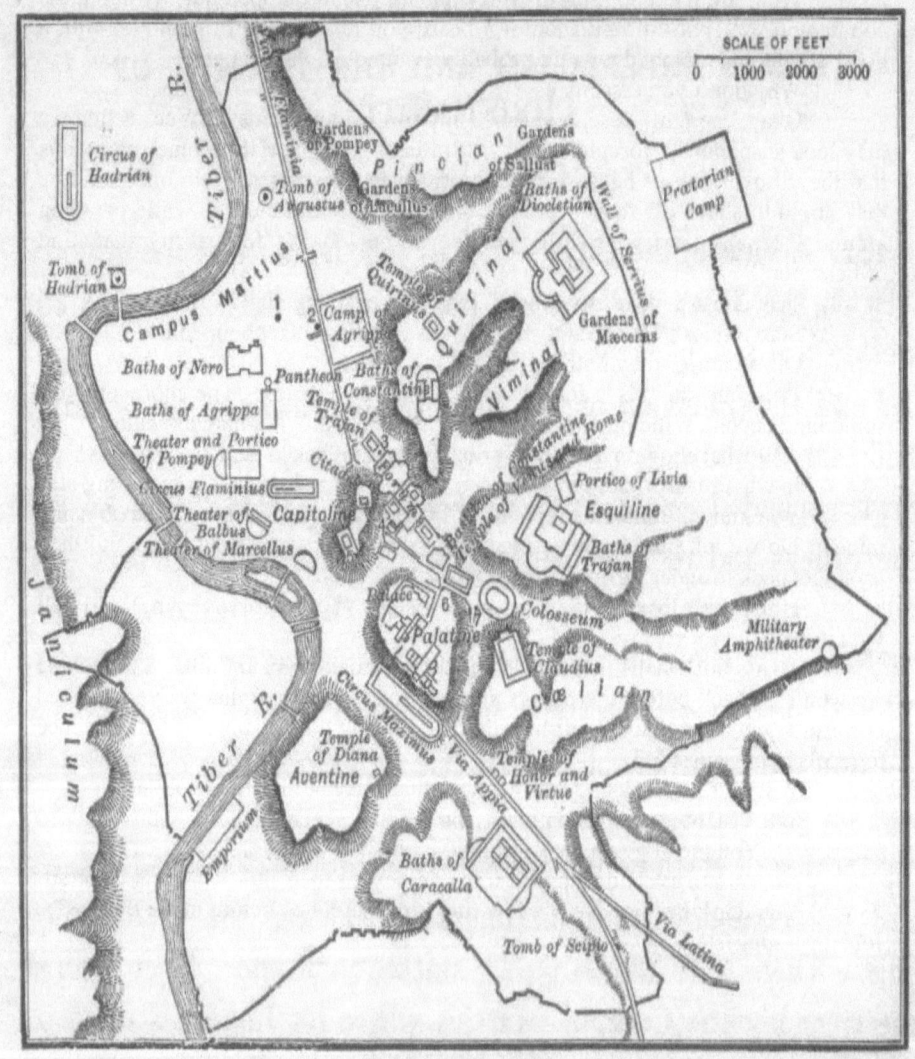

IMPERIAL ROME

The wall surrounding the city was begun by the Emperor Aurelian, A.D. 271.

# CHAPTER SEVENTEEN

## WHANGAREI; PRESENT

"You're expecting me to accept all this?" Pearce questioned in a ridiculing tone.

"Which part are you struggling with now John?"

"All of it!" he replied instantly. "Spies, weapons of mass destruction. This sounds more like CIA telling the story than someone I've come to see as a well heeled historian."

"Ah, I see you know your history," I scoffed. "They couldn't possibly have secret weapons. After all, this is the time of barbarians. Men with swords and running around in knee high skirts. Primitives! Science wouldn't be around for another fifteen hundred years. Isn't that correct?"

Pearce knew he was being ridiculed but wasn't certain how much sarcasm on my part was being cast in his direction. In fact he assumed incorrectly that it was perhaps fifty-fifty. I wasn't about to let up.

"The only time science disappeared for any real extent of time was during the dark ages. And that was only because the Church forbade anyone to practice it. The only reason it was dark was because they turned out the lights. Wherever they weren't in charge though, science progressed normally. And one of the best promoters of science throughout the ages has been munitions. We still do it now. Some of our best creations started out as weapons first, and only home improvements afterwards."

"But this was ancient Rome, Doc," he said pleadingly. "What could they possibly build? A better sling shot?"

"Go do your homework, John. The onager was a real weapon. In fact you probably saw it produced to perfection during the Hundred Years War, over a millennium later. It worked; in fact it worked very well. Rome had its scientists in metallurgy, architecture, physics, astronomy, and a dozen other fields of study. Don't ever cut them short."

Pearce was still finding it difficult to swallow

"Let me give you an example of what you want to call primitive science," I continued. The Byzantine Empire is fighting the advancing Muslims. There's a sea battle and the Byzantine sailors unveil a brass canon that shoots a streaming flame at the Arab navy. It literally burns on the water itself. Throw water on it and it burns even hotter. You know what they called it? Greek fire. And it wasn't until twelve hundred years later we were able to develop anything like it. We call it napalm."

215

"I've actually heard of Greek fire," Pearce responded. "I didn't realize it actually existed.

"Oh, it did. Some grand medieval murals even portray it. It didn't stick around though. Its inventor Carboni died and took the secret with him. What a mess the world would have been in if he had written his formula down? We'd be lucky to be around today if he did."

"Okay, Doc, I'll accept that perhaps one of your ancestors may have been involved in some secret spy mission going on in Rome. But I still refuse to believe in weapons of mass destruction!"

"I will concede that it sounds a bit far-fetched especially after the botch up in Iraq during the Bush era."

"So you're saying you probably made that part up," Peace thought he finally had caught me.

"I'm saying that everything is relative. A bioweapon or nuclear weapon today would be a WMD but only because we look at tanks or jets as being yesterday's toys of war."

"So what if this thing really wasn't a weapon of mass destruction?"

"Then it really won't make a difference to the rest of the story, would it? So if you don't mind letting me get on with telling it!"

"I can buy that," he smiled.

---

# ROME; 64 A.D.

As time rolled by, the legend of the daring spy had undergone several impressive revisions depending on the teller of the tale. The six and a half foot thief grew or shrank accordingly. Equally common was the change in his complexion, from the paleness of a Nordic raider to being as dark as a Nubian warrior. It was well known that the recent unrest in Alexandria was the promise of another revolt among the Egyptians. What better way to signal their unswerving resolve to break free of their Roman masters than to steal secrets that would provide them with the likely tactics to be used against them. In the minds of the public it was a settled matter and the search within the city continued for a renegade African that would be desperately trying to make his way back across the Mediterranean.

Among the female circles of the Roman aristocracy, there existed a far different version of the event. Theirs was not a story of a daring Nubian, but one of a handsome rogue, more determined to force his way into their boudoirs than into the halls of state secrets. It was often repeated that since the crime many a Roman lady would lie in her sleeping cubicle with her windows wide open, praying that this amorous scoundrel would venture her way. For rumor had it, that the lady he did chance upon was ravished in such a way that no other man could ever satisfy her needs ever again.    There wasn't a woman in Rome that didn't wish for such a lover!

Only the Praetorians thought differently and although they they had their suspicions, there was no way they could prove that the Judean guests of the Empress, living within the palace were the ones responsible for the espionage.    But since that time, the three Judeans found themselves being followed constantly and the fact that they had conspicuously altered their appearances only made the captain of the Praetorian guard even more suspicious.

It was two months following Jacob's harrowing escape that Joseph found himself being paid an unexpected visit by the Praetorian officer.  It was one of the few times that he allowed himself to become separated from his companions whom were attending to other matters in the company of Aliturius and he regretted his decision not to go with them. As soon as Joseph allowed the captain into his suite, he found himself being questioned rather uncomfortably.

"How many times do I have to repeat myself, Captain?" Joseph's voice clearly reflected his growing frustration with the man. "I told you, I had nothing to do with the events you speak of."

The captain was evidently from one of the Germanic tribes according to his accent, although for all intent his appearance was completely Roman.    It had become customary for the Emperors to select the Praetorians from their barbarian auxiliaries, especially the Germanic tribes.    In that way they bore far more loyalty to the Emperor than to Rome.    Ever since Caligula the Praetorians had grown in power to the point of being able to make or depose an emperor with the swing of a blade, so attaining their loyalty had become critically important to those in power.

"And I have told you," the Captain repeated himself, "I know it was your man that broke into the camp and eventually I will prove it.    So why not just tell me what I wish to know now and save us both a lot of time and trouble."

"If you are threatening me Captain, then I will have you know that the Empress is my friend and benefactor and she has sworn that on that day none of us ever left the palace."

"A point I am very well aware of," the officer showed no evidence of being impressed or threatened.    "The Empress has only gone as far as claiming that you alone were with her that morning and therefore it was impossible for you to have been responsible.    It is only the thespian Aliturius that has alibied your companions."

"So where is your problem?"

"The problem is that we know that the actor is lying.    He was with the Emperor that night and morning and if he is lying then so too might be the Empress about you."

"You would doubt your Empress then?"    Joseph tried to unnerve the Captain by cautioning him that he was treading on unsteady ground.

The Captain was wise to Joseph's little game and snorted a small stifled laugh. "I certainly am not the one to doubt the Empress. That I will leave for the Emperor to do. And you should know, he has many doubts about her already." The Captain in turn threatened Joseph with a sly all-knowing little nod to indicate that nothing remained a secret for very long within the confines of the palace, whenever the Praetorians were concerned.

"You are wasting your time Captain," Joseph responded. "You will find nothing out of order here. I am not responsible for any crimes you may believe I have perpetrated. If you want to find your criminal, then seek him among a people that could benefit from whatever he took."

"The plans that were stolen from our military warehouse will not benefit anyone," the Captain forewarned. "Already alterations are being made to ensure that the weapon cannot be easily disabled by anyone having advance knowledge of its existence."

"Well then," Joseph replied smugly, "If that is the case then there was no harm done, was there? You might even consider the intruder has performed you a favor by making you redesign your weapon for the better. The matter is therefore of little concern and might as well be forgotten."

"The matter is far from over," the officer rose from the chair and started to make his way towards the door of the apartment. "In fact it has only begun. Do not be surprised if we should have this discussion again in the future." Not waiting for a response from Joseph, the Captain exited from the chambers, slamming the door behind him. Joseph could tell that the Captain was a man of his word. This matter was far from over!

---

The Mediterranean spring was borne on wings of dissent. A ground swell of resentment directed towards the Emperor was fomenting with dire consequences as public displays of discontent were becoming more and more frequent. Each uprising was put down with a little more violence than the previous one, furthering the tension that fueled the city like a powder keg waiting to explode. The poor, the hungry and the homeless pressed into the city in greater numbers than at any time prior. The grain harvests of Sicily and North Africa were already being rumored to have suffered during the drought and would be the worst in years, prompting the Senate to begin the rationing of grain as a precaution. At twenty sesterces a modius, the price had been inflated well beyond the range of the city's poorer classes. The Senate was well aware of what empty bellies among the populace meant but as usual they would not release funds from the treasury to subsidize the grain until it was absolutely necessary.

For reasons of personal safety and security, Nero spent most of his time at his vast country estate in Prenaste. With the Emperor absent from the day to day affairs in Rome, the gossip concerning his personal life grew rampant. Stories of how he had murdered his step brother Britannicus, a favorite among the people, flowed easily off the people's tongues. Once they realized that there were no reprisals for uttering this particular accusation, the plebeians began to talk freely about the other atrocities committed. How Octavia, his first wife had met her untimely end, and how Agrippina his mother had been forced to drink the same poison she had used on so many others. All that was rotten and diseased within the heart of the city was laid at the feet of their Emperor, whom they had adored only a few months before when there was plenty of bread to share. The change in sentiment was a clear signal to members of the Senate that now might be the time to begin looking for a new candidate to sit in the curule chair if they intended to safeguard their own positions for much longer.

Not without his own network of spies, Nero was equally aware of what was transpiring in Rome, despite his continued absence from the city. Those that had once been his friends, but exposed as allying themselves with those enemies in the Senate plotting the Emperor's overthrow, had become the perfect fodder to feed to the starving masses. Nero had learned his lessons well from when Claudius was emperor, that the best way to placate the bottom dwellers of society was to provide them with spectacles that would take their minds off the haplessness of their existence. Each spectacle would be celebrated with a day of free grain to everyone that attended the events in the arenas. As expected, the daily flow of blood in the arenas and the generous gift of grain stemmed the anti-Nero sentiment among the people for the time being. The hundreds of thousands that lived upon the Seven Hills of Rome could for the moment overlook their hardship and suffering thanks to the kindness and benevolence of their Emperor.

It was a dreary Adar morning when Joseph, Jacob and Jonathias received an invitation to join the imperial entourage; an invitation that they knew they could hardly refuse. If Nero was making the effort to come to the city, then it would be expected that everyone made the effort to come to Nero. Headlining the festivities was another gladiatorial filibuster, quickly contrived by Nero to appease the still disgruntled people and make them forget that although their stomachs may not be troubling them as much, the outbreak of the swamp fever as a result of a wet and cool spring was claiming lives by the thousands. During the walk from the palace to the Circus Maximus, the Judeans remained unusually quiet. Perhaps they were growing tired of Rome and the ugliness of the city that was exposed each time the people packed the arena. Perhaps even the most sadistic of appetites would eventually be overwhelmed by the sheer atrocity of Nero's events. As for themselves, they had no tolerance at all to watch the obscenities taking place but they had no choice. One wrong word and it could be them that the people were watching fight to the death and Joseph remembered well the parting words of the Praetorian Captain.

Poppea, seated in her usual position beside her Emperor at his left hand looked as beautiful as ever. The rest of the royal entourage filled the semicircular rows of seats that were situated around the Emperor's box. As guests of the Emperor, the Judeans had no choice but to take their assigned places in the royal box, leaving them with no opportunity to leave unnoticed. Jacob wedged himself between Jonathias and a young woman dressed most appropriately for the equitae order, obviously a member of one of Rome's old, established families. Aliturius, whom was also there by special request, sat in the row behind them, alongside Joseph, which placed them even closer to the imperial couple and therefore more easily scrutinized by the Emperor, who used these opportunities to carefully evaluate all his potential enemies. Everyone in the Imperial stands knew they were being watched closely. And they knew exactly what he was looking for; Looking to see who might be offended, who wasn't laughing when he laughed, and who might be whispering suspiciously? They all knew that one mistake and they could be in the Imperial stands one day but standing in the centre of the arena the next.

In an effort to divert his attention away from the gladiatorial games, Jacob greeted the woman sitting to his side, practicing the little bit of Latin he had acquired over time. When she looked up towards him and returned his smile of greeting, he was overwhelmed by the most peculiar feeling that they had met before. He wracked his brain trying to determine how that could have been even remotely possible. Perhaps at one of the banquets in the palace he postulated but nonetheless he was certain he had seen her before, though for the life of him, he could not place the where nor the when.

It was only when she lowered her cowl, draping it around her shoulders, letting her auburn hair cascade down in ringlets, that it hit him like a blinding flash of lightning. 'The girl in the bath!' the voice inside his head screamed. His smile faded instantly and he his knees begin to shake uncontrollably. He felt the bile churning in the pit of his stomach, as it began to rise in the back of his throat. Fighting back the urge to run, he struggled to appear as calm and collected, even though the sweat began to cascade down his forehead as he flushed with panic. Jonathias could see that his friend was in serious trouble but had no idea why. Jacob tried turning and facing in other directions but his effort wasn't of any use as he found himself continually looking over his shoulders to see if she had drawn the connection herself.

The thought of running occurred to him again but there was no means of escape as he surveyed the exits and passages leading from the arena. There was no doubt about it, he was trapped! It would only be a matter of time before she recognized him as the man in her apartment. What happens then, he wondered? Would she scream, pointing a finger of accusation his way which would automatically bring the guards rushing to the Imperial box? Would she faint? That would be good he thought. It would create a diversion and he could quickly disappear during the commotion.

How could this be happening, he cursed his fate? All this time and now some quirk in fate was about to bring about his demise? There was one chance in a million that he would sit beside the one woman that could identify him as the thief from the Mars field, and here it was unfolding as impossible as it seemed. How could fate be so cruel to permit this to happen?

He decided best to face his fate head on. Jacob looked deeply into her eyes for any sign of recognition. To his horror, she stared back with equal intensity, but then to his relief, she blushed and cracked the most amazing smile. Did she know? Obviously, he assumed, she didn't care either way. Using his fractured Latin, he made an excuse to move closer and restart the conversation he had attempted earlier. Their exchange was highly animated and full of laughter which managed to catch the attention of anyone else that preferred to watch anything other than the fighting in the arena below. For the first time since he arrived in Rome, Jacob could say that he felt at ease. Why, this should be the case, when the person that brought him this tranquility could just as easily have him crucified the next day, he didn't quite understand, but he didn't care.

---

The last losing combatant had just been scraped from the field when the marshals led a girl looking no more than sixteen, from Joseph's estimation, into the arena. She was handed a shield and a spear, before the attendants left her standing alone mid field. From the opposite end of the Circus the huge gates used by the charioteers swung open and the spectators waited eagerly in anticipation to see what would emerge. The music became louder and bolder, urging the crowd to prepare for a magnificent entrance. Emerging from the blackness, much to the delight of most, ran a naked dwarf armed with only a small shield and a short sword. The audience suddenly cheered uproariously, expressing their approval, laughing hysterically at how they had been fooled into thinking it would be a bear or perhaps even a tiger. It was a masterful deception. This was what they had been waiting for, and they let their Emperor know that they were not disappointed with his selection.

Joseph looked at Aliturius dumbfounded, desperate for an explanation, and certainly not appreciating the expression of the crowd's satisfaction. "What the hell is going on here Aliturius?"

"Spring rites," he replied. "It's an old custom or ritual depending on how you look at it. Every year the Emperor presents it but every year the format of the presentation changes. Essentially, it is supposed to be about how wisdom and knowledge must struggle against hedonistic lust. Looks like we're going to see a more traditional presentation. The girl represents the goddess Minerva. The dwarf is the mischievous Pan. It is said that at the dawn of creation, Minerva pleaded with her father, Jupiter, to make men and women equal, so that they could be bound through respect for each other. Pan, being Pan, had a different idea. Man should be dominant and when he so desired, he should ride woman like a beast in the field, under his preeminence so to speak. Jupiter, to no one's surprise supported Pan. Minerva never accepted her father's decision and every year, during the spring, when young men are thinking about trying out their manhood, it is said that she sets aside her crown of wisdom and comes to defend the innocence of her female worshippers through the force of arms. It is why the Romans have always portrayed their goddess of wisdom with weapons. As intelligent as she may be, she is always at war with male foolishness. Man thinks more with his little brain and none can be more foolish than the demi-god Pan. So what you see before you is this theoretical conflict between these two deities and the winner decides what kind of year it will be for the sexes."

"Then this is merely a performance," Joseph surmised.

"Oh yes, quite the performance. A performance to the death I'm afraid!"

Joseph just shook his head in disgust. "Where do they find these poor creatures? A dwarf and a young woman both eager to disembowel the other."

"Desperation makes people do terrible things, my friend. I would suspect the girl is from the Christian community. Nero despises the community with practically an insane hatred because they refuse to acknowledge him as the ruler of the western world. She wins this, and she probably was promised her freedom. Most Christians aren't given that option when they are exposed. As for the dwarf, I would suspect this is what he does in order to earn a wage. It's either this or joining some circus where his life would be just as precarious. Do not underestimate the powerful lure the promise of a full belly, or money, or more importantly, freedom, can be. When you don't have any one of these things, you will do almost anything to gain any one. I can't say for certain what they're particular stories are, but it's almost always one of those three basic requirements."

"This is absurd," Joseph commented as the dwarf circled around the girl, searching for an opening in her defenses. "How can anyone bear to watch this immoral act. It's obscene!"

"Don't speak too loud, Joseph. Right now all Nero is listening to are the cheers and laughter of the crowd. That's all he cares about and Nero doesn't want to hear that any of his guests aren't having a good time."

"What's he going to do," Joseph tested how far Nero might go, "throw me in with the lions?"

"Most likely, so don't speak too loudly," Aliturius cautioned him again. "You wouldn't be the first Judean to end up as an appetizer for the big cats if you offend him."

"Is there any way we can leave?"

"No!" Aliturius was firm in his reply. "Just sit still, close your eyes if you must and cheer loudly when everyone else cheers. Do you understand me?"

Joseph swallowed hard and nodded. As much as he detested what was taking place in the arena, he knew there was nothing he could do.

Pivoting on her feet, the girl never looked away from her opponent. Circling and parrying a jab once in a while, the mood of the crowd was quickly changing. The inaction of the combatants was met with a volley of jeers and a hail debris from the spectators. The crowd was growing restless and eager for the first blood. The combatants looked up at the royal box and could see Nero with his hand over his mouth stifling a yawn. It was the usual signal that unless blood was drawn quickly he would send in a gladiator or two to finish them both off before an undercurrent of hostility spread through the spectators.

The dwarf made the first move, lunging at her legs, only to have his sword turned aside by the small circular shield Minerva carried. Steadily moving forward while jabbing at the air pointlessly with her spear, it was evident that the goddess was frustrated by her failure to land a single blow.

Seizing the opportunity, Pan made a quick thrust with his sword and the sharp edge caught her dress, slicing through and lightly grazing the girl's left hip. The people in the stands worked themselves into a frenzy as the first trace of blood trickled slowly down her thigh.

Finally awakening her savage spirit, the girl swung the spear over the top of her head like a club, only to have it knocked aside by the dwarf's shield. But as he focused on her spear he failed to watch her left hand as she slammed the edge of her shield against his exposed skull. Pan's legs wobbled, as he stumbled about on his now rubbery appendages, but he did not fall.

Thinking she delivered a near fatal blow, Minerva overestimated her advantage, rushing precariously at her adversary to strike again. Blindly, the dwarf swung his sword in a wide arc from left to right. The goddess had been too eager for the kill, and she caught the tip of his sword, slashing across her stomach, just above her navel. She stood motionless, her eyes glazed over in pain as she tried desperately to think about her next move but her mind was now in a fog.

The crowd stamped their approval against the stone floor of the Circus. The cut wasn't deep but the pain was excruciating. Though not educated in the art of poisons, she immediately sensed something had been painted on the dwarf's blade as she felt the strangest of sensations radiating outward from the wound. Whatever the toxin, it probably would have been far more serious if the cut had been close to a blood vessel but it was still having an effect, which meant she would have to dispatch her opponent quickly.

Joseph recognized something was amiss immediately. He could see that the girl's body was unwilling to respond normally and recognized that she was experiencing a mild degree paralysis, which buckled her at the knees until she was practically kneeling on the ground. "She's been poisoned," he alerted Aliturius, whom showed neither surprise nor disgust with the revelation.

"Quiet!" he warned his colleague to choose his words with care, "Nero obviously wants a year of men being dominant," Aliturius speculated. "I believe he is sending a message to the Empress. Something she may have done is evidently bothering him." Aliturius turned his head to look over at the royal couple only to see that Nero was staring back in their direction. "Keep looking straight ahead Joseph but I believe this message is meant for you as well."

"Why would you say that?"

"Don't look but Nero is watching your reaction as I speak. He may have been told that you have been visiting the Poppea's quarters quite frequently."

"Damn it!" Joseph cursed. "The Praetorian Captain threatened that he would say something to Nero. They know I have been sleeping with the Empress."

"It's not the sleeping that would bother Nero, it would be the frequency. If he thinks Poppea is treating you as more than a casual fling then he will put an end to it."

"How would he do that?"

"Picture you and Poppea down there in the arena instead of those two." Aliturius was deadly serious about the warning.

"You've been in Rome too long, my friend. This city could be filling you with terror but instead you have become numb," was Joseph's only comment.

The crowd grew hushed, anticipating the finishing blow. Still groggy from the wound to the side of his head, the dwarf raised his sword, ready to bring it slicing down upon Minerva's exposed neck, now that she had been brought down to his height. The audience began to scream its approval. All eyes were transfixed on that sword blade hovering in the air. With his weapon lofted, the dwarf rocked on his heels and then toppled backwards as if a strong gust of wind had bowled him over. Protruding from his chest was the spike end of the spear, quivering with each beat of his heart.

He had been too slow, allowing Minerva to regain strength in her weakened limbs. As he raised his blade, she lunged with her spear. With most of the toxin's effect waning, she was now able to rise to her feet, her clothes tattered and her skin splattered with a mixture of their blood. Retrieving Pan's sword, she skewered the dwarf repeatedly as the applause thundered from row after row in the stadium.

"It looks like this year you will have to listen to me," Poppea gloated to her husband loud enough that everyone in the Imperial box could hear. Joseph wondered if she had not interpreted the signs in the same manner that Aliturius had done. If she did, then why in the world would she deliberately antagonize him further?

"The year has just begun," those in attendance could hear the Emperor mouth repeatedly.

"Is there not some way we can make our excuses and be away from here," Joseph pleaded having seen enough and concerned that Poppea's taunting of Nero might cause him to react irrationally.

"Don't create an issue," Aliturius pleaded. "Just take a look at the next combatants. This is what happens to anyone that displeases Nero. Just remember that it could be any of us down there!"

Two gray haired, scraggly and overweight men dressed in faded togas were dragged in chains through the gates and onto the field. The pit guards undid the cuffs around their wrists and gave each a short sword, known as the Hispanic gladius.

"The one on your right," Aliturius explained, "is, or was, depending on how you assess his predicament, the senator Publius Valerius Cotta. Once a very prominent member of that esteemed college of legislators, but like most Cottas, he had a tendency to speak too freely and too often against the Emperor. The one on your left is another senator. The esteemed Gaius Fruggi Piso, whose crime, was one of being foolish enough to try and defend his friend Cotta when they placed him under arrest. What you will see now is how Nero is going to test their bonds of friendship."

"This is utter madness!" Joseph protested quietly.

"This is reality," Aliturius whispered back. "This is Nero's reality. You need to remember that! That is why I can say with all sincerity that if you are not careful it can be you and Poppea down there. Nero would take great pleasure in seeing how strong are the bonds of love."

"You were the one that set me up with the Empress," Joseph protested.

"I told you to ride her like a wild pony for all of us in Judea," Aliturius argued back. "I didn't tell you to become lovers. When did I instruct you to become emotionally involved?"

"What do you mean?" Joseph appeared shocked by the accusation.

"You heard me," Aliturius was blunt. "That is why Nero has become suspicious of your affair. Don't deny it. I can see it in your face every time her servant comes to your door and says the Empress requests your presence."

"That's not true!"

"Isn't it? Now that she has returned to Rome, you will have an opportunity to lower the intensity of your relationship. Prove to me that you can do so."

"How can I prove something like that," Joseph had no idea what kind of proof would satisfy Aliturius.

"The proof will be that she will start requesting you less and less. If you're not satisfying her any longer, then she will bring an end to your affair sooner than later. Her fading interest will be the measurement of your success to distance yourself."

"And if it doesn't happen right away?"

"Look down there Joseph and watch," Aliturius warned.

As the senators moved towards each other, Nero sported a grin spreading from ear to ear. Pointing to the two men, he shouted for the benefit of his guests, "See, I told you they would fight! They will do anything I tell them to. They love life too much to refuse."

But instead of engaging in combat, the two men lowered their weapons simultaneously and embraced in a final gesture of defiance. The crowd leaped to their feet shouting and cursing their outrage. Spontaneously, Nero attempted to stem the crowd's displeasure by signaling his archers stationed on the outer ring of the arena to slay the two men immediately. Under a shower of arrows, at least one arrow pierced the heart of each man, but the commotion among the spectators grew louder until it had become a horrendous clamor. They had been cheated, the crowd shouted and Nero sensed their anger was shifting and being directed at his presence. They had been denied their full ration of entertainment, this being the last bout scheduled for the day. Now they would take their hostility into the streets and vent their displeasure. Ordering the Praetorians to form a circle about his entourage, Nero and his guests were ushered from the Circus, making a hasty retreat back to the palace. The show was over!

The power of the mob was greater than any Emperor. It feared no one. It was the first time that Joseph felt overpowered by anything he had seen or done in Rome. Harness the mob and you are without equal. Direct its fury against a single focus and it can tear down mountains. He recognized that he had just witnessed the real power in Rome and it was a terrifying force to be reckoned with. Rome was its people, and they could even make an emperor flee in fear. If you wish to defeat Rome, then you must turn its people against itself. That was the secret to victory; not war, not spies, not having superiority on a battlefield. Rome could only die if it rotted from its core.

---

The twenty-fifth day of the month of Mars corresponded that year to the fourteenth of Nisan according to the Jewish calendar. It was a unique coincidence that both the spring and Passover festivals arrived on the same day. The influx of warm weather brought a feeling of euphoria to both the Jewish community and the closely related Nazorean community which followed the teachings of the one called Jesus Christ. Each community celebrated for a week and the Roman officials grew increasing worried that while the two communities reenacting an ancient rite marking the overthrow of tyranny and their people's flight to freedom that some of their enthusiasm could boil over into the streets if it was not closely monitored.

The Nazorean community resident in Rome had grown rapidly over the past few years appealing to the lower classes and the massive slave population that could only dream of freedom. Concerning the Jews, they had always formed a large proportion of the immigrants living within the confines of the seven sacred hills and for that reason had always been considered a threat from the day they first arrived. Recent population statistics said that they made up as much as ten percent of the city, but since so few were actual citizens of Rome, most never appeared on the census and their numbers may have been actually much greater.

More than ever, Joseph and his colleagues found themselves being closely observed during the approach to the festival week, as Nero's paranoid mistrust spread to friends and foes alike. To the Emperor, there was little to distinguish Jews from Nazoreans. Even if their beliefs had fractured the two communities from each other, the differences were immaterial to Nero. They were all easterners, harboring their hatred for Rome from the time they were born. They were dangerous; a cancer living within the body of the Empire; a disease that had to be eventually eradicated.    The garrisons within the city were placed on high alert as the Jews sat their seder meals speaking of past deliverance, while the Nazoreans talked and prayed for their future deliverance as they reenacted their last supper.

In an attempt to relieve the mounting threat, Nero went a step further, instituting a systemic program of hunting down nests of these Christ worshippers.    Flushing their lairs led to a stream of charges for treason, an easy enough crime to prove, since none of the Nazoreans would acknowledge Nero as their supreme ruler even under threat of death.    But the Jews of the city could not be handled with such ease as the Nazorean threat.    They had no qualms in declaring their recognition of Nero as their Emperor, only denying him godhood, which unlike Caligula, Nero had never demanded from the people.    Had he done so, then they would have found themselves sharing the same prison cells as their Nazorean brethren.

While the garrisons in the city paraded back and forth through the streets on the first night of the Passover ensuring that their presence was well marked by the citizenry, there were few incidents of any significance to report. The threat of insurrection materializing from messianic shadows never appeared and Rome relaxed with a collective sigh.    As far as Nero was concerned it was not a matter of if the revolt would occur, but when.    And that meant keeping a closer eye on any that he suspected might be involved, especially those emissaries that had infiltrated his palace and were now living off his kindness for about a year now.    It was all Poppea's doing he railed at the captain of his Praetorian guard. Could she even be considering elevating her Judean lover to a Senatorial position as a Roman citizen as the Captain had suggested.    Her misguided devotion to these eastern beliefs and philosophies had created an intolerable situation and at some point he would need to put an end to her foolishness.

The house of Elias had prepared the entire week for the Seder meal.    To have guests from Judea of such esteemed status only served to enhance the festive atmosphere among the congregation's worshippers.    Rituals preserved for twelve hundred years were reenacted with the utmost of care and    precision. If there was ever a defining moment of the Jewish heritage, it was the Passover meal. The past, present and future all telescoped into a single ceremony honoring them all.    As all the guests gathered around in the lounge, making themselves comfortable on the cushions scattered around the floor, Elias stood in order to make the introductions.

"We are extremely fortunate to have so many special visitors with us during these holy days," Elias began. "Some of you may already be aware of his presence in our city, but for those that have not met him as yet, we have the special envoy from the Sanhedrin, Joseph ben Matthias here tonight. From what I understand, Joseph will finally succeed in obtaining the release of the priests being held under house arrest by Nero for so many years, where so many before him have failed." The announcement was received with a round of applause by the score of guests.

"And I would like to welcome his two associates, Jonathias ben Elioneiai and Jacob ben Simon. Jonathias is the grandson of the High Priest Joseph Caiaphas who you may remember was also a prisoner here in Rome during the final year of the reign of Tiberius and that of Caligula. Jonathias some may also remember attended to his grandfather for years while in Rome and was able secure that Caiaphas could return to Jerusalem to spend his final months before passing away. If we could all please show our joy in having both Jonathias and Jacob here with us." Once again those in attendance applauded the visitors.

"Lastly, we have another very special guest that has been with us before and has just recently returned to Rome following his journeys through Greece. May we all welcome Simon ben Johan from Capernaum."

While reclining on several cushions, the elderly man in his mid-sixties raised his right arm and waved to those in attendance. At the same time, Jonathias had sprung to his feet and was practically frothing at the mouth. "You!" he shouted. "How dare you come here!"

Jonathias was already halfway across the room when Elias thought it to his best discretion to wedge himself between the two men. "This man is my guest, Jonathias. You will not lay a hand on this man, especially on this Holy night!"

"You're right," Jonathias responded. "I will lay two hands on his throat and see to it that he pays for what he did to my grandfather."

Both Jacob and Joseph were shocked by their colleague's behavior, neither of them ever seeing Jonathias this infuriated and irrational before. They had no idea who the man was and why he would stir such a reaction in relation to Caiaphas.

"Please control yourself," Elias urged, as he tried to calm Jonathias, whom was now only mere steps away.

"That's enough of that," Jacob commanded as he grabbed the scruff of his friend's tunic and pulled him back. As powerful as he was, Jonathias still struggled to break free of Jacob's grip, though his efforts were proving fruitless. "I don't know who you are stranger," Jacob commented to the one called Simon, "But I do apologize for my associate's behavior. It is obvious that he feels he has a serious bone to pick with you, though I have no idea why."

"I understand his angst," Simon smiled back. It was obvious that in his younger days Simon had been a large, muscular man, perhaps standing almost as high as Jacob's chin but with age most of the build had withered away and his shoulders rolled forward, giving the appearance of being hunched. "Once, long ago, I was also an angry young man, just like your friend here. And though I'm not as big as you, I certainly did not shy away from my share of fights. But all that anger served no purpose, but sadly I did not see it that way, at the time."

"Enough of this crap!" Jonathias still wiggled like a fish on a hook trying to break free. "Tell them what you did. Let them know what kind of man you really are. You're a liar, a coward, and most of all a murderer!"

"I did what I had to do," was all that Simon said in that respect.

"Bullshit!" Jonathias screamed. "You had one job to do, one simple job and you failed because you were a coward. Good men died because of you and my grandfather paid the price by being taken to Rome where he was imprisoned for the final years of his life. All because of you!"

"I cannot deny that I failed to do what everyone thought I was supposed to do that night but in truth, it was my true purpose in life to do exactly what I did."

The more Simon talked, the more enraged Jonathias became. "Is that what you tell yourself? That you were meant to let good men die because you were too frightened to say just a few words before the council. I thought he was your friend. You let him die. You let my cousin Judah die as well. They were depending on you and you turned, denying even knowing them! As far as I'm concerned, you killed them!"

"Calm down," Jacob instructed. "You keep pulling like that and I'm afraid I'll be left hold nothing but a torn tunic and you'll be standing stark naked in front of all these people."

"Why are you even here," Jonathias demanded to know. "You aren't one of us any longer. You don't belong here.!"

"He is my guest," Elias interceded. "No matter what you may think, he is still a Jew. All the Minians are still Jews even if they believe their messiah has come. Are we that much different in believing that our messiah will soon show himself?" With those words, several heads turned towards Joseph, who pretended not to notice.

"Minians, Nazoreans, they are no different," Jonathias insisted. "If we are not careful they will be the death of all of us. Nero makes no distinction as to which sects the Christians might belong too. They're all Christians as far as he is concerned and he intends to hunt them all down."

"Which is exactly why we should be extending our hands in aid to our brethren, in their time of need, even if they should be following a somewhat different path," Elias counseled.

"You still don't understand," Jonathias was not ready to extend any hand to someone he considered his adversary. "You have no idea what happened that night. But I do. As I tended my grandfather, he told me over and over again how that night became a disaster for all of them. And it was all because of this man," he pointed his finger accusingly at Simon.

"I did nothing," Simon stated in his own defence.

"That is true," Jonathias quickly jumped upon his statement. "You did nothing and that is your crime. Thirty-one years ago my grandfather held his tribunal in order to keep Yeshua out of the hands of the Romans and you were key to that plan being successful but you failed them all by refusing to testify."

"That is not the full story!" Simon insisted.

"That is the truth," Jonathias countered. "All the tribunal needed was two independent witnesses to deny the claim by the Pharisees that Yeshua said he was the son of God as a result of the Lord fornicating with his mother. Nicodemus had already asserted that the charge was absurd, but being a member of the tribunal himself, he could not bear witness. Judah had already sworn that the statement was not true but that you and Philip had been spreading such a rumor even though Yeshua condemned you publicly at Gerasenes for having done so. The charge was blasphemy and Yeshua had two options, to either say he was not a Jew and then the law would not apply to him, or else declare that he never made such a statement. He stated the latter and all he needed was two men to confirm it that could not be accused of bearing false witness."

"But I could not in truth say such a thing," Simone argued. "I believe he did say such a thing to me and that is why I spread that story. I felt I would have been bearing false witness and that was not who I am!"

"Fortunately, there was a Pharisee that rose from those assemble that declared he heard Yeshua recite the Shemah. We all understand there could be no Son of God if Yeshua recites such a statement.'

"Then you did not need me and this bias and unbridled hatred you bear towards me is unwarranted."

"Yes we did! If you had made such a declaration then the tribunal would have been over but because it came from a Pharisee, it provided them with another opportunity to level a charge. This time they accused him of saying he was the messiah and he would lead Israel into the final battle against Rome. What had begun as a religious court had now become political and that meant if this second charge was proven then he was to be handed over to the Roman Procurator."

Shaking his head, Simon refused to accept any responsibility for the new accusation. "What could I have done to deflect such a charge. As far as I am concerned, he is the messiah!"

"Yes, you could have confirmed Judah's defence when he told the assembly that the anointing in Bethany was not Yeshua's doing. It was Lazarus ben Simon's doing and as a descendant of the royal family, Lazarus had that right but it did not mean that Yeshua deaclared himself to be the messiah."

"Then blame Lazarus for the undoing of your tribunal but do not point your finger of guilt at me," Simon dismissed Jonathias's accusation

"You know that Lazarus had fled the city that night after you raised a sword against the captain of the Temple guard at Gethsemane. It had to be you. You were standing in the courtyard. My grandfather sent out a servant to bring you safely in but you refused. It was worse than that. You denied even knowing the man. Three times you denied knowing him and that meant you could no longer give any testimony. Because of you, what should have been a simple religious case to dismiss, became a civil matter, which meant it had to be handed over to the Roman authorities.    It was because of you that Yeshua was crucified.  It was because of you that my grandfather was sent to stand trial in Rome."

"I cannot bear the responsibility for that outcome," Simon still refused to accept the argument of his culpability.    "The wheels had already been set in motion and it was meant to happen.    How else could my Master rise from the grave if he had not been executed?    How could he prove he was the Son of God if the events did not unfold as they were intended?  What you call my denial was clearly ordained to be in order that we can share in the truth of his messages today."

"This is blasphemy," Jonathias yelled at Elias. "This is intolerable in a House of the Lord.    Rid us of this venomous tongue or else I will tear it out of his mouth myself," Jonathias threatened.

"You will do no such thing," Elias fought back.    "This is a House of the Lord and there will be no blood shed in His house.    There are many sects among us Jews that share different beliefs. Will you rip the tongues from the Essenes as well for their conflicting beliefs?    Sit back down Jonathias and let us find a way to find peace between you.    After all, this is Passover and it is a time to celebrate, not to make conflict."

"I will not make peace with this man," Jonathias shouted. "If you let him stay here then he will bring nothing but evil down upon your roof. He brings with him nothing but a trail od death and destruction!    Mark my words!"

"I will not turn any Jew away at the Passover," Elias refused.

"Then you need not worry about that as I will leave of my own accord!    I will not break bread with this man!    I warn you all!    Beware of letting this man under your roof, it will lead to nothing but death!"

Before Jacob even had an opportunity to try to convince his friend to change his mind, Jonathias was out the door and half way down the street on his way back to the palace unchaperoned.  Jacob stood in the door frame, watching as Jonathias disappeared from view.  Elias walked slowly to his side, looking like a mere child as he stood by the giant of a man.

"Let him cool his temper," Elias advised.    "In time he will see that the hatred he holds within his heart is a poison that must eventually be released, otherwise it will consume him."

"He is not one that easily forgets," Jacob commented.    "I fear he will take this grudge into the grave with him."

"I fear that many Jews will do so," the old priest postulated. "The more they show their hatred for the Minians, the more they will drive them away until the rift between us is irreparable. That will be a sad day when our brothers become our enemies."

"Sad indeed," Jacob agreed with him.

---

Once the situation had cooled and Elias was able to restore a degree of decorum within his sanctuary, he pronounced that the ceremony would begin. The washing of the hands was followed by the traditional blessings over the wine, the herbs and the flat bread known as matzoh. The two goats had been slaughtered earlier that day, and had been roasting in the synagogue's kitchen for most of the afternoon, braising in the somewhat famous spiced seasoning that was Elias's own secret recipe. Then the moment everyone had been waiting for finally arrived; the serving of the festive meal. The guests were ushered into a second room, very similar in size to the lounge but unlike the salon, it had several low tables placed end to end in a semicircle. All of the guests reclined on the pillows and cushions that were arranged around these low standing tables upon which the food was being brought out and displayed.

Elias took great effort in conducting the seating arrangements, making certain that any further conflicts that night would definitely not occur. At first it seemed strange that he sat the the one called Simon beside Joseph, but he had assumed correctly, as the two men quickly became engaged immediately in a heavy discussion. Joseph appeared intrigued by this strange man that was called a Minian and his story of why he considered Yeshua to be the messiah. Joseph was curious to understand why the people in general seemed so desperate to have someone they could label at the messiah in the first place.

Much to his surprise, Jacob was delighted when Elias sat him down beside one of the late arriving guests that he had not noticed had entered the synagogue. Now that he was separated only by a couple of feet, he recognized her as being none other than the woman whom he had now met on two very different previous occasions. She made a point of reclining on the pillows immediately beside him, smiling bewitchingly in response to his look of stunned silence that he wore the moment he first saw her. She did not appear surprised at all, as if she had known all along that he would be present. It almost seemed that she may have played some role in urging Elias to arrange the seating to her specifications, if that was even possible. Could this have been in some way planned, Jacob wondered. It surely could not be coincidence.

It finally dawned on Jacob that something other than mere chance and coincidence was involved though he still could not piece the why and how of the situation together. He was naturally elated by the prospect that in some way fate was forcing them together. Easier to think that it was the whims of fate rather than the alternative that this was a carefully crafted plan by this beautiful woman with the soft curved lines of her cheekbones, and the petal-like lips that she would purse to perfection when he spoke. Was she in some way toying with him, much in the way that Poppea had done with Joseph? No, it definitely had to be mere chance or fate as far as he was concerned. He could not fathom that it was possible for a woman to be crafty enough to manipulate the circumstances to make such things happen.

He struggled to say something pithy, and as he fumbled and failed to produce a single intelligible statement, she decided she would begin by conversing with him. Suddenly he found that his voice had returned and he was talking endlessly, all the time wondering why such a lovely flower of the Roman equestrian class would be present at a Seder in Elias's sanctuary. It was a fleeting thought, given only passing consideration because he felt if should start analyzing the situation infinitum, he would run the risk of losing this golden opportunity to become more than mere acquaintances.

The celebrations continued late into the early hours of the morning, as the guests recounted the tale of the Exodus of the Hebrew slaves under the leadership of the lawgiver Moses. Talk of Nero as a second Pharaoh was heated, especially fueled by the constant sound from outside of the marching soldiers patrolling the streets of this predominantly Jewish neighborhood. It was obvious that Nero had anticipated there would be a flare up of rebellion beginning in the Jewish quarter and his soldiers were a reminder that they would deal harshly with any signs of trouble. But if Nero was the second Pharaoh, then obviously there would need to be a second Moses, a new messiah to liberate the people. It only stood to reason. Simon ben Johan spoke up that he believed that liberation was at hand and that Yeshua would be returning soon at the head of a resurrected army, just as Ezekiel had prophesized. Considering that both Elias and Joseph were Saduccees, they quickly dismissed that idea, insisting there was no such thing as a resurrection of the dead. This led to an interesting debate among the guests, many who held Pharisaic beliefs, much to the amusement of Simon who kept raising the fact that these others were willing to accept the resurrection and a messiah leading the reborn dead in battle but just not Yeshua being that person. It was a debate that would obviously have no decision by the end of the night.

The wine flowed freely and the somnolence of the grapes eventually ended even the best of debates no matter how intense. Sleeping arrangements had been made well in advance for all the guests, making use of the synagogue's expansive property. Elias had anticipated correctly that very few would dare to challenge the patrols and try to make their way back to their homes that evening. To a Roman centurion determined to find an inciter of insurrection, no Jew would be innocent if found on the streets that night.

Oblivious to the debate that was carried on by the others around the tables, Jacob was still unable to fathom his unbelievable stroke luck. Firstly, this beauty beside him never bothered to report him to the authorities after their first encounter, not even to hand over his tunic as evidence of his break-in. He had always considered himself blessed for scraping through that situation unscathed but never knew why. Secondly, his being seated immediately beside the most enticing woman he had ever seen at the Circus only to strike up a conversation, even after her apparent recollection of him from their first encounter was more than he could have ever hoped for. And now fate had tossed them together once again and not even the fact that they were the only two not paying any attention to the other conversation, could tear them apart when others tried to engage them. In fact he was grateful for the debate, as it provided the opportunity to talk all evening with this mysterious lady that had miraculously entered his life without concern of having someone else listening in. Feeling it was the right time, they walked hand in hand, strolling into the deserted sanctuary adjacent to the house, exchanging glances as they fathomed the depths of each others eyes. Feeling his heart pounding within in his chest, Jacob leaned towards her to steal a kiss. Not even when he was fleeing from the Mars field did he feel so scared and apprehensive. What if she was offended he thought, but it was too late!

As he drew back, she whispered, "I do believe that you owe me a dress."

At first he was tongue tied, and then after what seemed a lifetime, finally found his voice to speak, "I thought you had recognized me. I wasn't certain but I suspected."

"Of course I did," she nodded in confirmation of his suspicions, her eyes flashing with girlish pleasure as she finally revealed her secret. "There are certain things a woman never forgets, especially the face of the man that breaks into her bed chamber."

"It would appear that you have me entirely at your disadvantage, my dear Mirah. All that you have given me thus far tonight is your name, but you obviously know so much about me already."

"Actually, Mirah is the name that Elias has given me. He says it is my Hebrew name but obviously as you can tell, it was not the name I was born with. That name from my past is Agrippina, the daughter of the late senator, Agrippa Marcius Rubrio. But please, continue to call me Mirah. I prefer it."

"I admit that I was confused by your name. Your features are not those of a Jewess. You are Roman then? I can assure you that it does not make you any less beautiful to me. Actually I find you more beautiful than any woman back home." He wanted to slap himself across his face when he realized how stupid what he had just said sounded. He prayed that the words escaping from his lips did not sound so ignorant that she was offended.

"I have to think about whether you have just complimented me or insulted me," she blushed, as a pinkish hue tinted the highlights of her creamy white skin. "If you are trying to say that you're fine with the fact that I'm not a Judean, then I am glad, for I am not one, but don't think for a moment that I am not a Jew. I may be the progeny resulting from several generations of Romans, but both my mother and father, God bless their souls, who have been dead these last nine years were every bit as Jewish as you are, having embraced the faith a long time ago. You should know that those that convert are often far stronger in their faith than those merely born to it! If you're telling me that you have no other woman waiting for you back home, then I am pleased, but I do think you might owe an apology to your mother and perhaps every other woman you just insulted back in Judea. "

"I apologize only for any insult you feel but I assure you none was intended.

If it helps for me to explain myself, had I found that you were not Jewish, I still would have pursued you to the farthest reaches of the earth.   I would not have settled for any woman but you, because since the moment I saw you, I can see no other face but yours in my dreams.   And that is what I meant by my comment. That I would have surely abandoned all that I hold dear, all my beliefs and the beliefs of my ancestors, in order to be with you.   I have to tell you that!"

"Now you do have me blushing," she glowed.   "No one has ever promised to pursue me in such a manner before.   To the ends of the earth is a long distance indeed!   To be willing to sacrifice your birthright is the highest compliment you could ever pay a woman!"

"And I meant every word."

"I know you did.   I knew it when we met that day at the arena.   I saw it in your eyes how you felt about me, and I knew there were so many things you wanted to say but didn't know how to express them.   But that was okay.   I could feel the words you could not speak."   She caressed his brow with a velvet touch of her finger tips.   "When I was eleven years old, Nero had just been proclaimed emperor.   He expressed an interest in me and was desirous of making a pact with my father that I would be betrothed to him when I reached the age of thirteen.   This was not unusual because in Rome although we have always considered a woman to be of marriageable age at eighteen, arrangements for the marriage are usually done several years in advance. My father was caught in a predicament.   For years he had hidden the fact that we had adopted the faith of the Hebrews.   Very few of his trusted friends even knew.   He did not wish me to become the wife of Nero but neither could he refuse such a powerful man.   For almost a year my father managed to stall the formal arrangement of the marriage pact but he knew that eventually Nero would uncover his maneuvering and avoidance.

Suspecting that he would eventually fall victim to foul play, he secretly made arrangements to have me spirited to the house of Elias upon his death, where I would be beyond Nero's reach.   Because then it would become obvious to all that I was a Jewess, and as such there could be no way in which I would be acceptable to be the next Empress of Rome. Someone took the lives of both my father and mother, and I became a ward of this house and I was raised here for four years until Nero eventually forgot about me and I doubt he ever learned of my Hebrew secret because his mother had taken over finding him a bride.

First there was Octavia, and then came Poppea Sabina.   Agrippina Rubria was now only a vague memory to the Emperor.   I was seventeen, free to return to my father's estate, and suddenly a very wealthy woman.   Elias saw to it that the house and land was transferred properly to my name and that my money was invested wisely.   The right people were hired to manage my estate, and with my investments I was able to buy an apartment in the Subura; an apartment by the way which you have already seen you shameful bully."   She raised his hand to her cheek, rubbing it slightly, then ushering forth a subtle sigh as she did so. "I have my investments to watch over now. They keep me busy."

"But do you come here often?" Jacob inquired.

"Under Elias's instruction I rarely return to this house. He felt that it would be best that I didn't provide people with a constant reminder that my family has a Hebrew skeleton in our closet. Rome is in a flux now. They care little if you are a Hebrew as long as they don't see you flaunting the faith in front of them. But whether they see me practice or not, has not diminished my faith. I do believe in our God! With my whole heart and my entire soul, I believe! And that belief has only served to make me so lonely, a recluse from any suitors, as I had no choice but to refuse any matrimonial proposal presented to me. I was different but they could not know why. I was different in my heart and I knew I could not go back to the old beliefs. Just as I knew that someday there would come a Jewish prince to sweep me off my feet and rescue me from my loneliness. And then it happened. Our first encounter," she giggled.

"You have me mistaken. It is Joseph that has the princely blood."

"No, you are mistaken to think blood makes a man a prince." She pressed her index finger against his chest. "It's what's in here that makes a prince!"

"But I hit you! I hurt you! I am so ashamed. How can you forgive me?" Jacob couldn't believe that he had actually struck her and she had swept that all aside.

"To me it was nothing more than a love tap."

"I could have hurt you."

"But you didn't. I spread a rumor of an amorous encounter among the ladies of the city knowing that somehow the prattle of women would eventually reach your ears and you would find your way back to me."

"But I could have been anyone. I didn't even have to be Jewish."

"My dear, foolish Jacob, I don't know how to tell you this but your features could be nothing other than Jewish. Over the years, my father had entertained countless guests from your homeland. I knew how they spoke, how they dressed, even how they gave off a scent from their skin that was peculiar to the spices from your homeland. And I still have your tunic under my pillow. The weave of the cloth can be from nowhere else than Judea. From the moment you entered my apartment I knew immediately where you were from."

Jacob began smelling his forearms to detect any trace of an odor. "I have a peculiar smell?" he asked, still unable to detect what she described.

"A very distinct odor," she confirmed.

"But I hit you and knocked you out," he repeated.

"You hit me, that is true, but you held back so much I doubt you could have cracked an egg with that blow. I feigned being knocked out because I knew it was necessary for you to believe I was unconscious in order for you to make your escape. I watched everything out of the corner of my eye."

"You watched everything?" Jacob asked incredulously.

"Yes, everything!    And next time you run your hand down my leg, it better be with my permission or you will be in a lot of trouble," she scolded him.

"I'm so sorry," he blushed.    "I don't know what I was thinking."

"You better have been thinking what I thought you were thinking," she jabbed her finger into his chest once more.    "That I am the most beautiful, alluring, woman you have ever laid eyes upon, and you couldn't help but to touch me.    Otherwise, I've made a fool out of myself chasing after a dream and going to all this effort of trying to be alone with you once more."

"I did not abuse you in any way," Jacob stumbled to release the words from his mouth.    "I assure you!"    He was still concerned with the fact that she had observed his momentary weakness.

"But you did, Jacob?    You did think about taking advantage of me as any man would do, but you put them all to shame by refusing to give in and respecting me.    And then you touched me.    Your touch, your gentle caress, was what won over my heart.    But should you be unable to give me your heart in exchange, then you will learn how dangerous I can be when I'm scorned," she threatened him.

Jacob could not tell if she was serious or not by her last statement.    Then he thought about their meeting at the Circus and he felt compelled to ask.    "How did you arrange to be at the Circus and sitting beside me if you no longer had any relationship with Nero?"

"Oh that was easy," she answered.    "I simply told Elias that you had violated me and therefore we must be brought together in order to erase the sin."

"What!" Jacob practically fell over where he stood.

"Don't worry about it," she continued.    "I simply explained to him what happened when you came to my apartment.    I then said that I wanted to meet you again.    The rest he took care of through Aliturius.    It was actually quite simple to arrange."

"So let me understand this," Jacob began putting together the pieces. "All this time that Aliturius, Joseph and Jonathias have been torturing me since that day I broke into your room, they already knew that you were never going to identify me to the authorities. They probably knew that when I sat beside you in the Circus that it had all been prearranged. So, as I was sweating in absolute fear that you'd recognize me, practically having a heart attack at any moment, they were all laughing at me because they knew why you were there,"

"Possibly," she smiled.

"That was very cruel," he recollected and assessed all that he had suffered through. "Even for them, that was very cruel."

"You probably deserved it," she giggled.

"That's    not    the    point.    This    is    the    point!"    Without    a moment's hesitation, Jacob embraced her between his massive arms, kissing her tenderly upon her full rubied lips.    As their mouths met, she let out another little impish giggle.

"Is my kiss that funny that you have to laugh?"

"No, it's not that," she explained. "It's just something I have thought about for a long time now. Ever since that night, I wondered what it would be like to kiss you with your full beard, but now I'm afraid I'll never know."

"That is not a problem. Over a lifetime together, a beard can always be regrown."

"Yes," she shouted at the top of her lungs. Loud enough to disturb some of those in the house that had retired and were now trying to sleep.

"Yes, what?"

"Yes, I accept your proposal," she continued to shout excitedly.

"But I didn't...."

She placed her finger across his lips before he could finish his sentence. "You said over a lifetime. Now don't you go making me angry! I've warned you already," she looked him sternly in his eyes.

"I guess I did," he said as soon as she withdrew her finger from sealing his lips. "Come to think of it, I most definitely did!" he was now quite jubilant.

She wound herself around him without concern for neither time nor place, ignoring the fact that they were standing in a hall of prayer. Jacob reciprocated as he wrapped his arms around her, She practically disappeared from view, concealed and sheltered in the bough of his embrace.

Unnoticed, old Elias watched benignly from the entrance to the synagogue, the delight and satisfaction etched into his face. He had lived the last few years of his life for one reason only; to ensure the future happiness of his ward when he was gone from this world. With a sigh and a smile firmly on his lips, he tottered back into the house to find his bed.

# CHAPTER EIGHTEEN

## WHANGAREI; PRESENT

"What is truth?"

"Are you getting philosophical on me Doc?"

"No, just giving you something to ponder. As a reporter, you know that truth must have a reliable source in order to be taken at face value. If the source has a sketchy background, then we tend to dismiss anything that might be said. Sadly, there are many truths that are lost because we cannot accept the source of the information."

"I suspect you're going to give me a lecture now, aren't you?" Pearce knew me well enough by now to have guessed correctly.

"Well, think about it John. If I believe something is true, and you don't, does that in any way make me believe whatever it is, is any less true? I doubt it. But unless I can convince others of its veracity, it will die with me should I be the only one to believe it, even if it was one hundred percent true!"

"And your point is....?"

"My point is something which my distant cousin living in Sydney made me examine, even though I was very reluctant to do so. And even though he strongly believed in what he was telling me, I could not accept it, that is, until now. Not that I totally accept it, mind you, but I will admit that I am more convinced that he was possibly on to something that defied explanation."

"And that makes sense, does it," Pearce challenged my remarks. "You don't, but you do, but you don't."

"Yes, I think you now understand the point," I answered, quite smug in my assertion. "You may choose not to believe in something, and even when it's shown to you, you'll try to dismiss it as some sleight of hand trick, but eventually you have to accept that it was true for all intents and purposes. That is what my cousin taught me then. As hard as it might be to accept, when the facts are there, you don't have a choice."

"At some point you're going to tell me what the hell you're talking about, right? This isn't going to be one of those hypothetical discussions that just spin around in circles, is it?"

"Ever hear of the Bible Code, John?"

"Sure, everyone's heard of it," he replied nonchalantly. "There are books, documentaries, videos, all talking about the Bible Code. Excellent marketing."

"But what did you think of it," I asked bluntly.

"I didn't buy it, if that's what you mean. Too much hype and after the fact solutions for me to give it much credibility.   In a nutshell, crap!"

"Exactly," I shouted.   "That's how I felt.   I told my cousin exactly that, and I was certain I could produce patterns saying anything I wanted, given a large enough manuscript like the Old Testament to work with.   Problem is, Dov's a computer specialist.   Designing software, he'd know the actual probability of hitting certain characters repeatedly. So, I listened, and agreed to buy the program so we could analyze it.   I bought it on the primary premise of proving it flawed. As far as I was concerned, God does not write computer based programs three thousand years ago for the sole purpose of us mortals uncovering it now."

"Sounds reasonable," Pearce confirmed.

"Well I thought so too. You may not be aware of all my university training but I'm also a bio-statistician, so I believe I have enough knowledge that I could present a reasonable argument why this thing is nothing more than a random combination of letters that has to come up in a certain order every so often.   And working with the Hebrew alphabet makes it even easier.   Only twenty-two letters and the vowels are not present, so this should be a no-brainer situation.   Right?"

"Right," Pearce agreed even though I doubt he had a clue what I was talking about.

"So I throw in the name Goldenthal into the code finder, and sure enough it finds the name once in the Old Testament.   I can't say I'm overly impressed. We're talking only seven consonants, so the odds aren't exactly huge.   Interesting, but certainly not impossible.   Computing the odds, one out of twenty–two letters multiplied by the seven times each one of those consonants must appear in the precise order is only a one in a billion chance of finding my name.   It's a big book; it was highly probable that it would occur at least once, even at one in a billion, and it did."

"Okay," Pearce drew out the expression as if to ask what my point was.

"But Goldenthal wasn't the family name, was it?   So why should a Germanic surname be found in the Old Testament? But Kahana should be since its origin is Middle Eastern.   And curiously enough it was but again, that's no big surprise.   Numerous times, as it's only four letters, so a one in one hundred and sixty thousand chance of that combination of letters coming up. That isn't really a big surprise.   But the Hebrew equivalent0 for Goldenthal were a definite possibility as well.   So I fed into the program 'amek zahov', golden valley, which is the translation of my surname from the German.   And suddenly it gets interesting because Kahana as a word is there intersecting with golden valley in a number of places throughout the Old Testament.   That alone is pretty spooky when you think about it. Separately, I can expect it, but intersecting?   Shouldn't happen, but it did.   I figured I'd let it pass though. Don't want to get excited and give the nod to my cousin that he was on to something.

And you know me, I'm not one to quit and surrender.   I became even more determined to prove this Bible Code theory was a sham. So I feed into the matrix even more words, like Allen, and Cohen, and Aaron. But the damn thing refuses to give up. Suddenly there are hundreds of places where these words are conjoined in a matrix throughout the Bible. This is not only defying impossible odds, it's just getting plain weird. I don't want to admit anything yet, so I figure I'll make it even harder. I start throwing other words into the matrix. Caiaphas, priesthood, Temple, and the crème de la crème to make it even harder, Aryeh-Zuk. There is no way there's going to be a matrix in the Old Testament that's going to have all these words intersecting in one place. It would be a mathematical impossibility. I press the return key and I admit I'm excited because I'm certain I've beaten it and it won't be able to do it.

It's churning away, struggling to get through the data, and every indication was that it was about to fail. And then the miracle of miracles happened, the screen came up and it was all there. Not as many locations in the book, but it was still definitely there. It shouldn't have been possible even once, let alone a few times! We're talking astronomical odds. Odds that say there was a better chance for the sun to fall into your backyard than finding this particular matrix. I even had a better chance to win Lotto ten weeks in a row. Odds so high, that they couldn't even be calculated. The Bible isn't big enough to have trillion-to-one odds, let alone whatever these would have worked out to have been."

"So what did you do then," Pearce asked eagerly.

"Oh, so now you're interested, are you? Suddenly becoming a believer?"

"No, but I will admit you caught my interest," he replied.

"I couldn't let it beat me. The impossible should not be possible. Actually I couldn't admit to Dov that the bloody thing actually worked. I tried to make it even harder so I threw in Nazorean, because you have to remember, they weren't Christians back then. That word came from the Greek and after all, this was a Hebrew program. Then I threw in the word Sadducee, chosen, and a whole bunch more. And still they kept coming up in an ever expanding matrix. I have a printout of one matrix that is an entire block of interwoven letters making up the mother of all matrices. When I saw that, I knew that this had gone way beyond any explanation that I could ever come up with. It was exhilarating and yet at the same time scary to think that somehow, my life, and that of my ancestors was incorporated into the holiest book ever written. What does it means exactly, I don't know and I probably never will. All I can say is that there are some things that have to be accepted on faith."

"Wow, that is kind of freaky," Pearce commented. "A long winded explanation to tell me about faith, but still freaky!"

"Well, here's a good one for an article. I haven't mentioned yet the number of hits for Aaron to Allen. Three thousand three hundred and five. Makes you think."

"I don't get it. What's the number got to do with anything?"

"Everything. It wasn't the number of hits, it was actually revealing the number of years. I was able to see that immediately."

"Good for you," he ridiculed, "but how about explaining it to us lesser mortals."

"Remember my family tree I showed you a while back?"

"How could I forget it?   It covered your entire living room floor."

"That number I knew from the tree.  That number was the time from when Aaron was born until the time I was born.   That's what it represented."

"So what year were you born again?"

"In nineteen fifty-five."

"If that's the case, then Aaron was born...let's see now...," Pearce started doing some very slow mental math.   "That would make it...somewhere around."

"Are you finished yet," I grew impatient.   "The answer is 1350 BC."

"Okay."

"I guess it doesn't mean as much to you as it does to me," I responded.

"Should it?"

"You see John that goes back to my original premise when I began talking about this Bible Code thing.  What is truth?   Is my truth the same as yours?  And if you believed in something strongly, and for so long, would I be able to change that truth if I was to provide the facts that presented a hundred and eighty degree turn from your beliefs."

Pearce pulled on his chin between his thumb and forefinger.    "I suspect Doc that you're going to lay down a big one that's going to challenge ever yone's belief.   Correct me if I'm wrong."

"The year 1350 BCE is huge, John.   I know what I've seen in my mind. I know what happened back then.    And this date from the Bible Code only confirmed to me that what I perceive as Aaron's memories are essentially correct."

"And that's why your wrote *Once A God*?"

"That's pretty much the reason I wrote that book."

"So Doc, you saying what you wrote in that book is actually what Aaron saw!   You have visions of back then."

"GLEEM, John! Not visions, genetic memories.   He was my ancestor, I share his DNA, I see those events that impacted upon him to such a degree that he synthesized and stored the memory protein into his genetic code.   As simple as that.   Just happens that his memories aren't exactly the story that everyone has come to believe over the past three thousand years.   So once again I raise the question;   If I can present the facts, do my truths become your truths?"

"Simple for you, maybe but hard to change what we've all been taught to believe.  But let me ask you, if you have Aaron's memories, then you must be able to go back even further, like to Jacob and Abraham.   Isn't that so?"

"No, can do," I deflated his enthusiasm quite quickly with that remark.

"How's that not possible?   You said you have your ancestors memories handed down to you.   Then you should be able to see what those guys saw too!"

"I do carry my ancestor's memories but not those individuals.    That should tell you something right away, John. Think about it!"

"But the Bible tells us that Aaron was a descendant of Jacob. That means the memories have to be there," Pearce insisted.

"Think harder John!"

"If you don't have those memories, then that would mean…"

"I told you at the start John that Aaron's origins had nothing to do with a tribe of semi-nomadic sheep herders that traveled up and down the valleys of Canaan all their lives. You have to start listening to me."

"You really shatter my beliefs Doc, in case you didn't know."

"Mine too."

---

# ROME: SUMMER 64 A.D.

Just like most months of late, July began with the usual unrest among the people. The intense heat from the summer sun after what had been a wet spring served to magnify the usual sickness that blew in from the swamps along the Tiber. But unlike previous years, these episodes of illness didn't naturally wane as was usual, and instead one family after another was ravaged by the fever that quickly spread well beyond the banks of the river. Nero was sympathetic to his people and emptied the public coffers in order to stem the tidal wave of misery and despair, but with little success.

Accompanying the burgeoning illness came a growing unrest that smoldered into a festering anger that pervaded every social layer within the city. Nero had witnessed a time when the populace was like this once before in his life. It was when Caligula was Emperor, and he recalled very well what happened when his relative failed to take the outcry of the people seriously. Not wishing to suffer the same fate, he considered it best to retreat from the city to his country estate once more where he felt safe and insulated. There was always the hope that with his absence, the people would find someone else upon which to vent their anger and frustration. In a city the size of Rome, there was always a component of society that others could find a reason to detest and blame for all their ills.

As usual, the Senate attempted to burn the swamps but it only proved to be a very temporary solution this particular year as the swarms of mosquitoes merely relocated each time they did so. Soon it was no longer just the very young and the elderly that succumbed to the illness. Something was different this year, as those that would have normally survived had to endure the added torture of the unending heat-wave that repeatedly dried up the aqueducts that brought fresh water into the city from the springs up in the hills. By the ides of the month, the death merchants and their wagons meandering through the streets had become a far too common sight, searching for just one more body to toss on the pile before they headed to the abandoned quarries where the corpses would be interred. The people shuddered as they saw the wagons approach, rolling slowly down the roads. At five sesterces a body, the undertakers often didn't wait for confirmation of death before a body was thrown on to the back of their carts.

It was early in evening of the eighteenth day of the month, when a lone spark hit a pile of kindling, unleashing a blazing inferno. The yellow spurts of flame gorged themselves on the wooden shacks that stood at the east end of the Circus. Their wooden frames dried by the relentless sun had become the perfect fodder for the fire. Soon the night sky was ablaze with the dancing lights spreading in every direction. Higher and higher the cinders scaled the air until they were captured by the swirling winds that blew from the southeast sweeping them carelessly into the residential sectors of the city. Each home that they lit upon was nothing more than a ripe tinderbox. In this part of the city there were no stone gates or mortared walls to stem the disaster. No white stucco walls to reflect the heat and impede the spread. Nothing stood in the path of total annihilation as the flames scurried along the rooftops.

The stores of dried wood and oil in the markets whipped the blaze to frenzied heights. Row after row of town houses were consumed without mercy, while the suddenly homeless survivors scrambled hysterically through the streets, filling the suburb with the wail of tears and haplessness mixed thoroughly with a cacophony of choking gasps and stifled breaths of those that would not make it through the night. While both the Aventine and Caelian hills smoldered under the intense heat, the winds urged the flames to probe even further northward.

Quick to respond, the fire brigades hastily assembled but found themselves stymied by the panic stricken citizenry that moved as an overpowering wave, surging along the main arteries, pushing everything and everyone they encountered in their path backwards. Almost all of the major accesses to the fires were blocked and there was nothing the brigades could do but try to find alternative routes that cost them an enormous amount of time. The warren of narrow alleyways and numerous dead ends only stymied their efforts further. But fighting the fires did not come free of charge. Those that wanted their properties saved had to pay. Those that could not afford to pay were offered a less than fair price to sell their homes by commander of the brigades. Those declining both offers had no choice but to fight each blaze on their own, their frustration boiling over from the futility of it all, screaming their rage into the towering pyre from which they could hear the horrifying screams of anyone unfortunate enough to be trapped within the belly of the burning beasts.

Panic spread even more rapidly than the flames through the city. The commotion outside finally stirred Jacob from his heavy sleep. The three Judeans had decided not to join Nero's exodus to the countryside for reasons of their own. For Jacob, the decision had been easy to make, being too preoccupied with Mirah these past few months, never even bothering to consider the proposal to leave. Whereas, Joseph decided not to join the Imperial entourage because of his overpowering intuition that Nero had had his fill of all things Joseph when it came to his wife's indiscretions, which were constantly reported by the Captain of the Praetorian Guard.   How much he may have been resented by Nero's was still unknown but the countless hours Poppea was unavailable because of the often repeated   excuse   that   she   was   being   tutored   in   middle   eastern customs behind locked doors by Josephus, definitely took its toll.   Recognizing that his time in Rome was rapidly approaching almost two years, he had to deal with the admission that he had progressed no further in his mission than any of the previous ambassadors sent by Jerusalem.   This was his one opportunity to make a name for himself, and it appeared that he was failing miserably by his own estimation.   The   only   scale   upon   which   he   had   proven   successful was that the Empress had certainly not tired of him yet.   Aliturius considered that to be quite an accomplishment even though it made his relationship with Nero precarious.

"Yoni!   Yoni, wake up!"   Jacob burst through his companion's bedroom door and brusquely shook him until the first evidence of his arousal.

"What's wrong," Jonathias muttered, still more asleep than awake.

"Something's happening in the streets.   I think the palace might be under attack."

"So what?   The Emperor's not here.   They'll figure it out soon enough and go home.   Why don't you just shut the shutters on your balcony and we both can get back to sleep."

Jacob instead trudged his way over to Jonathias' balcony and threw them wide open.

"I said go shut your own!" Jonathias shouted at him as the bright lights flooded into the room, forcing him to shut his eyelids.

But Jacob failed to answer at first, instead standing mesmerized by the brilliant spectacle that flickered all across the city's panorama.   "Jonathias, get over here.   Come over here now!"

"Leave me alone!"

"The entire city's on fire.   Everything!   The whole bloody city!"

"Yeah, right!"

"Seriously, come quick!"

Jonathias   finally   stirred   from   the   comfort   of   his   bed   and stumbled to the balcony, then became frozen like a statue as he watched in disbelief, standing in silence beside his companion.   The flaming ruins of once majestic buildings crumbled as he watched.   Drawn into a hypnotic trance, they failed to notice the crawling arm of flames that climbed the palace wall and was now feeding itself on the withered palace gardens.   It wasn't until a sheet of fire reared like a bucking bronco and thrashed violently alongside their balcony that they realized the danger that had now surrounded them.

Racing   to   Joseph's   suite,   they   found   him   still   fast   asleep despite the panicked screams that were echoing through the palace corridors. Half dragging, half carrying, Jacob never bothered to wait for Joseph to fully awaken as they fled the palace. Caretakers and servants valiantly attempted to quench the spreading nightmare that had crept into the palace itself but their efforts were in vain. Rome was doomed and there was no doubt in anyone's mind that it was true.

Reaching the palace portico, there was no one standing guard. The sentries had deserted their posts, placing their own lives before any of the palace minions. In their haste to flee, they had left the store of weapons in the guardhouse completely exposed and unprotected. Jacob urged his two companions to grab a sword belt each before leaving the palace grounds. His reasoning was solid, based on the basest of human instincts. When desperate men perceive no other choice they will kill in order to survive. There would be plenty of desperate men running through the streets. The second reason he explained was that during a catastrophe there would always be those that see it as an opportunity to rape and pillage. Once again, it was human nature.

Striding through the streets, the three Judeans approached the Palatine Hill, the one area of the city where the fire was only beginning to spread. Ignoring the pyres that fed themselves on anything and everything combustible, Jacob dodged and weaved his way through falling, flaming debris until he was finally standing at the entrance to Mirah's apartment.

Flying up the length of the staircase, he charged through her apartment and crashed easily through the locked door of her bed chamber. Instinctively, Mirah screamed before she recognized her savior. "No time for pleasantries my love," he apologized as he picked her up, wrapped he in a blanket he took from her bed, and carried her out from the apartment.

She was fully aware of the fire enveloping the city, but like so many others that night she had become immobilized with fear, locking herself inside her bedroom, thinking that somehow the inferno would pass harmlessly by and she would be safe.

"I knew you would come for me," she snuggled into his chest.

"Of course I would," he lowered her slowly so her feet touched the ground. "There is nothing in this world that could ever keep us apart."

"How very touching," Joseph commented patronizingly. "Now can we please find some cover before we are too late to save ourselves?"

Beneath the sheltering marble wings of the monument dedicated to the Fates, the four companions sought a moment of respite, finding the statue a pool of tranquility in a world gone mad. All around them the panic and hysteria was spreading as rapidly as the flames. While a city burned, all manners of debauchery were taking place, much of it happening right before their eyes.

"For God sake, Jacob, tell me what's happening," Mirah pleaded.

"I'd like to know the answer to that question too," Jonathias piped in. "It's as if everyone has gone crazy. I have seen people running around with torches that I could swear are purposely setting the fires."

Seeing one of the local magistrates attempting to organize a team of slaves that he hastily recruited and formed into a fire brigade, Joseph decided to find out for himself. "I'll be right back, Wait here."

Within minutes he returned to his companions huddled beneath the statue.

"So what did he say," Jacob inquired excitedly.

"I don't know if we can believe it or not. It's too astounding to even consider. I think we may have remained cloistered in the palace too long, my friends. There have been events recently transpired that I certainly was not aware of. Did any of you know that over the last few months they've been hunting down and slaughtering the Nazoreans with a ferocity that was unheard of before?" Joseph looked at his companions to see if they had any recognition of this fact.

"But why?" Agrippina questioned. "Why intensify their persecutions now?"

"There's more to Nero's fleeing to the countryside than just a holiday," Joseph criticized. "I thought he was merely arresting some of their ringleaders but the magistrate told me that he knew for a fact, none of those that were imprisoned are still alive. Nero had them all executed. That included any Minians as well. Jews like us that got caught up in the nets his Praetorians cast."

"And yet not a word from Aliturius. Not a single word." Jacob was furious.

"Not exactly like us," Jonathias corrected Joseph's statement. "Heretics like Simon. Jews that had gone over to the Christian beliefs. I have no sympathy for them."

"Well you should," Joseph admonished him. "There's very little that separates them from us. Minians today, the Jews of Rome tomorrow!"

"What does any of this regarding Christians have to do with what's happening," Mirah pleaded for an answer. "The city is being destroyed and you're talking about Christians. I don't understand."

Joseph took a deep breath while he prepared to explain the connection to the information provided by the magistrate. "It would appear from what he's heard, that this conflagration is somehow related to the persecutions. An act of revenge on their part!"

"That's ridiculous," Jacob insisted. "A bunch of Nazoreans managed to destroy the greatest city in the world. Impossible! Do you know the type of co-ordination it would take to set enough initial incendiary blazes to cause this kind of destruction?"

"No, but I'm sure your going to tell us," Joseph confessed.

"It takes a hell of a lot. The precision, timing, planning would be months in the making. The amount of material to act as igniters would be enormous. Calculation of the starting sites, the wind currents, ensuring there were no physical barriers to spread, takes careful planning. It's not something a group of religious fanatics cobble together at one of their prayer meetings in one night."

"They executed someone we're familiar with last week." Joseph added. "The one called Simon Peter. You should all remember him from the Passover meal."

"The fisherman," Jacob shouted in recognition, "The one who was a Galiean like me."

"You mean the one that got my grandfather arrested," Jonathias corrected his friend. "The man who betrayed everyone he was close to, even Yeshua of Nazareth."

"Hey!" Jacob seemed irate. "I should be mad at the man as well but it's too easy to blame one man for all our misery. My father believed until the day he died that Simon Peter was responsible for King Agrippa's death. He could never forgive himself for allowing the assassination to take place. He blamed himself for failing to protect his king. As soon as Agrippa had been assassinated, Simone Peter fled to Rome, beyond the reach of my father. Letting him escape was the second crushing blow my father could not forgive himself for. But just because someone sails to Rome does not make that person automatically guilty of a crime. My father died from a broken heart. He loved the King and he failed him. Failed him while alive and after his death in his own mind! My father was a good man but he could not live in dishonor! But over the years it was not Simon's fault that my father abandoned his responsibilities to his wife and family. That was a decision that he made alone and it did not matter if Simon was or was not involved in the bloody assassination. He didn't take my father away. My father did that all on his own. Do you understand what I'm saying?".

"But he was the one for wrecking my grandfather's strategy and placing the lives of so many in danger," Jonathias refused to change his opinion.

"Anyway," Joseph continued. "Apparently he was crucified a week ago. From what the magistrate said, he was preaching anarchy and the total destruction of Rome. He even went as far as saying that this city would be razed to the ground and upon its foundation would be rebuilt a new kingdom of God. Then, at that time, his messiah Yeshua would return. So, they crucified him! He was charged with preaching insurrection."

"And from this they can justify the burning of an entire city," Mirah tried to reason.

"Not from this, as the magistrate indicated. The burning he said is the result of Simon Peter informing his congregation that they must ensure that the Lord's plans do not go unfinished as a result of his own death. His followers are apparently carrying out his deathbed wish," Joseph explained.

"And that being the case, then the setting of these fires must have been well planned," Jacob affirmed. "Simon probably had everything worked out well in advance."

"A one week anniversary present to Rome, following the crucifixion," Jonathias spat. "That certainly would explain the individuals I saw running around with torches. They would have been given precise locations around the city to ensure the job is complete. You're right, someone would have planned this all out quite a while ago."

"I didn't understand what he was talking about when we were conversing during the Passover Seder," Joseph reflected on the night several months ago. "I thought it was just some improbable religious prattle on his part. It sounded like nonsense. Something about being resurrected on the third day once again. Except that a day is not a day when measured in heaven. He said he thought at first it would be three weeks but Yeshua did not return. Then he waited three months, then three years, only to meet the same end of no resurrection. It was three decades now and he claimed he realized that it was not about waiting for their messiah's return but actually preparing for his return. It was up to his followers to make it happen. I never bothered to ask him what he meant. I could have prevented this," Joseph was horrified by the thought, "and instead I ignored what he said and chose to do nothing."

"It's not your fault Joseph," Jonathias quickly dismissed Joseph's feelings of guilt. "You couldn't have known what kind of man he was. I did know, but I chose to leave that evening and in so doing there was no one there that could have challenged his insane ideology.

"My God," Mirah cupped her hands over her mouth. "They will find out that we were with him at the Passover. They'll blame all of us. They won't distinguish between us and the Minians. To the Romans we're all the same and when they trace his whereabouts to us, we are all going to suffer for his madness. They're going to kill us all!"

"No one is going to harm a single hair on your head," Jacob reassured her.

"We can't stay here. We have to find the rest of Elias's congregation and get them to a safe haven. Mirah is absolutely correct. Someone will talk and identify Simon being present at our feast. We all will be guilty through association. We have to act now. Are we in agreement?" Joseph asked his companions.

"You're right," Jonathias agreed. "We have to protect them! But how? We're probably as much in danger as they are."

Jacob only nodded while he held Mirah close, sheltering her within his massive frame.

"Perhaps even more than others," Joseph confided. "The captain of the Praetorian Guard is desperate to have us charged with some offense. If he finds out we had discussions with Simon ben Johan, he will certainly arrest us as willing accomplices. He'd relish the moment."

"So what are you suggesting?" Jacob wanted to know.

"We head to the Jewish quarter and ensure everyone is kept safe."

"Seriously," Jonathias questioned. "The three of us?"

"Three of us with swords," Jacob corrected his friend. "That should give us one advantage over a lot of trouble makers."

"As said by the military man," Joseph took exception to the suggestion.

"As said by the Jew that understands what it takes for us to survive," Jacob refuted his sarcasm. "Now's the time Joseph that you learn that unless we stand up for ourselves, there's no one else that will protect us. God won't intercede unless we demonstrate that we are willing to protect ourselves. We must show Him that we are willing to fight for our beliefs and our way of life. It's time you learn that there is no such thing as a benevolent occupation. There is them, and there is us and there is no in between. So grow a pair and let's go save our brethren if they're in danger."

"We go," Joseph agreed. "But we don't instigate any confrontations. That's the condition."

Jacob stifled a laugh. "If you think we're going to be the instigators by showing up with a sword, then you have a lot to learn about this world. It's time I open your eyes to the reality and show you exactly why Jonathias and myself are here."

Charging towards the Janiculum hill, they found the streets increasingly congested as the homeless milled about aimlessly. The closer they drew to the Jewish Quarter, they sensed the mood among the people swaying from what was viewed as the hysterical haplessness they witnessed most of the day to that of unbridled anger as the people became a mob seeking revenge. As Jacob had expected, there were those among the crowds that were fueling the people's emotions, screaming their rage that the foreigners were obviously responsible for the destruction of their city.

Joseph could not dismiss the fact that he began hearing the words being shouted more frequently: Jew, Nazorean, Christian! It was obvious the blame was already being pinned on three particular segments within the immigrant community and things were about to become very ugly.

"Be careful," Jacob warned his companions. "There is something more afoot here than meets the eye. Those people inciting the crowds, they are not dressed like the normal inhabitants of this subura. I wouldn't be surprised if they're Nero's own men inciting the mob to do his dirty work. Certainly would make his life easier if he could be rid of all of us in once shot."

Approaching the street where Aliturius's synagogue stood, Joseph became keenly aware of several cowled men that were moving about at the periphery of the mob with an obvious malicious intent. He pointed out to Jacob the few that he observed, watching them weave back and forth in the darkness, so that just as suddenly as they would appear, they just as easily disappeared out of sight.

Jacob spat his disgust on the ground. "Assassins," Jacob mouthed the poisonous words. "They'll pick us off one by one if we give them the chance. Let's get to Elias quickly. Don't stop moving for a second. I'm guessing your captain friend is not willing to leave anything to chance."

Up ahead a tight circle of the crowd jostled and swarmed angrily outside the exterior of the synagogue. The air was filled with the foul scent of the malevolent nature of the mob.    Though they could not see what was happening, it was apparent that at the core something had definitely whipped the mob into an irrational frenzy.

"Yoni, you stay here with Mirah.    I'm going to take Joseph into the center of that?    Have your sword ready!"

"But, you need me with you!" Jonathias protested.    "Leave Joseph to watch Agrippina.    You need a fighter with you."

"No!    I need you here.    Mirah needs you here. I need her protected by someone handy with a sword.    And so help me if she's harmed in any way, you better hope you're already dead!    And that's an order!"

Jonathias was about to object again, when Jacob placed a heavy hand upon his shoulder.    "Yoni, I love Mirah.    She is the most important person in my life.    I need you to safeguard her for me. Can you please do that for me?"

Lowering    his    gaze,    Jonathias    shuffled    his    feet    and acquiesced.    "Only because I'm a sap for a good love story. Don't get yourself killed you big jerk. Otherwise I'm going to marry her myself!"

"I'll never let that happen," Jacob warned his friend.    "Anyway, you're already married."

"Who says I can't have more than one wife.    Plus, I haven't seen my wife in over two years, so you better not do anything foolish," Jonathias warned again.

"By now you should know that I'd never do anything foolish," the giant laughed.    "Joseph, follow me!"    Lowering his shoulders so that he moved like a projectile almost horizontal to the ground, Jacob took off at a full gallop towards the mob."

"Now that I consider foolish," Jonathias commented to Agrippina.

Jacob's massive frame bowled over anyone that got in his way like a charging bull, as Joseph followed up the rear through the cleared path before the surprised and dazed bodies could pull themselves off the ground and determine what had just happened.

Breaking    through    to    the    centre    of    the    circle,    Jacob    and    Joseph discovered that three men were the source of the crowd's jubilant mood. Oblivious to their approach, two men were still kicking and punching the prone figure of a third man curled in a fetal position on the ground.    It was only when Jacob roared like a snared lion, as he recognized old Elias lying motionless on the cold cobblestone street, soaked in his own blood, that his attackers knew they themselves were under siege.  With a single blow, Jacob sent one of the assailants flying through the air, crashing down upon several spectators yards away. Seconds before the other assailant was about to deliver a kick to the side of Elias's head, Jacob seized his foot midair and then twisted it with every ounce of strength he could muster.    The man shrieked in pain as the ligaments of his knee gave way under the strain, his lower leg practically sheered at the joint as he tumbled to the ground.

Recovering,    the    first    assailant    was    about    to    launch    himself onto Jacob's back, sword in hand when he felt himself being wrenched backwards by his shoulder length hair. As he turned to see what had restrained him, Joseph's fist landed squarely in the centre of his face, flattening his nose to one side. The attacker took a couple of steps back, wiped away the blood that flowed across his upper lip and then stared momentarily at his own blood as it dripped from the tips of his fingers. He then waved his short in Joseph's direction. In response, Joseph unsheathed his own blade and adeptly parried the man's wide arcing swing. A second lunge and once again Joseph turned the blade, followed by the thrust of his own that caught the man squarely across the right shoulder, leaving a thin trail of blood as it swathed through the fabric. Joseph offered the man a wicked smile, hoping that it would deter him from fighting any further, but the gesture only inflamed his assailant further. The man closed in with a killing blow, swinging his sword like a hammer from over the top. Dodging to his right, the blade sliced within a hair's breadth of finding its intended target. But the sheer momentum of the intended strike carried the attacker's torso past Joseph, so that the area over his right kidney was exposed. Without any hesitation, Joseph turned his own blade, thrusting backwards. Joseph felt the sensation of the cold steel sinking deep into the man's flesh. It was a killing blow. As he withdrew, the assailant fell off the end of his sword, gasping for breath in his final death throes.

The dying man's final groans incited the mob into a blood hungry frenzy. Limping forward, the man that Jacob had hobbled was now on his feet and moving rapidly towards Joseph, his own blade bared. Jacob looked about the crowd and recognized at least a half dozen of the cowled men encircling them with their weapons at the ready. "It would appear that the assassins as well are preparing for a fight," Jacob assessed their predicament.

"Are you finding this entertaining?" Joseph found nothing about impending death amusing at the time.

"Not at all," Jacob retorted. "But I knew that when the day came for me to depart this world it would be in a manner similar to this. What more could a warrior ask for?"

"How about old age, a warm bed, and a young woman doing the warming?"

"Naw! Too boring. Let's welcome these bastards into hell," Jacob sang out as his blade flitted through the air so quickly that its movements could barely be followed. "Come on you sons-of-bitches," he shouted in perfect Latin. "Come and get me!"

"Back to back," Joseph shouted. "Let's make this as difficult for them as possible."

"By the way," Jacob took a moment to comment. "You surprised me. You are able to handle a sword."

"I told you when the time came to fight I wouldn't hesitate."

"Well, I'm glad you decided this was the right time," Jacob laughed.

The two Judeans pressed their backs up against each other, rotating constantly in order to face the onslaught. The tactic worked sufficiently, as they wheeled about blocking blow after blow until they found an opening to strike with deadly accuracy. There was a look of shock on the faces of the remaining assassins as they came to the realization that they had already lost three of their number without a single wound inflicted on the pair of Judeans. Jacob did a quick count; there were still four men with blades as far as he could determine. The rest of the mob had backed off having neither weapons nor a desire to be caught between the pincers of the two factions.

"Now this is more like it," Jacob bellowed. "Odds like this I believe we can handle without a problem."

But as he spoke a small squadron of soldiers, their hobnailed sandals rhythmically striking the cobblestones, was approaching swiftly from a position on their right. "Shit," Joseph cursed. "I think the odds have just changed. Looks like they're throwing the army against us as well."

Jacob performed a reassessment. "I don't think we're going to win this one." He watched as the helmeted men approached towards the inner circle, their blades shining brightly as they reflected the flames that continued to spread across the Janiculum Hill. The soldier moved towards them swiftly and were shouting at the mob to disperse, which it did so quickly, fearing for their own lives.

Taking down another of his attackers, Joseph turned his head to talk over his shoulder. "Only three left now from this bunch but I'm afraid that neither of us is going to succeed in our mission now," he advised Jacob. "I'd like to apologize for some of the things I have called you during this trip. I want you to know, that I do consider you to be a friend."

"Really, now?" Jacob sounded surprised. "You really think now is the time? Keep fighting Joseph. Apologize later!" Jacob slashed out at the attacker he faced, but he missed his target within inches.

"I don't think there is going to be a later," Joseph panted, his strength quickly waning from the uninterrupted battle. "I want you to know that even though I still think you took a foolish risk and jeopardized us all, I still admire you. You're a hell of a man, Jacob. A hell of a Jew!"

"And so are you," Jacob responded, "Even if I think you're still a pampered, spoiled aristocrat. But you clearly know how to fight and that makes you alright as far as I'm concerned." this time Jacob's sword did strike flesh and he could hear it grate against his opponent's forearm, who screamed as the sword fell from his hand.

By this time the dozen or so soldiers had completely surrounded the remaining four combatants, and both Jacob and Joseph became completely demoralized by their number. They had neither the strength nor the will to fight on.

Stepping through the circle of soldiers, their commanding officer thrust his sword into the back of one of the assailants, while another of the soldiers quickly dispatched the final attacker. Turning to face the Judeans while removing his helmet, both Joseph and Jacob were surprised to see the face of Aemilius Lepidus with a squadron of soldiers from the 1st legion of Rome. "I would suggest you throw down your swords, my friends. As long a you hold on to them my men might take it as a challenge." Their weapon hit the ground with a sharp metallic clang against the stones.

With the fighting over, Joseph ran towards Elias whom remained motionless in the middle of the street all this time. He turned the old man's silver ed head, looking at it from side to side, then placed his fingers along the neck to feel for a pulse. "We're too late," he cried out to Jacob. No sooner had he said those words, Agrippina raced from the shadows where Jonathias had kept her hidden all this time and threw herself across the old priest's body. She wailed in lament, rocking Elias's head back and forth in her arms.

"I presume it was your intent to rescue this man," Lepidus spoke to the Judeans.

"We obviously failed," Joseph replied.

"I am sorry for your loss," the commander sounded sincere. "Arrest that man," the Roman commander pointed at the one remaining attacker that was still alive, though for how much longer was questionable as his arm bled profusely.

The soldiers seized hold of the man, attempting to stem the flow of blood from his arm, which was hanging loosely from the elbow where Jacob's sword hit bone. They tied a quick tourniquet over his biceps and then proceeded to drag him away with little concern of dressing his wound otherwise.

"I'm going to have to report that both of you are responsible for killing several men as well," Lepidus explained to Joseph and Jacob. Looking at the faces of some of the men laying on the ground, Lepidus clearly recognized a few of them. "Considering they were Praetorians, no one is going to shed to many tears over them. Probably did the rest of us a favor. Obviously, it was an unprovoked attack on their part and you clearly acted in self defense. So as long as you agree not to leave the city, I am satisfied that it won't be necessary to put you both in custody as well."

"It was pretty obvious that it was self defense," Joseph argued.

"To most," the officer agreed, "But to someone that might have a bone to pick with you, making it necessary to send his Praetorians to do his dirty work, it could be made to look otherwise."

"What are you suggesting," Joseph picked up immediately on the Roman's partly veiled warning. "And come to think of it, how is it that you and your men are here. Have you been tailing us as well?"

"I told you long ago, Josephus, I take my orders of the Empress Poppea. She had reason to fear for you while she was away from the city."

"But doesn't that put herself at risk? The Praetorians take their orders directly from Caesar. You take your orders from Poppea. She obviously knew that Nero planned to do something tonight. In fact this entire night seems staged somehow by a lot of different factions.   What exactly is going on here?"

"Be careful Josephus," the Tribune cautioned. "Asking too many questions in Rome is the fastest way to sign your own death certificate.   I may not always be around when you need me."

"But what about the Empress?   Has she placed herself into a precarious situation by saving us?" Joseph pursued his line of questioning.

"The Empress Poppea can manage to take care of herself," he answered, looking directly at Mirah still cradling the head of Elias.   "Right now, I would be concerned about the Lady Agrippina. I will keep her out of my report but I will guarantee someone has already carried the news back to the palace of her presence here."

"They wouldn't dare to lay a hand on her," Jacob interceded.

"I see my big friend that you Latin has much improved.   I will tell you this.   They may not directly harm her but they now know of your weakness. Do not put it past them to get to you through her.   Be careful my Judean friends.   You have made many enemies during your stay and tonight you will have angered those enemies further.   I bid thee a good night."

Saluting, the Tribune departed into the night accompanied by his squadron, his mission completed for at least one more evening.

Joseph turned to see the rest of his retinue hovering over the slain Elias. Jacob was preparing to lift the frail body with such tenderness that he made the old man appear no different from a young baby.   Joseph stood silently in the street as he watched them disappear through the front gates into Elias's home carrying the body of Elias as if he was merely sleeping.   Several streets in the distance, Joseph could still see the flames dancing from rooftop to rooftop, but the wind was now blowing in a westerly direction, carrying the seeds of destruction away from where they were.   It would be safe now, he told himself.   Safe? What a meaningless word. Could anyone ever be safe again, he questioned after tonight?

# CHAPTER NINETEEN

## WHANGAREI; PRESENT

"Everyone knows the Christians weren't responsible for the burning of Rome," Pearce argued vehemently.

"And everyone thinks that Nero stood on some balcony, fiddling while Rome burned too.    But that didn't happen because he wasn't even in the city at the time," I challenged him.    "So don't believe everything you're told!"

Pearce dug his heels in.    "He used the Christians as a scapegoat.    It was possible he ordered the city burnt himself, just so he could build a new one?"

"History records that a fire started in the immigrant sector of the city.    It also records that just prior to the fire, Peter was crucified.    They say it was done in the head down position.    Do you know what that signifies?"

Pearce shook his head.

"I didn't think so.    That's the problem when people try to defend the early history of the Church. All faith, no understanding. How can you even try to argue the event when like so many others, you don't even comprehend the significance?"

"And I suppose you do?"

I shot him a glance that stopped him cold.    He knew that look. He's seen it before.    It basically said sit down, stay quiet and listen or don't bother wasting my time.    "If you're going to start challenging my understanding of history, Mr. Pearce, then you might as well pack up your pens and paper and leave right now."

"I'm sorry Doc.    I shouldn't have said that."

"Apology accepted," I responded.

"Okay Doc, I admit it.    There are certain things I don't want you messing with inside my head. Granted, I know by now that one of your ancestors was there, and you probably knew what did happen, but that's the one failure you have that you don't recognize when dealing with the rest of us.    Perhaps we don't want to know all the answers.    Maybe we're happy in our ignorance.    Have you ever thought of that?"

"If you didn't want my version, John, you wouldn't be here in the first place and if the people didn't want it, then they wouldn't be buying my books.    The simple truth is that you and everyone else probably knows what really happened but you find it easier to stick your head in the sand and point the finger everywhere else."

"What does pointing out the bad things achieve," Pearce asked, somewhat dismayed by my intransigence to budge even an inch on this matter. "Perhaps it's you that doesn't understand the ignorance is bliss motto?"

"Oh, come on Pearce! We've been through this so many times, I've lost count. No one's asking you to change your beliefs, nor is anyone else being asked to do so. Right from the start, you knew what your editor published was going to raise the hackles on a few people. ***Blood Royale, Caiaphas Letters***, both were written in order to have maximum impact. And if in the process they smashed down a few walls and opened up some light on the dark corners everyone has buried themselves in, then so much the better. I don't know about you, but I'd rather deal with the damage control than live my life in a total lie. And if I think that way, then there are others as well with exactly the same ideology. So if you want to still believe that the Christians had nothing to do with the burning of Rome, then so be it. My few words aren't going to change your mind, but they may certainly help others that are looking for meaning and understanding."

"How can you claim that the burning of Rome was tied to the Christian community when it's even recorded in history that the accusation was a lie."

"And who in history made the statement that the accusation against Christians was a lie I'll tell you who," I shouted unintentionally. I could feel my blood pressure rising and though I kept telling myself it wasn't his fault, he only knew what he had been taught, it still didn't keep me from feeling like hitting him with a few undeniable facts that would make his mind reel. "I'll tell you who!" I repeated but more under control. "The same people that ended up running the Empire into the ground. The Church. And do you think it's any amazing coincidence that they'd be the ones saying that it had nothing to do with the Christian community. You don't have to be any type of genius to figure that one out. Of course they'd say it wasn't them. It would be awfully hard to recruit new members into the religion if you admit to being responsible for causing a major catastrophe resulting in the death of thousands. I think we call that terrorism now. I've told you more times than I can recall John, history is written by the victors, and in this case the Church whitewashed any involvement. But the fact is Peter was crucified in a manner that was reserved only for those that were totally despised and detested by the Romans One had to have been considered a major threat to the government through treason or some hugely despicable act to have been punished in that manner Do you realize that not even Spartacus was crucified in the head down position. As much as he almost brought Rome to his knees, they still did not torture him in the same manner that they reserved for Peter. The head down position was selected for very few, but it was effective in delivering the message that this man was considered enemy of Rome and had deliberately tried to undermine the State. You can't swallow in that position. So if someone tried to give you water, it just falls out of your mouth. Your head is at a level that anyone that wishes can deliver a blow as punishment. Not to mention that the asphyxiation that usually led to early death in the normal crucifixion upright position is not an option. The chest doesn't collapse from the gravitational pull on the shoulders and sternum. Instead you have the weight of the organs pressing against the diaphragm, causing tremendous discomfort, shortness of breath, but even so, death will not ensue rapidly."

"And you're saying that as a result of Peter's crucifixion, his followers burnt down most of Rome?" Pearce questioned incredulously.

"I'm not saying they started it, but as soon as they saw it spreading then they certainly had a hand in ensuring it took out most of the city. Are you not listening to me? Just imagine your spiritual leader and master has just been killed. I don't care how much you've been taught to turn the other cheek; human nature says that you're going to demand revenge. And when all your religious training has taught you that Rome was an evil city that was going to be swept away in a torrent of Hell fire, because it was another Sodom and Gomorrah, then mankind's thirst for destruction will automatically kick in. I will confidently tell you that those sect members were going to help that happen. Think of it as a cult. That's all it was at that time. Look at the cults that we've experienced in our own lifetime and some of the horrible things they have done from Jimmy Jones to the shootout in Waco, Texas. Multiply that by several hundred times to get the feel of the size of the religious order back then, and add on to it the burden of suffering from slavery, oppression, and general lawlessness. Mix in a good helping of ostracization and prejudice, because you need to remember that the majority of these people were immigrants to Rome, not to mention a greater burden of taxation that had to be paid by those that weren't members of the thirty or so tribes that were considered the genuine citizens of Rome, and you have a delicious recipe for disaster."

"You actually believe that it was the Christians that burnt Rome?"

"Why are you having such a problem with that?"

"Because it can't be right," Pearce insisted it was a lie. "It was deliberately made up, a false accusation. Because it would be un-Christian"

"Oh, give me a break John! Like the Crusades was un-Christian. How about the inquisition? Not to mention the slaughter and eradication of every group that was branded as heretical over the centuries. Hey, even better yet, the Holocaust was un-Christian. Problem is that they were all committed by "so-called" good Christians and therefore the reality must be that they are very much Christian. Let's face it John, what Jesus preached, and what men have done in his name have been entirely different things for a very, very long time. Just like all these other un-Christian acts, the burning of Rome was not anything exceptional. In fact, as you probably figured out by now, it was par for the course!"

"Figure you'd bring up the Holocaust", Pearce lashed out, trying a last desperate attempt to defend his beliefs.

"Why shouldn't I. Do you think that I should somehow forget the names of the members of my own family that went to Theriesenstadt? They were sent there by their government. Their good, law abiding, Christian worshiping Austrian government.    A government that they had sworn allegiance to, had defended in battle as members of the military, and were culturally participant to.    Of all the European countries at that time, in Austria, the Jews were as close to being treated with the full privileges of citizenship than anywhere else    And in gratitude they shared fully their abilities in the arts, sciences and philosophies earning   Austria   the   acknowledgement   of   being   the   most   enlightened and progressive nation on the continent.

And what did my family get in return? A one way ticket to Theriesenstadt, that's what!    But because they were honored and respected citizens, they couldn't just load them into cattle cars like they did to the east European Jews.    No, they couldn't   do   that.    They   played   upon   their   loyalty   to   the   nation and told them for their own health and the benefit of their fellow Austrians, it was in   their   own   best   interest   of   safety   and   security   to   take   an   all expense paid trip to the Czechoslovakian resort, where they would be wined and dined as special guests of the government that loved them, until the war was over. And like good citizens, they packed their one suitcase per person that was allowed, while placing all of their estates into the care and custody of the government, and then boarded the train.    And when they got there, they still believed they were being   sent   to   a   resort,   until   they   suddenly   had   their suitcases ripped from their hands, and the gates of the city were slammed shut   behind   them.        They   eventually   died   from   disease   and dysentery that resulted from the overcrowded conditions.    Now that was the gift of the God-fearing, good Christian government of Austria.    Want to know the date?    February 1942.    That's when they took my relatives."

"They had no choice," Pearce anguished with the thought of the camps. "The Nazis were in control.  They couldn't resist, otherwise they would have been killed themselves."

"Not the point.    A true believer would not have let it happen. They would have fought it with their very last breath because that is what Jesus' sacrifice would have taught them; should have taught them.    You cannot succumb to evil, even if it is only momentarily, because the moment you do, in turn you will become the embodiment   of   evil.    There's   a   reason   he   said,   "Lead   us   not into temptation."    Because he knew you can't come back once you've gone over to the other side.."

"And   therefore   you   condemn   everyone   involved   and   blame   it on Christianity rather than the insanity of a few."

"That insanity of a few, took entire nations down with them.    They used or misused Christianity as their vehicle to commit murder because it could be used. Whether you want to consider it as a manipulation through force or coercion, or temptation, the fact remains that Christianity has this inherent glitch built into it that allows it every so often to go murderously insane.    Just look at the annals of history. Of course the Holocaust was a period of insanity, just as were the pogroms, the   crusades,   the   Inquisition,   the   Albigenian   and   Arian   massacres,   and even the burning of Rome. Incomprehensible, inexplicable, undeniable insanity that overwhelmed a normally God-fearing society that preached peace and love and benevolence. I can't explain it, you can't explain it. Maybe we shouldn't even try to. It just happened. But the more you or someone else tries to tell me that they weren't the real Christians, but some demonic evil that possessed a small group that amazingly was able to force and bend the majority to its will, the more pathetic the advocates of this particular explanation begin to sound."

Pearce tried to interrupt at that moment but I wasn't about to let him. He had hit a raw nerve of mine and I wasn't about to let it go without having my full say. Too often today's society tries to whitewash the actions of the past. History is meant to teach us so that we learn not to repeat our mistakes. You can't learn if you refuse to accept that we are capable of the most sinister and barbaric behaviors imaginable.

"And you want to know the strangest part. I don't hold it against them. I actually understand it. I see it as nothing more than the world behaving exactly as it was meant to. Man has his periods of baseness and that is the reality. When we believe we are more than we truly are, that is when we are willingly being deluded. Do I bear resentment of what happened? Of course I do. Anyone that lost someone in that way would. That's human too. But I do not hate anyone as a result of it. Those days, those people have gone and they are the past. This is the present. Some day it will happen again but that will be a long time from now. You want to know what I felt when I took my family to Austria to see my roots. I felt pride. Bet you didn't think I would say that. An overwhelming pride that my ancestors were integral to the development and history of that country. I am proud of my Austrian roots. I am proud of so much that was good and is good about Austria. I didn't want my children to dwell on the insanity of a horrific decade when there were centuries of greatness. I still remember the day when we were driving north out of Vienna and I parked alongside the Danube in a little park-like area. We all took our shoes off and ran into the river. We splashed around, skipped stones and admired then serenity and sheer beauty of the place. I wanted them to know what it was like to have that sensation; the same one that their ancestors would have experienced when they went into the country side and couldn't resist the majesty of that river drawing them into the water like a magnet.

You have to appreciate that there are terrible things done in God's name, all the time, and there may be a thousand and one reasons we should condemn those that perpetrated them, but there's a million and one reasons why we should just look past the event and continue on, acknowledging that it happened, it was tragic, but not letting it stop or impede us. And we certainly don't have to make up lies to conceal the event. Hard to explain, but when you can laugh and splash with your children, in the water of the past, like we did in the Danube, then you will be able to appreciate that life, just like that river, continues on into eternity, always flowing, even after bearing witness to some of mankind's worst moments."

Pearce's mouth hung open as I concluded my monologue. At the moment, I think he thought it more prudent not to say a word. Most perceptive because I wasn't prepared to listen anyhow. I had said what had to be said. And even though historians flatly deny that accusations leveled against the Christians of Rome after July of 64 AD it really isn't as great an issue as they perceive. Should they admit that it was true, it wouldn't change anything. Under similar circumstances we probably all would have done the same. Peter had just been executed in the most galling and humiliating manner possible. Paul was in prison, soon to be executed. Their community leaders and preachers were promising an end to the world as they knew it; an end to their suffering. A rebuilding of God's kingdom on earth as it was in heaven. But in order to make it happen, there had to be a cleansing. What better way to cleanse an evil and corrupt city than through fire. Cauterize the wound and stop the infection. Nothing more, nothing less.

---

# ROME; SUMMER 64 A.D.

"Then it's important that I make the Empress and the Emperor well aware of the distinction between us and them," Joseph reassured Agrippina by patting the back of her hand. "It won't be impossible. Just a few well chosen words." In an effort to distance Jacob's fiancé from any involvement with the Jewish community, they began to refer to her only by her Latin name, avoiding the use of Mirah, completely.

It had been days now since the fire was finally quelled and Elias had already been interred in the Jewish cemetery that lay outside Rome proper. As her guardian, Agrippina had prepared the shiva house according to the proper customs and traditions. For one week she resided in Elias's home, greeting his family and friends, accepting their condolences and fed them as they said their final farewells to both an old friend and religious patriarch of their society. During that time Jacob never left her side, always there to support her whenever she felt like succumbing to the tremendous sorrow of her loss. But with her constant presence in the Jewish quarter at that time, tongues began to wag and what may have been a well concealed identity at one time was now revealed to everyone. Having flagrantly ignored Tribune Lepidus's advice, it was now too late to force the genie back into the bottle.

Furthermore, with the royal palace having been reduced to ashes by the fire, both Joseph and Jonathias took advantage of lodging in Elias's home as well, rather than lodge in Aliturius's apartment. With Agrippina being exposed, they felt they could not afford to have Aliturius revealed as a secret Jew as well. Their time at the synagogue lodging, gave them plenty of time to think about the future and how they could best deal with the present situation.

"It would mean a total division, irreparable. If we emphasize the marked differences between our two beliefs, show how the Minians no longer adhere to all of our customs, there probably won't be any chance of their ever coming back into the fold." Jonathias sucked in his breath as he thought about his statement, which sounded like typical rhetoric from his priestly upbringing.

"Now you are sounding like your father," Jacob scoffed at the same time criticizing his friend. "You think it really matters to the outside world that the Minians need to toe the line or cast off. We've said that how many times in the past and take a look at us. Samaritans, Idumeans, Damasceans, Judeans, Nazoreans, Essenes, and on and on. Hell, there are people that look at me as a Galilean and think I'm from another part of the world. There are so many sects now that I've lost count. But the bottom line is no matter what we call these other groups, the to rest of the world they only have on word and that's Fucking Jew!"

"That's actually two words," Jonathias corrected him.

"No, my friend," Joseph intervened, "There has to be a complete separation laid out in terms that the rest of the world can follow. Yoni is right. If I do this thing, there will be no turning back. The Nazoreans, Minians, or whatever you want to call them will be lost to us. The severing must be complete. Nazoreans and Christians can no longer be thought of as Jews in Rome. I understand why God has sent me on this mission. Damneus may have chosen me to get back his priests, but God had another plan for me and that is apparent now. To convince Nero, and the rest of Rome that the Christians, whichever sect they belong to, are not Jews. That is the only way. Let them earn the hatred of the entire Empire but spare us that hatred."

"I don't understand," Agrippina failed to follow the conversation. "How do you separate one sect of Judaism from all the other sects of Judaism? It's all the same. We all worship the same God. You cannot make a distinction."

"Yes we can," Joseph advised. "What is it that Simon said to us that showed their difference? He said Yeshua was the son of God. We take it a step further. We tell everyone that they worship a different god. They worship a god named Jesus. We have no Jesus in our religion. They have nothing other than Jesus. They believe their Jesus is greater than Nero and will return one day to take away the throne in Rome for himself. We have no Caesar but Nero and our God does not exist on earth. Deny any similarities long enough and it will be ingrained into their belief system. They have no leaders from Judea to claim they are Jews any longer. All that's left are their heathen converts to lead them. If we emphasize Jesus is their god, I guarantee those leaders will take it up as their dogma. After all, their beliefs are far more Greek than Jewish, with this son of god concept. I just have to make certain that Nero sees it exactly the same way too."

"And what makes you so certain you will be able to accomplish this complete separation?" she asked bluntly. "Nero is a tyrant. He won't care about a distinction of who he throws into the arena! And as we already know, you're not exactly one of his favorites that he'd listen to anything you had to say."

"I know that you're worried about your own survival now that the rumors of your being a Jewess are widespread but I need for you to trust me on this. I have an idea. Every disaster has its other side, an opportunity waiting to be seized." Joseph smiled quietly to himself. "I definitely have an idea that should work but I haven't worked out all the details as yet."

"I agree with Mirah…I mean Agrippina. Didn't the Tribune warn you that the Emperor is looking for any excuse to have your head on the block?" Jacob cautioned Joseph. "You could be walking directly into the lion's den!"

"I have no doubt," Joseph agreed. "But I'm willing to offer him something he wants more than anything else."

"You still plan to go ahead with this craziness of yours and appeal to his better nature? He doesn't have one!" Jonathias advised

"There are some things that every man wants and I'm going to give it to him!" Joseph defended his actions.

"But you're not going to tell us?" Jonathias pressed him further.

"Not yet, it's still too crazy an idea," Joseph laughed.

---

News of the conflagration reached Nero quickly at his country estate in Cambria, thirty-five miles distant from Rome. He was told of the hopelessness of the citizenry and cautioned that his presence would do little to soothe the seething anger among the populace. Nevertheless, Nero felt it his duty to return to the city and take control of the emergency. Well aware that the situation was beyond control and beyond miracles, his first instructions to the magistrates were to make preparations for housing the homeless and supplying provisions to the needy. What little remained of the royal gardens was hastily converted into a city of tents providing shelter to all those that required it. Stores of grain were transferred from Ostia and doled out generously to the amassed crowds. For the time being, Nero's administrations appeared to be winning the people's gratitude and the tensions in Rome were calmed down.

For six days the people watched their city burn and for a further nine days they watched it smolder. By the time it was declared extinguished only four of the original fourteen districts remained unscathed; the rest reduced to nothing more than charred ruins and crushed dreams. Ancient Rome had become little more than a historic memory. What Hannibal had failed to accomplish three hundred years earlier, had now come to pass through the combination of an intentional spark and an unforgiving wind.

From his country estate, Nero directed the reconstruction of what he called New Rome. Into this enchanted country setting, far from the misery and sickness of the city, Joseph managed to secure the invitation of the Empress and gain her permission to introduce his plan to convince the Emperor that the Jews were innocent of any involvement in the city's destruction. Using his own influence as an emissary of the Sanhedrin, and the network of connections that Aliturius had established over his lifetime, he was able to divert the Temple tax gathered from all of the Jews residing in Italia and Italian Gaul into Nero's construction projects.

Achieving this feat proved not as difficult as Joseph had initially assumed. Every year, each head of a Jewish family all over the world would donate a half shekel, the equivalent to a stater, or about the value of three denarii in Roman currency, to the Temple in Jerusalem. Multiplied by the number of families of Jewish origin living in the Italian peninsula, the donation was close to twelve million sesterces and it went a long way in allaying any suspicions of Jewish involvement in the burning of Rome as far as the authorities were concerned.

Sending his appeal directly to Damneus, with the advisement that failure to co-operate might mean the end of any future donations to the Temple should Nero decide that the Jews were a threat to his Empire, was enough to convince the High Priest that the diversion of a few million shekels to the reconstruction of Rome on a one-time only basis was a sound investment for the future. Within weeks, Joseph had his reply from the court in Jerusalem to act as tax agent while in Rome and he delivered those monies gathered directly to Nero along with the expression of the Sanhedrin's sincerest support for the people of New Rome. It was not given as a loan, nor was it attached to any demands. As far as anyone could determine, it was a contribution from a very generous people extolling their profound friendship with their Roman overlords. As Joseph had calculated, every man, even an Emperor has his price. But there was more than just money that Joseph had to offer. The better nature he had spoken of was Nero's own vanity and narcissism.

Now that he had successfully catered to the greed, it was time to provide for the vanity. The opportunity to rebuild the fabled city in his own image was more important to Nero than any mistrust or hatred he may have borne towards Joseph and the Jews. Joseph knew that in the Eastern world there was no greater builder than Herod the Great. His palaces overhanging on mountain sides, the arenas, coliseums and basilicas he had constructed throughout Israel were considered marvels of modern architecture. So at the same time that he had requested permission to deliver the Temple tax, Joseph also requested that he be sent the architectural plans of some of Herod's greatest architectural achievements.

Greek, Oriental, and Egyptian craftsmen and architects were summoned to Nero's country estate, along with the Senatorial Princeps and military attachés to contribute to the designs of the new Imperial City; a Rome far greater and more glorious than the previous one. To everyone's surprise, Poppea, through further manipulations arranged for Joseph to present at the first of these meetings, much to the dismay and disdain of all those that were offended by the presence of this outsider that had the pretense to even pretend that he had the slightest nuance regarding architecture and construction.

Arms laden with blueprints delivered from the archives in Jerusalem, Joseph moved into a clear spot around the draftsman's table and dropped the pile onto the olive tabletop.

"Are you an architect now, Josephus," Nero made fun of the Jewish emissary with his mountain of plans and diagrams. Nero may have agreed to let him attend but it did not mean that he was happy with providing Poppea with her way. Jewish money he was more than pleased to accept but to have a Jew tell him how to build his New Roma, that was already too much but rather than have Poppea nag him incessantly, it was best to give in to her demand.

"No Excellency, I am not. But the men that designed these certainly were. May I offer this gathering of esteemed craftsmen a few of the design plans for some of the construction marvels of my homeland. As great as these buildings are, I believe that this assembly of artisans and architects can make them even greater. I speak of creating buildings in New Rome that would have no rival anywhere else in the world. Structures so magnificent, that when people gaze upon them, they think of only one word; Nero."

Unrolling some of the designs, Joseph pointed out some of the highlights that he knew would intrigue the specialists that had been gathered. "Let me show you buildings with domed ceilings that require no internal support structures. They seemingly float in the air high above your heads. Or this one," he unrolled another, where during the summer days the ceiling can be retracted to let the sun shine in and closed if the rain should fall." Laying out another plan, Joseph smiled at the Emperor, whom he could see was already very intrigued by the designs already unveiled. "Why not a building where the ceiling revolves. Paint it like the heavens above and it will mimic the movement of the stars and the planets." The craftsmen were already pawing the designs and discussing the intricacies of the construction as if the designs had already been adopted. "Or one of my favorites," Joseph continued, "A building where the walls are constantly moving and changing, a system of gears keeping them constantly in motion. An ever changing maze to amaze and entertain your guests. As I said, Excellency, I am no architect but the greatest architects of my homeland would be pleased if you would accept these blueprints as their gift to you. Anything we can do to make the city of Rome the greatest and most beautiful city in the world would be our pleasure. The city of Nero must be innovative, remarkable, and unique, so that all will be in awe of the greatness of Rome's Emperor."

Puffing out his chest, Nero was obviously pleased by Joseph's presentation and the support of the Jewish people. "The Empire is eternally grateful to its Jewish allies and appreciates the generosity of its government and its people. Let it be known by all that the Jews have earned the title as 'Friends of Rome' and an official decree will be sent to the Procurator and the provisional government in Judea saying that it is so."

Bowing, Joseph could not have hoped for a better outcome. As 'Friends of Rome' the Jews in the city had gained a protected status that should clearly differentiate them from the Minians and Nazoreans. Nero would from now on focus his attention on those groups and leave the Jewish community be. Though there would be those that would accuse the community of abandoning its responsibility of protecting those other Jews that belonged to the varying sects, the violence promulgated by these fringe groups could no longer be condoned or tolerated. Joseph was right, the time to sever the connections had come and he took satisfaction in making it happen.

After a mind spinning pace for four solid weeks, the first draft of the blue prints for New Rome was ready. Joseph had reason to be proud of his few contributions that had been incorporated, though by comparison to the overall plan, they were minor. The streets of the New Rome were to be both wider and straighter than before, providing a deterrent to the easy spread of any future fires. Gardens with pillared colonnades along both sides of the main thoroughfares and fountains at most crossroads would provide a very relaxing atmosphere, even when the streets were congested. Throughout the city there would be large open expanses designed to provide park like settings for the people to relax. New laws prohibited the construction of the first level of any building from being made of anything other than fireproof stone. All buildings would be separated by alleys and it was made mandatory that each structure would have its own picturesque garden, intended to further enhance the separation.

Nero's palace would be known as the Golden House, occupying an area of no less than one hundred and twenty acres, situated in the valley between the Palatine and Esquiline Hills. Three pillared arcades would stretch a mile in length, while in the vestibule of the palace would stand a lofty statue of Nero, one hundred and twenty feet in height. Around the palace was to be a forest, stocked with wild game, and in the midst of the forest, a lake. Nero's personal apartments would have gold leafed walls, lending to the appellation of Golden House.

The main hall of the palace was designed with a revolving ceiling, while the banquet hall had a roof levered and cogged to retract and shower the guests with flowers. These two architectural concepts stemmed directly from Joseph's personal contribution of plans for the rebuilding of the city. He viewed their inclusion enthusiastically, thinking there could finally be a mutual understanding between their two cultures. Over time he prayed, there might even be a peaceful co-existence between Rome and Judea. .

# CHAPTER TWENTY

## WHANGAREI; PRESENT

"He sold them out," Pearce protested.

"What are you talking about?   Sold who out?"

"Nazoreans, Minians, whatever you want to call them," Pearce was beside himself.

"He made certain that the distinction between the Jews and Christians was well understood if that's what you mean," I attempted to calm him down.

"What you're saying is he helped pin the blame on the Christian community by making certain he deflected it completely from the Jews in Rome."

"But the Jews didn't have anything to do with the burning of Rome," I insisted.

"That's not the point.   He made certain that everyone was thinking it was the Christians, like there were no other immigrants living in the city that could have been responsible."

"You have me confused here, John," I admitted to him. "Everyone already knew that the Christian community was involved with the burning.   He wasn't giving them anything new.   All he wanted to do was safeguard his own people by letting the Emperor know that they were innocent.   It was to avoid any confusion.   Where's the problem with that?"

"They said it themselves.   He drove a wedge between Jews and Christians that was never going to heal.   He caused it!   And later when Christianity took over the Empire, there was no turning back.   You couldn't expect the Church to say, that's all right, we understood your reasons for saying we're as different as night and day, but we don't mind.   We're still one people. There was no going back!"

"And your point is?"

"Don't you see Doc, a lot of that anti-Semitism that developed within the Church was created by you guys rejecting us first?"

"That is some of the weirdest logic I have ever heard, John.   The Greek influences on Christianity had already inserted enough differences into the two religious practices that they weren't harmonious any longer.   They weren't compatible by this time.   But the pagan world didn't see that.   They just lumped every Mideastern religion into a single basket.   All Joseph did was educate them to the differences."

"Right," Pearce agreed, "But in so doing made certain that everyone would view them as being different and that is precisely what happened.   There couldn't be any bridges between the two any longer."

"You're assuming that there were efforts to try and bridge the two. Trust me, there weren't. It was a case of a mother telling her daughter it was time to leave home, pack your things and live your own life. If the daughter manages to make her own way in life, she's not coming back. That's the way it is and that's the way it was back then!"

"Well I still think he made it impossible for the daughter to even come by to visit, let alone come home."

I placed my face into my hands and just shook my head in frustration. This was becoming a very long day.

---

# ROME: FALL 64 A.D.

Upon the Ides of the ninth month, early in the morning, the summons came from Poppea for the three Judeans to join her at the Palace of Caesar where she had taken up residence since returning to Rome from the countryside. There, surrounded by her retinue of servants, in one of the remaining large villas that had survived unscathed by the fire, she held court, greeting foreign guests and conducting foreign policy to a small degree, while the Emperor still remained at their Cambrian estate. Country life had proven too boring for her liking, and a city under reconstruction she deemed would be far more exciting. It also meant that she could be closer to Joseph in order to continue her private lessons.

Though transport had been provided in the form of litters, it still required a good portion of the morning for Joseph and his companions to reach the villa from their location on the other side of the city. No sooner had they arrived, they were escorted to the caldarium where the Empress was waiting for them on the other side of several veiled curtains. Laying on the massage table, Poppea's attendants continued to cover her with fine perfumes and luxuriant oils, while the masseuse kneaded her muscles with expertly guided fingers. She did not roll over and sit up to face her guests, maintaining the pretense of a limited modesty, though her state of undress, noticeable even through the curtains would betray otherwise.

"Forgive me Josephus for not meeting you in the salon, but I grew too hot with the rising sun, and a massage was what I desired most. I assume your companions understand the Latin tongue fluently by now." Both Jonathias and Jacob nodded though she could not see them. "I hope that they will permit me this minor digression of being disrobed without their being too discomforted." Once again they nodded while trying in vain to peer through the heavy lacework of the drapery but without success.

"How is my dear friend, Josephus? Have you grown tired of living in the Palatine districts? All these hours you have spent these past days traveling back and forth must have grown tedious. Perhaps it is time you think of packing your belongings and moving from there.    I am thinking it is time for a banquet.    Don't you think so?    A farewell banquet would be appropriate." She bit into her lip as she completed the suggestion.

"I hardly believe moving back to your palace requires a banquet in its honor," Joseph commented somewhat confused by her suggestion.

"You're right, it does not.    But this banquet will also honor your two companions.    I will have your belongings transferred from Lady Agrippina Rubria's estate to this palace before the evening is out."

"I think you are mistaken, Majesty," Joseph addressed Poppea in a stately manner because of his companions being present.    "We are staying at the old synagogue there, not at the Lady Agrippina's estate."

"As I said," Poppea didn't change her mind. "The Lady Agrippina's estate. After all she was the ward of the priest there, was she not?    As I understand it, Aliturius had given title to the property to the priest, so now that Elias is dead, it is inherited by the Lady Agrippina.    It becomes part of her estate."

Joseph was not totally surprised that Poppea was completely aware of Mirah's history.  There seemed to be very little that the Empress was not aware of when it concerned information about himself and those around him. "Yes, you are correct Majesty."

"What is this Majesty nonsense," the Empress chastised Joseph.    "Am I no longer your 'Little Poppy'.

Joseph cringed with embarrassment as soon as she said his pet name for her, while Jacob and Jonathias merely stared at him with bemused looks upon their faces.    Joseph hesitated to respond.

Poppea knew exactly what she was doing as she toyed with Joseph.    "Is that not so, Josephus?    But I can't hear you."

"Yes...you are my Little Poppy," he replied, turning his head away from his friends so that they could not see the colour red he had turned.

"That's much better," Poppea cooed.    "For the moment I thought you had forgotten all about me."

Joseph knew exactly the answer she was waiting for. "I would never forget you.  I could never forget my Little Poppy."

"I certainly hope not," she answered in response.    "We do not have much time left to us to spend together.    Sadly, tomorrow we must say our goodbyes."

"Are you planning to travel somewhere, my Little Poppy?"

Jonathias could barely contain herself, covering his mouth with his hand each time Joseph found himself in the inescapable position of having to refer to the Empress with his pet name for her.

"Oh silly boy," she tittered in that same girlish fashion they all heard the first day they were brought before the royal couple. "Not me, you! Your passage has been booked on a ship leaving from Ostia tomorrow evening."

"I don't understand," Joseph stammered, his knees feeling like they had become nothing more than sticks of gelatinous matter at that precise moment.

"Have I done something wrong?"

"Of course not, my Love. Actually it is because of the others. They all wish to sail immediately, so this was the first available ship I could hire. There were so many of you that I thought it best to secure the entire ship for your voyage. Are you pleased with me?"

"I don't understand." Joseph was baffled by her inference. "The others? What others?"

"Yes Josephus, the others. The priests that you wished released from house arrest. Your mission here has been successful. And Jacob, why don't you bring your fiancé tonight as well. I haven't seen her in such a long time and I have a trove of wedding gifts for you both. You better tell your future wife to be to pack whatever belongings she needs for the voyage, assuming that you both intend to return to your homeland. She need not worry about her estates. I will mind them for her until she decides what she wishes to do with them. "

Now it was Jacob's turn to flush with embarrassment. He and Agrippina had thought themselves so very clever in the manner in which they concealed their engagement from the Roman aristocracy. Obviously there was little that the Empress wasn't aware of happening within society's upper echelon.

Poppea turned her head ever so slightly so that she could see Joseph's face through a small gap in the curtains. As she gazed into his eyes affectionately, she knew the veils prevented him from seeing the faint stream of a tear that had rolled down her cheek. It was not meant for him to see as it would reveal exactly how much she would miss him and she could never let that be known to him or anyone else. It would betray a weakness and surviving as Empress in Rome meant she could have no weaknesses. She knew this night would be their final time together. There would be no tomorrows as they would never see each other again following this one last night. Of that she would make certain.

"See to it that my guests are well taken care of for the day," she shouted to her servants. "Now be off like good little boys," she giggled. "It's time for me to towel myself dry."

The three Judeans were led from the villa, along a path that stretched from the palace portico all the way to a stone cottage that stood by itself in the midst of the gardens that were central to the villa. As they ascended the granite steps, they were cheered loudly by a crowd that had already assembled on the porch. Some of the faces were familiar to them, many were not. A few they even recognized as guests at Elias's house from the Passover Seder. Swept inside by the crowd that milled about them, Aliturius, whom they had not seen in so long, stood anxiously awaiting them in the hallway.

"I thought you were off around the country doing some play? What is this all about?" Joseph demanded an explanation as he watched unidentified people scurrying madly from room to room. The Empress's intimation was that he was going home successful but he needed to see the priests for himself in order to confirm what she had said. "Who are all these other people?"

Aliturius didn't say a word, but instead took Joseph by the arm and led him into the main salon. There, in the middle of the room sat six men, lean and gaunt, old and wise, and very much alive. Joseph instinctively knew they were all that remained the priests that he had come to Rome in order to secure the future of Judea. "But what about all the others?" Joseph still was confused as to why there were so many people flitting about.

"Didn't Damneus explain it all to you? Of course the priests were held here in Rome but that didn't mean their families weren't here as well. You're looking at their wives and children and even their grandchildren They're all going back to Judea with you. You made it possible for them all to return at once!"

"That explains why the Empress hired an entire ship for our travels," Joseph now realized why she had done so.

"Not just for all these people, but for everything else as well," Aliturius explained. "This is not all," he remarked further. "Come with me!" Ushering Joseph swiftly into another chamber, he made him close his eyes momentarily, only to open them when he said so. "Now!" he shouted. "More gifts for you, you lucky boy!" Drawing back a linen sheet, Aliturius exposed a mountain of presents from the Empress. Piled high were clothes, much like the ones that had been given to the Judeans when they first arrived at the Palace, so long ago, but which had all perished in the great fire. "Most of these are for you but there are also gifts for Jonathias and Jacob along with wedding gifts in another room."

"This is too much. I am not deserving of all this," Joseph protested.

"Oh, but we both know that you are, Joseph. Let it not be said that the Empress does not take care of those that have won her favor. And you definitely are one of her favorites," the old thespian brandished his approval. "I guarantee that she will never forget you!"

---

For the remainder of the day, Joseph busied tidying himself in preparation for the banquet to take place that night. Aliturius had taken the liberty of laying out those clothes he considered the most appropriate for this special evening, as Joseph still had no sense of style, even after living a couple of years in Rome. Appreciating that Aliturius had a penchant for fashion, Joseph was glad for the assistance, never questioning his choices.

For Joseph he had chosen a scarlet toga, woven from the finest of oriental silks. About his waist, Joseph wrapped a pale blue sash that matched the border of his toga. Combined they provided the normal Roman attire with an Eastern accent. Upon his wrists were clasped gold bracelets and jeweled rings that covered his fingers. He was the last to get dressed and the last to enter the room where his companions waited impatiently.

Aliturius had also taken the liberty to arrange the clothing for the other two Judeans. Jonathias was adorned in princely fashion, but Jacob was far more of a challenge as this evening would be a prenuptial banquet in his honor as well. Therefore, it was necessary to ensure that Jacob and Agrippina appeared no poorer or less glamorous than the Empress of Rome with what they were wearing.

Not wishing to be outdone, Aliturius outfitted himself with the most exquisite of clothes from his own wardrobe. A black toga unlike that worn by anyone else, edged in gold thread and trimmed with the Greek geometric pattern seen only in Athens. His attire shone like polished onyx, while overall he radiated a statuesque beauty that earned him his reputation as Rome's most illustrious thespian.

"Come on Joseph," Jonathias urged. "We're going to miss our own farewell party! That would be a travesty to say the least!"

Joseph could not help but to be filled with awe as he looked his companions up and down, marveling at the transformation that had taken place. "Wow!" was all that he could say at the moment but they all knew exactly what he meant. "I don't know what to say. Mirah, you look absolutely beautiful. What are you doing with this beast of a man?" he teased her.

"Thank you Joseph. I ask myself the same thing but I think I'm going to keep him," she joked.

"Oh…you only think?" Jacob feigned being hurt.

"Of course not Baby, I know so."

"Baby!" both Joseph and Jonathias looked at each other simultaneously as they mouthed the word.

"Hey," Jacob stopped them. "If you can go around calling the Empress of Rome 'Little Poppy', then I can be Mirah's Baby."

"Yes you can," Jonathias snickered, only to receive a harmless punch on his left shoulder.

As the guests of honor entered the main banquet hall, the trumpets flared the fanfare followed by the herald announcing their entrance. "Joseph ben Matthias, ambassador of the Sanhedrin, Great Council of Judea. Jonathias ben Elioneus the Patriarch of Antioch. Jacob of Galilee and the Lady Agrippina, daughter of Agrippa Marcius Rubrio, late senator of Rome. Aliturius, esteemed playwright and prima thespian of Rome." The guests broke into riotous applause as the new arrivals seated themselves around the banquet table. Joseph sat to the right of Poppea as her most esteemed guest of honor, Aliturius to her left. Jacob and Mirah were a couple of seats down to Joseph's right, while Jonathias sat to Aliturius's immediate left hand.

They ate a sumptuous meal prepared by best chefs selected from the Jewish quarter, a careful consideration that Poppea had given to the arrangements to ensure that her guests would be free to eat whatever they chose that evening and not violate any of their strict dietary laws. Bottles of consecrated wine were carried about the room by scantily dressed serving girls, ensuring that everyone's glass was always full. Throughout the meal there was a continuous parade of entertainers. From the Nabataean sword dancers, to Cretan acrobats, assorted jugglers and musicians, there wasn't a moment throughout the evening that the guests weren't being dazzled by the brilliance of the performers.

Poppea rose from her cream colored settee to offer the customary toast as the evening events closed and suddenly everything came to a halt. She raised her glass and held it up towards Joseph. "Rome could have no better friend than a man who took part in her reconstruction. If the Emperor Nero was able to be here tonight, he would have spoken no differently. It is with deep feelings of remorse and regret that we bid Rome's good friend farewell, but it is with joy in our hearts that we part as not only friends but as allies. The memory you have borne within me I shall always cherish. You will go but there will be a part of you left inside of me." She winked suspiciously to Joseph as soon as she made that comment. "To good friends that we shall never forget!"

"Ave! Ave!" the crowd chanted in response.

Looking further to her right, she kept the glass raised towards Jacob and Agrippina. "And what better way for Rome and Judea to show our affection for one another than to consecrate that relationship in a marriage of our two worlds. May the wedded bliss of our dear Lady Agrippina and Jacob the Galilean be an eternal sign for us all of the bonds of friendship between our two peoples. Let us wish them happiness, love and lots of blessed children."

"Ave! Ave!" everyone cheered again.

"And lastly to the most overlooked member of this trio that came to our shores but who is a clear symbol of the loyalty and sense of honor that those in the government of Syria and Judea pay in homage to the Empire, a man who I see one day filling the shoes of his ancestors in the esteemed position of the High Priest of Israel, Jonathias ben Elioneiai, ben Joseph Cayafa. May the God of his people smile benevolently on his future and may he bless Rome in his function as both priest and loyal friend."

"Ave! Ave!" those in attendance shouted once more.

"Before this night ends, I have but one more presentation to make to my dear friend Josephus." Clapping her hands, two servants immediately brought the special parting gift into the hall and laid it at their mistress's feet. The reflective brilliance in the firelight was met by a series of oohs and aahs from everyone in the hall whom were equally impressed by the exquisite beauty of the item. "A personal gift from me to you, dear Josephus, may it be something by which you will always remember the Empress of Rome! Forged by the hand of Alexander of Rhodes, there is no finer armor to be found for design or craftsmanship. Honed by hammer and anvil through Vulcan's love, here is my personal gift to watch over you and protect you, wherever destiny may lead you. As Tribune Lepidus has remarked to me, you are apparently all too willing to enter into a fight without any protection, so then let me insure that never happens again!"

"Speech, speech," Aliturius struck up the chorus.

Joseph rose from his cushioned seat at the request of the guests. "Pardon me if my Latin is not correct but I will try." Having said that, Joseph became quiet as he looked about the filled banquet hall. " So many people. I'm not certain what to say," he stumbled awkwardly in a search for the words that suddenly eluded him. "I'm usually not this tongue tied. The Empress has been most kind and gracious for the two years that I have dwelled in Rome. She has been my patron, my friend, my mentor and on occasion with the help of the illustrious Tribune Aemilius Lepidus, whom she mentioned, my savior. And now, with this gift of armor, she will be my protector wherever life's road may lead me. I have but one regret in leaving Rome…" but the words failed him at that time and he could say nothing more as his throat became choked and he felt it necessary to take a drink from the wine goblet. He tried to speak again. "I regret, those that I leave behind that I will always cherish within my heart. I bid you all a fond farewell." With his last turn of the phrase, Poppea understood explicitly what he meant to say, and though no one noticed when they stared momentarily into each others eyes, they were both aware of the glistening tears that they quickly blotted away with a deft movement of their handkerchiefs.

His farewell speech was met with wild applause and everyone was in agreement that this night had been an amazing event and uncontested success. As the hour grew late, Joseph leaned over to his hostess and kissed Poppea's hand tenderly as he prepared to depart her company. Reaching upward she gently caressed his short bearded face, a face with which she had grown very familiar with over the years; the final goodbye between lovers who cared deeply for each other but due to the circumstances of fate could never be together.

"What should we do now?" Joseph asked her very suggestively.

"I think tonight you should be with your friends, my dear Josephus. If you stayed with me I fear I would not let you leave my bed in the morning. I could not bear to see you leave like that."

"I wish that there was something that I could give to you," Joseph apologized, ashamed that he had taken so much from Poppea and feeling as if he offered so little in return.

"Trust me when I say that you have given me more than you may even know," she smiled bewitchingly. "Now go on, your friends await you and your ship sails in mere hours from now." She waved him away with a royal dismissal of her hand.

Joseph could barely take his eyes from her as he stepped backwards, then bowed, before he made his final turn and stepped dirgefully in beat to his heavy heart. "Farewell Josephus, farewell my love," the words sailed from behind and pursued him until he had left the great hall.

"The fates are cruel, my friend," Joseph philosophized to Jonathias as they walked back to their apartments together. Jacob and Agrippina had already left earlier in order to make the necessary preparations for their voyage.

"Why is it so often that which we want most we are never meant to have?" Joseph pondered.

"Seriously?" Jonathias couldn't believe what he was hearing. "You actually thought you could spend the rest of your life with the Empress or Rome? How long do you think that would have lasted once Nero found out you didn't sail back to Judea."

"It was merely a thought. I know it was never realistic," Joseph admitted. "But why does God let us do these things in the first place?"

"You are actually asking me to provide you with an answer on God's infinite wisdom? I always thought that was more your domain, my friend!"

Joseph wore a half-hearted smile. "I know I must sound ridiculous but I am at a loss for answers. I had hoped that you could at least offer me a new perspective. After all, you are some day going to be the High Priest of Israel." Joseph nudged his companion in the ribs.

Clearing his throat, Jonathias was thrilled with the prospect that Joseph was actually asking him a question beyond matters of their mission. "I must first say that I disagree with you," he contested. "You have been granted that which you wanted most when you first arrived in Rome. You have gained the freedom of the priests. Whatever else you may have desired since your being here is only secondary to your primary wishes. But then again, that which we think we want may not be what we want at all?"

"Are you supposed to be my confessional priest or a philosopher?" Joseph challenged his friend's profound insight. "But what if it is what I want? The second thing that is."

"If it's meant to be, it will happen," Jonathias provided Joseph with his overall assessment of the world.

He clapped Jonathias across the back. "Sometimes you amaze me. If you think your 'what will be, will be' speech is going to win you any accolades as a high priest my friend, then you are sadly mistaken."

"I've been asked by Jacob to perform a wedding ceremony tomorrow morning and I've consented. I guess there is someone that still sees me useful as a High Priest."

"Well, so Mirah and Jacob are to be husband and wife before we sail to Judea. That is a wonderful surprise."

"Jacob wanted me say that he would be greatly honored if you would bear witness on their ketubah."

"And I would have been insulted if he hadn't asked me," Joseph replied as he slapped Jonathias on his back once more.

"And yet, you seemed troubled Joseph?" Jonathias sensed something was still bothering his companion.

"I feel as if Poppea was trying to tell me something all night but she never came out and said it to me directly."

"That's certainly unusual," Jonathias commented. "The Poppea I know always seemed to say whatever was on her mind. Perhaps it is just your grief over your separation that has you wanting her to say something more."

"Perhaps your right. Let's see if we can get a few hours sleep. Tomorrow will be a busy day." Joseph dismissed his concerns that Poppea was concealing something from him.

---

Shortly after the sun had risen the wedding ceremony conducted by Jonathias was just drawing to a close. No one had actually slept during the few hours following the banquet.

"You really are full of surprises lately," Joseph congratulated Jacob and Mirah as he signed the wedding contract. Once his signature was completed, he embraced Agrippina, lifting her from the ground and at the same time feeling the heaviness lift from his own heart. "Forget trying to get any sleep before we head to Ostia, there is much to rejoice. We can always sleep once we're all on board the ship. Time for another celebration. Aliturius, bring us some wine! We need to have a wedding party!"

"Yes," Jonathias shouted. "Let's celebrate the marriage of our good friends and because we're going home!"

"Home," Jacob repeated to Mirah as he hugged her. "This is the most exciting day of my life. I can't believe you are my wife and we're going home together!"

After consuming copious amounts of wine, Joseph found himself sitting quietly in a corner, enjoying his own company. He had a lot to muse and reflect over. A new bride, six priests and their families, precious gifts, a rebuilt city; he had been an integral part of them all. Life had taken him on an erratic voyage but in the end he was filled with an overpowering satisfaction. Yet at the same time, it had demanded a stiff price. Old friends had died, new friends left behind, a taste of forbidden fruits that fed an appetite that he never knew existed but now filled him with a desire that could never be fulfilled. Everything was in a balance but the scale was not always honest, he realized.

How was he to deal with this newest revelation regarding his own life? He contemplated the complexities of what was meant by true happiness, a concept that he had never understood, but now perceived it to be fleeting at best. He had come to the realization that unless one learns to savor those moments at the time they manifest then the alternative is to have them snatched away in the hour of triumph, leaving behind a bottomless pit of emptiness. How was a man supposed to deal with the iniquity of it all? Perhaps that was God's intention all along.    To measure a man's worthiness by his unwillingness to concede defeat. As long as there was hope that all would resolve into an equitable solution, a chance that dreams might some day possibly become reality, then there would also exist the impetus to carry on.    That no matter, even if everything within this universe was predetermined, it was still worth striving and living in the hope that one could actually obtain their dreams and change the future.    Cruel as life might appear to some, there was always the remote chance that a reversal of fortunes could take place.    He came to the realization that this is what God meant by free will.    There was the freedom of choosing one's own path even if the course of their   life   had   already   been   set.   We   all   had   the   choice   of moving from the beginning to the final destination in a straight line, accepting everything as the status quo and doing nothing to change our route, or we could take a route with many detours along the way to reach the same destination.    The outcome would be the same, but what we do along the way was up to us.    He wondered why so few could actually see it. That our destinies were preset no matter what we did but that should never stop us from trying to change the course of destiny, even if it was hopeless.    As he watched Jacob dance with his new wife carried about in his arms like a porcelain doll that he cherished and caressed, he was convinced that the joy of life should supersede everything else, even one's commitment to God.    Without those moments of happiness, there was no life!

As   the   hour   until   departure   rapidly   approached,   a   personal escort led by Tribune Aemilius Lepidus was sent by Poppea to escort the travelers to Ostia where their ship was berthed.

"Will you not come with us to Ostia," Jonathias begged Aliturius.

The silver coiffed actor placed his arms affectionately around the Judean. "It would not be any easier to say there that which must be done here.    Think of this merely as a play, and the curtain has been drawn on the first act.    More is to follow but the set and the characters will change in the next scene.    So take heart, as we may still meet in the finale."    Moving on to Jacob, as tall as Aliturius was, he could not even reach the giant's shoulders to fully embrace.    "Take that which has been entrusted to you my friend and use it wisely.    You have been given   a   heavy   burden   and   an   even   much   greater   task. The   future   of our people rests in your ability to glean as much as you can from your stay in Rome and to learn from it.    I know that you are up to the task."

Moving on to Agrippina, he gave her an affectionate little kiss. "Take care of your husband.    Sometimes he does rash things without thinking.    Grant him your   wisdom   and   keep   him   safe."        And   finally   the   master   thespian came to Joseph, and his voice began to crack as he choked back the tears.    "What we have shared together will be the source for legends and songs to follow.    You are the one that they will call Josephus, and it is written in the prophecies that your name shall never be forgotten.    I have been honored to have known you."

"No," Joseph corrected him.    "It is we who have been honored to have known you.    No finer friend could ever grace this earth.    It was you who rescued me when all seemed lost. The history books shall never forget your name. Whatever the future holds in store for us, none of it would be possible without your friendship. Farewell my friend, the day will come when we shall meet again!"

The wagons were already heavily laden with Poppea's gifts as the last of the party climbed aboard the final carriage. With tear glazed eyes, a hundred hands were lofted skyward, raised high in a final gesture of farewell. As the carriages and carts passed the corner of the villa where the Empress Poppea maintained her apartments, Joseph thought for a brief moment that he could see the outline of a woman watching from one of the upper windows. He strained to see more clearly and thought for the briefest of moments that he saw her pat her stomach as she waved. But before he could be certain, the wagon turned the corner of the gate and the window was no longer in view.

"What was it Joseph?" Jonathias asked as he helped his friend back into his seat after he nearly lost his balance while craning his neck to try and catch a final glimpse of that particular window.

"I'm not certain, Yoni. I can't really say. I think my imagination might be playing tricks with me. I think I might have seen Poppea."

Along the roadside, the Jewish community of Rome lined the periphery with row upon row, shouting salvos of admiration as the carriage passed by. Joseph returned their waves, smiling confidently as he rolled past the sighs of adoring young maidens and hero worshiping children.

Each clap of the horses' hooves took him further from Rome and closer to his homeland. He was returning to Jerusalem. It had been quite some time since that remarkable day when the high priest Damneus had visited his home. Months had become a year and one year became two. Whatever or whomever that person may have been on the day that the men of the Sanhedrin arrived to request his undertaking of their mission, he no longer existed. He had perished in the windswept sea of an Adriatic storm long ago. He knew in his heart that he had become something more, someone different; a man of prestige and stature; a soul that walked between two worlds with ease. A man that an Empress had called Josephus, who sat and dined with Emperors and Kings, and now craved far more than to continue an existence as an educated priest of nation located at the far end of the Great Sea. Life could never be the same! Once back home he would have to reassess where he belonged. It was a changing world and although he could not explain the reason why, he knew that he was instrumental in how that change was soon to occur.

# EPILOGUE

"Okay Pearce, that's it, time to go home!"

"What do you mean that's it?   We're just getting started."

"I'm tired and I'm cranky," I complained bitterly.   "The rest of the story we can do another day, but as of now, I'm officially on my break.   No, better yet, go back to Canada and release this second edition of Part One."

"That's   not   fair,"   he protested.   "We went all through the night when we did **Blood Royale.**   You didn't think it necessary then to stop in the middle of a story!"

"That was different. I was younger; hell, even you were younger! Plus you have to remember that was our first story together and you had taken me completely by surprise when you showed up on my doorstep that day and threatened me."

"I never threatened you."

"You certainly did.   But I forgave you for that," I reminded him. "So trust me when I say that the events surrounding the life of Josephus are far more complex than any of the Almyeri   They honestly can't be done in the same way."

"You're actually going to kick me out."

"Just   until the next time, John.   I'm certain you'll survive.   Much in the way that Josephus and his companions had to learn to survive.   Their world was changing and they didn't realize at first   how much of that change they were actually responsible for.   Our adventurers are about to return home but it definitely won't be the home they left and they are about to find out that it never would be ever again."

"So what about the next part?"

"Pearce, which parts of a trilogy don't you understand?   I told you at the onset of this story that I was going to deliver it to you in three parts minimum. So expect to be down two more times at least."

"But we're practically at the end," John tried to argue.

"Whatever gave you that idea John.   We're just getting started!"

For the continuing adventures of Joseph and his companions, get your copy of:

# DEFIANCE: Part Two of the Flavius Josephus Journals

Available from Amazon and leading bookstores around the world.

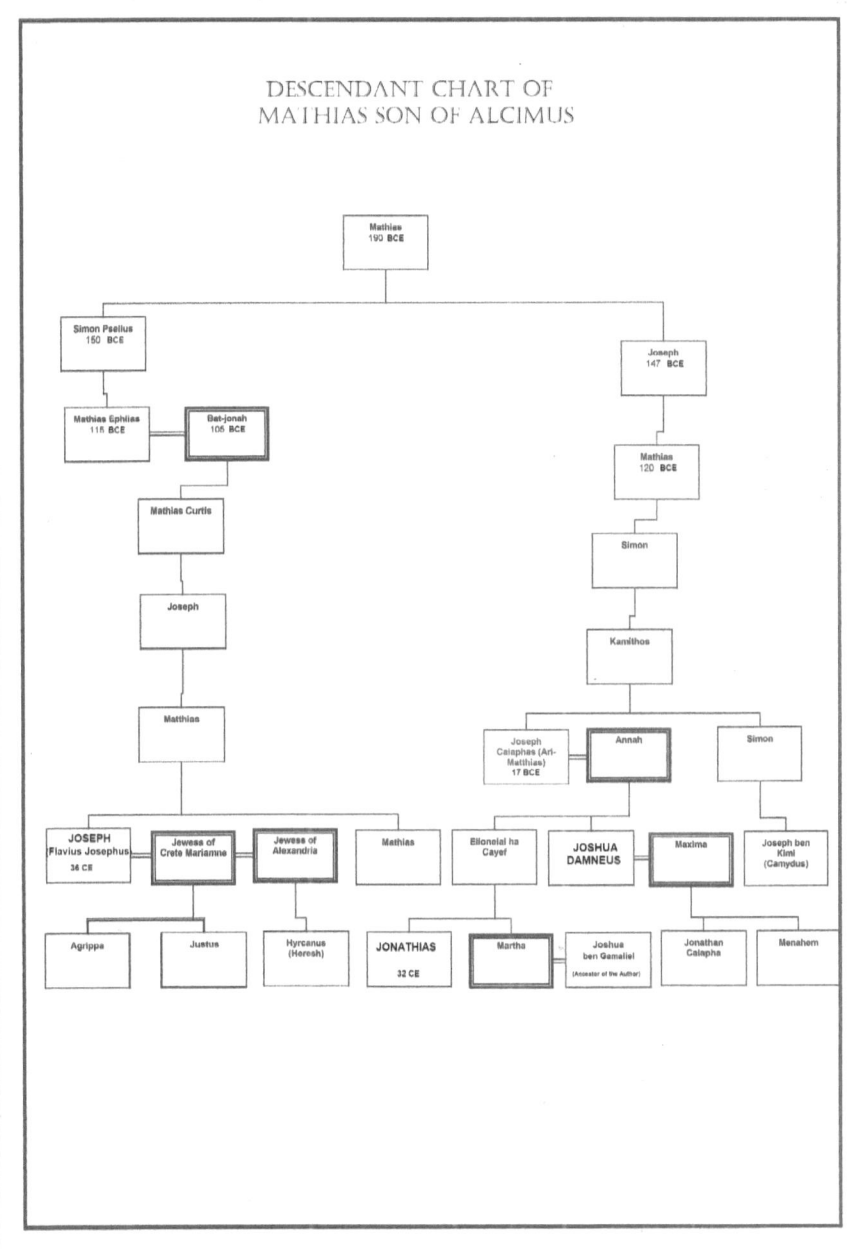

DESCENDANT CHART OF
MATHIAS SON OF ALCIMUS

*Allen E. Goldenthal*